Shifting Tides

PAINTING THE MISTS, BOOK 7

PATRICK G. LAPLANTE

Published by: Patrick G. Laplante
Editing and Interior Design by: Crystal Watanabe
Cover Illustration and Design by: Petros Stefanidis

First edition, 2020
ISBN: 978-1-989578-05-6

Other Painting the Mists Books:
Clear Sky
Blood Moon
Light in the Darkness
Pure Jade
Corrupted Crimson
Kindling
Shattered Lands (forthcoming)
Violet Fate Duology:
Violet Heart
Converging Fate (forthcoming)

Dedication

To my wife. No road is too long when in the right company.

Author's Note and Acknowledgments

It's December as I write this. The weather in Beijing, though cold, is far from unbearable. My writing continues to go well, and I can dedicate increasing amounts of time to it, having recently reduced my regular workload. Life is good, and it's about to get better: Soon my wife and I will be traveling to Canada to for our wedding reception, having been legally married in China a couple of months ago. I'll be taking a three-week vacation from writing during that time.

The more I write, the more I see things that I would have done differently had I known better. Some of these things cannot be fixed. Others, though they can be, shouldn't be. I think it's high time, however, that I fix one important thing: choice. Not for me, but for you, the reader.

Writing is a journey. Like any other profession, it's easy to find mistakes in retrospect. One that I noticed when writing an author's note for *Violet Heart*, the book before this one, was that I tended to frame my books for the reader. On a whim, I deleted it. I realized that I often fall into the habit of explaining what my books are about in advance, before even delivering the story.

This now strikes me as wrong on many different levels. For one, if I need to explain anything outside my story, it wasn't delivered properly, like a joke you need to explain after the fact. For another, everyone interprets a book differently. By explaining my intent up front, I take that away. I take away an important train of thought from the reader: What was the author trying to convey? That, and it makes my writing sound preachy. So from now on, I won't be doing that. I'll be keeping my author's notes short, if I chose to leave them in at all, and merging them with the Acknowledgments.

For this book, a special thank-you goes out to my wife, Xing Wen. We've been legally married here in China and will be holding our wedding reception in late December. Please wish us luck in the upcoming year. I'd also like to thank my parents and hers, my brothers, and my sister, who continue to support us.

I'd like to thank this book's beta readers: Dave Yeung, Aljoscha Volk, and Drew Kennedy. They helped me flesh out some parts of the story that were lacking and spotting many mistakes that I, as the auther, can easily miss.

Thank you to all my friends once again. We've kept in touch since moving to China, which has been a tremendous pillar of emotional support.

Many thanks to Crystal Watanabe for her excellent support while editing my novel. My writing continues to improve with her help, so I'm glad to have her on board. Thank you to Samuel Alves for the great cover.

Last, but not least, thank you to my readers. I write to tell stories to people, and a story is worth nothing if it isn't shared.

That's all for today, as I don't want to keep you away from Cha Ming, the others, and their story. I hope you enjoy reading this book as much as I enjoyed writing it.

Cheers,
Patrick

Prologue

Icy puddles cracked as Zhou Li walked on the hard clay road. It wasn't hard because it was dry but because of the rain from the night before. It was November—yes, that was the month's name—in the season called "autumn." A house burned in the distance, and many tendrils of smoke spewed out from cracks in its distorted walls. There were no screams, nor sounds of alarm. The inhabitants were dead, and their neighbors fast asleep.

He could faintly see the starry sky through the billowing clouds of smoke. The country skies, unpolluted by light and smog, revealed a vivid picture of swirling lights. Through his seer's eyes, he could see certain trails, certain signs; paths that he must walk but others he mustn't travel. But watching through the smoke wasn't perfect. And so he stepped up above the smoke, and then higher. He appeared on the edge of the stratosphere, where he looked back at Earth in contempt. It was an insignificant planet in an unnaturally large mortal plane. The small blue-and-white orb was a useless decoration in the black emptiness of space.

He wasn't sure why he was here in the first place. It was only a dream, after all. But he knew firsthand how real dreams could be. Ignoring his visions would be both foolish and risky. Therefore, he took his time looking over the planet and its crude, rudimentary technology. It had no conception of spirit, natural energy, and runes.

Surrounding it were several planets that orbited around a single sun in the surprisingly large solar system. But despite its impressive size, it was still a drop in the black void surrounding it.

Four groups of stars were particularly noticeable. One represented the Sage, and the vision it had given him previously was one of preemptive action. His time in the Song Kingdom and his rebirth during this period were related to the wise constellation. He'd thought that by striking the Song Kingdom at its weakest point and at many different crucial junctures, they could win over the plane without much effort and bloodshed. He couldn't have been more wrong.

Zhou Li sighed as he recalled the consequences. A karmic anomaly had appeared, completely derailing his carefully laid-out plans. Now war was a necessity. The Merchant was watching, as was the General. The plans he'd drawn up based on their advice were already in motion, and in a decade at most, the South would come bearing down on the North with both coin and sword.

And then there was the void. This fourth constellation was a path he hadn't given much thought. It was a road filled with death and destruction, and even his seer's eyes couldn't fathom where it led. It was a path of desperation, a path he would avoid unless given no alternative.

As he looked into the brooding darkness, Zhou Li caught a glimmer out of the corner of his eye. It was a small light that moved slowly across the starry backdrop, almost unnoticeable to the untrained eye. But his eyes *were* trained, and they narrowed upon discovering that all around the light, the stars in the sky were shifting and realigning. That small light was causing a chain reaction, and as it moved, the Merchant shifted. A bad sign.

Don't look. Don't you dare look, Zhou Li thought. If only words and thoughts could change the stars. The Merchant slowly turned its attention toward the light, which was actually a small star. The Merchant's grace was now focused away from the South, where he'd carefully guided it. *Damn it. How could this happen?* He needed to do something about it.

Gritting his teeth, Zhou Li traveled through space, completely disregarding temporal laws in the process. This was his world, his own domain. He appeared beside the star in an instant, and what he saw made his blood boil.

The star's soft yellow light was surrounded by trinkets, each one more interesting than the last. Foxes of light and darkness danced around it, and so did some familiar-looking coins, as fuzzy and obscure as they were; they were only visible due to their proximity to a strange flame that both chilled his mind and seared his soul.

Zhou Li looked around and sighed in relief when he didn't see a spear or a rosary. Those two were tricky, but fortunately, they were busy with something else. The coins and the flames were somewhat distant as well. Only the black and white foxes were close enough to influence it. That, and those four insignificant stars. But were they growing?

Wait a moment, Zhou Li thought. His eyes narrowed as he realized the star looked familiar. He focused his seer's eyes on its blinding light and saw a clear brush surrounded by clouds of gray mist. *No wonder.* The star represented the karmic anomaly, Du Cha Ming. And now, he was alone and unprotected.

According to his sight, the young man from the Song Kingdom was headed toward the ocean. He was on a collision course with one of Zhou Li's most promising plans and would likely derail everything if left unchecked. He thanked his lucky stars he'd noticed. He still had time, if he acted quickly.

Zhou Li woke, his grogginess and blurred vision disappearing in less than a second. He washed his face and fixed his robes, then walked through the blacksteel door of his personal chambers, passing his deathsworn guards on the way out. These slaves, bound by devilish contracts, followed him and ensured no one approached him unbidden.

Several turns and a long staircase later, Zhou Li entered a room. Twelve men sat there discussing plans, while others stood off to the side. He nodded slightly to the man he'd needed to call "master" a few years back, and the man returned a deep bow. Fate was funny that way. He, a mere mortal cultivator, now enjoyed a higher ranking than a transcendent. But when you played a game as long as theirs, cultivation realms hardly mattered. Only a few individuals in the room had the standing to discuss matters with him, and even then, barely so. When he spoke, others listened. For he had the sight, the plan, and the vision.

"There's been a change of plans," Zhou Li said. "We need to accelerate phase sixteen or forever lose the opportunity."

The men at the table frowned. They exchanged confused glances, and their looks toward the maps on the table were very telling. Some were nautical maps, while others were trade contracts and promises.

"Would you care to elaborate?" a man finally said. He was a transcendent, and his position in their hierarchy made his standing only slightly inferior to Zhou Li's.

"The complexity of the situation makes it difficult to explain everything," Zhou Li said in an annoyed tone. "But long story short, the karmic anomaly known as Du Cha Ming is moving again. He's returned from Jade Moon Planet stronger than ever."

"How certain are you that he'll derail our plans?" the man asked.

"Sixty percent," Zhou Li said. "And that's if we accelerate the plan but don't otherwise hamper him. Ninety percent if we do nothing in response to his actions."

"And if we add you into the mix?" the man said.

Zhou Li grinned. Those were the words he'd been waiting for. "Fifteen percent chance of derailment, but sixty percent chance of removing him permanently. He might be strong on this plane, but compared to me, he's weak. He's also separated from most of his friends."

"We should just remove him," a gruff-sounding man said from the side. The gray-haired man had sharp teeth and bloodred eyes. Despite these frightening features, his tanned skin and chiseled jawline made him unusually attractive.

"Sure," Zhou Li said. "Which of our transcendents would like to volunteer for this mission? Lu Tianhao only has two men guarding him as we speak, so in all, we'd only have to sacrifice three transcendents to get the job done."

His sarcasm was biting and served to highlight their greatest weakness—fear of death. Despite all their power and tens of thousands of years of effort, death and reincarnation wasn't something anyone wanted to go through needlessly. It was due to this weakness that, despite his vision and planning, they'd yet to succeed. Their fear wasn't unfounded, of course. Who could truly know if there *would* be a next life? They'd already lost half of their original members through spiritual erosion, and any one of them could be next.

"We'll cede to your better judgment," the original man said, defusing the situation. "When are you leaving?"

"Immediately," Zhou Li said. "Meanwhile, please contact the Spirit Temple. They need to remain vigilant and push for early completion. It will cost them, but they'll regret it if they don't."

The man sighed. "I'll try, but you know how stubborn they are."

"I do," Zhou Li said. "But if they fail again, I won't be able to guarantee their standing in the Alliance. I'll let the Buddhists come at them with everything they have, and they'll soon learn that even monks can harbor grudges."

The man gulped. "I'll pass on the message."

"I don't doubt you will," Zhou Li said. Then, he turned to a taciturn man in a corner, a man who'd yet to say anything. "Is everything going well on your end?"

"Peachy," he said. "Run along and don't meddle with my plans. You're not good at this sort of thing."

"I suppose I'm not," Zhou Li said. He hated war, as it was a boring, chaotic mess. As he left the room, the building, and his associates, he began fleshing out a plan. Countless threads of possibility danced before his eyes. He plucked them, one by one, evaluating his future actions.

Elsewhere in the universe, an old man with white hair and timeless eyes gazed at a trickling stream in a mighty canyon. The man was Yama, and like any good CEO, he was doing research. Market research. The River of Souls, which usually delivered a constant flood of fresh clients, had receded. It now ran at less than ten percent capacity, as though the mighty lake from which it flowed had been dammed, preventing it from escaping downstream.

Such a slowdown was unusual, especially given the current political climate. It was like the river had been purposefully slowed, stopped up until the reservoir was full to bursting. Eventually, it would burst, and given their stretched resources, Yama wasn't sure how he'd deal with it.

I need more employees, Yama thought. *Good ones.* He shifted his thoughts back on the solution: politics. He hated politics. Unfortunately, winning the election was now more important than ever. If they didn't get more workers soon, the entire universe might collapse within an Underworld millennium, and he really didn't know how he'd answer to the board if that happened.

Then again, he thought, *I might just be the only one to survive a universal collapse.* Maybe the Jade Emperor could survive, or even the Curse Sovereign. Neither of them, however, were good company. Shuddering, he whipped out his phone and sent a message to Han Yu. He waited for a second before following up to her reply: Yes, he wanted all of them. All the books in the universe. He'd take all the movies too, but unfortunately, data storage devices got atrociously expensive once they reached a certain size.

Han Yu soon appeared beside him wearing her trademark gray dress suit. She pushed up her black-rimmed glasses and flicked through a tablet before pulling up an appointment. "It's time for the rally at Time Square," she said. "I've taken the liberty of having your reaper's robes dry cleaned."

Yama nodded and motioned for the package in her hands. It disappeared and reappeared on his own body, replacing the jogging suit he'd been wearing and making him look like the Western depiction of the god of death. His bony, albeit strong hands looked skeletal enough; all he was missing was a scythe, but he loathed to carry that archaic tool. Like the farmers before him, he, too, had outgrown the traditional cutting instrument. He now relied on machinery and highly skilled labor to harvest souls.

Han Yu held out her hand, which Yama grasped. Their surroundings lurched as they reappeared in a square where a large clock tower was present. True to its name, Time Square was inhabited by the Sea God and his wife, the goddess of time. The giant clock tower presiding over the square could house billions of spirits within its independent space. It was a great place for holding a speech.

Speaking of which, Judah, his candidate for mayor, was just stepping up to the podium beneath the giant clock. His short stature didn't matter much, as everyone present was able to zoom in on him and hear him clearly. He held his hands up and waited for everyone to quiet down.

"Ladies and gentlemen, buddhas and spirits, angels and devils, demons, and those who belong to a species but don't wish to be associated with them… we have a crisis on our hands," Judah said gravely. "The cycle of reincarnation is under threat. Though it's true that the demand for souls and soul products is greater than ever, we are struggling. We're struggling to bring our resources to market.

"Our neighbors have abandoned us; they've changed their tax policies to attract the best and the brightest. Meanwhile, all we're left with are hardworking devils, lazy demons, and slightly pompous angels who've decided they want to live in this great country without contributing anything to it. It isn't enough."

"Those angels are arrogant!" a man suddenly yelled out in the crowd.

"They think they're better than us!" a woman yelled.

"I don't know about that," Judah said reassuringly. "I'm sure there are some very fine people on both sides."

"Send them back!" a voice yelled.

"Send them back!" another dozen voices yelled. And suddenly, the bewildered Judah was drowned out by chanting voices. "Send them back! Send them back!"

What the hell is going on? the wide-eyed Yama thought. This was supposed to be a campaign rally, not a gathering for spirit supremacists. He wondered if he should do anything, but then he decided that forcefully reincarnating the lot would be counterproductive to his efforts to gather votes.

Then, his eyes narrowed when he saw Judah's response. The man pumped his fist almost encouragingly and did nothing to stop them. The chanting lasted far too long before Yama, fed up with the spectacle, coughed lightly in intimidation. The crowd quieted instantly.

"Right," Judah said awkwardly. "That was… unexpected. Like I said, we don't have a lot of spare spirits in Diyu, and it's important to draw people in. Not everyone, mind you—only the best and the brightest."

"No angels!" a man said.

Yama didn't wait this time. He snapped his finger, and the soul was whisked away to a special hell he reserved for pedophiles and people who talked in movie theaters. That would teach him.

"That's why it's important that you come out and vote," Judah continued. "Vote for the Diyu Advantage so we can bring the best and the brightest to this city. Together, we can prosper. Together, we can win."

The remainder of the rally was uneventful. The few scattered voices that tried to egg on the crowd were forcibly detained, and the mayoral candidate got down to business. He talked about fiscal responsibility, taxes, and recognition of professional accreditations. He talked about legal immigration, and for some strange reason, a wall to prevent illegal immigration. Finally, he mentioned destroying some unpopular art, the proposed ban on time travel literature—which, to Yama's surprise, the time goddess approved of—and finally, a message to make Diyu great again. Like it wasn't already.

The crowd dispersed, and soon they were back in Yama's office. The spirit that used to be a mere mortal trembled slightly as Yama curled his lips in disapproval.

"Do you know why we're having this meeting?" he asked, tapping his bony fingers on the desk. Fortunately for the object, it was an empyrean god-grade artifact. It could handle the abuse.

The short man gulped. "It's about the wall, isn't it? Yes, I know it's inhumane, but we really need to make sure everything is legitimate. And as much as it isn't practical, there's a certain amount of symbolism—"

Yama cut him off. "No. Great circle of reincarnation, no. I've been arguing that we need a wall for decades. I want as many immigrants as possible, but only legally, which isn't rocket science as long as you hire a few government employees to file the paperwork." He sighed. "No, I called you here because I'm disappointed. I'm disappointed in your behavior. You should have condemned those bigots. Instead, you almost egged them on."

"That's not true," Judah said. "I wasn't happy with it. I disagreed with it. And I didn't say that. They did. I started speaking very quickly."

"Thirteen seconds," Yama said sharply. "You waited thirteen seconds. Do you know what people can do in thirteen seconds?" Seeing that Judah was speechless, he picked up Han Yu's tablet, which conveniently listed off many things mortals on Earth, Judah's home planet, could do in thirteen seconds. "An earth mortal can run 100 meters in thirteen seconds on Earth. He can buy something online in thirteen seconds. He can down a pint of beer, solve a Rubik's cube, or can break into someone's home in thirteen seconds. Hell, he can probably peel and eat a mandarin orange in that time. And you're going to tell me you started speaking very quickly?"

"Point taken," Judah said. "I'll cut in faster next time."

"It's too late for a next time!" Yama said. "Thirteen seconds is all it takes to form a first impression. Now we need to run damage control." He breathed deeply and controlled his emotions. "Now we need to deal with the media. Those politically correct news anchors will tear you to shreds. We need to demonize them and tell everyone their news is fake. Or we could just reincarnate anyone who dares publish any bad articles."

"That sounds a bit harsh," Judah said. "Can't we just do some serious backpedalling and apologize like reasonable people?"

Yama paused. "What does apologize mean?"

"Are you serious?" Judah said.

Yama nodded.

"It's when you're, you know, wrong. And then you admit that to everyone."

"But I've never been wrong in my life," Yama said. Which was true. Every time someone had told him otherwise, he'd obliterated them from the face of the universe, which, as far as he was concerned, cut at the root of the problem.

"Right…" Judah said. "Which is why you have me. I was wrong, and I can do the apologizing. I'll save some face, and you won't have to do anything drastic. Make sense?"

"Somewhat," Yama said. "I may need convincing. Just do what it is you do, but don't hesitate to tell me if I should annihilate someone. Do we have a deal?"

"Sure thing," Judah said, wiping the sweat off his brow. "I'll be going now." The short man walked out of his office, looking back nervously before closing the door.

"Mortals," Yama muttered in bemusement.

Han Yu came in moments later, ushering in his next appointment.

Chapter 1: True North Country

Cha Ming and his four disciples looked around in marvel as they entered Beihai City, the largest coastal city in True North Country. They saw boats entering and exiting the busy harbor in the distance, their sharp eyes aiding them in rendering it in the finest detail. The buildings in the old city had a rustic charm to them; their stone construction and the salty air reminded Cha Ming that he'd yet to see an ocean in this lifetime.

"Where's Mermaid's Place?" Huxian asked eagerly as he jumped onto his older brother's shoulder.

Cha Ming scratched him between the ears and smiled.

"It should be near the western docks," Cha Ming answered. "Coffee first?"

"Coffee," Huxian said. It was another life and another time, but somehow, the beverage had found its way into this world as well. They entered a crowded building where people discussed both business and their daily lives. Most of them were mortals. Despite this fact, their group of four cultivators and a demon drew little attention as they made their way to a bar staffed by moderately attractive women who made coffee while desperate men ogled them.

"My friends and I will each have a large cup of... True North Blend," Cha Ming said. The name was purely coincidental. As it were, True North Country resembled Cha Ming's Earth home in many ways. For one, it was colder than all other human-inhabited territories. For another, it was the only democracy on the continent. Like that would last.

"Do you mean a dabei or a chao dabei?" the lady asked. She wore the innocent smile of someone who'd completely given in to her corporate overlords.

"Chao dabei," Cha Ming said, massaging his brow. Whether it was corporate culture or strict branding regulations, some things never changed.

Soon enough, they sat on a balcony enjoying their steaming hot beverages. The scent of rotting fish was thick in the air, but as a body cultivator, Cha Ming dulled himself to these external smells. He reserved his senses for sip after sip of blessed coffee, enjoying the dark but slightly bitter taste as it danced around his tongue.

"This is life," Cha Ming said to the others.

Unlike him, they weren't taking kindly to the stimulating beverage. Some of them had even polluted their drinks with milk, sugar, and flavoring. A travesty if he'd ever seen one.

"I'd wager I could make something with a similar taste, if a little more potent," Jin Huang said, smacking his lips in appreciation. "A thousandfold increase in strength might do the trick."

Cha Ming's eyes lit up. He took the young man by the shoulders and spoke sternly. "I knew when I first laid eyes on you that you'd be my favorite disciple."

The others groaned. Noticing that his abrupt movements had surprised other patrons, Cha Ming sat back down and continued to drink. As he did, he pondered his disciples' paths and how he might help them. His way of thinking had changed during his journey to Jade Moon Planet. The ten years he and Huxian had spent there made him much more suitable to guiding them compared to who he was before he left. As a late-marrow-refining cultivator and a middle-core-formation cultivator, only transcendents could bully him now. As for Huxian and his friends, well, they were only middle-core-formation demon beasts, but he wasn't the least bit confident about taking them on as a team. All of them had power in spades now.

Power. It's something we gained in our ten years on Jade Moon Planet, Cha Ming thought. We got techniques, alchemical manuals, and even an entire herb garden.

But he'd give it all up in a heartbeat for one more day with Yu Wen. Now he only had one chance at seeing her again: finding her in the cycle of reincarnation and restoring her memories. And for that, he'd need to become an immortal. His sights were set on the higher realms now, conveniently aligning with Huxian's ambitious goal of savoring everything in the universe.

Older brother? Huxian asked, jumping on his shoulder and breaking him from his reverie.

Yes, Huxian? Cha Ming asked. He took another sip of dark coffee.

There's something interesting going on just outside our building, Huxian said. *I think it deserves a second look.*

I noticed a short while ago, Cha Ming said, focusing on the blip in his intangible field of transcendent force. A teenage girl, surprisingly strong for her tender age, was running away from two men. She had a large lead on them and would soon escape their pursuit.

Is there something I'm missing? Cha Ming asked. Huxian wouldn't bring it up if it were trivial.

Embrace my shadow qi, Huxian said.

Cha Ming obliged. The world changed as black and white inverted, and a completely different scene appeared. In the shadows, he saw people appearing and disappearing as they entered the dark world for seconds at a time. There were also the usual creatures of shadow that were born one moment and died the next. He ignored these and focused on the area near the girl, where he now saw several dozen deadly pursuers. They didn't exit the shadows but clung to them with purpose.

"I need to go," Cha Ming said to his startled disciples.

He and Huxian jumped off the balcony and onto the street below. Vendors and mortals shouted in indignation as he zipped past them. He soon reached the two men chasing the girl in the open. They were normal thugs, nothing more, so he gently tapped their skulls and sent them tumbling to the side of the road, unconscious. He then appeared next to the girl, who looked at him in alarm.

"Who are you?" the girl asked, clutching her right hand warily. He saw it flash as she retrieved something from her storage device.

"A friend," Cha Ming said gently. "Are you aware that there are forty men trailing you in the shadows as we speak, all of them armed and dangerous?"

Her eyes narrowed. Before she got a chance to reply, Huxian yelled out in warning. *Incoming!*

Explosions of blades, flames, ice, and gold erupted from the shadows. Cha Ming summoned a barrier of sigils and blocked the bulk of these techniques, picking up the surprised girl as he did. She might be strong for her age—a middle-bone-forging cultivator—but she was nothing compared to these men. His body tanked damage from several blades, healing instantly from the shallow cuts and lacerations. Cha Ming summoned his Clear Sky Staff, then, seeing the nearby vendor stalls, chose to block an incoming blow rather than kill the assailant.

It's a little hard to fight back against them, Cha Ming said. *Can you take them out without destroying the city?* He was, after all, responsible for all damage both he and Huxian inflicted.

On it! Huxian said. He entered the shadows, and all around them, puddles of blood appeared out of nowhere.

Do you have any parents or guardians I could take you to? Cha Ming sent, clutching the girl closely.

I have two guardians near Central Square, the girl sent back, shivering in his tight embrace. Fire came out of nowhere, and Cha Ming summoned a shield of qi to protect them. He reached out into the shadows and plucked out a cultivator by the throat. The surprised assassin transformed, his skin instantly transforming to the purest gold.

"Wrong move," Cha Ming said. His eyes turned pale jade as he poured Devil-Sealing intent into his fist and crushed the devil's throat. It howled as it became gold shavings that littered the city streets. Civilians and cultivators alike screamed to get out of the way as a burst of fire erupted around them. Cha Ming summoned two icy formations, one for them and one for their audience. The strain was ultimately too much for their own shield, so he expanded his qi to surround the girl with a protective bubble.

Huxian appeared beside them, his maw covered in blood.

"Was that all of them?" Cha Ming asked.

The small fox nodded.

He loosened his grip on the girl, but just as she left his embrace, Cha Ming felt a burst of power and a glint in the distance. It shot toward her at lightning speed. He threw up three hasty combat formations, but what looked like a small golden pin pierced through them all in an instant. He threw up his qi shields to block for her, but it was too little too late—the pin pierced her in the chest, knocking her backward and into his arms.

"Get him, Huxian!" Cha Ming growled. He lay her down on the ground and realized there wasn't any blood. A quick inspection confirmed what saved her: a golden medallion with mystical blue runes nestled behind her clothes. "It's better to be lucky than good," he muttered.

His eyes flickered as two powerful presences appeared. To his surprise, they were both peak-marrow-refining cultivators. He doubted there were more than a handful of these on the continent.

"Unhand her," the man said calmly. "If you release her now, we'll grant you a swift death and won't hunt down your entire family."

"I think there's a misunderstanding," Cha Ming said with a raised eyebrow. But before he could react, the man appeared behind him and put a sword at his throat. The woman slipped in front of him and carried the girl off to the side.

"Any last words, savage?" the man said.

Cha Ming shrugged. "Do you really think an assassin would kill his own men?"

The man paused. He looked around and noticed pools of blood in the surrounding blocks, along with puddles of water and heaps of gold. Vicious, poison-coated weapons littered the streets around them.

"I suppose not," the man finally said, pulling back his blade. He walked over to the girl, who'd just woken up. She was coughing and rubbing the spot where the pin had struck her medallion.

"Thank you," the girl said, looking up at Cha Ming. "Thank you for saving my life."

It was only now that Cha Ming noticed how strange she and her guardians were. Her hair was long and white, and her skin was a slightly blue shade of white that was covered in blue-and-gold runes; it was completely at odds with the normal clothes she wore. She looked fourteen, fifteen at most. Her guardians, unlike her, did not sport any runes on their skin. They did, however, have strange white hair that seemed to float about, despite the absence of wind.

"Haijing thanks you for your assistance," said the woman. "My name is Gong Rufeng."

"And my name is Gong Su," the man said.

To Cha Ming's surprise, the two mighty cultivators bowed at him with arms raised and fists clasped. "We thank you for saving our young mistress."

"It was no problem," Cha Ming said. He looked to Huxian, who'd just come back with a man in tow. He threw the late-core-formation cultivator to the ground. Cha Ming moved in to interrogate the man but noticed he was already dead.

"Poison," Huxian said. "Ate it when he knew he was caught. I hate eating poison, so I brought his body back."

"An assassination attempt that could have been avoided," the man said with a scolding tone to the teenage girl. "If only you'd stayed by our side. Have you learned your lesson, young lady?"

The girl, who'd somehow grown a little paler, nodded. "I'll stay beside you from now on." She then looked to Cha Ming. "I'm not sure what I can give you in payment."

"No payment required," Cha Ming said. "It was my pleasure."

"Nonsense," the girl said. "I, Gong Shuren, owe karma. Karma is something Haijing cannot owe, so I must somehow repay you." She thought for a moment, then her expression lit up. She reached around her neck and pulled out the blue-and-gold medallion."

"You mustn't!" Gong Su said.

"I must," Gong Shuren said, berating her guardian with her gaze. "And this as well." She pulled out a blue-gold disc, and within it, Cha Ming could see a swirl of something intangible. Huxian stopped him as he moved to refuse her.

That disc contains the essence of time, Huxian said. *Accept it!*

"Thank you," Cha Ming said, taking the disc but leaving the medallion. It was clearly very precious. He closed her hand around it. "No need to give us any precious treasures. My friend here says this disc is extremely valuable. It will do. You owe us nothing."

"But—" she started.

"No buts," Cha Ming said. He clasped his hands and bowed to the two cultivators. "I'd better get going. Do be careful as you travel. Those assassins weren't normal cultivators but devil cultivators. They're more dangerous than they seem, and the lives of others are meaningless in their eyes."

Seeing Gong Su's grave nod, Cha Ming rushed back to his disciples, who'd been waiting anxiously in the café. They were greeted by angry guardsmen and a civilian police officer.

Well, that could have gone better, Huxian grumbled as they walked out of the guard office.

"How so?" Cha Ming said. "They just want us to leave within twenty-four hours and ban us for a year. I think it's reasonable, given how many things we wrecked."

But it's their fault for letting assassins into the city to attack people! Huxian exclaimed.

"They frankly don't care what people do, as long as they don't commit crimes and destroy buildings," Cha Ming said. "Though self-defense is allowed, collateral damage is not."

It's so unfair, Huxian said.

All four of his disciples rose as they exited the prison.

"Master, we missed our appointment with Lan Xue," Yue Bing said. The woman, who used to be a gentle spirit doctor, now wore red robes. Her temperament had changed drastically since he'd left for Jade Moon Planet.

"Yes," Cha Ming said, "I heard he's a little eccentric. I hope he's still willing to take us."

They walked down several roads until they reached a poorer area of town. The buildings there were dirty and worn, and they wondered if they were in the right place. They soon discovered the place they were looking for: The Deep Sea Emporium.

The Deep Sea Emporium was, admittedly, a bit of a dump. Scattered, disorganized treasures littered the shelves, and a man was sleeping at the counter. He seemed to be dreaming. Cha Ming felt a tingling sensation as he walked across an invisible boundary. He frowned and repelled the invading dream, while Huxian ate it. All his disciples but Zi Long suddenly crumpled to the ground as they were dragged into a dream.

"It'll do them some good to suffer a mental technique, especially a non-offensive one," Zi Long said, shrugging.

"My thoughts exactly," Cha Ming replied. "You've learned a few extra tricks. Illusionist, right?"

"Something like that," Zi Long said. "I'm now a heart-force cultivator, majoring in illusions. It might seem like a small distinction, but it makes a world of difference."

"I'll bet," Cha Ming said. Through his transcendent soul, he could see a violet hue staining his disciple's soul. A spirit resided there as well, much like Sun Wukong resided in his own Clear Sky Brush. It didn't seem malevolent, so he left it alone.

Yue Bing's eyes snapped open first, followed by Jin Huang's. Ling Dong came last, and he awoke with bestial fury. Cha Ming appeared beside him and placed his powerful hand on his shoulder, holding him down to prevent any misunderstandings. They might not know how powerful the sleeping man was, but he did.

"Let him at me if he wants," grumbled the man, who'd clearly been feigning sleep. He yawned and stretched out his arms. "I could use a warmup."

"As much as I care about their education, Lan Xuan, a peak-core-formation cultivator bullying juniors isn't exactly educational," Cha Ming said.

Ling Dong's eyes widened as he realized the mistake he'd almost committed.

Lan Xuan grinned. "You're too soft on them, Cha Ming."

"I feel people learn best by example," Cha Ming said. "Why don't you tussle with Huxian? It seems dreams make for good eating."

The black-and-white fox was salivating, almost begging the man to oblige.

Lan Xuan grunted. He walked over to a desk and pulled out a piece of pure white paper with blue lines. Beihai City was a single dot at the edge of the ocean, and Haijing City was a bright golden dot in the center of it. The two points were separated by a gap ten times wider than the plane's single continent. He handed white discs to each of them. Unlike normal compasses, they contained two needles, one blue and one gold.

"The gold needle points to Beihai City, while the blue one points to Haijing City," Lan Xuan said. "If any of you get lost, you only need to follow the needle along the sea floor or the surface, and you'll find your way back to Beihai. The pressure near Haijing is intense, even for peak-core-formation cultivators, so I don't recommend heading back there."

Cha Ming nodded. "Do we need anything else?"

"City passes," Lan Xuan said. He held out blue tokens with gold writing to each of them. "Haijing issues a limited quantity every decade, and they're expensive. Don't lose them."

"Not a problem," Cha Ming said.

"Everyone should get some sleep," Lan Xuan said. "The darkness down there can be unbearable. I want everyone in good mental shape before we go down. Understood?"

"Yes, sir!" everyone said.

"Great," Lan Xuan said. Then, to Cha Ming's surprise, the man snapped his fingers. Everyone but he and Huxian fell asleep.

Cha Ming chuckled. "Saves on hotel rooms, I guess."

He found an empty room. Then, instead of sleeping, he summoned a gray portal and entered the Clear Sky World.

"Took you long enough," a gruff voice said as Cha Ming entered Jade Moon Garden, the single landmass floating within the Clear Sky World. He looked toward a nearby mountain and appeared beside a tall red-bearded man holding a large stone staff. Now that his soul was healed, Sun Wukong sported a furry red monkey tail as well.

"My apologies for keeping you waiting, Teacher Sun," Cha Ming said.

Sun Wukong grunted. "It's not as lonely here as it used to be. The fish and the nymphs taking care of the garden are pleasant company. Especially the nymphs if I look past their dreadful, soul-sucking habits."

Cha Ming cleared his throat. "What's next on the agenda?"

"So impatient," Sun Wukong said. "So hardworking." He lifted his hand, and a cauldron appeared. "Today, we're going to learn about fire."

"Again?" Cha Ming groaned. It was his least-favorite subject.

"You have your strengths, and fire isn't one of them," Sun Wukong said. "You might cultivate five elements, but your proficiency in each isn't balanced. You're going to have to work ten times as hard as anyone else to be an alchemist, and the only reason you have half a chance is because of your absurdly strong soul."

Cha Ming closed his eyes. "What will it be this time?" he asked, accepting his fate.

Sun Wukong grinned. "You're finally accepting your place. Great! To celebrate, I've thought up an extrafun activity."

He closed his fist, and Cha Ming disappeared and reappeared inside the cauldron. Sun Wukong's voice came from all directions. "Evade the flames for as long as possible."

Ten flames appeared in five different colors. "You're to evade them while keeping five different flames summoned and circulating, as I taught you."

Cha Ming gulped. After all, unlike before, he was here in the flesh; whatever had brought Jade Moon Garden into his Clear Sky World had changed the Clear Sky World on a fundamental level.

He summoned five different alchemical flames, one for each of the five elements. The blue flame controlled flow while the red one controlled temperature. The brown flame separated while the golden one lacerated. Finally, the green one gave life. He circulated all five of them along a complex runic pattern he didn't understand, using over nine-tenths of his transcendent force to make it happen.

Meanwhile, the ten flames in the cauldron danced. He used his remaining soul force as a sort of peripheral vision, twisting and turning to avoid them as they attacked. Before long, he made a mistake; his soul projection suffered a minor burn.

As time passed, the drill gradually became easier. When he finally managed to control his flames and resist the attacks, ten more flames appeared for a total of twenty. Then, when he bested twenty, ten more appeared. Their training session ended after ten hours. Cha Ming's body and soul were scorched, but he had to admit that his gains were noticeable.

He appeared as a collapsed heap outside the cauldron, where a flurry of rainbow fish appeared to greet him. The smallest among them was grinning ear to ear. "Cha Ming! Cha Ming! Do you want to play a game?"

He smiled sadly. "Sure, what game would you like to play?"

"Chicks and eagles," the fish said. "You make a great eagle, and it's so difficult to run away."

Memories of playing the same game with Yu Wen surfaced in his heart, and the warmth eased the pain of the burns he'd just suffered.

"Sure," Cha Ming said. He looked to Sun Wukong. "Are you game as well?"

The Monkey King snorted. "I'll be in my cave. Go ahead and play your childish games."

The game soon started, and for thirty brief minutes, Cha Ming knew peace. Then, he woke.

Chapter 2:
Journey into the Deep

The Northern ocean was cold, far colder than most mortals could stand, even in this magical world. Yet despite the frigid temperature, its salty waters stubbornly refused to freeze. They were laced with something—a trace of gold qi that kept its molecules from forming an orderly structure. No ice could form, so no icebergs or ice sheets ever graced these Northern waters.

Cha Ming shivered as he plunged directly into the vast ocean, escaping the howling winds and open skies. The cold intensified as he dove, but as a late-marrow-refining cultivator, the pain it caused him was tolerable, almost pleasant. And as they descended, Huxian and his friends changed.

The small fox's fur became oily and coated with thick demonic energy; his swimming changed from a slow wade to an effortless rush. Likewise, Silverwing's feathers receded, making his wings more like flippers. Lei Jiang's weight adjusted his buoyancy, and small extensions of demonic qi extended from his short legs. Gua was the only one who didn't change; his amphibious nature made him more or less immune to the trials they'd face in the depths of the ocean.

How are you four holding up? Lan Xuan asked. The man had donned a necklace that enveloped him in a powerful blue membrane. He wielded a trident, a suitable weapon given the oceanic environment. The dreamer had vanished upon awakening, leaving a fearsome warrior in his place.

Did you study the diagrams as I instructed? Cha Ming asked the four.

We did, but we didn't have the knowledge to understand it, Zi Long said. *What was it for?*

Cha Ming was disappointed but not surprised. They'd progressed far on their own path, putting the runic arts he'd taught them to the wayside. He held two fingers to the front and summoned a swirl of ink from the Clear Sky World. It separated into mostly blue runes and complementary red, gold, brown, and green runes. Once the last of the runes had formed, they shot out toward the four and imprinted themselves on their skins. A membrane spread out from the runes, completely encapsulating their bodies.

The suits can be banished at will, Cha Ming sent. *They'll decrease your friction underwater, fight pressure and cold, and enable you to control buoyancy. While you don't need to worry about breathing, it will also supply you with air if you so wish.* They nodded in thanks, but their embarrassment was clear. This was fine by him, since shame was a great motivator.

The ocean grew darker, and a few miles away from the rocky shore, the slightly tapered seabed plunged down into the black unknown. Their vision almost instantly lost its effectiveness, making it necessary to rely on their souls to probe their surroundings. The transition was a bit jarring, but soon they were introduced to a whole new world.

Mostly blue and purple reefs littered the sandy landscape while smaller demonic fish swam merrily between corals. Crystal starfish laid on the seabed while amorphous but living agglomerations of salt and metal floated around, absorbing whatever stray particles they could. There were few predatory demons here, and Cha Ming wondered if it had anything to do with their proximity to the shore. Perhaps the residents of Beihai hunted them? It was one of many questions that would invade his tranquil mind as they descended.

Time stretched on as they worked their way through the ocean, sometimes barely above the bottom. At other times they could see only vast, endless waters in every direction. Sound traveled far here, but aside from the soft swishing of their movements, they were surrounded by a deathly, suffocating quiet.

Concurrently, the pressure mounted. As they dove deeper, Cha Ming's body felt a steady push against his skin, which was quickly remedied by the blue runes he'd painted on himself. They were a mile down now, and his eyes barely functioned. The only "sight" he could rely on were faint emanations of demonic qi that stood out thanks to his violet irises, as well as his morphed eyes from the Seventy-Two Transformations Technique that allowed him to pick up remote traces of light. He also had his transcendent soul. All three incomplete pictures were superimposed, leaving him with only a faint vision of a purple void.

At the two-mile mark, they finally saw movement in what resembled an underwater graveyard more and more. It was a school of demonic tuna, and the group was happy to swim through the large number of peaceful demonic fish. They swam with them for a while until they suddenly scattered. Giant squid zipped into the school and caught one of the students, dragging it into a dark fissure on the ocean floor. Cha Ming didn't know what he expected, but he found himself inexplicably disappointed when the other tuna continued on, as though the disappearance of one of their thousands of members meant little. It was a testament to the cold and merciless nature of the ocean that, in a strange way, resembled the darkness of a magma-filled volcano.

That thought bred others, and soon he thought of his days on Jade Moon Planet. The days in the quiet waters became more like an ethereal dream of what once was and what could have been. A gentle smile, a calming embrace. Grief unlike anything he'd ever felt. And hope. Hope to see her again. The reason for his mission here. These thoughts were more potent in these dark surroundings, the perfect incubator for dreams and nightmares.

Some of them were of the mind, and others were real. As someone with a transcendent soul, he knew what was lurking in the deep. Demonic creatures measuring hundreds of feet long roamed the darkness below them, probing at them as they passed. Some looked like monstrous abominations with hooked maws filled with nothing but teeth. Others had massive eyes that, despite the absence of light, could still see. It was as though they'd morphed, and instead of taking in light, they drank in darkness.

Yet as interested as those things were, they all shied away. When Cha Ming asked, Lan Xuan was only too happy to elaborate.

Sea God Command, he said, pointing to an amulet around his neck. *Won't go anywhere near it.*

Cha Ming relaxed a little when he heard this. Though he was confident in his strength, he had no desire to tussle with those fanged and tentacled creatures that, as far as he was concerned, belonged in the seven hells.

They swam some more, and the darkness deepened. They swam and swam, and then, when light seemed like nothing more than a distant memory, they saw a beacon in the distance.

At first, Cha Ming didn't know if it was real or just a figment of his imagination, a hallucination created by his starved mind. Then the others noticed it too. It grew clearer with every hour, and before long, a tower appeared where the light had been. It stood tall beside a large bone that resembled the skull of a deceased god. It bathed the now-visible sea floor in a soft blue light.

Whatever the light touched came to life. Where there used to be rocky outcroppings and sandy floors, they now saw various forms of algae that survived despite the lack of oxygen. Multicolored schools of fish appeared, dancing joyfully beneath the enchanting blue glow. Human swimmers soon appeared, and flora and fauna of all kinds.

The tower grew clearer as they swam, and soon a large circle appeared on it. No, it wasn't a circle—it was a clock. The tower was actually a giant clock tower that overlooked the entire seabed, and just below it was an assortment of bubbles. There was one large bubble stretching out wider than the tower was tall, while many other small bubbles floated around it. All the bubbles were connected by clear bridges, and each one hosted its own source of light.

The bubbles were cities, and Haijing was the largest of them. Its delicate porcelain spires and soft blue lights were a wonderful sight to behold in the alien deep-sea world. The small bubbles appeared to be villages, farms, and other facilities that supported the capital of the Sea God Empire. Patrols mounted on dolphins, manta rays, and strange crustaceans roamed around, fighting stray demons that came too close to Haijing's exterior.

It's beautiful, Cha Ming thought as he floated there, paralyzed by the city's beauty.

Lan Xuan chuckled and swam up beside him. "Most people react the same way the first time they see it. It's unlike anything on the surface, and to be honest, it's this scene that keeps me doing what I do."

Cha Ming looked around and noticed that many humans were swimming around, whether it be guards or other cultivators swimming below the ocean. To his surprise, their qi reserves were almost nonexistent, and their soul cultivation even more so. Further, many of these people had a blueish or pale tinge to their skin, while many sported gills or runes on the sides of their throats. A few even had white hair. Everyone was either toned or muscular, without exception.

Seeing Cha Ming's inquiring gaze, Lan Xuan explained. "Most cultivators in the Ling Nan Plane ascend through qi cultivation, or demons through demonic cultivation. But the citizens of Haijing City are different. They aren't normal humans like the rest of us. All of them are descendants of the Sea God. A trace of divinity runs through their veins, and as a result, body cultivation comes naturally to them. They're especially well-adapted to pressure. The constant stimulation from their environment is very helpful to their advancement."

God's blood. Now that's interesting, Cha Ming thought. He'd never heard of gods until now and had previously thought they were only myths from his old world, a fable conjured by hopeful men and women to push through difficult times. Which was fine, given the virtues they represented. But to hear that they were real flesh and blood creatures and that their blood had very real impacts on their descendants, that was something new to him. He resolved to find out more about it.

Haijing loomed closer as they swam toward it. The journey was much farther than they'd imagined due to an optical illusion stemming from the water. Or perhaps it was the hope in their hearts that made it seem nearer than it really was. The very sight of the city made the fear and despair that had built up in Cha Ming's heart vanish and bloom into a tiny speck of light. It was his desire for immortality. It burned fiercely, and with it came all hope he had of seeing Yu Wen again.

The feeling grew stronger, and because of it, he almost missed a dreadful pressure coming from a chasm near the city. It was a wide fissure that people and fish both avoided. Try as he might, Cha Ming couldn't fathom the bottom. But he *could* see the cliffs that traveled down, and what he saw made him wary. In the caves that peppered the rocky walls were demons that glowed both violet and ochre. Fiendish demons.

Huxian growled as they passed over. Cha Ming wondered why they stayed there, but he soon noticed a light-blue barrier covering the fissure. Was it to protect the fiendish demons or keep them inside? Perhaps both.

Finally, they passed the fissure, and Haijing reappeared in all its unblemished splendor. What had seemed like densely populated oceans now seemed like empty waters in comparison to the sight that greeted them. Tens of millions of cultivators swam around, playing, talking, and working. Convoys of merchants traveled to and from various bubbles, and so too did guardsmen in golden armor riding demonic mounts.

Meanwhile, billions of fish swam all around them. Despite the various fishermen that caught them and dragged them back to the city, they still hovered around in the strong glow of Haijing's blue light. It was as though they obtained nourishment from the light, and the small reduction in their massive numbers was the price they paid for it.

Everyone, I'm pleased to present the main attraction: Haijing City,

Lan Xue said, holding his hands out to a massive golden gate.

It glowed with blue runes and contained three doors. The largest door, the central one, was closed. A large string of cultivators lined up at the door to its right, where guardsmen inspected them prior to entry. A much smaller line of cultivators swam straight through a door on the other side. They all had white hair, the mark of a Haijing noble.

As commoners, they could only wait, but compared to their long swim to the city, the wait was pleasant. A few hours later, they finally swam through the golden gates—only to flop onto the stone streets face-first.

Thank goodness, Cha Ming thought as he picked himself up. He'd wondered long and hard about how he'd do alchemy underwater. That worry behind him, he headed farther into the city.

Chapter 3:
Haijing City

The group followed Lan Xuan straight to Clock Tower Square, the area immediately beneath the giant clock tower. "This is our agreed-upon destination," the large man said. "I'll be returning to Beihai in a week if you need me to pass on any messages."

"Thank you for all the trouble," Cha Ming said.

The man grunted. "Come see me anytime you like. Especially if Jin Huang creates a stronger version of coffee. If it's good enough, I'll help him start up a franchise." The man walked away, leaving Cha Ming, his disciples, and Huxian and friends to do as they pleased.

They didn't have to look long to find their destination: a large white stone complex just opposite the clock tower. It consisted of a series of adjoined buildings including a library, a residence, workshops, and a guild hall for just about every occupation on the continent. A squadron of guards kept careful watch over the entrance as they approached. They allowed people in and out with flashes of their identification badges, some bronze, others silver.

Cha Ming presented his letter of introduction. One of the guards took it inside, and soon they were brought into the complex by a plump but jovial man. Unlike the many members of the academy he'd seen before, this man wore a golden badge.

"Welcome to the Haijing Academy of Science and Technology," the man said. "My name is Gan Quan, one of the residing elders of the Alabaster Group faction in the academy."

"I've heard so much about you from Lu Tianhao," Cha Ming said, bowing slightly. "He says you're the best spiritual blacksmith on the Ling Nan Plane. It's an honor to finally meet you."

Gan Quan flushed. "I wouldn't call myself the best, but I'm definitely in the top twenty," he said proudly. "I happened to get lucky while researching armor-link construction and made a breakthrough to the peak of spiritual blacksmithing. One day, I hope to craft a half-step transcendent treasure." His eyes glimmered as he said this. "But where are my manners? Let's go to the registration bureau."

They crossed an empty grass-filled courtyard on their way to a building with a large door flanked by marble pillars. Four pictographs were shown on the wall—an ankh surrounded by two serpents and angel wings, a hammer, a medicinal cauldron, and a runic diagram. These were the four main professional schools, and many other schools were subsets of them.

"Senior Partner Lu has vouched for your competence as a grandmaster formation master and talisman artist, so I've already submitted your application for a silver membership badge," Gan Quan said. "As a silver member, you can sponsor up to five master-level professionals as bronze members. However, they'll need to obtain approval from their respective occupations here in Haijing."

"I was unaware of this detail, but it shouldn't be a problem," Cha Ming said, nodding. "Spirit doctor, alchemist, spiritual blacksmith, and formation master, right?" he asked his disciples. He regretted not discussing the particulars since his return.

"Actually…" Yue Bing said, stepping back. "I'm afraid I won't be able to obtain the approval of my association. I'll wait outside if that's more convenient."

Cha Ming frowned.

Jin Huang winced. "I may have upset a few people in my organization, so I'll have to recuse myself."

Cha Ming's frowned deepened.

"Same here," Ling Dong said.

Cha Ming facepalmed and cursed himself for being so negligent.

I really should have taken the time to talk to them, he thought. He'd neglected his duties as their master for far too long. Now, it seemed only Zi Long might be allowed inside, but he figured that, given his stubborn temperament, he'd refuse to enter without his brother and sisters.

"Is there really no other way?" Cha Ming asked. He'd hate to have wasted their time in bringing them here. Haijing was a haven for professionals, and anyone who studied here advanced by leaps and bounds. Their motto was "For Science." He hadn't imagined there would be any problems in bringing them here.

"There is," Gan Quan said, nodding slowly. "They would need to become members by obtaining grandmaster qualification in any profession. If they are unable to do so through regular means, we happen to have a means unique to Haijing Academy: the Nine Illusions profession trial. It's costly to activate, but if your disciples can prove to the formation that they have the skills of a grandmaster professional, they'll get their membership regardless of sponsorship. Their professional organizations would be unable to object.

"This isn't an uncommon thing. Some people feel they've been discriminated against or denied advancement due to status or wealth. They journey to Haijing City to prove their mettle through the trial, and as a result, certifications obtained here are universally recognized. It won't earn them forgiveness if they did anything too egregious, of course."

"When can they take this test?" Cha Ming asked.

"Allow me to report this matter to the headmaster," Gan Quan said. "It won't take long, but expect an audience."

With that, the man excused himself and entered what seemed like a mansion not far from the administrative building.

A few hours later, Cha Ming, Gan Quan, and a few other elders were chatting in a large audience hall. Huxian was somewhere else in the city, doing whatever it was that demons did to alleviate boredom.

Many normal members had trickled in. All four of his disciples, including Zi Long, had opted to take the test. They were seated before a golden arch etched with blue runes representing various professions. The four main ones were glaringly obvious, but some of the lesser ones piqued his interest, like pyromancy and herbology. There were thousands upon thousands of runes, many unknown to him. He wondered if there were thousands of professions as well.

"Is this arch truly able to evaluate any profession objectively?" Cha Ming asked. "Such a thing doesn't seem possible with a mortal artifact."

Gan Quan smiled. "That's because it's a transcendent artifact with its own intelligence. Not only can it evaluate known professions, it can also name new ones if the profession deviates significantly from the original occupation it's based on."

Cha Ming nodded. "I was negligent. I returned to this plane from Jade Moon Planet just a week ago and didn't take time to question their abilities or what they'd been through over the past year. I'd thought there would be more than enough time when we got to the city."

"They'll all pass," a voice said from behind him. "But whether or not you wish to accept their results is a different question entirely."

Cha Ming's eyes narrowed. He knew that voice. He summoned his Clear Sky Staff, and the air around him crackled as he turned to look the new arrival in the eyes.

"Zhou Li!" Cha Ming growled. A soft boom echoed through the room as he broke the sound barrier, his powerful body appearing right before the unsurprised Zhou Li. The man smiled and lifted a black flame shield, repelling his attack. Flaming black chains darted out and tried to entangle Cha Ming, whose staff whirled around and deflected them.

"Order!" a voice yelled loudly.

Cha Ming calmed down and noticed everyone staring at him as

though he were a madman. Zhou Li smirked.

"Don't worry about it. It was only a small scuffle," Zhou Li said. "He just doesn't know the rules here. Haijing Academy doesn't discriminate against the South like the North does. Members are forbidden from attacking each other within Haijing City. Moreover"—he flicked one of the gold medals on his robes—"as an elder, I should be benevolent and educate my junior."

Cha Ming's face twitched as he realized that Zhou Li's cultivation had improved drastically since he'd last seen him. Somehow, he'd reached the peak of core formation. The two violet-gold medals on his robes marked him as a peak grandmaster seer and a peak grandmaster painter, of all things.

Seeing that his behavior was somewhat inappropriate, even if justified, Cha Ming straightened himself out and bowed slightly. "My apologies. I wasn't aware of the rules here. I will make sure to hold myself back in the future." He would find a more covert way to deal with Zhou Li, though the fact that he was an elder irked him.

"Be at ease," the same loud voice from before said. It was the amplified voice of an older man with white hair. He wore one gold medal, several silver medals, and a gray medal with a set of weighing scales engraved on it. "As the headmaster, I, Dai Yijun, invite Yue Bing to enter the Nine Illusions profession trial. The sponsor should supply ten top-grade spirit stones to drive the trial."

A single top-grade spirit stone was worth ten thousand high-grade ones.

Cha Ming flicked his sleeve and sent forty top-grade spirit stones, one set for each of his students. He wasn't rich by any means, but he had certain obligations as their master. The older man nodded and placed ten stones on a dais beside the arch. A thin blue membrane appeared, and Yue Bing walked through it.

"She'll be entering an illusory world," Zhou Li explained. "I got my elder designation through this formation. Grandmaster seers and painters are far too difficult to find in this backwater plane, so I couldn't have any organization vouch for me."

Cha Ming, having calmed down substantially, nodded. "You

seem to be uncharacteristically helpful today."

"Oh, I'm not being helpful," Zhou Li said. "I already know what the results will be. I'm a seer, after all. I'm mostly here to rub in the disappointment. Her exploits over the past year are well-known. Three quarters of the medical profession see her as an abomination. I wonder how you'll react when you see the results?"

Not much time had passed, and suddenly a medal appeared beside the arch. It was a bronze medal—a peak master spirit-doctor medal. He heard murmurs of disapproval from a group in the crowd, however. Things like "not a doctor," and "traitor." He wondered how she'd gone from being a prized student the year before to a pariah.

"You're going to get a shock at the next one," Zhou Li said. "She ended up dabbling in some dark arts, things you only see in the South. If you ask me nicely, I'll ask her profession to sponsor her and grant her cultivation materials. For a favor, of course."

Cha Ming ignored the man's taunts and focused on the second medal being formed in the air. It was a bronze medal affixed with bloodred characters. Peak-grade blood master. Somehow, his disciple had gone down the same path as Gong Lan and cultivated it to peak mastery, all without him knowing. He shook his head. Though he didn't trust Zhou Li in the slightest and figured there must be more to the story, he was less than pleased.

"I wonder how you'll react to your youngest disciple's results," Zhou Li said, summoning an apple from a spatial treasure. He bit into it noisily and talked while eating. "Probably not so badly. You're acquainted with a member of that profession, though its headquarters are still in the South. For a simple favor, I'll—"

He frowned. His gaze shifted to the arch, which was letting out a third light and generating a third medallion.

Cha Ming chuckled when he saw his reaction. "It seems you're not as all-knowing as you say. Let's see what her third profession is." He highly doubted it was a runic profession.

A faint hint of silver appeared in the swirling cloud as it formed the badge. Soon, a silver medallion appeared. The bloodred characters for "initial grandmaster blood doctor" appeared on it. Murmurs ran through the hall as Yue Bing walked out of the gateway and accepted the badges.

"Interesting," Gan Quan said. "Though I don't approve of the blood master profession, I've never heard of the blood doctor profession before."

"It appeared once in the past," Dai Yijun said, walking up beside them. "There was a famous doctor called Hua Tuo tens of thousands of years ago that claimed a medal for this profession. She must have found his inheritance somehow. It's all in the history books if you know where to look.

"Still, I must congratulate Cha Ming on raising such a fine disciple. She'll be welcomed as a full member, the only one in her profession. I doubt her two other professions will be happy about this, but I, for one, welcome the addition of new knowledge to our academy. For science, of course."

Then he turned to the three remaining disciples with glittering eyes. "Jin Huang, step into the formation." He flicked his sleeve, and the formation activated. The younger man stepped through, and Cha Ming's eyes flickered over to the silent Zhou Li.

"Any predictions?" Cha Ming asked smugly.

"None I can taunt you over," Zhou Li said. "He'll have two, and my offer still stands. He won't be able to procure materials without my help." A minute later, a bronze badge with the words "peak master alchemist" appeared. Then a bronze mid-grade runic alchemist badge appeared; that one raised many eyebrows. Finally, a minute after that, a silver badge appeared. Jin Huang was apparently an initial-grade poison grandmaster, the same profession as Zhou Bei from Quicksilver City.

"Looks like you were wrong again," Cha Ming said, grinning. "Perhaps they should strip you of that seer designation."

Zhou Li's eyes narrowed. "I absolutely despise karmic anomalies like you. You just stroll around, messing up well-laid plans wherever you go, tearing apart centuries of planning and causality."

"Anything that makes you upset makes me happy," Cha Ming chided. "Let's see how Ling Dong does."

A few minutes passed. Unsurprisingly, Ling Dong was a peak master spiritual blacksmith.

"He ruffled a few feathers some months ago," Gan Quan muttered. "While I don't care personally, I heard some of the older and more traditional elders say he was ignoring technique and convention. As a result, his works couldn't be replicated and had huge variations in quality. He tried to share his secrets with the rest of the profession, but no one could even understand them." As he spoke, a second medallion appeared. Peak master beast tamer.

Interesting, Cha Ming thought. *It seems Huxian's eyes weren't a waste.* He could hear a group of elders dressed in beast hides muttering in approval. It seemed at least *this* profession wouldn't be an issue. Just when they thought the results had stabilized, a third medallion appeared. To everyone's surprise, this one was silver. It contained violet characters that read "initial grandmaster demonic blacksmith."

"Your apprentices are simply remarkable," Dai Yijun said, rubbing his hands. "It's a victory for science, an overwhelming success. I've never heard of such a profession in all my life. For all I know, it's unprecedented, unknown! Think of the possibilities!"

"Don't wet yourself," Gan Quan said drily. "There's still one more to go."

"Of course, of course," Dai Yijun said. "Your disciples will be available for interviews, correct?"

"They're free to do whatever they wish," Cha Ming said. "They're their own people."

Inwardly, though, he was grumbling. He had taught them all runic arts, but they'd squandered them. They hadn't even gotten medallions for these professions, and he wondered whether their skill was just too low or if they'd just wanted to save face by not showing off meager skills before experts. He was determined to remedy the situation, willingness be damned.

Zi Long was the last to go. Just as Cha Ming predicted, he was a high-grade formation master. To his surprise, however, he was also an early-grade grandmaster illusionist, obtaining a golden medal for a tiny faction in the academy. There was no muttering or bitterness, a fact that brought much relief to Cha Ming.

"Is there anyone else who wishes to challenge the formation?" Dai Yijun said.

Everyone shook their heads, but just as he was about to call the meeting to a close, Cha Ming raised his hand. "I wish to challenge the formation."

Though he was on good terms with his respective professional bodies, Cha Ming had a few tricks up his sleeve. He figured that if Zhou Li was an elder, he should be one as well. Besides, the creepy man hadn't said anything or taunted him. Just the fact that he wasn't provoking him into trying out the formation meant this was exactly what he should be doing.

"Are you sure?" Dai Yijun asked with a strange look. "Your standing as a member won't change, and with your cultivation, you won't be able to obtain a higher result than normal membership."

"I'm sure," Cha Ming said, supplying the man with ten more top-grade spirit stones. Then, under everyone's confused gazes, he walked through the arch's blue light.

Chapter 4:
Through Will Alone

The blue light faded, revealing a circular disc surrounded by mountains. Nine tall slabs of stone surrounded him, each one with different characters dancing within. They channeled power into a runic array that was etched into the solid stone floor. He immediately recognized it as an illusory formation.

"Welcome to the profession trial," a voice that sounded like thousands said. "Please stand by while we analyze the potential of your various occupations." Several runic characters began floating out from him and spinning above his head. The first ones that came out represented formations, and they were closely followed by those representing talismans. A bit more time passed before a fainter character appeared, one representing alchemy.

To Cha Ming's surprise, a fourth set of characters appeared for herbology. These characters quickly took on a black iron hue, followed by bronze, then silver, and finally, gold. Then it disappeared into space.

"Low-level, knowledge-based profession quantized," the voice said. "Herbology has achieved peak grandmaster rank. Further growth in this field of study can only be achieved by blending and combining with other occupations."

Interesting, Cha Ming thought. He hadn't studied herbology as a profession, and he'd assumed all professions required soul-force manipulation. Even the Jade Moon Library hadn't mentioned it was a profession. He now realized this was likely due to the limitations of knowledge and calculation. It couldn't transcend its mortal shackles without a fundamental change in the nature of the profession.

Seeing the three remaining characters floating around, he noticed that the runic alchemist designation hadn't appeared for him as it had for Jin Huang. That was another thing he needed to talk to the younger man about. For now, however, he would focus on proving his worth.

"Which challenge do you wish to accept?" the voices asked. "Time contraction is in effect. Additional time is available with supplementation."

Cha Ming looked at all three characters and decided to select his least-skilled occupation, alchemy. He would use the results to adjust his approach for the other trials. The world shifted as he touched the character, and he found himself on a lonely mountaintop next to an alchemical cauldron. There were fields of medicinal ingredients below, and he instantly knew that, should he wish it, he could pluck any of them to use for the trial.

"How do I pass the trial?" Cha Ming asked.

"One does not pass the trial but simply walks as far as he can go," the voices said. "Simply concoct the most difficult pills you know. We will record your skills and achievements and quantify your professional rank."

Cha Ming nodded. He brought a relatively simple alchemical recipe to mind, a foundation consolidation pill. Herbs floated into the air beside him; he threw them into the cauldron and used five flames to simultaneously roast and mix the ingredients as they reacted. A few minutes passed before he retrieved a gold-seal pill from the furnace.

The ingredients behave like real ones, including the many variations one can find in nature, Cha Ming thought. They were very realistic illusory replicas, ones that responded perfectly to his flame. The cauldron, on the other hand, was a very well-made one. It didn't have any impressive capabilities, but it did have excellent heat distribution and durability. There would be no amplifying his creations with imbued runes, nor would there be any medicinal infusions from the seasoning accumulated by the cauldron. It was a pure test of ability.

Understanding the situation, Cha Ming got to work. As he used his alchemical flames, he noted that the flame training Sun Wukong had put him through was bearing fruit. He no longer made as many temperature-control errors as he used to, and he could now control many wisps of flame simultaneously. Ingredient preparation was no longer an imprecise mess but a routine, even robotic task. Before long, he'd created ten or so successful batches of pills.

Alchemical skill quantified, the voices said. *Mid-grade master rank achieved.*

Cha Ming nodded. This was the rank he'd expected, though inwardly, he'd hoped his rank had grown under the Monkey King's tutelage. Unfortunately, flame control wasn't everything when it came to alchemy. His knowledge was sorely lacking.

Cha Ming's surroundings blurred, and he found himself back inside the runic circle. He rested for a quarter hour before reaching out for the next rune, formations. The next thing he knew, he was in the ruins of a temple. His eyes narrowed when he realized he was surrounded by layer upon layer of runic traps.

"Break out of the room to proceed to the next level," the voices said. "Performance is timed. You have fifteen Ling Nan standard minutes to complete this stage."

Cha Ming smiled at the mention. He hadn't heard people say minutes often in this world, but now that he was in Haijing, people used minutes and even seconds everywhere he went. The large clock tower had apparently standardized time measurement for the entire plane. Despite this, most of the non-scientific, non-Haijing population still preferred to use breaths, incense times, and hours. Even double hours in some places.

He cast out his transcendent soul force and analyzed the various formations in the room in a split second. They were mid-grade formations, and he figured the room had pegged his general skill as a mid-grade master professional due to his previous results in the alchemy trial. He grinned, and without using his brush, sigils, or even qi, he prodded the formations at hundreds of key points with his soul. The formation collapsed instantly. His surroundings shifted again, and he found himself on an icy plain.

"That's a fairly steep increase in difficulty," Cha Ming noted, sensing the various middle-core-formation traps laid around him.

"We previously misjudged your skill based on past performance," the voices said. "The new starting point is equivalent to your cultivation level and will reduce or increase as required. Performance will be assessed from here on out."

Cha Ming nodded. By taking this test, he was planning on revealing a hidden fortuitous encounter from Jade Moon Planet. This was also what would allow him to transcend his cultivation in this trial.

He shrugged and got to work. It was no longer possible to complete the trial using only his soul force, so he summoned his sigils and summoned runes and runic fragments. Three hundred and sixty gray sigils floated around, hovering for a few seconds before finally setting themselves down on the innermost formation. Runes glowed, and runic lines short-circuited as the first trap was deactivated. Eleven more traps were disabled in short order, each one touching on different aspects of formation arts appropriate at this level. Then, more traps appeared.

This continued for four hours before finally, he destroyed the last formation. His surroundings changed again, revealing Clock Tower Square in the middle of Haijing City. It was surrounded by high-grade formations. He sighed and began channeling his qi. High-grade combat formations, while simpler and faster than normal formations, not only required a powerful soul but a denser qi. He couldn't summon the appropriate formations with his core qi alone, but thanks to his transcendent soul, he didn't have to.

He used his transcendent force to compress and refine his qi as it traveled through his body until finally, its volume shrank by half. The purity of this compressed qi was twice as high as the original. He poured it into the sigils and guided 720 of them into the appropriate combat formation. Then, something clicked, and the trap shattered from his interference. He moved on to the next one.

High-grade formations aside, the test was much more difficult than the one before. It wasn't a challenge on an intellectual level, of course, but refining and controlling dense qi put much strain on his qi pathways. Moreover, he wasn't just feeding qi into the pearls, but his heart and soul, managing the impossible through sheer will alone. He paced himself as he solved the puzzles one at a time, making careful use of the entire half day he was allotted for the trial.

Before long, he arrived at the final puzzle. This one could not be solved using combat formations, so Cha Ming was forced to use formation flags for the first time. He summoned the Clear Sky Brush in its large form and painted white lines where required and black lines to destroy certain key links. The process was arduous and time consuming, and every brush stroke was excruciating and raw. It would have been expensive too if not for the illusory supply of ink for his brush.

By the time he completed the high-grade counter to the complex puzzle, a half day had passed. Finally, the last formation collapsed. The room shifted, and the voices spoke.

"We have sensed that you require time to rest," the voices said. "Please be advised that based on your performance, this formation will require a top-up of ten top-grade spirit stones. In addition, as this test will take twenty-four time-contracted hours, you are advised to rest before starting."

Cha Ming nodded. He threw ten top-grade spirit stones up, which vanished into thin air. "I'll be resting for three hours before starting," he said. He'd never really practiced concentrating qi before, and the process was both physically and mentally exhausting. He sat cross-legged and adjusted his condition, and once three hours had passed, he stood again. He was now in a plain blue stone room that reminded him of the Bridge of Stars or Fuxi's Library. He wondered if it was a certain building style that made them look the same, or whether it was simply available or cost-effective materials that spurred their construction.

Cha Ming's transcendent soul scanned for a full minute before determining that thirty-six formations were present, each one overlaid with the next. Solving this puzzle would be especially difficult compared to the others. He compressed his qi again, not once but twice, in all five elements. He imbued them into 1,080 gray sigils that then floated out to their necessary positions.

These combat formations were insufficient to break the formation, of course. Rather, he saw through the crux of the test: A single grand formation was required to break all thirty-six superimposed formations simultaneously. It was impossible to get to the necessary positions to lay the flags without first slipping through the smaller formations one at a time without actually breaking them. By doing so, he proved his skills as a formation master.

The next twenty-four hours were excruciating. Cha Ming worked tirelessly, and his soul burned with overuse. To make matters worse, a spirit hounded him ceaselessly.

Now we know where to focus our practice next, Sun Wukong taunted from the Clear Sky Brush.

Though Cha Ming dreaded the hellish training that was in store for him, he knew it was necessary.

With less than a minute left on the clock, he laid the last flag. The formation activated and drank in ambient illusory qi. Five colors lit up, combined, and clashed with the puzzle beneath it. The earth was torn, and buildings shook. When the dust finally settled, he saw that the formation had also suffered and broken under the devastation.

"Peak-formation-grandmaster rank achieved," the voices spoke. "One hundred top-grade spirit stones are required to power the next trial. Proceed?"

These words made Cha Ming's heart skip a beat and confirmed that his goal wasn't just a pipe dream. He thought of his current objective—crafting a transcendent-grade pill from inside a mortal plane. Was it possible?

"Can a mortal pass the trial and become a transcendent professional?" Cha Ming asked hesitantly.

The voices paused for a moment before answering. "Yes. This

option is only offered because the strength of your soul is sufficient. A transcendent soul is required for transcendent performance in a profession. Evaluating transcendent-grade performance was considered a vital function for this formation and imbued into our programming."

Cha Ming thought for a moment before shaking his head. "I won't proceed."

"Very well," the voices said. "Please instruct us when you've fully recovered and wish to proceed with the other professional trial."

He nodded and sat cross-legged to replenish his energy. Replenishing qi was easy, and his body was durable to begin with. His soul, on the other hand, had been greatly strained in the last trial. He estimated his ability to cross ranks was limited to two levels above his qi cultivation rank if he used no external assistance.

Five hours passed before he stood and touched the talisman artist mark. His surroundings changed to a familiar scene: Elder Ling's cabin. The older man and his cat were missing, but the devil- and spirit-repelling talismans were still there, as was the *Angels and Devils* board. To his surprise, despite his elevated strength, there were still talismans he didn't understand on the wall. Their power was clearly far greater than he'd originally imagined.

Was Elder Ling a transcendent? he wondered.

A slip of paper appeared on a desk in the living room. "Paint a talisman," the voices instructed.

Cha Ming nodded. He settled on a mid-grade core talisman that focused on stagnation. As he painted the talisman, he took note of the behavior of his ink compared to the real world. To his surprise, it was identical. This illusion seemed indistinguishable from reality.

Are the consequences of failure just as real? he thought. Then, he licked his lips and carefully traced the miniature formation and its delicate blue lines. When he finished those, he added even more detail and depth into the talisman.

Soon, six hours had passed. At his level, each talisman was a masterpiece, a composition of perfect balance. With the current strength of his soul, even with the Clear Sky Brush, he only had a fifty-percent chance of success. He finished on his first try.

"Based on your current and past performance, proceed to the high-grade test immediately," the voices said.

Cha Ming nodded and concentrated his qi. This time, he was instructed to paint ten different talismans, one after another, using only a single attempt for each one. To make the best use of his limited qi, he chose a variety of talismans. One could summon a rain of boulders, while another could summon a flame dragon. Another, a storm of blades. The last one could summon invisible spores that bonded to any nearby humans or demons. They wouldn't harm them, but rather, they would absorb ambient qi and demonic energy and channel them into the bonded recipient for healing and recovery.

The process took him five days, and compressing his qi was a much more comfortable experience this time than the last two. After completing the last talisman, he poured his transcendent soul into it and activated the green sheet of paper. The spores flew out and spread into his surroundings while a few latched onto his body, rapidly increasing his rate of recovery in the process. It only took ten minutes for him to recover.

Cha Ming looked up at the glowing formation eye where the voices originated from and wondered about his result. He'd only succeeded in four out of ten talismans, but then again, he'd been able to complete the others to the final steps before making a mistake. His anticipation increased as endless moments trickled by.

"The formation requires an additional thirteen top-grade spirit stones to continue," the voices said. "Ten for the trial and three for your wanton plundering of the formation's energy."

Cha Ming slapped his forehead in realization. No matter what he did here, the energy was limited. It made sense that the formation's time could be reduced if top-grade spirit stones increased it.

"High-grade grandmaster qualification achieved. The result is based on overall competency in the entire process. Success rate is above the minimum threshold."

"What are the requirements for the peak-grade trial?" Cha Ming asked.

"Paint five unique talismans at peak grade," the voices said. "Truths converge, and choices are limited. You must succeed in creating two and make sufficient headway on others."

Cha Ming nodded and offered up the thirteen top-grade spirit stones. At this point, even he was feeling the pinch. He'd had a good haul on Jade Moon Planet, but his resources weren't unlimited.

Concentrating qi took twice as much qi for each level of concentration, meaning that his qi usage was four times higher than normal. For his first work, he painted the peak-grade version of the Mount Tai Talisman, a gravity-based suppression talisman. It was ideal to use against qi cultivators, as their bodies weren't as resilient as body cultivators. To him, it was doubly useful. If he used it against a qi cultivator, he could use it to increase gravity and still be fit to fight in its confines. It took a day to create it successfully.

He moved on to the peak-grade versions of the Inferno Dragon Talisman, which he failed miserably nine-tenths of the way in. Then he tried his hand at creating a withering talisman using wood qi. Unfortunately, till now, he hadn't had time to think up more talismans from the Myriad Truths Diagram. He tried it despite his terrible mastery of wood and failed eight-tenths of the way through.

Cha Ming was feeling the pressure. He proceeded to paint the Blade Storm Talisman. His paintbrush was reminiscent of a sword, a sword that he used to cut through his exhaustion and strained qi pathways. Line after line, slice after slice, the golden talisman took shape. Then, only three strokes away from a complete product, he failed. He only had one chance remaining.

"Best for last," he muttered aloud. His experience indicated that his odds of successfully crafting a top-grade talisman were roughly twenty-five percent. But that didn't apply across the board. He'd succeeded with earth because of his high affinity with earth. He was betting everything on his success with a Stagnation Talisman.

His soul ached, and he wanted nothing more than to rest in the gentle embrace of crashing waves. Every stroke of his pen made him want to pause and take a break. He pushed through these negative thoughts and poured them into the brush. Where his soul and qi weren't strong enough, he used the strength of his heart to push the lines into place.

If it were any other talisman, he would have failed. But this was stagnation, an emotion he was far too familiar with. He knew better than anyone else how the world sought to make him bow, to stop him from moving forward. And he'd overcome it every time, building unstoppable momentum in the process. Would a silly trial like this halt his journey? Would it prevent him from reaching immortality and seeking Yu Wen's soul? Of course it wouldn't.

He struggled every minute of the way, but this struggle only strengthened the talisman, strengthened its intent. Then, after twenty-four hours of hard work, he completed the final stroke. The talisman pulsed, and unlike the others, which had evaporated and returned to the illusory qi pool, this one *solidified*. It became real, and when Cha Ming touched it, he knew the tangible object was something he could take with him.

"Using emotion to supplement creation," the voices said. "Admirable. Your performance before did not meet the minimum threshold, as you had failed too miserably on the other three attempts. But with this feat, you have exceeded expectations. My verdict… is a pass!"

Cha Ming sighed in relief. Even if he'd been allowed another attempt, he would have needed days to recover.

"Proceed to the next level trial for talisman artistry?" the voices asked. He declined and chose to leave the runic circle.

His surroundings faded, and he found himself walking out of the archway and collecting three gold elder emblems and one silver emblem. The spectators looked at him with slacked jaws. He had no idea how much time had passed outside the formation, but given that not a single person had left, it either hadn't been very long, or his performance had impressed them.

After carefully observing the figures at the front, Cha Ming realized the reason for their expressions. All the elders, every one of them, were peak-core-formation cultivators. Moreover, most of them only had one golden badge, while he now had three.

"Congratulations, Elder Cha Ming," Dai Yijun said. "As per our rules, you'll be awarded with three voting quotas on the elder council and all other resources and stipends awarded to elders, including unlimited library access and a standard allocation of time-contraction medallions. Everyone, please give Elder Cha Ming a congratulatory bow."

Everyone in the room bowed, whether due to fear or reverence. But Cha Ming only had eyes for one man: Zhou Li. The man who'd been taunting him earlier was now glaring daggers at him. Respect was one thing, but seeing the man he loathed looking at him like he'd swallowed a fly was priceless.

Chapter 5: Unfamiliar Home

Gold Leaf City was just like Wang Jun remembered. It was autumn, and every tree in the city was adorned with the very leaves it was named after: golden ones. Here and there, he spotted some with violet-gold edges. They were beautiful, and if not for the strict laws against picking them, he was sure they'd have made their way into someone's collection.

"We don't have all day, young master," Elder Bai said, walking up beside him. The older man was trying hard to put up a strong front, despite being weary from their travels.

"I just missed the sight of them," Wang Jun said, smiling. "To me, home is where golden leaves grow."

Golden leaves, along with blood, death, and the brother who killed his sister. The city boiled his blood and chilled his heart, but unfortunately, that didn't change the fact that it was his home, the place where his family lived. He followed Elder Bai as the older man coaxed him back into the carriage. Their destination: Gold Leaf Square.

Unlike most central squares on the continent, Gold Leaf Square was less a mercantile area and more a public park. The ban on stray hawkers and open-air salesmen made the public area more family friendly than most. Parents roamed with their children, and mortal elderly did tai chi off to the side. Cultivators meditated while pondering the Dao of golden leaves, soaking in the beautiful but temporary nature of these natural ornaments.

There were only four businesses in the square, each one occupying a large corner. The Jade Bamboo Headquarters, a much larger facility than the auction house that occupied every major city in the North, sported its usual green bamboo décor. The Red Dust Pavilion, a premier entertainment venue featuring the most popular courtesans on the continent, attracted both the curious and the lecherous with its red lights and decorations.

The Greenwind Pavilion, on the other hand, was more subdued—the mediocre-looking building seemed to slink into its surroundings. But despite its deceptive exterior, every person in the city worth his salt knew there was no better place on the continent to obtain information.

The Spirit Temple was the last of the four businesses. It was the least conspicuous of the lot but also the most sinister-looking one. Why it could exist in the city, where the Church of Justice reigned with an iron fist, was a mystery to all. No one knew what truly happened within its forlorn walls; they could only guess based on hearsay and myth.

Wang Jun, however, knew of a very special function it served: The Spirit Temple was home to the mysterious Spectral Assassins, who would kill anyone for the right price. Their money-back guarantee and their low failure rate ensured their popularity within certain circles. They also never seemed to target royalty or Church officials. Wang Jun guessed this was the real reason for its continued existence.

We're back, Wang Jun thought as the carriage stopped before a bamboo garden. Protector Ren stepped out and opened the door, allowing Wang Jun and his assistants to get out of the cramped carriage. Some minor servants ran up to the carriage and began pulling out their belongings. Along with them came an elder. A lesser elder, Wang Jun noted. The man bowed deeply before speaking.

"We're all overjoyed with your return after a successful venture for the family," Elder Ting said. "The Patriarch has arranged a banquet to celebrate your return. He expects your presence at six o'clock sharp, so please manage your time wisely."

Expects, not requests, Wang Jun noted. And judging by the height of the sun, he only had twenty-two minutes to prepare.

"Please inform the Patriarch that I'll be there promptly," Wang Jun said. "Also, aid Elder Bai in everything he requires. I'll be in my quarters preparing." Then, noting the man's awkward expression, he raised an eyebrow. "Is there anything I should be aware of?"

Elder Ting coughed awkwardly. "Your room was reassigned to your youngest cousin, Wang Jie. Perhaps we can arrange a temporary room for you to prepare."

Wang Jun pondered that for a moment. From what he recalled, though Wang Jie's family did not approve of his eldest brother, Wang Ling, they didn't support Wang Jun either. Still, he couldn't displace them without upsetting those in their neutral faction, as a residence in the main household was highly coveted.

"Is Wang Xinyi still residing in the main household?" he asked. Wang Xinyi was a low-ranked member the last time he saw him, and unlikely to amount to anything in life. However, his household was extremely supportive of Wang Ling.

"He is," Elder Ting said. "Do you have any instructions?"

"Please have his room vacated for my temporary accommodation in the next five minutes," Wang Jun said. "I'll be getting a higher-grade room soon enough, but his room should do fine for the next few nights."

Elder Ting smiled lightly and bowed. "Your wish is my command, young master. You three!" he yelled. Three higher-ranked servants ran up and snapped to attention. "Vacate Wang Xinyi's room and prepare temporary amenities and robes befitting Young Master Wang's status. You have four and a half minutes and can recruit up to five helpers."

"Sir!" they said without a hint of hesitation. The servants, who were also cultivators, ran into the house with inhuman speed. After exchanging a few more pleasantries with Elder Ting, Wang Jun walked into the house, down a few familiar hallways, and smiled as he passed Wang Xinyi, who was only half dressed.

"How dare you!" Wang Xinyi yelled as he passed. "You'll get what's coming to you for this, mark my words."

His possessions had been placed outside the room. Wang Jun noted that an unhealthy amount of liquor bottles and potentially harmful medicinal pills were present, along with many much more embarrassing things.

"No need to apologize for taking so long," Wang Jun said. "I'm sure these quarters will do fine for now." He closed the high-quality door, blocking out any further screaming from his younger cousin.

The bedding in the room had already been changed into the plain ones he preferred, and a pot of tea had already been prepared for him.

He took a sip of the clear cup on the desk and hummed in approval as he rummaged through the various toiletries. Then he noticed the robes: green with gold trim and black runic highlights. The green symbolized the Wang family, of course, and the gold symbolized not only the main branch but his status as a competitor for the family leadership. The black runes were unusual. They represented his identity as a personal disciple of Daoist Obscurus. He frowned when he saw them.

Wang Jun looked to one of the many clocks on the walls. *Twelve minutes,* he thought, then walked into the washroom and entered the rune-mist shower. The soap-filled mist cleansed his body and washed his hair simultaneously. Then he stepped into the neighboring drying formation. His whole body and hair were freed of any dampness or wetness within seconds. As per his usual habits, he brushed his hair with an enchanted comb and put on his ceremonial robes. After taking two minutes to pick fitting shoes and an appropriate belt, he walked out of the room. His cousin's things were no longer there.

On his way to the dining hall, he gave a nod to Wang Jie. She was apparently aware of the awkward position she'd been placed in and was thankful that Wang Jun had retaliated on the aggressing party instead of taking the easy way out. They headed inside the dining room with two minutes to spare. Servants poured them both tea and wine as they took their seats. Wang Jun ignored the alcoholic beverage and instead savored the fermented tea. The Wang family had many shortcomings, but tea was not one of them.

The room filled almost instantly. Then, when the clock struck exactly six o'clock, their host arrived. Everyone stood up as the Wang family's current leader, Patriarch Wuling, walked over to his seat.

"Everyone, thank you so much for accepting the last-minute invitation to the welcome banquet of one of our most promising juniors, Wang Jun," he said. "Please, feast on this delicious fare. I have some important announcements to make after the feast, but for now, enjoy!"

Servants poured into the room and placed platters of exquisitely prepared dishes on the table. Wang Jun looked around as they moved, evaluating the competition as they spoke.

The Wang family had many juniors, but the main family only kept fifty in the main household. Forty-three had attended the banquet, but that could have been for various reasons, like seclusion. He noted that Wang Ling wasn't there, but many of his fiercest and most powerful supporters were in attendance. Being a junior didn't mean being young. Though many of them were in their twenties, many of their members were in their nineties. The only requirement for being a junior was being less than a hundred years old. Those worthy of becoming protectors or directors were core-formation cultivators. They would be appointed upon their hundredth birthday. Others would become elders and managers. While this was technically an honor, it was tantamount to failure in the eyes of many. Elders and managers were part of the side family, and elevating oneself out of the side family could take generations.

"It's been a while since our last meeting," Wang Bing said, smiling from a few places away. Apparently, her assignment in Quicksilver was over. Like him, she was in the main family, and given her abilities, she'd likely be assigned to something greater than managing an empire's auction house. This came as no surprise to Wang Jun, who'd always been impressed by her performance.

"You're just as pretty as ever," Wang Jun said. "Many thanks for your help in Quicksilver. Be sure to come and see me if you need anything."

She sniffed. "I only did my duty as an interim manager. All my decisions benefited the family and made us a fortune."

"If you say so," Wang Jun said. "But just the same, let me know if you need help, and I'll be there." He said it and he meant it. The public announcement was for her benefit, as it would be shameful to retract an official offer.

She nodded, and a man beside her he'd never seen before waved. Or at least, he thought he'd never seen him. It took him a few moments to realize that it was Wang Tong, yet another distant cousin. Wang Tong's family wasn't very influential in the inner circles. They were too honest and insufficiently shrewd.

Still, the man's cultivation talent was high enough that the family had overlooked this unfortunate fact. If he played his cards right, he would be named a protector by the age of fifty. Directors were expected to be intelligent and possess good business sense, and only members of the direct line like Wang Jun could vie for the position of patriarch. The strong became protectors, which were essentially guardians for the family.

"Have you had a chance to visit the Red Dust Pavilion?" Wang Tong asked between mouthfuls. "They've gotten a new headmistress, and a young one at that. The whole city's talking about it."

Wang Jun smiled. "You know I don't like to frequent such establishments," he said. "Still, I'll be sure to pay a visit. The Red Dust Pavilion's influence is substantial, and I'd be foolish to dismiss them."

Other juniors greeted Wang Jun one after another. He expressed heartful congratulations to some and accepted compliments in return. To others, he traded unspoken barbs and aggressive but polite banter. An hour later, he'd spoken to everyone at the table. It was at this moment that Patriarch Wuling cleared his throat. Everyone immediately quieted down.

"As you all know, Wang Jun has returned after successfully completing our family's difficult task," the Patriarch said. "By doing so, he has proven his worth and will be considered in the family's leadership selection."

Some quiet murmurs ensued.

"This is only the beginning of a difficult journey, however. Wang Jun must continue to prove himself and his suitability for the position. I have every confidence that he won't disappoint.

"After discussing with the clan elders, we've decided that Wang Jun's excellent performance deserves an appropriate position in the family. It is with great pleasure that I appoint Wang Jun as auditor general of the Wang family. All powers of investigation and prosecution will be under his supervision."

Wang Jun's eyes narrowed. Given his goals and the information in his hands, this appointment was too good to be true. There had to be a catch.

"However," the Patriarch continued, "while this position might come with many benefits, it also comes with heavy responsibilities. The extra information at one's fingertips can skew the playing field between our members. As such, we ask that Wang Jun restrain his financial activities to remove even the mere suspicion of impropriety."

Ah, there it is, Wang Jun thought. *The expected leash.*

Unfazed, he stood, smiled, and bowed. "It would be my honor to accept this heavy responsibility," he said. He accepted a golden sash he was meant to wear on his arm while performing his duties, as well as the corresponding family seal. Any Wang family member who saw the sash would know his identity as an auditor and supply him with any information he requested. The seal was meant to approve official documents.

"Thank you for your hard work, and thank you all for attending," the Patriarch said. "I'm sure you all have much to speak of, so I'll be retiring to my chambers to cultivate for now. You may continue with your celebration." Then he stood up and left.

Though Wang Jun wished to escape the room full of gloating opponents, reassuring allies, and clueless—in other words, less talented—family members, he forced himself to finish every painful conversation, his current feelings be damned.

It was dusk when Wang Jun finally left. He sighed as he walked down familiar hallways and passed familiar pieces of art. He and his sister used to play a game while walking through the mansion, taking turns spotting the many details others ignored. As the most talented and intelligent family member of her time, she'd occupied the room closest to the Patriarch's. He'd spent most of his free time there accompanying her.

There was one place where others didn't go, however. A hidden place that others couldn't see without permission. Wang Jun's light smile faded as he turned to enter a hidden hallway, a hallway of darkness. He merged with the shadows and entered another world, a world of light. There, a long corridor containing many closed doors stretched on endlessly. He walked through the corridor despite the seemingly unbreachable distance, for he only had eyes for the door at the end of the hallway, the door that led to his master.

The door opened to a plain stone chamber. Two candles were lit beside a large, throne-like chair where no one sat. Wang Jun took a seat at a low table and began brewing tea. He prepared a wash batch and threw it away, then brewed a second, and this time, best, cup and placed it on the other side of the table. Shadow smiled and accepted the cup. A near-invisible hand swirled its contents before a man cloaked in obscurity drank it.

"Oh," the man said, moving his imperceptible lips and smacking them. "That's a new one."

"Violet City, reserve blend, aged nine years," Wang Jun said. "It's raised just outside the Violet Heart Sect's headquarters in Violet City. As such, it absorbs much of the ambient heart force, giving it a distinctive but soul-nourishing flavor. And with the fall of the sect, it's unlikely you'll be able to taste it again."

The man nodded. His name didn't need to be spoken or said,

and save his disciples and others he chose, whoever heard it would forget it in an instant. "Do you understand your current situation?" he asked.

Wang Jun nodded and took a sip of his tea. "I've been hamstrung, given an honorary title, and shoved in a corner. I'm effectively not allowed to compete with my dear brother Wang Ling—at least not in any businesses he has a significant hand in. This happens to be the most profitable ones."

"Their purpose?" Daoist Obscurus asked.

"They're likely trying to get me to perform important, essential duties for the family while trying to make me realize it isn't so bad working under someone else's leadership," Wang Jun answered. "Meanwhile, Wang Ling will continue growing his influence while I just upset people."

Daoist Obscurus nodded. "You assessed correctly, but you don't seem displeased."

"I happened upon some useful but damning information," Wang Jun said. "All I need now is irrefutable evidence, something made possible by my title as auditor general. Soon, Wang Ling will be brought down to his knees."

Said damning information had been obtained when he'd killed Li Ming. It had been an ironic reward for defeating the difficult-to-handle assassin.

"It seems so simple," Daoist Obscurus said, drinking from his small cup. "It would be even simpler if you just planted or fabricated evidence. And faster too. I have no doubt that you could make something convincing with what you keep in your spatial treasure."

Wang Jun thought for a moment. "I'd rather he suffer the consequences of his own actions, not mine. Worse comes to worst, I'll kill him myself. But I'd rather the elders and the Patriarch recognize their mistake. Besides, we have family rules. Without them, the family is nothing."

"It's your life," Daoist Obscurus said, shrugging.

They drank tea in silence for a bit.

"It seems like your family duties will keep you busy for some time. If you ever need help, you know where to look."

Wang Jun took the hint and got up and bowed. "Many thanks for your instruction, Master," he said before retreating from the shadows.

He walked back through the hallway of light and returned to the mansion proper. Then he proceeded to the second room from the Patriarch's, his new chambers. He didn't go to bed but began poring over documents that assistants dropped on his desk in a slow but steady procession. There was much to do and a lot to get used to. He was back home, yes, but he hardly knew the place anymore.

And Gold Leaf City was *not* somewhere you did business uninformed. Those who did didn't live long.

Chapter 6:
Remnants of Red Dust

Hong Xin looked around the mid-sized audience chamber, her gaze cold and impassive. Her burning anger was hidden beneath a thick layer of ice that was impenetrable to the untrained eye. Two dozen beautiful cultivators kneeled with bowed heads on the gold-and-red marble floor. They seemed like precious ornaments that adorned the beautiful though plainly decorated hall of red and gold.

"Is this all of them?" she asked.

"Yes, that's all of them," Mistress Huang said. "After some… convincing, they let us know about some secret chambers where half a dozen members were hidden. We weren't able to find anyone else."

Hong Xin rapped her fingers on her large redwood chair. These two dozen women were the remnants of the Red Dust Pavilion in Gold Leaf City. Or at least, those who were stationed in the pavilion itself. Some had long black hair and white skin, the generally accepted vision of beauty, while others had shorter, sometimes colored hair and bronzed skin. Everything a man could look for was present on these women.

"Have we verified how many courtesans were stationed in Gold Leaf City prior to our arrival?" Hong Xin asked. She'd originally thought they could catch them all in one net. In hindsight, that had been naïve of her. An intelligence agency would never put all their eggs in one basket.

"Roughly three times as many as were stationed here," Mistress Huang replied. "We'll have a more accurate count once we verify their documentation."

The documentation she spoke of was a mismatched pile of jade slips, paper sheets, and scrolls, all shoved into a small filing room using a cryptic system. She had no doubt there was a method to the madness, but finding it would take time.

Hong Xin clenched her jaw as she thought of the implications. Between seventy and eighty beautiful seductresses were out there, using their carefully honed skills to manipulate the local populace and extract useful information. For each one, there were likely dozens of informants and at least a few loyal thralls ready to sacrifice their lives at their mistress's request. That wasn't even counting their employers.

Hong Xin stood up and expanded her chilling aura. A thin layer of frost began forming on her regal red-and-gold dress. "Congratulations to all of you," she said to the frightened women. "By sheer luck, you happened to be present when I, Headmistress Xin, decided to inspect the pavilion's branch in Gold Leaf City. As such, you will be the first to swear your undying loyalty."

Silence. The cluster of calculating women chose to bide their time instead of speaking up. It was a wise decision in most situations, but not this one. At Hong Xin's signal, the enslaved Mistress Meng held her hand up. A frozen prison appeared around one of the women, starting at her feet. It crawled up her body, completely covering it in painful crystals. The icy coffin ended in a sharp icy blade that barely touched the woman's neck and drew a single drop of blood.

Hong Xin walked up to the woman. She looked down into her fearful eyes and summoned an item in her hand. All the other women gasped when they saw the blue orb. She felt their emotions plunge and dread fill their hearts, flushing out their earlier defiance. Any who'd thought she was an illegitimate and powerless usurper now realized they were mistaken. They'd tasted the orb's control, and their subservience to it ran deep within their bones.

The woman in the prison, however, reacted differently from the others. Her eyes turned cold with icy hatred. "I'd rather die than get sworn in again," she spat, fighting against Hong Xin's dousing magic.

But beneath these brave words, Hong Xin sensed fear. Fear for her life and fear for other things. Slender threads of karma joined the cold-hearted woman to many individuals in the city. There were people she cared about in Gold Leaf, people she couldn't live without. She was likely seeking death to protect them.

Hong Xin thought for a moment, then touched the icy prison. The restraints on one of the woman's hands melted away, but the rest of the prison remained. The icy dagger stayed firmly in place. It dug into her tender neck even more viciously now that Hong Xin was closer.

"I can feel it," Hong Xin whispered, stroking the woman's cheeks. "I can feel their connections." The woman shivered. "I can feel friendly connections, even family. So amazing for a vicious person like you to have friends, people you care for. It would be a pity if anything happened to them."

The woman's eyes widened. They welled up with tears that froze and dropped to the cold marble floor.

"I won't do anything to them if you swear yourself to me," Hong Xin continued. "It will be just like before, but better. Believe me when I say I'm a far more merciful master than my predecessor." She gestured to Mistress Meng, Mistress Shan, and Mistress Yuan, who were dutifully guarding the chamber. "They tried to kill me, but I don't mistreat them. I know they want me dead, but that doesn't matter to me. If they don't act on it, such small indulgences can be forgiven. I want your obedience, not your heart and soul."

Hong Xin twitched her finger. The icy spike forced the woman's chin upward, and blood began to pour out more liberally. It pained her to do this, but she knew the weak and tender part of her would be unproductive in this situation. "Swear to me or die along with them. It's your choice."

The woman grimaced in pain as she reached out toward the blue orb. "I, Du Ai, swear on my frozen heart to serve Hong Xin to the best of my ability, unless certain provisions are breached," she said, some of her prior bravery surfacing. "I will do everything as instructed and will continue to do so for the rest of my life. In exchange, Hong Xin will swear to do her utmost to protect my family and dependents and provide for them should I be unable to do so. These dependents are my husband, Ling Baoshan, my children, Ling Xi and Ling Ye, and my friend, Hou Li."

Then she let go of the orb and glared at Hong Xin. There was little doubt that the woman would rather impale herself than agree to any other terms.

"How brave," Hong Xin said, kneeling and looking the woman straight in the eyes. "Despite being practically devoid of emotion, you've still managed to nurture some level of loyalty and caring in that ruthless, uncaring heart of yours. I confess myself impressed." She grasped the icy orb and circulated her icy power within it. "I, Hong Xin, accept Du Ai's oath. I swear on my frozen heart to do my utmost to protect her dependents, Ling Baoshan, Ling Xi, Ling Ye, and Hou Li. Should I fail to do so, her oath will immediately dissolve, and my cultivation will regress by a single sub-realm."

The orb pulsed, and two portions of blue mist shot into Hong Xin and Du Ai. The woman shuddered, but Hong Xin remained unaffected.

"Is anyone else willing to serve?" Hong Xin asked. "If not, I'm sure there are customers with unique tastes who would be glad to make your unwilling acquaintance. It matters not to me either way."

Most of them shuddered. Hong Xin proceeded to those who hadn't first, and after a few swift, gruesome executions, the others fell in line. Their deaths would surely lead to trouble, but this was a small price to pay for stability and secrecy.

The oaths she took were nonbinding, of course, but they didn't need to know that. Hong Xin's heart was no longer frozen, but a hybrid between forces of kindling and dousing. Still, she personally swore to fulfill them, as she wouldn't be herself otherwise. Minutes after swearing them in, she sent Mistress Shan and Mistress Yan to collect their close acquaintances and bring them back to the pavilion.

Hong Xin nursed a headache as she sat at a tea table in a small room. Mistress Huang, Ji Bingxue, and Bai Ling were there. Ji Bingxue served tea as they mulled over the information they'd just obtained.

Ji Bingxue was the first to speak. "Was it really necessary to oath-bind them all?" she asked. "Couldn't we have attempted to thaw their hearts first and obtain their loyalty?"

Bai Ling snorted. "That's all different kinds of stupid." She was sitting at a different table in front of an *Angels and Devils* board. She played a fierce game with herself. "For one, they don't have the same background as we do, so their loyalty would be limited even if we succeeded. If they decided to betray us, we wouldn't have a backstop like an oath to limit the damage they caused."

Ji Bingxue shook her head. "We almost had to suffer the same fate. I just can't imagine what they're going through."

"I can," Hong Xin said. She sipped on a cup of tea that Ji Bingxue had poured and nodded in approval. "I didn't do it because I wanted to; I did it out of necessity. Mistress Huang, could you please explain?"

"Of course, Headmistress," Mistress Huang said.

Hong Xin flinched at the mention of her title. Unfortunately, any attempt at correcting the behavior had ended in failure.

"We need to oath-bind them for the same reason that we needed to oath-bind Mistress Meng and Mistress Shan," Mistress Huang said. "Unlike Mistress Yuan, who'd secretly been doing everything she could for the students this whole time, and who was able to thaw with barely any outside assistance, these women are cold-blooded schemers with an entire network of people in the city. They don't just report to the pavilion—they also speak with business partners and informants. If we didn't oath-bind them, not only would they leak out our information to others in the city, but those same people would also see it as a sign of weakness. We're racing against time, and every second is precious."

"But much of the news we fed them was true," Ji Bingxue protested. "Some of the information was even conflicting. You ordered some mistresses to tell their acquaintances you were residing here, while you told others to report you were living in a safehouse. Some will report that you're a cold-hearted, murderous, ambitious devil, while others will report that you seem unconfident, implying that Mistress Huang is controlling you in secret."

"And this is why you're not part of the planning department," Bai Ling said, placing another stone on the board. "Just leave that to us. You can be our... sweet talker. The innocent-looking one who stokes ambitious youths into action."

Ji Bingxue pursed her lips in response.

"I'm just as uncomfortable with this as you are," Hong Xin said, shaking her head. "But it's a necessary evil. We have seventy to eighty unbound members, many of whom have switched their allegiance to their retainers after feeling their oath dissolve. This is the single best chance we have at gaining a foothold in the city. Gaining control of all former members or eliminating particularly dangerous ones will be like walking on a tightrope. We need to suppress any dissent while telling the city we're still open for business."

"I still don't like it," Ji Bingxue said.

"None of us do," Hong Xin replied.

"I'd like to discuss something before we get to work," Bai Ling said, standing up from the completed *Angels and Devils* board and sitting beside the others. She accepted a cup of hot tea from Ji Bingxue. "It's about you and your information on the Wang family. I want to know what it's about."

Hong Xin closed her eyes. She'd known the question was coming. "I have history with the second young master of the Wang family, Wang Jun," she said. "Romantic history."

Bai Ling groaned while Mistress Huang looked at her pensively.

"I just want to make sure everything is all right for him," said Hong Xin. "I want to make sure he's safe."

Bai Ling rapped her fingers on the table. She looked Hong Xin in the eyes as though trying to peer straight into her soul. "Looking into personal things is fine," Bai Ling said. "But we need to be clear on something: We're not here to do favors for your ex-boyfriend, nor are we here at your whim. We're here because we have some sisters to free and some psychopaths to put down. If, one day, I find that you're straying from this purpose, I'm out of here. Freeing sisters is one thing, but your love life is something else entirely. I'm not willing to die for it."

Hong Xin looked to the two others, who avoided her gaze. "You both feel the same way?"

Ji Bingxue nodded sheepishly.

Mistress Huang, on the other hand, shrugged.

"I don't see why both can't coincide," Mistress Huang said. "If the man is worth your attention, it's very likely that he'll be fighting against some very bad people. The Red Dust Pavilion tends to align with those very bad people. Or, at least, the members we're after tended to."

"My thoughts exactly," Hong Xin said. "I promise, rescuing our members is my top priority, but there's bound to be some overlap."

Bai Ling sighed. "Good enough." She slapped her thighs twice, stood up, and stretched. "There's a lot of work to be done, and very little time to do it. Are you both free for the next hour?" The two women nodded. They followed Bai Ling, leaving Hong Xin alone in the room.

A few minutes passed before Hong Xin composed herself and brewed tea for two. A red-clothed woman appeared in a puff of red dust. "I take it you heard everything, Sister Yinyue?"

The powerful transcendent woman took her small glass teacup and sipped. "Though I don't dare probe the entire city recklessly, there's not much in the pavilion that escapes my notice."

Hong Xin nodded. "What can you tell me about this city?"

"Very little," Hong Yinyue said. "As a transcendent, my every action is under much scrutiny. There are five others in this city: a powerful angel within the Alabaster Group, the grand elder of the

Wang family, the chief informer of the Greenwind Pavilion, and the shepherd of the Spirit Temple. Oh, and the vice chancellor of the Church of Justice. None of these people will interfere in the affairs of mortals unless it serves a strategic purpose.

"As for other matters, I can't tell you much. Our former members were mostly lent out to noble houses and to the Spirit Temple. A quarter of our members have historically been assigned to the Spirit Temple to facilitate their… unwholesome activities."

"Do I want to know?" Hong Xin asked.

"You don't, but you'll find out soon enough," Hong Yinyue said. She didn't speak further on the matter.

"It seems we'll have trouble reclaiming our stray members," Hong Xin said. "Not only will they want to avoid us for fear of being oathbound, but their employers won't want them to leave."

Hong Yinyue shrugged. "It's not like you're forced to use the stick. Given a sufficiently large carrot, a rabbit will be willing to run through a pack of wolves."

"That's true," Hong Xin said. "Besides, now that they have new employers, I don't need to deal with them directly. I can just entice *them*, and they'll send them back, won't they?"

"And how are you planning on doing that?" Hong Yinyue asked. "I'm sure those courtesans have told their employers about the threat you pose to them."

"But I happen to have a very large carrot," Hong Xin said, summoning both ice and flame in the palm of her hand. They executed a captivating, heart-throbbing dance. It wasn't enough to affect the transcendent being before her, but it was enough to get her point across.

"Kindling," Hong Yinyue said. "You'll tempt them with the power of kindling."

"That's right," Hong Xin said. "A week from now, we'll be hosting a free introductory performance. We'll attract drunks, deadbeats, and lechers, but with them there will be people who're down on their luck, or who are marginalized for no good reason. People whose cultivations have stagnated, and others who just need a little encouragement."

"Many won't be very happy with your meddling," Hong Yinyue cautioned.

"That's good," Hong Xin said. "With any luck, they'll send some of our stray sisters back to appease me. I could always use a few more helping hands."

Chapter 7: Marginalized

A violet staff came whooshing out of nowhere, leaving behind a stream of air as it hurled toward Cha Ming's face. He slapped it away with practiced ease, using nothing but his bare hands to do so. The floor lit up with a violet formation, which he immediately recognized as an early-grade illusory formation. He immediately sent a combat formation of equivalent grade bearing down on it, like a lock in a keyhole. To his surprise, it opened, revealing a gaping maw of death and destruction.

An illusion, he thought. It was difficult to know whether anything was real or imaginary when sparring with Zi Long. Especially when he used his trademark violet qi and heart force. Unlike with most people, his soul was cloaked in mystery. Furthermore, according to Sun Wukong, a holy spirit had taken residence in his disciple's spiritual sea. It was a good thing, so Cha Ming hadn't mentioned it. He simply took the disadvantage in stride and used it to hone his own skills.

The maw began shutting on Cha Ming's foot. He quickly coated it in a halo of golden runes. His impromptu armor groaned as the apparition bit down, threatening to burst at any moment.

It'll hold, Cha Ming thought decisively. The most important thing he'd learned when dealing with illusions was that belief was power; a single doubt would amplify his opponent's techniques manifold.

While his foot remained stationary, Cha Ming summoned a least-grade formation.

Hundreds of characters joined in formation and fluttered around the room like burning eagles. They seared the invisible formation webs Zi Long had cleverly hidden in the room, neutralizing his inevitable counterattack. Then they congregated around an ethereal shape bearing down on him. Cha Ming twirled his staff in a defensive circle of creation, a move that proved wise. Zi Long, who was only twenty feet away, burst into five avatars, one for each of the five elements. Each one possessed most of Zi Long's original strength, albeit only in a single element.

Cha Ming jerked his leg free from the fading jaws and danced between the apparitions. His staff was a blur as he used nothing more than initial-core formation and initial-marrow-refining powers to face off against the purple-robed man. He had the advantage but didn't press it. This spar wasn't for him but for Zi Long's sake. He counted the seconds as their struggle continued, and after exactly forty-two seconds, the figures blurred, and Zi Long reappeared in front of him, panting.

Light returned to their stone chamber, and a surge of qi repaired the minor damage the protective formation had suffered.

"An improvement," Cha Ming said, smiling. "Your ability to conceal your movements has improved. Your formation arts have improved as well. If I'm not mistaken, however, you're relying a little too heavily on illusory formations."

Zi Long shrugged. "With heart force, I can control illusory formations beyond my current cultivation realm. I need to use every advantage I have, though it's far from enough."

"Far from enough for what?" Cha Ming asked, slumping down against a wall next to his disciple.

"The war," Zi Long said. "I have little doubt that it's coming soon. I need to be as strong as possible when it does. Many members, including..." He shook his head. "Many members will die. Many friends will too. I can only do my all to protect everyone who's dear to me."

"That's all we can do," Cha Ming said. He tried his best to hide the pain in his heart, but he knew this disciple was especially observant. Fortunately, he was also considerate and didn't pry into other people's matters. "You're a smart man, and I know you're progressing well on runes, formations, and sigils. The guidance I can offer is limited unless you ask for specifics."

Zi Long nodded and sat cross-legged, as they usually did with these sessions. "The five elements. I'm able to use them to superimpose with my true self using my Nine Illusions Staff Art. My true self is an illusory avatar, allowing the other five to coexist with me. Yet I have trouble wrapping my mind around the last three avatars that can be generated."

"Ah," Cha Ming said. He summoned five elemental balls and caused them to swirl in his palm. "I still don't know how to mimic your illusory qi, but I will help as much as I can. Let me take you through it one more time."

The five elements began exchanging qi in a clockwise motion, establishing a white ring connecting them and generating wind. The wind blew around Zi Long before returning to his palm in the form of an orb.

"Creation is birthed from the five elements," Cha Ming explained. "It's propagation. It's fueling. You know that."

"I do," Zi Long said. "Though I have much trouble harnessing this power."

The five elements shifted in Cha Ming's hand, forming a crackling black energy that sought to destroy everything. It darted around the room before Cha Ming caught it and condensed it into a ball. The black and white orbs orbited around the center of his palm between the five elements.

"Destruction is like the lightning of judgment. It wishes to coexist with nothing, which is why I'm so amazed that you were able to superimpose it with creation qi and form illusory qi. As for the ninth element..." He dispersed the two balls and had all five elements come together simultaneously, concentrating all their power on a single point. A small gray dot appeared. "I think it's less the specific mixture and more the focus on a single point that matters."

The gray ball vanished in a puff of mist, and Cha Ming tapped his finger on Zi Long's mind. He imprinted an image of himself executing three staff arts: Splitting Heaven and Earth, Crushing Chaos, and Origin Strike.

"Don't focus on qi for now," Cha Ming said. "Focus on absorbing the essence of these techniques. They're formidable battle techniques, but more importantly, they allow you to gain inspiration on the elements and their origin."

"Thank you, Master," Zi Long said. "By the way, the others have been asking about you."

Cha Ming nodded. "I'm thinking about how to best help them. They've changed so much, and it's difficult to give blind guidance. I'm afraid I'll harm more than help."

"I'll tell them," Zi Long said. "But letting them know directly would be best."

Cha Ming smiled. As he left, he saw Zi Long imitating the techniques Cha Ming had imprinted in his mind. They were simple, crude strikes, but he knew firsthand that enlightenment on them would be extremely beneficial. Still, nothing was a given on the path of cultivation.

He sighed as he made his way through the halls of Haijing Academy. While he'd acted all mystical in front of Zi Long for the sake of appearances, he was stumped. The most difficult case was Yue Bing. He wasn't sure how he felt about her being a blood cultivator, even after assurances from Feng Ming that she hadn't turned into a battle-crazed maniac like Gong Lan had.

From what he knew, blood masters were only found in the South. They were evil cultivators who drank the blood of their enemies to heal themselves and fight harder. Yet despite all this, Yue Bing had been acknowledged by a modest contingent of spirit doctors on the continent. Her new profession, blood doctor, had formerly been an illustrious profession in Haijing Academy. That spoke volumes.

He had blood on his hands, yet he couldn't shake the feeling that there was something wrong with siphoning blood from his enemies.

Did that make him a hypocrite or a bigot? He wasn't sure. He knew he couldn't avoid the problem forever, though. Besides, he'd seen the white hair on her head. She'd sacrificed a quarter of her lifespan while he'd been gone at Jade Moon Planet. Evil people didn't do that.

He passed her on his way to his chambers. She smiled, and he nodded back. Then she continued reading as she went back to her chambers. Reading seemed to take up most of her time, since she had very few patients.

Cha Ming yelped in surprise as a smaller man bumped into him as he rounded a corner. It was Jin Huang, the youngest of the bunch. Despite having a spatial treasure, the skinny man always carried pouches that reeked of danger on his body. He radiated an aura of fear not unlike Zhou Bei's.

"Greetings, Master," Jin Huang said, bowing quickly after picking himself up.

"Greetings," Cha Min said. "How fare your experiments?"

"Quite well," Jin Huang said enthusiastically. "In fact, I got some very good results while studying woodcap infusion with bloodfeather sprouts and blue phenol—" He stopped, blushing. "Sorry for blathering on. I'm sure it wouldn't be of interest to you."

"Alchemy interests me greatly," Cha Ming said. "But your skill exceeds mine. My offer to instruct you in runic arts still stands, but if you wish to discuss alchemy, I'm afraid you'll be the one teaching me instead."

Jin Huang smacked his forehead with his palm. "Don't worry about it. One of these days, we really need to talk about runic alchemy. I've been reluctant to practice it since the fiasco in Evergreen, but I think it has a lot of potential."

Cha Ming wasn't sure what the Evergreen fiasco was, but everyone seemed to be tight-lipped about it, even the alchemists in Haijing. Given their rhetoric about science, they didn't seem to want to touch Jin Huang's profession with a ten-foot pole. He could only assume something disastrous had occurred. Just the thought of exploring runic alchemy with the younger man made him sweat bullets.

"We'll definitely study it together in the future," Cha Ming said. "Have you seen Ling Dong?"

"The last time I saw him, he was training with the City Guard," Jin Huang said. "Something about training demons. Or arming them. Or both."

Arming demons? Now that was interesting. Speaking of which, it seemed like Huxian had said something about getting a wardrobe change. He wondered if those two were related.

"I'll have to go pay him a visit one of these days," said Cha Ming. "For now, I'm off to see the elders."

"Take care, Master," Jin Huang said, bowing. Before Cha Ming could tell him bowing wasn't necessary, he scampered off.

Cha Ming made his way through the stone alleyways in the academy. He walked past the library and the workshops as he did. There were no storefronts here, as commerce was prohibited within the school's grounds. Any buying or selling had to take place outside the building. The move was largely symbolic, meant to show that science and commerce should be kept separate. He liked that idea, as inconvenient as it was.

For science, he thought, chuckling inwardly as he walked onto a short street. The walkway was mostly empty, save for members on both sides glaring daggers at each other. Some things never changed. He ignored the Alabaster Group and Obsidian Syndicate guards as he made his way into the white building. Some friendly faces nodded and greeted him according to his station as junior partner. Since there were no storefronts in this branch, nor accommodations, he made his way to the back offices and entered the only boardroom in the building. Six older cultivators were seated there, including Elder Gan.

"Sorry I'm late," Cha Ming said, taking a seat.

"Not at all," Elder Gan said. "Though I really wish you'd let us know before secluding yourself like that. Your disappearance was... inconvenient to say the least."

"What happened?" Cha Ming asked. He hadn't been aware that

his presence was required, and Lu Tianhao had said nothing about this.

"You're new, so you naturally don't know these things," Elder Gan said. "Every few months, the elders get together to vote on some matters. Things like dissemination of knowledge, time-disc allocation, facility allocation, etcetera."

"It all sounds rather boring," Cha Ming said. "Time-disc allocation?"

"They're things like these," Elder Gan said. He summoned a bronze disc inlaid with blue runes and a small blue dot. "We can use the concentrated time essence to research faster or even speed up experiments without speeding up time for our physical selves."

Cha Ming thought of the disc in his possession. How much was it worth? "Can I pass on my votes instead of voting in person?" Then it struck him. "I forgot to pass on my votes, didn't I?"

"That's right," Elder Gan said. He passed a jade to Cha Ming. "Please review this and imprint your soul signature. With it, we'll be able to represent you in the next meeting. Our members were rather disappointed to hear that our newest addition, a full quarter of our voting power, didn't deign to defend their interests."

"I take it Zhou Li fanned the flames?" Cha Ming asked.

"Dealt with that ray of sunshine before, have you?" Elder Gan asked.

"I have," Cha Ming said. "It sounds like he's been cooking up trouble."

"More than just cooking," one of the two female cultivators present said. Elder Xia's age was difficult to tell, since any gray hairs were either hidden, removed, or nonexistent. However, her gaze seemed far too experienced to have lived less than a few centuries. "He's rallied many neutral factions and wrestled away some key research facilities and funding. He was also rather blatant about trying to curb our influence."

Cha Ming frowned. "While that *is* concerning, Elder Xia, I'm more concerned about his ulterior motives. Most of his actions, while detrimental to us, are likely a smokescreen." There was a pregnant pause. "Have we done anything to fight back?"

A black-haired, bushy-eyebrowed man snorted. "We have no trump cards anymore," he said. "We've fought tooth and nail all these years and have nothing to hide. Despite all our best efforts, our membership is dwindling. We simply have nothing good to offer new members, which limits the generation of new elders. We each have about twenty apprentices, and unfortunately, most of our knowledge isn't exclusive. Meanwhile, the Obsidian Syndicate has a private library for study should members join and sign a confidentiality agreement."

"Hm…" Cha Ming pondered. He had a fair amount of higher-tier knowledge, but he was a little concerned about protecting it. Seeing his hesitation, a scholarly looking man with blue hair, Cang Fuxi, spoke up. "We've been approached by the grand elder, Dai Yijun. He's offered to supplement our research budgets handsomely if we donate any new information. It's only…"

"He wants to make it available to all sides," Cha Ming finished. "For science."

"For science," the others in the room echoed, almost religiously.

"I'm afraid I can't do that," Cha Ming said. "The right knowledge in the wrong hands is too dangerous."

"We understand that," Elder Gan said, "which is exactly why we limit people in our faction to those who at least have neutral merit glow."

"Neutral?" Cha Ming quirked an eyebrow. "That's much lower than the merit-glow threshold the Alabaster Group usually asks for."

"Much lower, but we've had little choice," Elder Gan said. "If we didn't, we'd lose almost all our new members. It would only be a matter of time before our faction was relegated to a group of crabby old men. And women," he added, looking to the two others.

"Who are you calling *old*?" Elder Xia said.

Cha Ming massaged his brow. He didn't like revealing too many cards, but if things were truly so desperate for them in Haijing, it wouldn't be long before they were forced out. And if they were, it was only a matter of time before the South had a substantial technological edge over them.

"I can help, but I have some conditions," Cha Ming said finally.

"What are your conditions?" Elder Gan asked cautiously. "Our finances are rather limited."

"I don't need funding," Cha Ming said. "Just assurances. And information."

Elder Gan sighed in relief.

"Don't be too excited. My conditions are that the bar be raised back up to a requirement for positive merit glow. In addition to any standard nondisclosure contracts, we'll also need to amend the contracts and have them swear to never discuss dissolving their contracts with Zhou Li, whether directly or indirectly, nor to allow him to interfere with their karma."

"What does Zhou Li have to do with nondisclosure contracts, exactly?" Cang Fuxi asked.

Now that Cha Ming got a better look at him, the seemingly argumentative man looked every inch a lawyer.

"Zhou Li cultivates fire and fate," Cha Ming said. "He can burn karmic obligations, which is why I think he's been so good at hiding. I don't know what he can do from a distance, but at least we can stop his open and above-board meddling."

Cang Fuxi hissed between his teeth. He evidently hadn't thought of the possibility.

"Is that all?" Elder Gan asked.

"I have two more conditions," Cha Ming said. "My second condition is that, since a war is brewing, any members must not seek employment with anyone from the Southern Alliance. If that's too hard a pill to swallow, we don't need them. I will *not* be divulging knowledge to aid my enemies.

"My last condition is that you help me find a seller for Waters of Life, a peak-demon bone relic, and Water Source Marrow. There's no need to purchase them for me—I'll do the buying myself. My information-gathering abilities are fairly limited, so I'll need to lean on you for this.

"If you meet these requirements, I can gift our group my interpretation of peak grandmaster herbology, formation arts, as well as talisman arts. I'm also in the middle of comprehending an ancient inheritance. Should I succeed in obtaining it, I'll be able to add comprehensive elder-level alchemical arts to the list."

"We'll have to think about it," Elder Gan said hesitantly. "The formation arts are tempting, and so is the herbology. Still, it's just too risky."

Cha Ming shrugged. "You have my votes for now. In addition, I can take on some in-name and personal disciples. You also have my permission to approach my disciples and convince them to share their knowledge. However, the same conditions would apply for them as well. I will *not* be teaching them only to have others convince them to share knowledge with ill-meaning individuals."

"We'll consider it," Elder Gan said. "Now, if you'll excuse us, we have many other matters to discuss."

"No need to rush," Cha Ming said. "I'll be in seclusion for a while. It could be weeks or even months." He got up and left the meeting room, returning to his cultivation chamber. He had little desire for boards or meetings. As far as he was concerned, they were the least productive use of a man's time.

On his way back, he summoned two balls of qi, one white and one black. He twirled them around playfully, just like he had when he'd been speaking to Zi Long. Then, using his transcendent soul, he nudged them together. He didn't force the two to coexist; no, that was impossible. But the *suggestion* of what could be and what might be caused black and white to overlap for a short moment. And in that instance in time, that slice of reality, a wisp of violet smoke flew into the air just before the two spheres annihilated themselves.

"Illusory qi," he whispered. He pondered chasing the idea, pondered replicating the phenomenon. But in that moment, he made a decision that would forever define his cultivation. His Dao was real, and his qi should be too. Zi Long was following a different path, and guiding his path was just as important as confirming his own.

Chapter 8:
First, Master the Elements

Cha Ming appeared in a world of all-encompassing white and immediately headed toward the floating garden in the distance. He passed schools of flying fish and passed over nymph-tended woods bursting with medicinal plants. He reached the mountain plateau a short while later. There, Sun Wukong was busy executing a fearsome dance with his staff. The five elements hovered around the Monkey King, but now that Cha Ming looked closely, he noticed an imbalance. Earth was substantially stronger for the monkey, which made sense given the legends that he was born from stone. The strong earth focused the other four elements, centering them around a common purpose.

The dance reminded Cha Ming of his own fighting style in an abstract way. His water and earth techniques were strongest, followed by gold. Fire came next, and finally, wood. It was little wonder that the red-haired man forced him to practice his flames so much.

The earthen staff in Sun Wukong's hands was *heavy*. As far as Cha Ming could tell, the other four elements were like lynchpins or guides, preventing it from veering off course. Should any of them be lacking, the staff would miss its mark. In some cases, the consequences would be devastating.

"So, you finally asked those old geezers," Sun Wukong said, ending his routine. His soul body was covered in a layer of slick sweat that Cha Ming thought might be imaginary.

"The demon relic and Waters of Life are the key ingredients for the Nirvana Pill," Cha Ming said. "They're both valuable and notoriously rare. As for the Water Source Marrow, call it my backup. Should I fail to heal my core, I'll be able to transcend via body refining and craft the Nirvana Pill in a transcendent realm.

"Still, I'm a little nervous about its creation. Are you sure you're up for refining it? The strain of crafting a transcendent-grade pill might be too much for your soul." The memory of Sun Wukong fighting off Huxian's tribulation and nearly dissipating was still vivid in Cha Ming's mind. It was only thanks to sheer luck that he'd found a way to heal it.

Sun Wukong shrugged. "It should be fine. I'm not as frail as I used to be. Besides, you can't exactly ask the transcendents on your plane to make it for you." He shook his head. "I'm not afraid of crafting the pill, but the tribulation that will follow concerns me. I've never tried making such a strong pill on a lesser plane before."

"Will it work?" Cha Ming asked worriedly.

"It should," Sun Wukong said, his eyes narrowing. "But the plane might have different thoughts. To make matters worse, we can't just ask it. Life throws a lot of curve balls, Cha Ming. Keep looking for the Water Source Marrow. It's never a bad idea to have a backup plan. Now, heads or tails?"

Cha Ming closed his eyes. "Heads." He braced himself as his body jerked, and he found himself upside down in a familiar cauldron. "I'm starting to think you don't care about my answer."

Flames appeared all around him, causing the temperature in the cauldron to rise. Cha Ming used his control over fire to suppress them. Meanwhile, he summoned fifty flames, his current maximum. He used some of them to deflect incoming tongues of flame while protecting others through dodging and qi-protected fist strikes.

"Nonsense," Sun Wukong said from the outside. "I care very much for your answer. You're just unlucky, that's all."

Cha Ming gritted his teeth and continued with the drill. With his soul split into fifty, it was difficult to sense and avoid Sun Wukong's attacks. Whenever he grew used to the temperature, the room warmed or cooled. Whenever he thought his flames were strong enough to repel the opposing army of fire, it varied the intensity of its attacks, forcing him to reduce his power to avoid wasting qi.

Their battle continued for what seemed like days before Cha Ming finally collapsed due to fatigue. This session had been particularly fruitful. By the time it ended, he'd gained control over five more wisps of flame, a personal best.

"Still not good enough," Sun Wukong muttered. "You'll waste more batches than you succeed with such bad flame control, and that's only at core grade. How do you expect to have any chance in hell at making a transcendent pill?"

Cha Ming panted. "Aren't you going to be making it?" His sweat dripped onto Jade Moon Garden soil, watering the parched ground on the plateau. A pillar of stone crashed into his head, forcing him to nurse the large bump that immediately swelled up.

"You think I can craft a pill in soul form?" Sun Wukong asked sternly. "I can assist. Assist only. You'll be doing the heavy lifting, and the more weight you can take off my shoulders, the better."

Cha Ming could only nod.

"What's next?" Cha Ming asked.

"Next is gardening," Sun Wukong said.

Their surroundings shifted, and they appeared in the forest. Dryads and elementals poked their heads out curiously from behind trees as Cha Ming and Sun Wukong appeared within the grove. It contained several trees of various colors, along with a few brightly lit herb stalks. Some moss grew on a black rock on the eastern end of the garden.

"That's new," Cha Ming said. "Did you plant it all yourself?"

"I did," Sun Wukong said. "I also personally installed a ripening formation around it. These are the plants you'll be needing to craft the Nirvana Pill. You're to spend at least six hours growing them every day. While you do so, you'll also be tending this larger, less important garden." He motioned to a massive plot of land just outside the woods. "Catalyzing both slow-growing and quick-growing herbs will allow you to train your catalysis skills in a well-rounded way. You'll also have a stockpile of herbs for when you start doing real alchemy."

Cha Ming shook his head impatiently. "I know enough to advance by leaps and bounds," he said. "Do I really need to practice all these skills first? Isn't it better if I gain practical knowledge?" He felt a sharp pain as Sun Wukong's staff rapped him on the skull.

"I'm the teacher here, and you'll do as I say," Sun Wukong scolded. "For your impertinence, you'll be distilling the liquid in this barrel while you work." He tossed a small keg to Cha Ming, who raised an eyebrow.

"Is this moonshine?" he asked.

"Training liquor," Sun Wukong corrected.

"I don't exactly like drinking," Cha Ming said.

"That's a good thing, because it's not for you," Sun Wukong said. "Now hurry up and distill. And don't forget to grow the garden!"

Sighing, Cha Ming felt out with his wood qi and infused the two gardens, big and small. Using his knowledge of herbology, he guided the different plants, pruning them and urging their growth spurts as required. He soon fell into a trance.

He didn't forget the keg, of course. For that, he'd lit up a brown flame beneath the barrel's ironlike wood. Both the barrel and the contents heated up, and Cha Ming began the tiresome process of separating the well-mixed alcohol using the gravity generated by the brown flame. To his relief, it wasn't an inseparable mixture, just a very tedious separation.

Cha Ming opened his bleary eyes as he regained consciousness. A small rainbow fish was nudging his cheek. He recognized the fish. "Yu Gen," he said, lifting his hand and stroking the rainbow fish. "How are you doing these days?"

"Pretty good," the small rainbow fish said. "We've all been very busy. Master Sun has a very important task for us, and we dare not slack off. We fear his big stick."

A full school of younger fish, who kept a safe distance behind Yu Gen, nodded in unison. They eyed Cha Ming curiously from behind the smaller but braver rainbow fish, who had always been the friendliest of the bunch.

"If you're working hard, then I can't slack off," Cha Ming said, pushing himself up. He swept the dirt off his robes and used qi to purge the rest. He looked around for Sun Wukong but failed to spot him. "Where's that dirty old man gone to this time?"

"Master Sun said you could find him on the north end of the garden," Yu Gen said. "Our work will keep us busy for some time. Go on ahead without us."

Interesting, Cha Ming thought as he left the fish for the white space beyond the garden. *I wonder what he's got them doing.*

Before long, he passed over the edge of the garden and into the empty whiteness of the Clear Sky World. The soil ended abruptly, and from the side, it looked like the entire garden had been uprooted like a tree, with a rather large shovel.

"Took you long enough," Sun Wukong said, appearing beside him. He took a drink from his small keg of liquor.

"I might not be as strong as I was on Jade Moon Planet," Cha Ming said, "but you'd be hard-pressed to find anyone with higher regenerative abilities than me on the Ling Nan Plane."

"Is that what you think?" Sun Wukong said. "You're gravely mistaken. There are thousands of demons out there with better recovery powers than you. Dozens of devils on this plane alone. In Haijing City, there are at least a hundred body cultivators that could put you down without breaking a sweat."

Cha Ming gulped. "Isn't body cultivation difficult?" He'd expected the demons, but the devils? And even normal cultivators?

"You shouldn't be surprised," Sun Wukong said. "Devils are mostly body cultivators. While your Seventy-Two Transformations Technique is strong, devils and angels are naturally stronger than you. You've chosen the neutral path. The easy path."

"But why would the path of devils or angels be stronger?" Cha Ming asked. "I just don't understand it. I've heard others speak of balance, how fortune and power are opposites. Currently, good-aligned people are favored by providence, but devils by power. If that's the case, why are angels also stronger than neutral cultivators?"

Sun Wukong chuckled. "You've felt it, right? Your body, your affinity with the elements. Everything got stronger when you received what you call half an angelic endowment, right?"

"That's right," Cha Ming said. "Even my flames got stronger."

"Thank the painter for that," Sun Wukong muttered. "If not for that blessing, we'd still have years ahead of us in flame practice. It's not actually wood that you're worst at but flames. Even with half an angelic endowment on a flame-aligned path, you're only barely better at controlling fire qi than wood qi. But let's ignore that for now." He summoned five sigils in his hand. They morphed into the five elemental sigils that Cha Ming knew too well. "Recognize them?"

Cha Ming nodded. "They're like I remember them. Only…" From what he could see, there was nothing wrong with the characters. They just seemed… dull. Lifeless, even. "They're missing something."

"But what if I do this?" Sun Wukong said. He clenched his fist, and suddenly the dull sigils burned brightly. New feelings overwhelmed Cha Ming. He felt the burning rage of flame. He felt the cold indifference of water. He felt the calm rebirth of wood. He felt sharp, surgical failure. Finally, he felt unrelenting, unbowed, unbreaking earth. The sheer determination of the fifth character caused Cha Ming's jaw to slacken in awe.

"I showed you mine, now show me yours," Sun Wukong said.

Right. These were Sun Wukong's emotions.

Cha Ming gulped. He summoned the same five sigils, but despite being identical in form, they differed greatly in feeling. His own characters screamed balance. A man crumpled before pulling himself together, stronger than ever. A man overcame the ocean called life and fate, breaking through crashing waves to swim ever faster. A man sharpened his dull blade with the whetstone of experience. Hope was kindled amid the loss of a lover. Only wood was empty, out of balance with the others.

"They don't only feel different; they *are* different," Sun Wukong said softly. "Those four flames are stronger because you're stronger as a person. Feelings have weight since they're the manifestation of your Dao. Angels have strong feelings, as do devils. Everything they do, everything they are is stronger than a lukewarm mortal who doesn't take sides.

"In this generation, devils are stronger because they are persecuted. Their feelings are stronger because it's the only way they can survive in a world that's overwhelmingly prejudiced against them. Angels, on the other hand, just haven't had to deal with the same pressure. They're stronger than those who haven't chosen a side, for sure, but they're not like devils. They're like…"

"A blade that hasn't been oiled or sharpened," Cha Ming finished softly.

"That's right," Sun Wukong said. "But back to the main point. You're not as tough as a lot of people on this plane. Haijing is full of strong body cultivators because they're descendants of a god. They're naturals with respect to body cultivation, and they're better at it than you ever will be without even trying. And it takes far less resources for them to train.

"Still, there's a workaround. By increasing your control over the elements, you'll be stronger, faster, and tougher. You'll regenerate faster too. And it'll make a world of difference with your alchemy. Now, are you ready?"

"Ready as I'll ever be," Cha Ming said. The moment he spoke, the world of white lurched around him. A viscous, clear substance appeared. It was like water but thicker. Sometimes, however, it was thin as air. Boulders floated all around him, some big, some small. Their densities varied, but through his transcendent force, he could barely tell the difference. As one of the boulders headed his way, he summoned his Clear Sky Staff to bat it away; to his surprise, it was shaped like a glaive. Frowning, he tried slashing at the boulder with the swordlike staff. The blade cut into the boulder but not completely through it. He was forced to yank his glaive out as another, denser boulder struck him in the back, breaking several ribs in the process.

"Is this some kind of joke?" Cha Ming asked, wincing as his strong bones healed.

"No, it's your training ground," Sun Wukong said, appearing behind him. "I didn't want to waste time with three separate training grounds since you're good at all these elements. Meanwhile, we need to fix your hand-to-hand skills. They're garbage. Complete garbage. I mean, I've literally seen newborn monkeys fight better than you."

Cha Ming glared.

"Anyway, I'm sure you've noticed the chaos in your environment, yes?"

Cha Ming nodded in apprehension.

"The goal is to last as long as possible before passing out," Sun Wukong explained. "To succeed, you'll need to do three things. Firstly, you'll need to sense the relative threats of the boulders hurtling toward you at breakneck speed and use your control over gravity to navigate, repel, or attract them. Second, you'll need to sense the relative viscosity and density of the fluid around you, which will be constantly changing due to my direct manipulation of the fluid.

"As a note, that's also how I'll control the rocks and how they hurtle toward you. If you don't sense the changes on time, the fluid will affect both your reaction speed and the speed of the boulders. It will be impossible to avoid them all, which brings us to the third part of the training—evaluating the relative hardness of the boulders and judging how much slicing power is required to cut them in two or more pieces. Many situations will arise that make it optimal to choose between lopping off a chunk, completely shattering a boulder, or just cutting it in two. Or evading. Any questions?"

"You're really pulling out all the stops on this one," Cha Ming said. "How long do you expect me to last on my first attempt?"

"The first?" Sun Wukong thought while rubbing his chin. "Seven seconds. You ready?"

"Born ready," Cha Ming said. He gripped the glaive and dove into the field as the boulders were hurtled at him. He barely had time to react before the first one reached him. He cleaved it in two before pushing off one half toward another one. As he floated toward it, the currents changed, and suddenly he saw a boulder heading at him from the bottom.

He activated his control over gravity and repelled three more boulders headed toward him from the sides while manipulating the turbulent fluid around him, neutralizing it. He struck down with all his power, reducing the boulder beneath him to rubble. He grinned triumphantly. Then he noticed a small metallic orb heading for the back of his head. He tried pushing it away, but to his surprise, it completely ignored his gravity field. He tried increasing the fluid's friction but realized it was impossible to stop the fast-moving object with friction alone.

Finally, he realized it was too late to slash with his glaive. He did his best to cut it down, but the glancing blow wasn't enough to stop the golden orb from crashing into his skull. It threw him into a large boulder that happened to be heading in the opposite direction. It seemed like a failure, but as he closed his eyes, he smiled in satisfaction. He'd lasted nine seconds. Two seconds longer than expected.

Chapter 9: Shark Bait

It's nice to finally get out and stretch our wings, Silverwing said. He effortlessly pushed through the water using his morphed wings, a crude but essential trick when navigating the watery terrain. Lei Jiang darted around him, carefully limiting his electric powers to his own body. You didn't fry friends, only food.

This feels just like home, Gua said, floating around. He hadn't changed his body in the slightest, and his webbed feet were perfectly suited for navigating the cold high-pressure environment. *I hate being away from water. It's terrible for my beautiful skin. This saline water is just the right thing to revitalize my youthful, unblemished appearance.*

I'm going to need you to stop for a second, Huxian sent, using his now-webbed paws to travel through the dark waters. *Okay, you can keep going now. I threw up a little when I heard you bragging so much.*

You're just jealous that you're not so good looking, Gua said. *Though I'll admit, your fur coat looks wonderful down here. If you weren't my friend, I'd consider skinning you here and now and taking it for myself.*

Huxian rolled his eyes. The toad's interest in fashion had bloomed after he'd met Ling Dong, one of Cha Ming's apprentices and technically Huxian's apprentice nephew. He wasn't sure if today's business would tone down Gua's itch or spark a lifelong obsession.

Huxian hoped it was the former; he hated shopping.

Their surroundings grew lighter as they approached a lonely bubble in the distance. Ten miles away from it, they began hearing the clanking sounds of a hammer on metal. It was a melodious song, far easier on the ears than the unnatural sounds human smiths produced. It was a demonic tune that altered nature and soothed demonic souls.

Soldiers patrolled the area with dolphins, crustaceans, and seahorses. No sharks, Huxian noted. It seemed shark taming was too dangerous for humans. Compared to the last time they'd visited, several of the sea demons now wore significantly nicer harnesses and saddles. Many of them now wore armor, a thin layer that seemed to offer barely any protection.

But that was only to the untrained eye. Huxian could see a healthy purple glow pulsing through living runes in the thin armor. They resonated with the sea, drawing power from it and delivering it to their bonded master.

"Business?" a human asked as they approached the bubble. It was a human guard captain, one they'd seen before.

We're here to see junior Ling Dong about a job he's working on, Huxian said. *We won't be long.*

The guard captain waved them through. They entered the bubble, reverting to their unadopted forms as they shook off the seawater that drenched their fur and feathers. Gua's skin, which used to look old and weathered, was now covered in a healthy layer of slime. The toad hadn't been lying; the sea was really doing wonders for his obscenely ugly skin.

"Ah, you're here," Ling Dong said. The usually stern man dropped what he was doing. "Follow me to the back. I've got something for each of you."

Gua practically shivered in excitement as they followed the short-haired man, who walked more like a predator than a human artisan.

To Huxian's knowledge, no other human had ever become a demonic smith. It was a registered occupation in larger demon realms, though only a few demons chose to practice it. Most of those who did lived near metallic deposits or demon graveyards. They'd adapted to their natural environment by creating weapons much like humans did. They were well-respected among their kind. Therefore, Huxian's three friends gave the man a wide, respectful berth, while the younger fox simply trotted just ahead of Ling Dong. The large man purposefully kept two feet back, a ceremonial distance, to show due deference, like a proper demon should.

"Who wants to go first?" Ling Dong asked.

Me! Me! Gua said, hopping forward. *I've been thinking about this all night. Did you make me a coat? Or a dress?*

Huxian raised an eyebrow but said nothing. While the toad was undoubtedly male, there were no clothing customs among demons. Instead, clothing was universally looked down upon, like a crutch. Huxian didn't share their naïve feelings, of course. Perhaps Gua would look fine in a dress.

"I didn't make you a dress," Ling Dong said. "Or a coat. I'm sorry, it just didn't feel right, and I couldn't force it."

Gua looked down, his large eyes resembling those of more subservient demon throwbacks like dogs or horses.

"But I did make you an accessory."

Gua's eyes brightened as Ling Dong took out a thin blue metallic object. It was forged out of blue-gray metal called deep-sea cold iron, and its surface was covered in the familiar blue-gold runes that appeared everywhere around Haijing. Unlike those sterile imitations, however, these runes seemed realer, more natural. The shape was unusual, consisting of a wide flat plate affixed to a long, thin pole. Upon further inspection, the plate was a seashell, flattened through countless hammer blows until it fused with the deep-sea cold iron and demonic runes seeped into its surface.

Gua received what appeared to be a fan with reverence. It grew and shrank in his grasp, and when he swung it, murky water filled with whirlpools and artificial flows appeared.

"When I saw your fight earlier," Ling Dong explained, "I noticed you like constricting opponents, choking them out. You stagnate everything like a bog. This fan will help you do that better using *movement*. Whirlpools and tides can also help you trap opponents. Sometimes redirecting is much more effective than friction and weight."

I love it, Gua said, teary eyed. He slashed a finger open, allowing a drop of red blood to fall onto the fan. It glowed softly before disappearing in a violet puff of smoke and reappearing on Gua's back in the form of a violet tattoo.

That's seriously awesome, Lei Jiang said. *What did you make me?*

"Exactly what you asked me to," Ling Dong said. "You're a little… thick-hided, so defenses aren't a priority. You're also very fast. But you lack attack power, and your lightning strikes can't focus very effectively." He pulled out a white cloth, revealing four minimalistic gauntlets. Huxian noticed that each gauntlet was tipped with metallic claws that were, in fact, real claws pillaged from other demons. He approved. No sense in reinventing the wheel. The intricate runes that covered their surface channeled lightning into the tips of the unusually sharp claws. These would be a substantial upgrade to the swift mouse's repertoire.

"Silverwing is next," Ling Dong said. He revealed a pair of three-clawed gauntlets.

I don't lack offense, Silverwing said bluntly.

"I know you're not happy, but hear me out," Ling Dong said, holding up his hands defensively.

Either give me a proper explanation or apologize, Silverwing said. His claws were fierce, fiercer than Huxian's teeth in many cases. Improving their offense was tantamount to an insult.

"Here's what I figured," Ling Dong said, holding up the clawed contraption. "You have three modes of attacking, right?"

That's right, Silverwing said. *Whirling blades of windy death created by flapping my wings, concentrated wind blades generated by flying into enemies with my wings, destroying them in the process, and my deadly claws. Which, might I add, can tear through mid-grade core armor like it's paper.*

"That's fair," Ling Dong said. "Actually, these gauntlets don't change the offense of your claws in the slightest."

Explain, Silverwing said.

"What the gauntlets do is focus your wind affinity and generate a current *toward* your claws," Ling Dong explained. "Not suction. Suction is far too weak. Rather, it triggers the wind around you and uses it to force things toward your claws when you activate the gauntlets. It'll make it much easier to grasp swift or slippery creatures, especially small ones, with your extremely deadly claws."

Silverwing blinked a few times, processing the explanation. Then he grinned. *I approve. Small pesky creatures are my biggest frustration in life.*

"All a matter of the past," Ling Dong said, wiping the sweat from his brow. "I naturally saved the best for last." He paused for dramatic effect before opening a small box.

Huxian looked inside briefly and looked back up. *Those are goggles,* he said.

"They're goggles," Ling Dong said, nodding slowly. "Your goggles."

This isn't what I asked for, Huxian said, noting that this was a large departure from the super-mega armor—the one that weakened oncoming attacks while making him much stronger and faster—that he'd requested. His gauntleted paws should have been able to crush any opposition, while the eyes on his helmet would unleash beams of concentrated light on his enemies. This wasn't it.

"I know it's not what you asked for, but it's what you need," Ling Dong said, shaking his head. "You're a Godbeast, Uncle Huxian, so it's extremely difficult for me to improve on perfection. Your claws are sharper than Uncle Silverwing's, and you're almost as fast as Uncle Lei Jiang while much tougher. Your suppression and trapping powers are much better than Uncle Gua's."

All true but irrelevant, Huxian said. He hated not getting what he wanted.

"What you're missing is perspective," Ling Dong finally said. "I thought long and hard about your weapons, and eventually I thought to use the illusory steel left over from Brother Zi Long's staff. I infused it into deep-sea amber retrieved from the fissure, and the band is made from peak core-grade shark skin. Meanwhile, the runes I inscribed are my best work to date."

What do they do? Huxian asked, pawing at them curiously. He didn't like the goggles, but he knew quality when he saw it.

"They let you see things as they could be," Ling Dong whispered. "I won't even pretend to know how that works, or how I did it. It was a mad moment of inspiration, something I won't be able to replicate. From what I understand, it can help you better unleash your abilities by noticing causality and the very nature of things.

"Right now, you're looking at life through an unfocused lens. What these goggles do is focus on minute details and overlay them with your regular sight. When I wear them, I catch glimpses of what could happen just a split second before they do, greatly enhancing my reaction time. And that's just when *I'm* wearing them. I have a feeling they'll be much more effective when you do."

Fine, Huxian said, dripping his blood on the goggles, which appeared on his head instead of blending in with his fur like for the others. *At least they're stylish. Unlike someone's accessory.*

Gua glared at Huxian, who used his paw to adjust the new addition to his wardrobe.

"About your trip..." Ling Dong said sheepishly.

"You'll get first pick as agreed," Huxian said. "You can keep picking until you make a fair profit from our gear. Though like I said before, your master and I need some items. Those are off limits, but everything else isn't."

"Of course," Ling Dong said. "The guards outside want armor and accessories for their mounts, more than I have materials for. I can buy any surplus from you for a decent price."

"You helped me, now I'll help you," Huxian said. He and his crew departed the bubble and floated off into the darkness. They were headed toward the fissure.

Here it is, Huxian said as they swam up to a dark crevice on the ocean floor. They effortlessly bypassed the blue shield around it with his spatial powers. The aptly named fissure was a deep gouge in the rocky ground that hid beneath a sandy exterior. Shelves and caves peeked out every few hundred feet, hinting at dangerous creatures that attacked both the clueless and the brave. People, demons, it didn't matter to these darker creatures.

Huxian stared down an eel with his violet Demon-Subduing Eyes as they swam along the length of the crevice. The fissure soon widened into a large outcropping on the side of the stone cliff.

Would you look at that, Gua whispered, swimming ahead to get a better look.

The cliff was covered in floating green and blue plants. Multicolored flowers grew everywhere in what appeared to be a wild but fiercely protected garden. The most vicious predators in the sea swam about as they guarded the stockpile of natural treasures. Sharks. Fiendish ones. Lots of them.

I don't think this is a good idea, Silverwing said, flying forward. He'd summoned his new claw armor and spread his massive wings, signaling for their squad to stop. *There are too many of them, and some are even stronger than we are.*

But the treasures, the delicious treasures, Huxian said. *Seeing but not touching just isn't my style. How about we take a quick look? A discreet one?*

Silverwing frowned in disapproval as Huxian blended light and shadows around them, cloaking their small group against the hundreds of carnivorous fiends down below.

Why do they grow plants? Huxian thought as they swam. *Can they even eat them?*

Maybe they add them as spices to their prey? Lei Jiang suggested.

Likely, Huxian said. *It can't be anything else. There's not enough here to grow livestock.*

As they swam, the sharks grew larger and larger. Smaller, obviously infant sharks could no longer be seen amidst the dangerous frenzy of demonic predators. Their small compressed forms darted between them, carefully taking note of the various treasures growing in the garden. To their surprise, small octopuses were busy pulling weeds away from more valuable herbs while guard eels scared away smaller fish the sharks ignored.

Huxian's breath quickened when he found what he was looking for. Apparently the information he'd purchased had been accurate. A single white flower grew atop a large, juicy bud on a mountain deep within shark territory. It was a seabreeze lily. Several peak core demon beasts watched over the precious flower with obvious hunger. But they didn't dare consume it; the chief monarch in the frenzy, an old hammerhead shark with metallic streaks lining his sides, floated silently beside it. The flower was clearly about to mature.

Just as they were about to turn around, a faint glimmer caught his eye. It was a fist-sized gem located just below the seabreeze lily. Huxian's eyes widened when he saw it. *It can't be,* he whispered.

What is it? Silverwing asked, floating up beside him.

A Water Essence Core, Huxian said, gulping. *And it looks like the marrow inside it hasn't been claimed. My guess is that the sharks have been using it to nourish the seabreeze lily. They won't harvest the marrow until it ripens.*

Isn't that what boss's brother is looking for? Lei Jiang said.

That's right, Huxian said. *Brother needs it, so we need to get it for him.*

But there are too many sharks here, Silverwing said. *We'll die if we try.*

Huxian nodded slowly. He was brave, not foolhardy. *Even with Gua running a distraction for us, we wouldn't make it a mile before being torn to shreds. We need something bigger, something that will keep them busy for quite some time, distracting even ol' hammerhead* here. *Now tell me, who hates sharks more than anything else in the world?*

Dolphins, Lei Jiang, Silverwing, and Gua replied instantly. *Dolphins will mess them up. For fun. The only problem is convincing them. They're incredibly lazy.*

Huxian nodded. *Dolphins are the perfect match. It's just...*

Just what? Silverwing asked.

I just don't trust them, Huxian said.

Why not? Silverwing said. *Everyone loves them and gets along with them. They always look happy, and they don't do anything bad.*

That's exactly my problem! Huxian said. *No one is that perfect. They must have some deep, dark secrets they don't want anyone noticing. Their niceness is just a façade.*

Well, it's dolphins or orcas, Silverwing said. *And I'm not luring orcas, no matter how effective they are against sharks.*

Huxian shuddered at the thought of dealing with those murderous creatures. Sharks were brutal and bloodthirsty and naturally tended toward the fiendish way. But even *they* fled at the drop of a pin if they heard orcas were in the vicinity. Yes, dealing with dolphins was a better alternative. With any luck, their hatred for each other would result in a bloodbath for dolphins and sharks alike. The world would thank him for his actions.

But how do we convince them to act on it? Lei Jiang asked with a voice full of innocence.

How do you convince a bunch of angry, pent-up males to do anything? Silverwing said mockingly. *Are you doing it, or am I?*

I'll do it, Huxian said, sighing. He retrieved a tiny recording orb from his storage collar and got to work.

Chapter 10: Interference

I just don't see why this is our problem, the leader of the dolphins said. He was one of the five leaders who occupied a large territory on the sea bottom. Those who traveled in dolphin territory gave those of his tribe a wide berth, lest they get chosen for their next meal. *Sharks do their thing; we do our thing. Sometimes we fight to the death. No need to go out of our way for it, though.*

Huxian facepalmed mentally. They'd caught them in the middle of breeding season, meaning that these dolphins were especially lazy.

Dinner is ready, a nervous-looking female dolphin said, bringing a net full of dead demonic fish up to the quintet of male dolphins. The entire school was under the jurisdiction of these five peak-core-formation demons. This included feeding and social structure, among other things. All of them had cute beady eyes, but Huxian could swear he saw a hint of darkness within them, a blemish on their otherwise innocent demeanor. One day, the world would know the truth. One day, but not this day.

Thanks, hun, the dolphin said, nibbling on one of the fish that was thrown his way. He gave his—or the group's—mate a loving smile.

Huxian almost retched at the over-the-top show of affection. Sharks might be bloodthirsty murderers, but at least they were honest about it.

Did you see the loads of herbs they were harvesting? Huxian asked, placing the recording orb in front of them. Detailed pictures of the garden appeared. The seabreeze lily was conspicuously absent from the picture, hidden by his illusions. *These could all be yours if you chased them out. All you'd need to do is brutally murder their entire family.*

The dolphin shrugged. *There are loads of places like that around here. Nope. Can't be bothered. Especially with such nice company around here.* He tapped a passing female dolphin with his fin and winked at her. The dolphin scampered off, obviously frightened.

Huxian and his four friends suppressed a shiver and turned a blind eye to the demon's leering.

Look, I know you have a lot of things to do, dolphins to... meet, Huxian said. *Thing is, I've got a problem with these sharks. I have it on good authority that they fought an orca not too long ago. Killed it, but they're bleeding badly. All that's left out there is a few strong males and defenseless women and children.* The orb's image shifted to other select images, never showing their full forces.

I... I dunno, the lead dolphin said, reclining against an algae-covered rock. *It just seems so troublesome.*

What's troublesome about it? Huxian said.

Fighting and killing is troublesome, even if it's sharks, the dolphin said.

But it's the right thing to do, a female dolphin suddenly said, swimming up to them. *Sharks kill anything in sight. They kill our family members all the time. We have a perfect opportunity for vengeance, and you're going to give up on it. Think about it, hun. They're not half the dolphin you are.*

Huxian struck while the iron was hot. *That's right, they're not half the alpha dolphin you are. With your crew, they wouldn't stand a chance.*

The dolphin's mate nodded enthusiastically.

Besides, the dolphin's mate said, her body wiggling in a way Huxian didn't understand. *When I think of you heroing it up, I just can't help myself.* She cuddled up to the alpha. Something seemed to ignite inside him.

All right, that's it, the alpha dolphin said. *It's our time to shine. We're going to grab the boys and go beat up those sharks. Where did you say they were?*

Fifty miles from here, Huxian said. *Due east.*

The dolphin trilled, and soon a contingent of five hundred fully grown dolphins scrambled to attention.

Here's the deal, the alpha dolphin said. *Our friends here say they found a den of sharks.*

Some dolphins hissed, and others groaned.

They're hurt, and bad. I talked it over with my babe, and she said we should go out there and do something about it. I think it's high time we did the right thing once and for all. What do you all think?

Seems a little fishy to me, a lone dolphin said, glaring at Huxian and the others. *They don't even look like deep-sea creatures. They're just badly morphed surface dwellers. I—*

The dolphin was smacked upside the head by another's flipper.

What do you all think? the alpha dolphin repeated.

I think it's a great plan, the large dolphin who'd slapped the other said.

I agree, another said. *It's high time we bring justice to the seas.*

Plenty of other voices joined in, leaving the glaring dolphin alienated, and it eventually joined the group that agreed.

Then it's settled, the dolphin said. *We'll head out in four hours. What do you guys say?*

The dolphins nodded profusely.

Great! Do your thing. And we're off! The alpha was then urged away by a few teasing females, leaving the four surface-dwelling demons shaking their heads in amusement.

So, Lei Jiang said, *what's next?*

We follow the dolphins, sneak out amid the chaos, and pillage the treasure mountain, Huxian said. *And if all goes well, we double back and kill off any stragglers to look like heroes.*

He turned to Gua. *Are you all right, bud?*

Gua blinked and looked around in confusion. *Did something happen? How did the meeting go?*

Just fine, my friend, just fine, Huxian said. *Just make sure you bring your A-game in four hours. We'll need all hands on deck when the fighting breaks out.*

The fighting broke out suddenly and violently. Blood splashed as razor-nosed demonic dolphins impaled weaker sharks and toothy demons of death and despair ripped each other apart. The water turned dark almost instantly, providing helpful cover for the hundreds of weaker creatures in the immediate vicinity.

While the dolphins and sharks killed, Huxian and the others slipped away under cloak of darkness. They made their way toward the small underwater mountain where the seabreeze lily grew. Only two of the original four guardians were still there, and the remaining two swam about nervously.

They'll need to send out the rest, Huxian said. *Those five dolphins are more than a match for them. It'll take ol' sharkhead to give them an edge.*

Time trickled by. Stray blood radiated from the small bubble of slaughter at the entrance, prompting two more sharks to leave. Huxian and the others observed with tense nerves, hoping the powerful demon would join the fray.

Then, after much indecision, he did just that. Huxian sighed in relief and summoned an illusion of light and darkness that hid their presence on the mountain.

The seabreeze lily, Huxian said as he approached the flower. *So beautiful, yet so bold. The very best nectar for maturing demon eggs, but also the best catalyst for transcending.* He looked at it longingly but shook his head. He and his friends didn't need such help, but the egg he'd obtained on Jade Moon Planet was in dire need of it.

Huxian willed the egg to exit his storage space and carefully placed it above the seabreeze lily. A violet mist seeped out from the bud below the lily and drifted into the stone egg. As he supervised the process, his three friends got to work. They pillaged the valuable herbs growing in the immediate vicinity, leaving nothing but the weakest, youngest herbs to continue growing on the sea floor for whatever replaced the sharks and dolphins after they killed each other off.

As Huxian stared at the egg, he fantasized about what it would become. What kind of variant demon or Godbeast would it be? Would it be male or female? His thoughts wandered off. For some reason, he imagined a pale black-robed man with red pupils. No, it would be terrible if his demon became a human. Huxian wondered why he suddenly thought of Zhou Li as he woke from his stupor.

Let's go see what other goodies there are, Huxian thought. He swam around the small mountain and noticed that it contained not just a Water Essence Core, but many other valuable things. Priceless shells, high-quality spirit stones, and other baubles were piled high. Demon bones were the most common treasures, however. He noted that while most were just normal bones filled with vital energy, some of them were covered in intricate runic patterns. Were they demon-bone relics?

Demon-bone relics were very valuable, to humans and demons alike. The odds of them dropping were tremendously low, and to obtain one, a demon would have to kill countless others. They tended to form inside monarch-level demons or stronger, and while they were more common in peak-level monarchs, they were still extremely rare.

Yet somehow, on this mountain alone, he found three peak-grade relics and a dozen high-grade ones. Hundreds of mid-grade relics were also there. Excited, he took all of them and put them into his storage space, barely noticing a flicker out of the corner of his eyes. But when he looked, nothing was there. Only ocean.

I should fetch these treasures as quickly as possible, Huxian thought. He scooped up precious ores and precious stones. He harvested precious shells and even normal demon bones. He even recovered many core-grade weapons, the only metallic objects that had survived their time at the bottom of the ocean. He found over two dozen initial-core-grade sabers, swords, and staves. There were no spears, only tridents, the regional variant and the official weapon of Haijing's City Guard.

Time to retrieve the pièce de résistance, Huxian thought, looking up at the rocky egg and the rapidly shrinking seabreeze lily. The beast-nurturing nectar was two-thirds consumed by the egg, and it was only a matter of time before it hatched.

Huxian swam over to the Water Essence Core and saw that the Water Source Marrow was still there. That was a good thing, given how much time it took for the core to generate additional marrow after it was harvested. As he reached out with his paw, he caught another flicker out of the corner of his eye.

He growled and put on his goggles, activating his battle armor and growing to his largest form in one swift movement. Once was a fluke, twice a coincidence, but three times? He looked around, and to his surprise, he saw thousands of threads dancing all around him. He hadn't seen them before, but with the goggles's help, they were clear as day. The threads spread out from his body and in many directions. They were there to confuse him, he concluded. Then he noticed a figure darting toward the Water Essence Core, a figure he could finally perceive. It was an obvious void in his otherwise unremarkable surroundings.

Huxian sent out auras of light and shadow at the intruder, who simply waved his hand and kept them at bay. In response, Huxian sent three suppressing spheres, one each for lightning, wind, and swamp. The figure slowed as Huxian rushed forward, contracting time slightly as he moved, allowing him to close the distance almost instantaneously.

His strong body collided with the assailant, who jerked his hand back in surprise and came into full view. *Zhou Li!* Huxian shouted furiously. His cry alerted Silverwing, Lei Jiang, and Gua.

Zhou Li clapped and smiled as the four beasts assembled in

front of him, blocking him off from the Water Essence Core. "Very well done. Who would have thought that you'd foil my plan after all the trouble I went through in facilitating the absence of those guardians?"

Huxian's eyes narrowed. *What facilitation? What trouble?*

"What indeed?" Zhou Li smirked. "You couldn't perceive it before, but you can now, can't you?"

Huxian thought for a moment and nodded. *Karma. You've been burning the karma around you, hiding your presence and how we perceive you. Meanwhile, you lured the sharks away using the same trick.*

"I do hate being caught, but it's so refreshing when it happens," Zhou Li said. "I was really hoping to be in and out this time, but it looks like I'll need to put in some extra effort."

Cut the crap and fight, Huxian growled.

"What, and cut down on the ceremonial banter?" Zhou Li said in a wounded tone. "As a demon, I thought you'd be more respectful of traditions. According to the demonic council, it's appropriate for each dueling party to taunt the other for a reasonable amount of time. An extension may be granted in the case of a particularly good monologue."

You! Huxian barked. *How did you know?*

"I know a lot of things," Zhou Li said, his burning eyes peering into Huxian's. "I know all about your father and mother, and your brother especially. I know about the birth of the universe, and the curse that pervades it. I know of the painter, his creation, and how he left the world split in two ever-warring factions. I know—"

This is getting boring now, Huxian said, cutting him off. *You can monologue all you want as long as it's good, but this just isn't cutting it. You really ought to rehearse every now and again.*

Zhou Li chuckled. "Fair enough. I was just buying time anyway."

Dozens of roars echoed through the waters. They sounded nothing like sharks, and nothing like dolphins, and they caused shivers to run down his spine.

What have you done? Huxian asked gravely. *What did you unleash?*

"What I had to," Zhou Li said, his expression cold. His surroundings erupted in a sea of flames that bore down against the mountain, forcing Huxian and his friends to erect some hasty shields. They reacted just in time to protect the Water Essence Core and the stone egg, which had already absorbed ninety percent of the beast-nurturing nectar.

"Let's see how long you can keep it up," Zhou Li said as he formed hand seals. His black sin flames writhed and formed dozens of dragons that probed their combined suppressive barrier, forcing it to retreat or be burned to cinders.

Huxian panted as he fought against the flames with all his might. Lei Jiang, Silverwing, and Gua were evidently hit much harder by the sudden attack. Surprisingly, however, Gua was the first to act. He summoned his giant rune-covered fan and swished it through the water, creating turbulent eddies that collided against the encroaching flame dragons. They broke up the dragons and gave their squad just enough time to reform their formation. They huddled around Huxian and linked with the stars using the Greater Friendship Circle.

Ninety-five percent. The egg was almost done absorbing the nectar. The moment it was done, they could retrieve the Water Essence Core. Zhou Li, seeing the situation was dire, summoned a sword. It pulsed with transcendent might as he slashed down with it.

Huxian howled and clashed with it, only to bounce back with a gaping wound on his shoulder. Zhou Li struck out again, and this time Lei Jiang clashed with it. He wielded his claw weapons and infused them with lightning. The entire friendship circle fed Lei Jiang with as much power as it could spare. The small rodent managed to deflect not one but seven blades of dark fire before being forced back.

Since Gua was busy fighting off the dragons of black flame, Silverwing took point. He channeled all their power into his metallic wings, which he closed into a shield. His massive body completely obstructed them from Zhou Li's attacks, and due to Gua's interference, Zhou Li couldn't get around the giant bird.

I just hope we have enough time, Huxian thought. The roar they'd heard was disconcerting. He looked at the egg, which glowed softly as it completed absorbing the last of the nectar. Huxian grasped the hatching egg in his giant jaws and raced toward the Water Essence Core.

Unfortunately, it seemed that Zhou Li had predicted this move. He saw causality shift and match up. As he'd retrieved the egg, Zhou Li had pulled out a large scroll. Now the beautiful painting of death and destruction came to life as it battered against Silverwing. But Zhou Li was nowhere to be found. He had severed karma to duck beneath Silverwing's guard and shot out a concentrated burst of sin flames.

No! Huxian thought. The black and white threads around him representing space and time tightened as he willed them to change to the limit of his ability. He spent a portion of his vitality, his very existence, to try and snap them into a more favorable position.

Unfortunately, this wasn't Jade Moon Planet. He was far weaker here without the Jade Moon Blessing. Even with the power of his brothers, all he could do was give them a chance. The black and white threads snapped into place, and Huxian found himself just beside the Water Essence Core. He used his purifying light and devouring shadows to purge the sin flames that had just touched it. Then he took the damaged orb into his storage space, protecting it from further damage.

It's time to run! Huxian sent to his brothers, who nodded. They'd heard the growl. Zhou Li had disappeared after his failure, but they didn't have time to chase him. What was coming was far worse. It was a three-hundred-foot-long, psychopathic creature of death and destruction. Its bright blue eyes, strangely adorable to humans, bored holes into the four terrified demons.

It was an orca.

Zhou Li had somehow summoned an orca, and a peak-level one at that. As much as sharks were known as the killers of the sea, and dolphins were known as the playful friends of the ocean, they would rather fight loads of them at a time than fight a single orca.

Scatter! Huxian yelled, blanketing them in a cloak of light and darkness.

Gua swung his fan, pushing them out as quickly as possible, all the while congealing pieces of water as they retreated. The shadow behind them grew larger despite the interference. It grew closer, and Huxian, through his mysterious violet goggles, could see exactly why.

Shit! Huxian shouted. *He tied a karmic thread between us and the orca!*

The black-and-white bringer of death appeared before them, its toothy, deceptively friendly smile ready to bite their flippers off on a whim.

Can you deal with it? Silverwing asked.

Huxian nodded.

Then I'll buy you the time you need.

The brave bird flew out against the unspeakably powerful demon. It flew through the waters, raking the creature's body with sharp feathers and steely claws. The orca barely registered the vicious blows, shrugging them off like mosquito bites. His flesh regenerated as soon as it was cut, leaving only barely visible trickles of blood in the nearby water.

Work quickly, boss! Lei Jiang shouted. He too jumped into the fray.

While Huxian carefully fashioned a saw out of light and shadow, slowly but surely severing the thread of karma, the brave mouse flew onto the orca and dug four claws into its back. Then he summoned unrestrained, unfocused lightning. The orca roared in anger as black-and-violet lightning raged through its body, causing it to twitch uncontrollably.

Demon dung, Huxian thought. *We pissed it off.*

He heard a soft pluck as a quarter of the string of karma peeled off. It was soft light in a dark tunnel. A dark tunnel that contained a psychopathic killer. Lei Jiang's lightning wore off, and the creature grinned. It flung the mouse off its back and bit at it. Fortunately, Silverwing had anticipated the move and caught their brave friend.

As the orca moved to eat them both for the insult, he was

suddenly distracted by waves of disgusting water. Gua was below them, waving his shell-shaped fan like filthy merchandise in a cheap body house. The move confused the creature and caused it to forget the annoying pests who'd slightly wounded it. He was intrigued by the frog. He wanted to eat it.

Gua fled frantically as two more thin strands of the thread peeled away. Huxian gathered energy from Lei Jiang and Silverwing, redirecting most of it to the fleeing Gua and using the rest to continue cutting. He poured his heart and soul into severing the connection that could only lead to one possible end—their death and destruction.

Finally, after much gut-wrenching effort, the thread snapped. Huxian summoned light and shadows once more, enveloping Lei Jiang and Silverwing. They swooped down to pluck Gua out from the literal jaws of defeat. As they fled, Huxian severed another thread to Zhou Li he'd discovered during his inspection. They looked down almost in pity as the orca, confused, wandered over to the crowd of warring sharks and dolphins.

Look here, look here, Lei Jiang exclaimed as they swam away on Silverwing's large back. The stone egg was now glowing brightly. Huxian and Gua moved forward excitedly while Silverwing craned his neck. The bright white egg began to show fissure after fissure until it finally cracked.

Revealing nothing.

Huxian was confused. There should have been something. He looked around, but to no avail. Then, as though thinking of something, he slipped on his goggles once more. Through the violet lenses, he eventually spotted a soft violet mist.

Holy hell, it's an illusory demon, he whispered.

An illusory demon? What's that? Lei Jiang asked, sniffing at the water curiously.

An illusory demon is a rare demon that can turn corporeal and incorporeal on a whim. It imprints a shape at birth, which becomes unchangeable. Normally, given where it was raised, it would have turned into something awesome like a rockwurm or a clay dragon. Possibly even a worldborn titan.

But we're now at the bottom of the ocean, Silverwing concluded. *Which means it could have imprinted something from the seabreeze lily, the underwater environment, or both. Basically, it's a gamble.*

But doesn't boss need a mountain-aligned demon? Lei Jiang asked. *What will we do if it isn't?*

Huxian shook his head. *It doesn't matter. We'll take him in as our friend regardless. We owe the mountain elemental that much. I just hope it's not something wimpy like a pet rock or a clown fish. Or worse, something feline.* The others hissed.

As though sensing something, the violet mist shifted. It took the appearance of many things at the same time. A cat without ears. A giant earthworm. A silver fish. An eel. A tree demon. A mighty serpent. It shifted through many forms, never settling on one. It was like rolling a dice with more than a hundred facets. Huxian's inner gambler sweated as he waited for the inevitable, unchangeable result.

Finally, the shifting began to slow. Ten forms a second became one per second, and then one per five seconds. The illusory demon could settle on any one of these shapes. The first one, surprisingly, was a many-tailed fox like Huxian. But instead of his bagua variation, it was just a normal many-tailed fox. The next one was a falcon, tall and proud.

Any one of these would be all right, Huxian thought. Until it turned into a mountain cougar, a feline creature of earth and stone. *Anything but a cougar,* he thought, shuddering. Then it became an orca. *On second thought, cougars are wonderful creatures. Anything but an orca.*

A few more forms passed by. It became a hammerhead shark, likely due to their recent contact. Then it became a demonic flower that resembled the seabreeze lily.

Finally, it shifted one last time. It was obviously the last, because this time a cloud of violet smoke erupted all around it and began to drink in the surrounding demonic energy. Even through their enhanced demonic senses, they still couldn't see anything. It was the necessary drama that came with a demonic transformation.

They gulped as the violet mist took its time to clear. First, it revealed a rocky horn at the edge of the mist, which was a good sign for Huxian since he wanted something mountain aligned. Then his eyes narrowed in confusion as the horn became larger and larger, eventually making up half of the mist.

What the... he started. And then it hit him. It wasn't a horn. It wasn't a claw. It wasn't any kind of lethal appendage on a self-respecting demon.

It wasn't a demon at all, in fact. It was a mountain. The egg had been kept by a mountain elemental on a giant mountain, where it drank in demonic mountain energy every day. Then it drank in the seabreeze lily's essence, which was effectively leeched from a mountain for thousands of years. The creature's final form, which was a forty-foot-tall initial-purification demon, was a perfectly conical mountain.

Hello? Huxian asked, cautiously greeting the newborn creature. *I'm Huxian.*

His friends held their breaths as they waited for the creature's response. It might have just been born, but it was born as an initial-purification demon. Moreover, it was an illusory demon. They were confident it had tons of ancestral memories to draw from.

I... the mountain started.

They edged forward expectantly.

I... the mountain said, just a little louder.

I am a mountain! it finally said. Its weight increased, and Silverwing cawed in shock as he plummeted down toward the sea floor.

I am a mountain! the illusory demon shouted, and the four demons wailed as they were propelled to the deepest depths of the ocean.

I am a mountain! it yelled again.

This time, Huxian responded.

We get it, you're a mountain, he said. *We got that. But we're falling fast, and this isn't the best place to crash, if you get what I'm saying.*

I am a mountain! it yelled in acknowledgement.

Huxian facepalmed. He really hoped this wasn't a case of demonic retardation, where the demon barely had the intelligence of a three-year-old human.

I get it, you're a mountain, Huxian thought, trying to guide the newly born creature. *But you can stop being a mountain sometimes, right?*

Illusory demons could shift between corporeal and incorporeal. Maybe this was something it could remember despite its childish mind.

I am... the mountain started. *Not a mountain!* The forty-foot peak that had been weighing down Huxian and friends suddenly vanished. It floated over to Huxian and nuzzled against him. They breathed in a sigh of relief.

Well, that was interesting, Silverwing said, adjusting their trajectory to return to Haijing. *Maybe we could teach it to do that on command?*

Maybe, Huxian said, looking at the violet mist uncertainly. Then, recalling what had transpired on the mountain, he retrieved the blue orb they'd recovered. The previously immaculate orb was covered in burn marks, but otherwise it seemed perfectly fine. Or that's what he thought until he noticed its glow had diminished.

Demon farts. He wasn't trying to destroy the core. He cut straight to the chase and destroyed the marrow.

Is that really a big deal? Lei Jiang asked. *Won't more marrow grow back?*

Huxian shook his head. *It'll take too much time,* he replied. *Cha Ming and I might share a lifespan, but it takes tens of thousands of years to generate source marrow. To make matters worse, a mortal plane probably won't have more than one of these cores inside it.* He sighed. *Zhou Li did exactly what he planned to do. He distracted us with the orca to slip a wisp of sin flames into the Water Essence Core and burn away at the marrow while our new friend hatched. It was meticulously planned and perfectly executed.*

Huxian sighed. *We can only deliver the bad news for now. On the bright side, we got something Brother needed. We got three peak-demon bone relics, an essential component for the Nirvana Pill. With any luck, the Water Source Marrow won't matter.*

Despite his reassuring words, the young fox knew deep down that it wouldn't be so simple. If Zhou Li was clever enough to find what Cha Ming needed most and eliminate it, he would move to block other avenues as well. This fight was just an appetizer to the feast of troubles they'd face in Haijing City.

Chapter 11: A Special Flame

A large ball of dense earth hurled toward Cha Ming at deafening speed. His eyes were closed, though that didn't stop him from barely moving his head as he sensed the approaching projectile. In the distance, thousands of large and small, dense and light earthen balls shot at him and tried to wound him. Some, he evaded. Others, he pushed ever so slightly, altering their direction.

He used the big spheres differently; by increasing his attraction to the spheres, he pulled himself toward them instead of the other way around. The pull complemented his movements, allowing him to avoid many boulders he couldn't have otherwise.

This tricky display of power was only possible after many months of extended practice with the earth element. The few projectiles that snuck past his gravitational defenses were struck down by his glaive. Not only could Cha Ming regulate how much power he used, but he could also extend the blade as required. Sometimes he struck with a razor-sharp edge. At other times, he struck with the dull edge, forcing away stray stones with a light tap. Either way, he conserved his power; the strongest attacks weren't needed yet.

Cha Ming always kept a thin layer of fluid around himself. It was dense but slippery enough to allow smaller pebbles to run past him. He no longer fought the turbulent eddies like he used to; instead he chose to navigate them like a surfer on a wave. Further, he'd discovered that forcing an entire current away wasn't necessary. Sometimes he simply needed to redirect a simple stream away from a larger wave to obtain the right effect. Context was key.

Like this, he floated around in the monkey-made deathtrap, patiently conserving his energy as the lethality of the test intensified. Smaller stones that took lone strikes to dispatch became larger ones that required dozens of lacerations to take down. Simple waves became unrelenting tsunamis he resisted with everything he had. When his environment thickened, he thinned a small layer around himself, avoiding most of the friction while he navigated his environment with gravity. It was a dance with death, and the stage was a razor's edge.

An hour passed in this way, after which the turbulence intensified, as it had the time before. He was sucked toward the middle of the field with nowhere to escape as rocks hurtled toward him. He used everything he could, including gravity, glaive, staff, and fist strikes. He used some of the rocks for leverage as he clashed against others.

Finally, only three seconds remained. The most important three seconds. He'd failed many times before, but this time, it would be different. His staff became a blur of blades that extended as an omnipresent shield of slashing energy. As rocks collided with the shield, a thick layer of debris entered, and he used his control of flow to force it out and deflect rocks in other directions. Due to the high density of rocks, he didn't use gravity to navigate the field. Instead he redirected rocks to crash against each other. The slightest mistake could easily cost him his life—or at least, it could have if Sun Wukong wasn't around.

Finally, the storm of boulders ended. The last of the rocks had been demolished by Cha Ming, their remnants forming a small mountain of gravel beneath him. He heard a clapping sound from behind him.

"It took you long enough," Sun Wukong said as he clapped. "Now wash yourself—you need to take care of the garden again before I grill you."

Cha Ming bowed and motioned with his wrists, creating water

and wind in midair. He cleansed his body and robes using an impromptu misty shower and made his way toward the lush plot of land. The field grew peacefully as he sat cross-legged in the center, feeling out the needs of the respective plants and balancing their growth. Some plants cried out for sustenance they needed while others for sustenance they wanted. He was forced to interpret these and prioritize. His qi and time were limited.

Six hours passed as he tended the garden. Though he wasn't great at manipulating wood, he felt peace as he worked the soil and fed the growing greenery. He didn't need Sun Wukong to prompt him when things were done. The plants knew when he would leave, so they stopped issuing requests when that time came.

"Are you ready?" Sun Wukong asked, grinning. "Heads or tails?"

"Tails," Cha Ming said, knowing his answer was pointless. Regardless of the answer, he would end up in the cauldron and upside down. He appeared in a sea of flames, summoning his own multiple tongues of flame to counteract it. Before, he'd felt attacked. But now, especially given his experience with the other four elements, he knew how silly that mindset had been. This wasn't a battle; it was a happy game.

The game was best played using everything he had to his advantage. He would use flames to correct heat imbalances around him, but there was no use trying to force everything to the same temperature. Instead of making things comfortable for his body, he made things tolerable. He economized where he could but also kept careful watch over nearby temperature gradients. Where the gradients were strong, he amplified flow to push heat into more desirable directions.

Sometimes Cha Ming even used gravity. Things flowed from hot to cold, but gravity also meant that denser things sank while others rose. Therefore, he manipulated the density of the hottest air, forcing it to move away. Meanwhile, he manipulated the coldest air in a similar way, increasing its density and using gravity to attract it toward him.

Heat manipulation, flow, and gravity. Sometimes he fed flames with wood qi, creating a high-temperature area that would distort the overall heat field and keep cooler areas around him. At other times, he used metal qi to absorb ambient heat as it melted. It was a dance of five elements, and he was king.

Flames are just like the five elements, Cha Ming thought. *They follow many different sets of laws, not only the laws of fire. It's why I can use five colors of flames and use them for different purposes. By that same token, the flames can all affect each other. It's all one big circle, one big star.*

As he struggled to survive for just a bit longer, that feeling intensified. It echoed through his mind like a mantra uttered by a monk seeking enlightenment.

Finally, he saw something he'd never seen before. Beyond the billowing trails of white, beyond the crackling blackness, he saw a small spot. It didn't have a color, yet it shared all colors. The spot was gray, and it had no beginning or end. It just was. It existed outside of the flame's influence, but intuitively, he knew they had a relationship. It was the birthplace of flames, the mother of all of them. And then it struck him: he could make that flame.

Cha Ming abruptly ended his training and sat cross-legged in a trance. He relied on Sun Wukong to protect him as he focused on this modicum of enlightenment. The flames dispersed, but Cha Ming's flames remained. He kept five wisps, which he split into many smaller ones. They combined experimentally, merging at lightning speed. Green flames jumped into red ones, creating blue-green flames of living inferno. Metallic flames merged together with watery ones as flames of acidic corrosion. Before long, ten sets of flames were present outside the original five colors.

He didn't hesitate. He threw one more wisp into each of the ten bunches and ended up with ten more. Five combinations were dark while five others were lighter. The dark ones were stronger, more concentrated. Lethal, even. The white ones, on the other hand, were larger and more accommodating.

He added one more flame to each bunch, and unlike what one might think, he didn't end up with five flames. Rather, the combinations of four elements were different depending on the way the flames had been added. Fire, wood, water, and metal could combine in two ways, one creation aligned and one destruction aligned. As a result, he still possessed ten flames. After adding the last color, he was left with five black flames and five white flames. Combining each pair could only result in two things: an illusory superimposition or annihilation. Therefore, he disbanded them.

He summoned five more flames, and instead of combining the different flames, he took out two streams from each of them, feeding them in creative and destructive ways. The wisps thickened, and he brought the flames closer together, observing the changes as they happened. The flames were being refined and destroyed at the same time, and he knew that if he continued this, they would eventually run out of fuel. Or would they?

He had seen something among the flames, a shade of gray that defied his understanding of how fire worked. So while the flames circulated, he began forcing them together, gently at first. Their auras clashed as the different elements in the flames began to affect each other. The transfer in creative and destructive energies intensified to the point that they threatened to destroy the subtle balance between the flames. He kept forcing them ever closer until finally, he did what he'd done with the Dao sigils and his core. He *twisted*. The flame configuration kept creating and destroying itself, but the twist had lessened the strain. Cha Ming effortlessly brought them together until finally, something appeared: a small gray spot.

He licked his lips as he decided on his next course of action. It was possible that only a single wisp of gray could be formed this way and forcing the flames together could cause something akin to annihilation. He shuddered when he thought of the combination that had once destroyed over half his body. He'd recovered, but he'd been scared he wouldn't.

He took a deep breath and steeled his resolve before continuing along this path. He continued forcing the five flames together into the gray point, which expanded as he continued pressing against it inch by inch, until the five flames, along with the gray and white lines connecting them, almost touched. Then he gritted his teeth and gave it one final push. He pushed with his body, with his qi, and with his transcendent soul. As it came together, he felt a soft pulse.

Surprised, Cha Ming opened his eyes. In his palm was a small gray flame unlike anything he'd ever seen before. As he poured five-element qi into it, growing and shrinking it, he realized that he'd created a flame seed out of thin air, no flame focus required. The flame winked out of existence at his command and reappeared again when needed. It felt hot and cold, sharp and dull. It felt fluid and stagnant, brittle and hard. It felt living and dead. This flame, he instinctively knew, could be used to control flames in ways he hadn't thought possible. He no longer needed five flames to perform each function, just one.

"I'll call it a Grandmist flame," Cha Ming whispered.

Sun Wukong appeared beside him and nodded gravely. "A very appropriate name, much more appropriate than your supposed Dao sigils from before."

Cha Ming chuckled. "Then I'll rename the Dao sigils. From now on, they'll be Grandmist sigils. Fair enough?"

"Much less conceited," Sun Wukong said solemnly. "I'd hoped to polish your flame control a little more before proceeding, but that's now unnecessary. Your understanding of flames has transcended the limits of mortals. So too has your knowledge of water, earth, and metal. Wood is on the cusp of breaking through, but only because you haven't infused your poetic insights and incorporated them into your angelic aspirations. But who cares about wood? Wood isn't the be all end all in alchemy, flames are."

"What next?" Cha Ming asked.

"Next?" Sun Wukong said pensively. "Next we use what you've grown in this garden to make every damn pill you can think of. By the time you get out of here, you'll be a real heavy hitter in alchemical circles, but probably not quite elder level."

"That fast?" Cha Ming asked, surprised.

"Compared to the progress you could have made before, you'll be flying," Sun Wukong said. "A lot about alchemy involves quickly spotting problems and then reacting appropriately. I beat that into your bones, and with your affinity for plants, you'll be able to sense even the slightest deviations and make corrections on the fly. There shouldn't be many low-level curveballs you can't handle, and with every pill you make, you'll learn that much more."

"Good," Cha Ming said, invigorated. Alchemy was only a means to an end, a way to heal his core and advance quickly. He'd now be able to find Yu Wen that much faster.

Time flew by quickly. Once Cha Ming formed his Grandmist flame, he was no longer required to undergo trial after trial. He only had to concoct pill after pill from a seemingly endless library of knowledge he gleaned from Yu Wen's Space-Time Camera. Occasionally, he read her letter. It made his desire to see her grow and egged him on. After a year's time, he pushed his way to early grandmaster in alchemy before finally running out of medicinal herbs.

One year after beginning his seclusion, Cha Ming roamed the familiar streets of Haijing Academy once more. The familiar living quarters were just like he remembered them. Scholars argued and played *Angels and Devils* while others drank. Some meditated beneath the trees, while others played musical instruments. It was almost picturesque. Almost. He frowned as he looked around and realized something.

Cha Ming let out a bright laugh and summoned blades of destructive energy. They tore through violet strings that were otherwise imperceptible to him, revealing five shadows that advanced toward him.

"Interesting," Cha Ming said. "Come at me with everything you have."

His opponent attacked with a formation and staff, using his superior weapon and incarnation techniques to fight like five men at once. He used different runes than before. They sometimes combined in defense and sometimes in offense. They linked together between avatars, using clever elemental combinations to wear away at Cha Ming's defenses.

At the start of the battle, Cha Ming had restrained his qi and body to initial core formation and initial bone forging. This clearly wasn't enough against this aggressive opponent. He thought for a moment before upgrading his qi to early grade and manipulating it in a new way. He then summoned creative wind and destructive lightning. The lightning ravaged his opponent's formations, striking at their weakest points as wind reinforced certain elements, throwing his opponent's formations off balance as Cha Ming sparred with the avatars. They continued this dance for five whole minutes, and every time his opponent found a way to fix his weaknesses, Cha Ming found new ones to pick on.

Finally, when it seemed his opponent could learn nothing more, Cha Ming summoned a gray flame in his palm. He threw it out at his opponent's web of formations, and everything burned. Wood, metal, even flame itself burned under its world-ending, world-birthing heat.

"Grandmist!" Zi Long said as he appeared where his clones had disappeared.

"Indeed," Cha Ming said. "I thought it would benefit you to see it. I'm relieved to learn you took my teachings to heart. Your runic arts now match your cultivation."

"I still have a long way to go, it seems," Zi Long said. "Though I have some ideas now that I've seen you wield creation, destruction, and Grandmist so exquisitely."

"I'm glad I could help," Cha Ming said. "Has anything new happened?"

"More of the same," Zi Long said, following Cha Ming through the garden. "Uncle Huxian went on an excursion and found something you might like, and the elders want to speak with you. Something about getting destroyed at council meetings."

"I'll bet," Cha Ming said, adjusting their route. "And your brothers and sisters?"

"Ling Dong is doing better than ever," Zi Long said. "It seems Huxian and his friends are great teachers for him. I doubt you could outdo them. As far as their bunch is concerned, Ling Dong is an honorary demon. That aside, he's got the entire City Guard in his back pocket. Everyone is fighting to get on his waiting list for demonic arms."

"Jin Huang?" Cha Ming asked.

"Concocting away," Zi Long said. "He's gotten to early core formation like us, and his alchemical arts have caught up. His poison arts are still devastating, and he's managed to frighten the Alchemists Association in Haijing to supply him ingredients. It seems his reputation from the Evergreen Kingdom influenced their decision."

"What exactly happened there?" Cha Ming asked. He'd heard Jin Huang's journey mentioned many times, but he'd never asked for specifics.

"They tried to bully him into giving away runic alchemy secrets," Zi Long said. Seeing Cha Ming's eyes narrow, he continued. "It didn't work, and he paid them back in spades. They were so scared of him that they did everything he asked. The rest of the alchemists boycotted him because they thought he'd grown too big for his britches. Seems they've changed their mind."

Cha Ming chuckled. "And Yue Bing?" She was the one he was most worried about.

Zi Long winced. "Her case is… complicated," he said. "You should really go talk to her. She's cold and withdrawn, but if someone asks, she'll help. Unfortunately, those in our faction don't take kindly to her blood doctor and blood master occupations. It puts her in a very bad position, both financially and emotionally."

Cha Ming sighed. "I'll talk to her. And to them. It's my fault for avoiding the issue."

"Please don't judge her before hearing her out," Zi Long said, stopping suddenly. "The rest of us think she's made all the right choices, and it wouldn't sit well with us if you keep giving her the cold shoulder."

Cha Ming stopped as well, then nodded. "I'll talk to her. I can't say I like blood arts, but I'll keep an open mind."

"That's all we ask," Zi Long said.

"Brother Cha Ming," a voice called out. Elder Gan walked out from a building behind them and caught up. "Do you have a moment?"

"I'll excuse myself, Master," Zi Long said, bowing and retreating.

Cha Ming nodded and followed the elder down the familiar road to the Alabaster Group headquarters. Compared to last time, it was much quieter.

"As you can tell, we've taken quite a thrashing," Elder Gan said wryly.

"Zhou Li is a difficult opponent," Cha Ming said. "Unless you have a genius on par with the Wang family's Wang Jun, you need to play hardball with him. Force things in a way he can't easily manipulate."

"So we've learned," Elder Gan said, leading him inside a room, where a half dozen men and women had hastily been gathered. No, it was five now. They'd apparently lost a member. "We've been considering your proposal, and after our latest council meeting, we've decided to take you up on it. If you're still willing."

"I'm always willing," Cha Ming said. "Same Alabaster Group rules as before, and my offer for knowledge still stands. I'm also willing to take on some disciples." He saw them visibly relax that he hadn't added any conditions. "In fact, since it seems Zhou Li is hellbent on ruining us here, I'll add to my initial offer. I'm willing to dispense alchemical knowledge as well."

Elder Gan frowned. "I don't mean to look down on you, but what level alchemist are you?"

"Early Grandmaster," Cha Ming said.

"Impressive, given the short time, but it will be difficult to compete with that," Elder Gan said, shaking his head. "In fact, it would only highlight our disparity."

"And what if I added this?" Cha Ming asked, placing a vial on the table.

A hand motioned at it and whisked the jade vial over. The vial opened, and a pill floated out.

Elder Cang Fuxi, the one who'd summoned it, looked at Cha Ming with curious eyes. "Is this even a pill?" he asked, rolling the colored item in his hand. Unlike most pills, it didn't have a bronze, silver, or gold seal. Instead, the seal was gray. It also didn't leak any medicinal scent like pills did.

"Put that down this instant, you foolish man," Elder Xia hissed. She grasped the pill with her soul force and forced it back into the bottle. She then looked at Cha Ming gravely. "Where did you get this?" she asked.

"I made it," Cha Ming said, smiling.

"Prove it," she said.

Cha Ming, still smiling, swept out his hand. The table was instantly covered with hundreds of vials, each one containing a different pill.

"Are those what I think they are?" Elder Gan asked, rubbing his eyes.

"Undoubtedly," Elder Xia said, looking over another pill. "Grandmist seals. The little-known perfect grade that's seemingly only achievable in transcendent realms or higher. How did you do it?"

"It's not exactly something anyone else can replicate," Cha Ming said, summoning a gray flame. "But you and I both know how valuable the mediating properties of pill seals are. Studying them and how they bring the ingredients together would greatly improve an alchemist's abilities. And with so many pills available…"

Elder Xia nodded. "Then your offer of knowledge, combined with these pills, is more than adequate to start poaching. What's your price? And terms?"

Cha Ming picked up a jade vial. "Gold-seal pills sell for fifty percent higher than list price, yes?" he asked. "Then we'll sell them for three times the list price."

"Cheap," Elder Xia said.

"Too cheap," Elder Gan agreed.

"Let me finish," Cha Ming continued. "Three times list price for members who join our group and forsake the others. They must swear stringent oaths, and the pills are only for their consumption or study as enforced by contract. The usual Zhou Li clauses apply.

"In addition, our clients who meet Alabaster Group requirements can request to purchase pills for personal consumption at five times list price. Since I'm always very busy and will disappear for months at a time, the Alabaster Group can be my middleman. You can take orders and payments for the next time I come to stock up on medicinal ingredients. For now, I can craft up to early-core-grade pills, and I will inform you when my level rises."

"A very ruthless move," Elder Gan said. "If the only place where members can study the Grandmist pills is with us, people will come flocking over. Furthermore, selling to good-aligned nobles will strengthen our faction and deter bad behavior. In fact, they may stop dealing with the Obsidian Syndicate for fear that we might not deal with them at all. Young man, you never cease to amaze me."

"Then that concludes that part of our business," Cha Ming said. "Now I need you to do something for me. I need you to approach Yue Bing and give her the respect she deserves."

"But she's a blood artist!" Elder Cang exclaimed. He cleared his throat and apologized. "It just doesn't sit well with me."

Cha Ming stared him down and looked each of the five elders in the eyes. "I will speak with her with an open mind and determine the nature of her abilities," he said. "If I find her arts are appropriate, wholesome, and aligned with the forces of good, I expect you to respect my decision. Do I make myself clear?"

Elder Cang nodded slowly. "If you feel so strongly about it, since you're contributing so much, we won't alienate her," he said. "But you're the one with the stringent standards. I expect you to vouch for her and her actions. If you approve of what she does, I'll give it my blessing."

"Fair enough," Cha Ming said. "How goes the search for Waters of Life?"

"We've found a seller, but there's nothing they currently want," Elder Gan said. "The sole supplier of Waters of Life is the Sea God royal family. I doubt even Grandmist pills can tempt them, as their cultivation rarely encounters any bottlenecks."

Cha Ming nodded. "I'll try to think of something. Now if you'll excuse me, I have a long-overdue meeting with my disciple to attend."

"Then we won't hold you up," Elder Gan said. "By the way, an elder will be undergoing his transcendent tribulation outside the city soon. Thousands of us will be there to watch, and it's a good place to exchange pointers and compete."

Cha Ming nodded. "I'll be there. Save me a seat."

Cha Ming hesitated outside Yue Bing's door. His hesitation wasn't because of her but because of his own actions. He felt guilty for judging her so quickly without speaking to her, and even more guilty for putting off the discussion for a year.

What's done is done, Cha Ming thought. *I can only move forward.* Overcoming resistance and building momentum was an undeniable part of what he'd begun to identify as his Dao. He knocked on the door and held his breath as he waited.

Yue Bing, the lone inhabitant of the small office in Haijing City, opened the door. Then, seeing who it was, she smiled. "Please come in, Master," she said, welcoming him inside. She led him to a table and began serving tea. They used to drink together every day before he'd left for Jade Moon Planet. It was only now that he realized he hadn't done so since his return.

"I'm sorry," Cha Ming said, cutting the tension after a few warm mouthfuls.

"Whatever for?" Yue Bing asked, averting her gaze.

"For waiting so long," Cha Ming said. "It was unfair of me to neglect you."

She continued brewing tea and averting her eyes. "It's not much different than the way anyone else treats me. In fact, you treat me much better."

"People are scared of what they don't understand, myself included," Cha Ming said. "I made a mistake, and I own that. Do you want to talk about what happened?"

"Ah, you're seeing me as a victim," Yue Bing said, smiling lightly. "A poor girl who must be saved from the darkness. Have you ever wondered how patronizing that sounds?"

Cha Ming thought for a bit and nodded. "How's business?" he asked, looking around. Her office was empty save for a lone bed. The usual concoctions and needles spirit doctors used were nowhere to be found. Neither were their impressive libraries or artworks.

"Surprisingly good," Yue Bing asked. "Especially given my client restrictions."

"Which are?" Cha Ming asked.

"I treat people and demons, both are fine," Yue Bing said. "But anyone with a sin glow is rejected, even if they're dying."

"Seems a tad cruel," Cha Ming said.

"It is," Yue Bing said. "But to be kind to the righteous, you must be cruel to the merciless. Life taught me that. It's not too late for you to learn the same lesson."

Cha Ming nodded, tasting her words. "Anything else?"

"That's it," she said. "I'll only refuse people beyond my ability to heal, but you'll be surprised how few people in the city that applies to. Perhaps a dozen, excluding transcendents. I charge according to cultivation level and severity of the injury."

"Far better than most doctors," Cha Ming said. "They're prone to daylight robbery. And when they fail, they blame the patient's condition." He also remembered Li Yin's story about how he'd been forced to flee his city because doctors didn't like him treating their patients.

"That's right," Yue Bing said. "But I guarantee treatment. I can do so because once I take on a case, I hardly ever fail. It's only happened two or three times since I came to Haijing, which is better than most spirit doctors can say." A soft ring sounded, and two figures appeared in the reception area. An attendant greeted the guests for her.

"Would you like me to leave?" Cha Ming asked.

"Stay," Yue Bing said. "They won't complain about your being here if I treat them for free."

Cha Ming nodded and sat cross-legged in a corner as he waited. Her patient was apparently the son of a noble, a Haijing royal. The white-haired young man was an initial-marrow-refining cultivator, so the injury had to be extremely severe to warrant immediate treatment.

The Haijing nobles were a surprising addition to my clientele, Yue Bing sent mentally as she touched several acupoints to stall blood flow. *Traditional medicine is extremely ineffective on body cultivators, who mostly rely on their own regeneration to recover. Usually, it's best to feed them some pills that replenish vitality. Those who come to me are too grievously injured for that to work.*

After exchanging a few words, Yue Bing glowed red with blood. Wings of blood sprouted out from her back as a red mist enveloped her and her patient.

Just where is the vitality coming from? Cha Ming thought. *From a treasure?* He dismissed that thought, as he didn't see her ankh anywhere. Yue Bing used no fancy techniques, nor did she use acupuncture needles or specialized knowledge. Instead, she poured the bloody energy surrounding her directly into the man. It seamlessly combined with his own vital energy. Then, to Cha Ming's amazement, the man's lethal injuries began healing faster than he thought possible. What should have taken several days to recover from—far too long for anyone to stand such a grievous injury—took only a single minute. It was the fastest recovery he'd ever seen for an initial-marrow-refining cultivator.

The treatment ended as quickly as it began. From start to finish, all she'd done was pour blood vitality into the man. By the end of the process, Cha Ming realized the mist hadn't come from an artifact—it had come from the void in Yue Bing's bones. She wasn't supplementing the man's vitality with captured blood, but her own. Could he really fault her for that?

A while later, they were drinking tea again. "How do you cultivate your art?" Cha Ming asked.

"By fighting the South in various battlefields," Yue Bing said. "I steal the blood of others to strengthen my body cultivation. Alternatively, I can use pills as supplements, but I figure why not kill two birds with one stone?"

Cha Ming bit his lip. "Then why haven't you joined the City Guard or groups of adventurers? It would be easy to find blood vitality out there while fighting demons."

"I'll shoot that question right back at you," Yue Bing said. "You could make a lot of money by hunting demons with Uncle Huxian. Why don't you do that?"

"I just don't want to hurt demons," Cha Ming said. "Call it a silly, idealistic thing to do. I just don't want to hurt anyone unless it's necessary." He felt thin white hands land on his.

"I'm the same," she said. "I might be a brutal killer, a bloody angel on the battlefield, but I hate hurting others. I hate killing people. If I didn't have to, I wouldn't. But sometimes you just do what you have to. There are evil people out there, and they'll stop at nothing to get what they want."

In that vulnerable moment, Cha Ming realized she was no different than he was. Many called him a hypocrite: How could a lover of peace kill so many people? But sometimes being kind to the many meant being cruel to the few. And cruel to yourself.

"All right," Cha Ming said, summoning a bloodred cloud of vitality from deep within his marrow. The process was visibly draining as opposed to Yue Bing's effortless display, but it would do the trick. He willed the vitality to assume the first shape he could think of: the vitality sigil. "Your power is great, but let's work on your delivery, shall we?"

Yue Bing smiled. It was the first real smile she'd shown him since his return.

Chapter 12: Transcendent Tribulation

Cha Ming massaged his temple as he read through a stack of applications. There were hundreds of them, some on plain white paper and others colored and scented. While he was surprised that he'd received so many resumes, he was more amazed that resumes even existed in this world in the first place.

They exist, all right, Cha Ming thought. *Along with all their problems and drawbacks.* He sighed as he scanned through a hundred-page document. Admittedly, it was short compared to many of the others. Cultivators did many things, studied a lot and fought a lot. It was difficult to stand out in such a competitive marketplace.

As he read, other applications trickled in like a never-ending flood. His Grandmist seal pills were apparently a huge addition to the knowledge base, as were his runic arts. Herbology was less in demand, but a surprising amount of spirit doctors and alchemists found it to be a very useful secondary occupation.

"Wait, who actually puts this on their resume?" Cha Ming exclaimed, startling his disciples, who were helping him with the tedious task. They weren't looking for personal disciples, but applications for the classes they would soon be holding.

Zi Long walked over and looked at the resume. "I don't see anything glaring," he declared.

"Jin Huang?" Cha Ming called.

The young man hustled over from his own pile and picked up the ten sheets of paper. He broke into a grin when he saw what Cha Ming had his finger on.

"Blood vitality donation—contributes daily to the Haijing City blood vitality pool," Jin Huang said. "It's a funny but shameless way to sell yourself."

"Too shameless," Cha Ming said. "Yue Bing, are you interested?"

"In blood vitality donations?" Yue Bing asked, quirking her eyebrow. "If I started harvesting from hundreds of cultivators, not only would it only be a drop in the bucket, but even *my* terrible reputation would take a dive. I'll pass."

"Rejected it is," Cha Ming said, tossing it onto a Grandmist flame he kept in the middle of the room. It was difficult to maintain the flame, but that was what made it good training. The paper was torn up by the flame in a converging whirlpool. It evaporated into nothingness by the time it reached the center.

By the end of the day, he'd reviewed ten thousand resumes. He kept one hundred of them and scheduled interviews over the next few days. Teaching disciples was troublesome, but he had to keep up his end of the bargain. He refused to let Zhou Li win, especially when the man was doing so much to sabotage him.

Huxian's report about his interference with the Water Source Marrow had both frustrated and chilled his blood. Just like that, what was likely the only Water Source Marrow existing on the plane had been reduced to ashes. He wouldn't have taken it so personally if someone had wanted it for a legitimate reason, but what Zhou Li had done was spiteful sabotage at its finest.

There's nothing I can do about it, Cha Ming thought, breathing deeply and calming his mind. All he could do now was get this disciple recruitment over and done with and practice alchemy. Only one path was barred, and another remained. Crafting a transcendent-grade pill might be tough, but if anyone on this plane could do it, he could.

"Tell me about yourself," Cha Ming said, sipping on a black beverage Jin Huang had concocted. It wasn't strong for a body cultivator, but he appreciated how the burnt-tasting drink gave normal cultivators jitters for days. Apparently it was now a popular staple in Haijing. His junior disciple had signed some very savvy business deals and was now effectively printing money. Though the young man had said it was more about acquiring real estate than the actual product, Cha Ming found the parallels to earth very entertaining. Conquering the world with a single beverage. He doubted the tea market would sit still in response.

"I'm a mid-grade-marrow-refining cultivator, a proud member of the Haijing nobility," the young man with white hair said. "I fight demons and fiendish demons to protect the city."

"I hear you're good at formation arts," Cha Ming said as he reviewed the man's resume.

"Yes, I find they're very useful when fighting demons and fiendish demons to protect the city," the man said excitedly.

"What do you plan to do with my teachings?" Cha Ming asked.

"I plan to get better at making formations," the man said after some time. "To better fight demons and fiendish demons—"

"—to protect this city. I've got it. Next!"

***

"I see you went to law school," Cha Ming said to the beautiful blond-haired cultivator seated before him. "Why did you choose to study law in a world where violence solves all problems?"

"Because violence *doesn't* solve all problems," the woman said, adjusting her glasses. "As evidenced through hundreds of thousands of successful prosecutions."

"Fair enough," Cha Ming said, mildly impressed. It wasn't often that he met people with such a reasonable mentality. "What do you want to learn from me?"

"I want to learn how to bring justice to those the law unjustly shielded," the woman said with a faint hint of bloodlust in her eyes.

Cha Ming mentally facepalmed and immediately began winding down the failed interview.

"Are you sure you want to use fighting to decide the results of your interview?" Cha Ming asked from the other side of a sparring ring.

"Definitely!" the scholarly, frail-looking man said from behind the circle. "All I ask is that you go easy on me."

"Go ahead and do your worst," Cha Ming said lazily. "Don't worry about blowing me up. As long as I don't lose more than a limb or two, I'll be all right." He readied his staff to jump in once the man showed any weaknesses. He didn't plan on testing his abilities, but his willingness to learn and to change.

"Great Phoenix of the Void," the man intoned, holding out his hands. A vermillion bird of flame appeared behind him, its wings obscured in darkness. "Lend me your favor and destroy my foes. Channel your wrath in a fiery ring of doom." His eyes flashed.

"Ring of inferno!" The phoenix shrieked and surrounded Cha Ming with mild flames that seemed rather weak compared to the level of the technique.

Cha Ming didn't react. He just stood there. He was speechless at the needlessly theatrical display. "How many fights have you been in, exactly?"

"Fifteen!" the man said proudly. "My fighting skills have impressed everyone so much that no one dares accept my challenges anymore."

"Right..." Cha Ming said, coughing lightly. "I think there's something I can work with here. I'll be in touch."

He tossed the man's resume into the flames when he got back to his office. He didn't bother witnessing his final form.

Eventually, Cha Ming settled on six prospects. They weren't as promising as his four original disciples, but they were the least awkward amongst the scholars who'd applied through the Alabaster Group. After a small ceremony, he announced that he was also willing to teach others. He gave similar terms to what Lu Tianhao had—teaching time for confirmed devil kills. In addition, after discovering that the branch had a merit measurement stone, he laid out a system for teaching time through merit accrued.

Before sending them off, he gave each of them some individual advice based on their interview and gifted them with the remaining instruction jades from Fuxi's Library. He'd given a sigil instruction jade to each of his four original disciples, so all he had to do now was wait until they mastered their contents. It would only take a few months until his karmic obligations to Fuxi were fulfilled.

Finally, he slumped on a sofa. His four original disciples were equally exhausted, as they had just taught their first classes. Jin Huang taught poison arts, Yue Bing blood doctor arts, and Ling Dong demonic smithing. Ling Dong knew they wouldn't be able to learn his art in depth. His students just attended to gain inspiration from nature and infuse it into their craft, which was fine by him.

They settled into a lull, and before they knew it, two weeks had passed by uneventfully.

"Master! Master!" a voice yelled.

Cha Ming opened his eyes and saw Zi Long shaking him. "Didn't you get the message?"

"Message?" Cha Ming asked.

"Elder Yang's tribulation," Zi Long said in exasperation. "It's happening soon."

"I guess I lost track of time," Cha Ming said.

The two men zipped out of the Alabaster Group's building in Haijing Academy and flew outside the city. They traveled in the ocean for ten miles before arriving at an open space on the seabed where people were floating. A lone man sat cross-legged nine miles away from them. Nine miles was the maximum size for transcendent tribulation clouds. Intruding into his personal space might be mistaken as aiding him, which would drag the offender into the tribulation.

Excuse me, excuse me, Cha Ming said, moving through frowning cultivators who ultimately backed down when they saw his elder badges. They soon arrived near the other Haijing Academy elders in a reserved area near the edge. Zi Long excused himself, leaving Cha Ming to speak to the other elders.

They spoke for a short while as Cha Ming observed the terrain and his opponents. The Obsidian Syndicate was ready for battle, as were many other groups in the academy. Some scholars were here just for the show, of course. While they were mighty cultivators, they just couldn't compete with battle-oriented experts in the upcoming struggle.

He watched in silence, taking note of the major players and their potential techniques. Many were devils, and many others were angels. Most of them, however, were normal qi or body cultivators.

In the distance, he saw another smaller crowd. The nobles in Haijing City were seated next to the royal family. All of them had long white hair that flowed in the water, while many had white or blue skin. Some even sported runes on their skin, but that was apparently much rarer. Cha Ming recalled the girl he'd rescued and the blue-gold runes she'd sported.

She must have been a member of the high nobility at the very least, he thought. *Perhaps even the daughter of a duke.*

His thoughts were interrupted by a sudden crackle of lightning that appeared above the man, despite them being fifty miles below the surface of the ocean. Familiar black clouds accompanied the lightning and spread out for three miles before stopping. The tribulation wouldn't be a strong one, meaning that the man wasn't too strong himself.

According to the statistics Cha Ming had read, everyone had a fifty-percent chance of overcoming the transcendence ordeal. The odds might seem high, but considering that the man had successfully carved his core despite the five-to-one odds against him and not died, one could forgive the heavens for being merciful.

The man rose up from his meditative position and raised his sword, which crackled in the dark depths of the ocean. He was surrounded by the nascent domain projected by his core that also extended onto the blade of his sword. The clouds responded by sending a dragon of lightning onto the man. It was the weakest of lightning, white lightning, but the dragon was far thicker than any Cha Ming and Huxian had faced before.

Cha Ming's eyes narrowed as the man's power erupted and slashed through the lightning as though slashing through reality itself. He had no doubt that this slash could kill him instantly. The first dragon was eliminated effortlessly, and the clouds rumbled and accumulated lightning for the next strike. This time, the lightning was red.

White, red, orange, yellow, green, blue, and violet. Six rounds were defeated with very little effort on the cultivator's part. Then the clouds shifted and went from black to gray. Violet and gold mixed and formed another, stronger dragon. The sheer power the lightning dragon contained eclipsed anything Cha Ming could generate. It resembled a living being that existed on a higher plane of existence.

As the violet-gold lightning bore down on the man, he finally made his first serious move. His sword glowed, and he sent a giant gold projection against the lightning dragon. His domain fought against it, and the plane shook as they collided. Black and gray cracks appeared all around them until finally, reality began to break apart. It was time.

Most of them hadn't come to see him transcend. Instead, they'd come due to the cracks generated by the battle. The spatial fragments created during each transcendent's ordeal were priceless. Cha Ming jumped into the air along with several others. They unleashed their techniques with mild reservation, aiming to injure each other rather than maim or kill. It wasn't that Cha Ming didn't want to kill Zhou Li and his ilk, but that the consequences of breaking Haijing's peace were far too great.

As he flew, he scooped up several spatial fragments and stored them in his Clear Sky World. The others also had treasures capable of collecting these tears in space-time. They collected the smaller fragments casually, leaving the smallest to fall to the weaker cultivators below. Those would be forged into normal spatial treasures like bags of holding and storage rings, assuming they were stable or large enough.

The real prizes were mid-sized or large fragments. Those had uses beyond simple storage treasures and were extremely valuable. Cha Ming winked to Huxian and his friends, who'd apparently grown a level in his absence. The high-grade beasts fought aggressively against competing demons in their section. Apparently, fighting to the death among demons wasn't seen as a big deal to either Haijing's rulers or the beasts themselves. Cha Ming managed to retrieve seven mid-size fragments during the exchange. Larger pieces had yet to fall.

The cultivators beneath the clouds panted as they fought, accumulating energy for the next strike. The clouds seemed to pulse as they also recovered. This wasn't a judgment against the cultivators, but a test along with an implicit threat. The test was to see whether the cultivator was worthy of the power he wielded, while the threat was very straightforward: If the plane wanted to, it could end him. Remaining on the plane was a privilege, not a right.

The man wiped the blood off his mouth, and the eighth lightning dragon began to form. This one wasn't violet gold but pitch black.

Both the audience and the man felt pure dread as it accumulated in the gray clouds. It was blacker than the deepest night, blacker than the deepest pit in the ocean. It was destruction itself, and even light couldn't coexist with it.

The bolt shot down, and the cultivator let loose. Thousands of metallic blades rose up to fight against the heavens. They crumbled into motes of qi as the lightning broke through them, but not without slowing down. The technique was imbued with the man's domain, so each blow caused further fissures in space. This time, three large chunks flew down amidst the cultivators. One toward the demons, one toward the nobles, and one toward Haijing Academy. Their positions had been chosen with this distribution in mind.

Cha Ming pushed off the ocean waves and whirled his staff. A white line of creation formed a barrier that repelled a few oncoming cultivators. He reduced the drag around himself while using his qi to propel himself toward the fragment. A few loose blades and techniques flew his way, but he deflected them with his staff just in time to see a flaming black dragon flying toward his face.

He threw up a hasty combat formation that doused the unexpected sin flames, only to find that his limbs had been bound in black chains. He broke the chains apart with brute strength and banished the black smoke around him, only to see Zhou Li pocketing the void fragment. The man smirked but said nothing. Cha Ming glared at him, then looked to the man in the clearing, who was now covered in blood from head to toe. His sword, evidently a half-step transcendent treasure, was cracked.

I wonder if he'll make it, Cha Ming thought. It would all come down to the last confrontation. Though he wasn't interested in the rest of the tribulation, this stage greatly interested him. Unlike the lightning tribulation he'd faced, this one had a special bolt. A gray one.

All the power in the clouds slowly converged on a single point as the cultivator bit on a medicinal pill and gathered his strength. He used the ten-breath window to heal some of his more grievous wounds and recover as much qi as possible. Then the single point arched down in a monochromatic gray lightning dragon. The water around it didn't crackle or fizzle; instead, it vanished. The bolt itself was very strange as well. It didn't move through the water but instead ceased to exist in one location while coming into existence in another. It was the strangest sight Cha Ming had ever seen, utterly devoid of supposed friction, weight, energy, shape, and life. Yet, at the same time, it seemed to possess all of these.

The Grandmist dragon and the man's domain, strengthened with every ounce of his power, collided, letting out an apocalyptic boom. Space shattered in the surrounding hundred miles closest to the man, with some of the fragments piercing his skin and causing grievous injuries. Nine large panes of space broke apart and flew down, three in each direction like before. Huxian barked instructions to his friends in a move to secure at least one piece before the ordeal was over. The lesser cultivators below Cha Ming and the elders cheered as flecks of raw spatial fragments rained down on them. The Haijing royal family also issued orders.

Everything around Cha Ming erupted into chaos. He wasted no time and used his concentration technique to summon a Myriad Truths Formation, something akin to a nascent domain. He used his power over the five elements to force people apart as he snaked toward where two of the spatial fragments were headed. Predictably, Zhou Li did the same. They flew neck and neck toward the same two objectives, launching long-ranged attacks toward each other as they traveled.

A black cloak of flame appeared around Cha Ming, who directly projected destruction qi to break it apart. He whirled his staff, creating shackles of pure creation power to wrap around Zhou Li. Zhou Li sent scythe-like bundles of sin flames to cut them down, then barely erected a shield as Cha Ming's staff came bearing down with Crushing Chaos.

The world erupted in black flames as Cha Ming felt himself being tugged in ninety-nine directions at once. He couldn't see them but sensed ninety-nine threads of unfair, sinful karma tying down his nascent angelic wings, threatening to tear them off. He countered by sending out a thin string of destruction to sever the ninety-nine threads, letting his half-corporeal wings manifest, boosting both his body and four of his elements in the process.

Cha Ming's energy reserves plummeted, but he didn't care. A strict edict by the Haijing royal family stated that killing was punishable by death in this friendly competition. He funneled the remainder of his five-element, creation, and destruction power into a ball of flame in his fist. Then he threw it out and formed a gray wall of flame between everyone and the two spatial fragments. He, as the owner of the flames, dove through them. No one followed.

He grinned as he pocketed the two spatial fragments, and Huxian pocketed another in the demonic battlefield. Then he pulled back the gray flames. They were a bluff, of course. There was no way he could generate enough power with his middle-core-formation cultivation to threaten so many peak-core-formation cultivators.

But they didn't know that. His gray flames were strange, unknown. In addition, they were all still shocked at the display of raw power from the Grandmist Lightning Dragon from the tribulation beside them. As a result, he'd managed to secure two of the four prizes that had landed in their area.

"Better luck next time," Cha Ming said to Zhou Li, who looked like he'd bitten into a lemon. The man glared at him murderously but could only sheathe his weapon and head back down. The elder who'd been fighting the tribulation had survived. Barely.

Cha Ming flew down to the other elders, who congratulated him on his heavy haul. Then, glancing into his Clear Sky World, he noticed the greedy brush had devoured one of the fragments, and to his surprise, the disc of concentrated time essence. He smiled bitterly and hoped something good would come out of it.

Now, what to do with my one remaining fragment? he thought as he reunited with his disciples and Huxian. Large spatial fragments were in short supply, so he was in no hurry to spend it.

Chapter 13:
Sea God Royal Family

Cha Ming spent the next six months completely engrossed in alchemy. He carefully raised his alchemical skill to the middle of core grade before leaving seclusion. Zi Long, who was often practicing in the courtyard outside his chamber, greeted him as he exited. After some quick sparring exchanges and a few pointers, he proceeded to the Alabaster Group's headquarters.

"Master, master!" a voice sounded. It was a middle-aged man named Wei Yu, a talisman artist and one of the six he'd recruited. "I have some good news!"

"Everyone who's received instruction slips has mastered their contents," Cha Ming said, smiling. "With that, my karmic duty is fulfilled."

The man scratched his head sheepishly. "That takes away the excitement. Yes, we mastered them, and the effects on my talisman arts were profound. Most of us advanced a full sub rank in our respective crafts."

"That's good to hear," Cha Ming said. "Tell me, has much happened while I was gone?"

"You'd have to ask the elders," the man replied.

"Not a problem," Cha Ming said. "Could you do me a favor? I'd like you to gather your brothers and sisters. I want to give everyone pointers after I've finished speaking with the elders."

"Right away," the man said. He bowed and left. Cha Ming wandered through the bustling Alabaster Group with great difficulty, as there were many more members than the last time he'd visited. He eventually reached the meeting room where several elders had already assembled. Cha Ming took a seat beside some familiar faces and waited as several more elders trickled in. There were now two dozen of them, four times as many as the last time.

"Order, order," said Elder Gan, the chair of the meeting. "Let's first go over the agenda. First on the list is time-essence allocation."

The entire room broke out into arguments over who should get what. Cha Ming didn't squabble with them. Instead, he drank tea and exchanged mental conversations as the others settled on who got what.

"Cha Ming, do you have anything to report?" Elder Gan said, a whole hour later.

Cha Ming directly summoned a batch of mid-grade Grandmist pills he'd created recently, prompting excited murmurs from the elder-level alchemists in the room. "As you can tell, I've advanced to mid-grade grandmaster alchemist. I'll trouble Elder Gan to deal with fair distribution of these new pills."

"Thank you kindly for your report," Elder Gan said. "That will be all for individual presentations. Are there any private concerns anyone wishes to discuss?" Silence. "All right, then. Everyone is dismissed."

Cha Ming walked up to Elder Gan as the others filed out of the room. "You seem both tired and busy," he said.

"If you're tired and unoccupied, you're depressed," Elder Gan said. "But if you're tired and busy, you're winning. Never complain when you have too much on your plate. Anyway, it's a good thing you came to find me. People have been asking about your spatial fragments."

"Did they offer anything worthwhile?" Cha Ming asked.

"It depends what you want," Elder Gan said. "Their items would interest one person or another. Of particular import was a request from the Emperor himself."

Cha Ming raised an eyebrow. "Didn't he capture two fragments on his own? And his vassals captured two more."

"They don't want to share," Elder Gan said, shrugging. "Which is fortunate, given that the royal family's well of life has just produced another nine cups of Waters of Life."

"When do we leave?" Cha Ming asked.

"As soon as possible," Elder Gan said, waving Cha Ming to his side. "That gnat, Zhou Li, has been stuck to the Emperor's son like a fly on excrement. The Emperor's been holding off on a decision since there are only two spare fragments in the entire city. The others who've obtained some have been using them to craft some impressive treasures, however. He might crack at any moment."

Cha Ming nodded gravely. He followed Elder Gan out of the academy and down Haijing's stone streets toward Clock Tower Square. He didn't know where the royal palace was, having only ventured through the city on a single occasion. He was surprised when Elder Gan headed not north or south, but toward the clock tower itself.

"Surprised?" Elder Gan said, noting Cha Ming's expression. "Not many people expect the main monument in a city to be the royal palace. However, this clock is special. It's a city-protecting treasure, the Sea God Clock Tower. There is no safer, more valuable building than this clock on the entire plane. Moreover, since the artifact controls time, it also holds dominion over space. The clock tower's insides are larger than half the city."

A pair of gold-armored, blue-skinned guards stopped them at the entrance. To Cha Ming's surprise, they were late-marrow-refining cultivators; just a single one of these guards was an army unto himself and could fight armies without tiring.

"We, Elder Gan and Elder Cha Ming, are here on request of the Sea God Emperor," Elder Gan reported.

"One moment," one of the guards replied. His partner headed inside and came back out a few moments later. "You may enter. Do not stray from the main hallway, and head straight to the audience chamber."

"Many thanks," Elder Gan said. They walked through a few outer doors before arriving at a beautiful golden inner door with blue-gold runes. As they passed through it, they entered a land of dreams. Cha Ming whistled between his teeth as they entered the sunny interior, complete with flowering trees, massive gardens, and large white stone buildings everywhere he looked. Everything was either gilded with gold or inlaid with blue-gold runes. He'd never seen such a massive residence in his life.

An attendant received them after they passed through the doors and ushered them to the largest white stone building with a large golden doorway. It opened into a long marble corridor adorned with lifelike paintings and sculptures. Though the sculptures stood still as they displayed their timeless grace, the paintings moved.

In the first painting, soldiers drew blood as they fought an unwinnable battle in the depths of the ocean. In the second, trees swayed in the wind while a volcano erupted in the background. In the third, a whale the size of a planet gobbled up a fish that wasn't much smaller. Even Cha Ming, who'd been to a whole other world, couldn't help but gape in amazement.

Several dozen paintings later, they arrived at a small waiting area. Their attendant exchanged words with the guards, and after waiting for a half hour, the wall they guarded opened. Unlike the others, this door was a carefully crafted mosaic of black, white, blue, and gold. Cha Ming wondered about the mosaic's meaning but soon dropped the subject in favor of admiring the chamber it opened into.

The first thing Cha Ming saw was a golden throne. It was inlaid with purple-gold runes instead of the blue-gold runes from earlier. A powerfully built man in regal cultivation robes sat atop it. To his left, Cha Ming saw a thin-framed, blue-skinned woman seated on a smaller seat. Off to the side, below the royal stage, two men were standing. One was a young man with long white hair and blue-gold runes adorning his pristine white skin. He looked familiar to Cha Ming, but only slightly. But beside him was someone he recognized a mile away: Zhou Li.

"Greetings, Your Highness," Cha Ming said, clasping his fists and bowing at a ninety-degree angle. He'd been briefed on etiquette before arriving by the nervous Elder Gan, who also bowed beside him.

"Rise," the Emperor said. "It's nice that you could finally make time to speak with us. We were beginning to tire of waiting, and to be honest, we were very close to trading for Nephew Zhou's spatial fragment."

Cha Ming cursed inwardly when he heard the king refer to Zhou Li in such an endearing manner. Evidently the man he stood beside was one of the king's sons, and this son was addressing him as brother.

"My apologies for the delay," Cha Ming said. "I was in seclusion, slowly but surely raising my rank in alchemy."

The Emperor nodded. "We have heard you can create Grandmist seals on alchemical pills. Not unobtainable by us by any means, but still rare. We would be interested in discussing your services should your grade increase to the level of an elder."

"Of course, Your Highness," Cha Ming said. He didn't miss the implication that his occupation, while respected, wasn't too valuable to the royal family. He didn't have the qualifications to use it as a bargaining chip.

"As you both know, we have been crafting a treasure for our most talented daughter in preparation for the Sea God Trials," the Emperor said. "As such, we require an additional large spatial fragment. Both of you possess one, and one of you has already stated they require Waters of Life, a treasure we are loath to part with. Elder Cha Ming, what do you wish for in exchange for your fragment?"

Cha Ming winced at the mentioned waters; it seemed that Zhou Li had already beaten him to the punch. "I regret to inform Your Highness that I, too, require Waters of Life," Cha Ming said. "I require them to craft a complex pill that is very important to me and my cultivation."

"I see," the Emperor said. "Then we are at an impasse. Both parties require the same thing, with no way to differentiate between themselves. What do you say, my empress?"

"Perhaps they could provide some additional treasure to compensate Your Highness?" the empress, who'd been silent until now, said. "It is perhaps the only fair way to break a tie."

"It is fair but below us to hold an auction," the Emperor said, shaking his head. "A spatial fragment's value is equivalent to the Waters of Life we possess. As their request is reasonable, I will not gouge them." He sighed and looked at Cha Ming. "Your reputation precedes you. My friend Lu Tianhao has spoken well of you, and you have a great future ahead of you."

The prince, who'd been standing beside Zhou Li this whole time, suddenly stepped forward. "Father, I ask that you favor me by trading with Brother Li," he said, bowing at a forty-five-degree angle. "He might not have an illustrious reputation like Cha Ming, but Brother Li is an academy elder in two disciplines. He is definitely worth the favor."

"I also agree with the third prince," the empress said from the side. "Nephew Li has gifted our halls many fine paintings, and his foretellings have been useful in making big decisions."

The Emperor sighed. His look was conflicted, and Cha Ming could tell that while he was looking for an excuse to trade to Cha Ming, his family wasn't making it easy. Cha Ming didn't know how to alleviate the situation, and it seemed like offering his services wasn't enough. Just as Cha Ming was about to excuse himself, another voice sounded in the throne room.

"Royal Father, I heard an interesting guest has come in to see you," the voice of a young lady said. "Brother and I were interested in meeting him."

"You may enter," the Emperor said, waving her inside.

Cha Ming heard two sets of footsteps walking in from behind him, and soon a young woman and a teenage boy walked up beside him. They bowed, though he noticed that the woman didn't bow as deeply as the younger boy. They both had white hair like their brother and were also covered in blue-gold runes. Moreover, the young woman, who couldn't be any older than sixteen, looked familiar.

"I'm so happy we decided to indulge in our curiosity," the woman said, smiling toward Cha Ming. She then looked back toward the Emperor. "Do you remember the incident a year and a half ago?"

The Emperor frowned. "We should not speak of embarrassing events in front of unrelated parties."

"Fortunately, he's not unrelated," the princess said. "This man, Cha Ming, was the one who saved me back then." The princess bowed toward Cha Ming, bending her brother down with her at a forty-five-degree angle. Almost as deeply as she'd bowed to the Emperor. "I, Gong Shuren, thank Brother Cha Ming for his lifesaving grace."

The Emperor looked startled for a moment, but then he broke into peals of laughter. "Good! Great! Our tight-lipped daughter had refused to divulge who'd saved her, lest she implicate him in our court politics. Who could have known that it was you, Nephew Cha Ming, who'd saved our most gifted child, the crown princess?"

"I was just helping in passing," Cha Ming said humbly.

"Since that's the case, there's no point in arguing over this," the Emperor said. He summoned a small golden receptacle from his spatial treasure. "Would you still be willing to trade your spatial fragment for these Waters of Life?"

"I would be honored, Your Highness," Cha Ming said, summoning the crackling black spatial fragment from his Clear Sky World. He kept it carefully coated in transcendent force as he sent it toward the Emperor, who sent the golden receptacle back toward him in return.

"We would invite you for dinner, but unfortunately, we must make the best use of our time and finish our daughter Gong Shuren's treasure," the Emperor said. "Why don't we invite you some time in the future to properly thank you?"

"I would be happy to attend to Your Highness at your earliest convenience," Cha Ming said, bowing once more.

"Good, let us be on our way," the Emperor said. "Shuren, Yuhan, you will remain with us."

"As you wish, Royal Father," the two siblings said.

Cha Ming, understanding that he'd been dismissed, bowed down and walked out of the room while still mid-bow. He only straightened himself out once he'd walked out the door.

Karma is a wonderful thing, he thought.

"You won't succeed, even with the Waters of Life," Zhou Li said from behind him as they left.

To Cha Ming's surprise, the prince was also glaring at him, though he couldn't remember when he'd had the time to offend a Haijing royal.

"Even if I don't succeed, I'll take pleasure in having gotten them when you tried your best to stop me," Cha Ming said.

Zhou Li chuckled. "I'm touched to be held in such high regard." Then he walked up to Cha Ming, only stopping a couple of feet away from him. "But you're mistaken about something. I wanted the Waters of Life, and I still want them. So I'll tell you what: Give me half, and I'll give you a way to heal your core. Without the Water Source Marrow, you're left with only two options to heal your core: my way or crafting a transcendent pill. Do you really want to tempt fate by trying the latter?"

Cha Ming placed a hand on Zhou Li's shoulder and squeezed tightly. "I won't know unless I try. Besides, if you say there are only two options, there must be at least three." He pushed Zhou Li back slightly. The prince caught him before he could tumble too far.

"Come, Brother Li," the prince said. "We still have much to discuss. Not obtaining the Waters of Life was only a minor setback, nothing more."

"Quite right, Brother Xuandi," Zhou Li said. "I keep forgetting the bigger picture whenever I see this annoying gnat. In the end, he's nothing more than an itch." The two entered a door to the side of the corridor.

"Let's go," Cha Ming said to Elder Gan. They left the palace and returned to the busy streets of Haijing City.

Chapter 14: Red Dust of the Mortal World

Gentle zither music filled the air of the Red Dust Pavilion as elegantly dressed guests chatted and made merry. Wang Jun, Wang Tong, and Protector Ren entered the establishment after paying a top-grade spirit stone each. They grabbed their complimentary drinks and took note of both the guests in attendance. They also observed the beautiful ladies accompanying them. It was easy to tell the difference, for there was a rule here: only courtesans wore red.

"I didn't think it would be so expensive," Wang Tong said apologetically. "I never would have suggested we come here otherwise."

"No need to apologize," Wang Jun said. "The key to successful price discrimination is that each customer be willing to pay. Given how much the Red Dust Pavilion has flourished over the past year and a half, I can only assume the price is worthwhile."

Protector Ren coughed. "I've heard that many cultivators come here for inspiration when they reach a bottleneck in their cultivation. One minute they're stuck with an unbreachable obstacle, and the next, they break through as though the wall they struggled with had never existed. If that's not worth a king's ransom, I don't know what is."

"I'm quite looking forward to Miss Bingxue's performance," Wang Tong said. "She's the most popular mistress—that's what they call the courtesans here. Dozens of high-profile men have their eyes set on her."

"Then they're living a fool's dream," Wang Jun said. "Courtesans manipulate the hearts of men for money, and anyone chasing them can expect to lose their life's savings, if not the savings of several generations."

The two men beside him shifted uncomfortably as dozens of guests shot them hostile glares. The ladies in red said nothing, however. They simply smiled in stride as though he'd never uttered the hurtful words in the first place. That's what made them frightening: their cold indifference to the words of others. Nothing was scarier than a woman who tolerated the insults of others.

"You could have been nicer about that," Wang Tong whispered. "Besides, I brought you here for a reason. You've not been yourself lately."

"No point flogging a dead horse," Wang Jun said.

"I think that's what he's talking about, young master," Protector Ren said wryly. "And I must say I completely agree with him. You've always been a fighter, not a doorstop."

Wang Jun sighed. He knew they were right. The past year and a half had taken its toll on the confident young man. He'd made progress, but not much. Meanwhile, his brother was outpacing him in every metric that mattered. As they walked over to an empty table, a nearby crowd gasped. Intrigued, Wang Jun edged a little closer until they saw a fit but graying man with short-cropped hair. He wore fancy black-and-gold robes and a thin silver rapier on his belt.

That's Bei Mu, heir of the Bei Clan, Wang Tong sent his way. *Very influential. Their families control several mines in the North. They also own several moneylending agencies.*

Wang Jun nodded as he listened to the man's story. "And that's when negotiations fell apart," the man barked. A woman in red, clearly the man's target audience, showed a slightly shocked expression while holding her wineglass. Other ladies—clearly not part of the establishment—gasped louder as they fell over themselves fawning.

"Six men jumped out from behind the amber curtains without

any warning, swords drawn and qi flaring," Bei Mu said. "My own guards, two of the most outstanding gentlemen I've ever had the pleasure of knowing, stepped up and met their blades without any hesitation. They fought with full confidence against these assailants because they knew I was no slouch.

"I drew my rapier, a short, thin blade, but deadly if you know how to use it. And use it I did. I executed Seven Flourishing Clouds, a wind-based technique, to close the distance in an instant. The six assailants couldn't react before I zipped past their defenses and straight toward the one they served.

"The first stab was for breaking his oath. He'd invited me to his house for food and drink, and everyone under the heavens knows what this promise entails. Not only should he not have attacked me, but by all rights, he should have defended me if I were attacked on his property. Such a ruthless move by my opponent took any thoughts of mercy out of my mind.

"The second stab was to his neck, for uttering those vile words when he did. His slander had ruined my reputation in town until I had no choice but to turn to him as a business partner, where he then whittled away at my fortune." Then he paused.

"The third stab was through his heart," Bei Mu said quietly, causing his audience's ears to reach out toward him. "He couldn't speak because of the hole in his throat, but I didn't want to hear another word from his filthy mouth. When he died, his guards died with him. They'd apparently been life-bound servants, little more than slaves since he trusted no one but his enemies. I made my name that day, and no one has ever dared betray me over a business deal ever again." The crowd clapped and whistled as he bowed in thanks for their time.

"You speak such bold yet flowery words," the woman in red said. "If I didn't know any better, I'd think you were a writer."

The man cleared his throat. "I've dabbled. Nothing major, but I admit to having done that at least."

"You should show me sometime, Master Bei," the woman said.

Wang Jun's eyes narrowed as he saw a subtle but still detectable use of fire qi. It did nothing offensive, but as it appeared, the man's behavior changed. He seemed to grow slightly taller and even more confident than his previous self.

"I think I'll do just that," Bei Mu said with a charming smile. "Alas, I have many friends to entertain tonight. Next time, perhaps?"

"Next time," the woman said with a faint smile. She took a sip of her wine as the man left and looked around at the dispersing crowd. She smiled warmly as her eyes met Wang Jun's.

"If it isn't the second young master of the Wang family," the woman said as she walked over. "This lowly one's name is Bai Ling, at your service."

"A pleasure," Wang Jun said. "This place is much livelier than I'd expected."

"We do all right," Bai Ling said. "Our performances are both beneficial and entertaining. You should come by more often."

"I'll p—" Wang Jun started.

"He'd love to," Wang Tong interrupted. "Especially if its Fairy Bai Ling who'll be doing the entertaining."

Bai Ling smiled. "I don't usually perform, but if it's Young Master Wang, how can I not pounce on the opportunity?" Her words turned heads, and Wang Jun felt an impending headache.

"What exactly do you play?" Wang Jun asked, carefully steering the conversation toward one of the many musical instruments she might know.

"Play?" Bai Ling said innocently. "Yes, play is a good word to use." She let him hang for a while before continuing. "I play *Angels and Devils*. I heard you're quite good."

He hadn't expected that. He moved to refuse but noticed many people edging forward. Some servants had even fetched him tea and were in the process of bringing over a small board. He'd been cornered. "I dabble," he said.

"If you dabble, not many men will dare say they know the basics," Bai Ling said. "I'd offer a teaching game to others of lesser skill, but with you I might have to play seriously."

Her bait was too strong to decline. "I'd be happy to accept your challenge," he said, holding his hand out to the board and the two bowls of stones that had just appeared. "Please, play first."

They both took a seat. A moment later, a stone came crashing down with lightning speed. A four-four opening, nothing exciting. She responded by playing a white stone in a mirror position. Unlike Cha Ming, who liked to play a flexible game, she liked to play strategically and safely with everything under her control. She slammed down another black stone.

"If you continue playing so slowly, Young Master Wang," Bai Ling said, "we'll infringe on sister Bingxue's performance. Many guests wouldn't be happy with that."

"Then what do you suggest?" Wang Jun said, placing another stone.

She slammed one down immediately after his.

"One second, one move," Bai Ling said. "If you can handle it."

Wang Jun's eyes narrowed. He used his resplendent force to summon a stone and smacked it down with matching ferocity. "If that's how you want to play." The crowd cheered as he accepted the challenge.

They played one stone after another, and as they did, Wang Jun tracked strings of karma that enveloped the board, linking past, present, and future moves together. She was good, there was no doubt about it. And while it might seem like playing quickly was to her benefit, he knew the truth full well: He had plenty of time to calculate, so he didn't make any mistakes. She hadn't made any either, as far as he could tell. It was an even game with a predictable outcome.

Their audience grew; they cheered as they saw battle after battle in their dance of black and white stones. Their clicking moves sounded rhythmically in their small circle, providing something akin to music to their spectators. To them, it seemed like a battle to the death, but to him, it was a dance. A coldly calculated dance. Their audience was seething with excitement, but she was cool ice while he was heartless shadow.

They quickly crossed the middle game, and now it became a

back-and-forth tussle over existing threats. They traded, threatened, and prodded for every point.

It looks like it's her win by half a point for starting, Wang Jun thought. He wasn't too depressed about this fact. It was her job to play, after all.

In their subtle exchanges, he barely noticed as their rhythm was interrupted. She made an unusual move. A bad one, which he punished immediately. They exchanged a few more moves when he realized what had bothered him about the interruption.

She's toying with me, Wang Jun realized. She'd made a mistake on purpose—her goal was to let him win. *If that's the case, I won't let her.* A few moves later, he also made a suboptimal move. To most people watching, it wouldn't register as a mistake, but they both knew what had happened.

They continued in this way, both playing a believable game while discreetly trying to lose a point. Their moves were growing more limited, and Wang Jun quickly realized he'd run out of proper opportunities. He couldn't make any big mistakes—that would be too obvious. Therefore, he started a ko fight and began making threats in dubious-looking areas. To others, it would look like she had to defend. They both knew she didn't, but defend she did.

Wang Jun's frustration mounted. He didn't want to win a thrown game, but he didn't want to throw a game too obviously. This game was less a fight between two expert players than a fight between his personal pride and the face he showed to others. They had ten real moves remaining, but he sweated as he placed stone after stone, agonizing over the decision.

Damn it all, he thought. *I refuse to be toyed with.* With three moves remaining, he finally spotted an opportunity. Before the stone could fall, however, Bai Ling did something he hadn't expected.

"I concede," the woman said. "Thank you so much for playing such an exciting game with me. You didn't disappoint."

He'd been duped. This whole time he'd been trying to play within the bounds of the game, but he'd failed to realize she had a way out.

She could end the game at any time she chose. "You let me win," he said with a wry chuckle.

"Nonsense," Bai Ling said. Then, she looked up toward the second floor, which had previously been unoccupied. A lady in red now stood alone on a balcony above them. "Ahem. It seems our headmistress has requested a personal audience with Young Master Wang. She says she was impressed by your performance and would be happy to make your acquaintance." The crowd had already dispersed, and through some strange technique, Bai Ling had sent these words to his ears alone.

Wang Jun looked up to Protector Ren and Wang Tong, who were discussing wine vintages, of all things, then back to Bai Ling. "I'd love to make her acquaintance."

"Then please follow me," Bai Ling said.

She took his hand and walked over to a marble staircase he hadn't noticed before. The staircase, which evidently led up to the second floor, was made from the purest black stone etched in red runic lines. "No one can scale these steps without the headmistress's permission. Just head up the stairs and walk over to her balcony."

Wang Jun nodded and took his first cautious step. The runes shimmered, revealing countless specks of red light around him that quickly dispersed. He took another, and the specks reappeared. As he began climbing the steps at a normal pace, he realized that the lights resembled a fine red dust. The symbolism was apt—in this house, more than anywhere else in the city, temptations of the mortal world haunted one's every footstep. Trying to rid oneself of every speck was a futile struggle that only fools and buddhas undertook.

The red dust faded as he entered the second floor. A red-crystal chandelier in the center of the vast three-floor chamber cast alternating lights and shadows on the floor's pristine alabaster surface; it was a show only *he* could properly appreciate, as the shadows seemed livelier to him than their bewitching red counterparts.

A short figure dressed in red and gold grew closer and closer as he walked, and he couldn't help but feel nostalgic. He mocked himself inwardly. In the Red Dust Pavilion, you could never trust your feelings. Therefore, he ignored his rushing blood and the fierce pounding of his heart as he walked up beside the alluring woman whose face he hadn't yet seen.

She turned toward him and smiled lightly. His heart caught in his throat for a moment as he was overwhelmed with inexplicable familiarity—only to breathe normally once he realized that she was a complete stranger. Assuming that was her real face, of course. The headmistress of the Red Dust Pavilion was beautiful beyond compare, but he could see faint red and blue runes dancing on the white paint that covered her adorable cheeks.

"Well met, young master," the woman said. She curtsied slightly. "This headmistress is pleased to finally make your acquaintance. I've heard so much about you, and your show down there took my breath away."

"She let me win," Wang Jun said.

"Didn't you try to do the same?" the headmistress asked, causing Wang Jun to raise an eyebrow. "It's the end result that matters, and if she says you win and can convince everyone else, win you did. You should be happy; she doesn't let everyone win."

Wang Jun coughed awkwardly. "You're... different than I imagined," he said finally.

"So straightforward," the headmistress said. "What did you expect? A cold, bloodthirsty owner of a body house that ruled with an iron fist?"

"Never," Wang Jun said. "I just expected you to be older."

The headmistress chuckled. "A woman always loves to be called younger, but in my case it's the truth. In fact, I'm about as old as you are, if you'll believe it."

"I'll take your word on it, though you don't look a lick past twenty," Wang Jun said. "I notice this place is packed, despite the steep admission price."

"Pricing is an art," the headmistress said. "And we have nothing but satisfied customers. For example, do you regret paying what you did?"

Wang Jun thought for a moment. "I suppose I don't. Just that game alone was worth it."

"Then you've already made a tidy profit this visit," the headmistress said. "I hear that's important in your family, to the point that everything else is meaningless. But back to admission and satisfaction. The truth is that our performances are both effective and addicting. They just need a little push, and they'll keep coming."

"Some would call that unethical," Wang Jun noted.

"Is it unethical if it helps them?" the headmistress said. "Cultivation is addicting, and so is making money. So is tea, I suppose, if everything I've heard of your expensive habit is true."

"You've got me there," Wang Jun said. "I can't say I treat my customers any differently. They keep coming if I do well by them, and they leave if I don't. If only that were enough." He stopped himself as he realized he'd said too much.

"If only it were enough," she said, echoing both his words and his feelings. "I find myself thinking the same thing every day. We might seem like we're doing well, but we could be doing so much better. My sisters and I have to hustle every day to pitch clients and close deals, but it's so difficult to find people who appreciate what we sell."

"Which is?" Wang Jun asked.

"Inspiration," the headmistress said. "Clarity of mind. The heart is a fragile thing that's only too easy to break."

Wang Jun felt a hint of discomfort, but the headmistress caught it and quirked an eyebrow. "Interesting. I never expected the illustrious Wang Jun to have suffered heartbreak."

"Not the broken but the breaker, I'm afraid," Wang Jun said. "I'll spare you the boring details."

"I can imagine," the headmistress said. "You're the rich young master of the Wang family, but your situation is far from stable. I take it you fell in love but realized your mistake. She was in danger, so you let her go. You knew it was the right decision, but she didn't understand. It was her sadness that broke you."

Wang Jun raised an eyebrow. "Have you been *spying* on me?"

"Lucky guess," the headmistress said, sighing. "You aren't the only one to have experienced such a situation. Now, where was I? Value. As you know, we sell information. But our most valuable service is inspiration, and it's something your brother isn't buying now. I know you're not doing too well, but I'm sure you can see how new ideas and a productivity boost for your many businesses could come in handy. For the right price, of course. And if you pay well enough, we could even do the opposite for your competitors. Covertly, of course."

"It's something I'd consider," Wang Jun said. He paused as the audience quieted and the lights dimmed. A red curtain opened, revealing a beauty and her zither. He heard a soft pluck, and his mind went empty. An entire day of stress and gloom flew away like a bird given wings.

"Her performance is amazing, isn't it?" the headmistress whispered. "Just a few notes are enough to calm the most restless hearts. It's difficult to put down your worries when so much rests on your shoulders. But you can do it for a few moments, can't you?"

Her words didn't distract from the performance but synchronized with it. He let his awareness drift toward the stage, where a cold winter was just ending. Everything was frozen and without life. But a few seconds later, a new note sounded: the chirping of a bird.

"It's easy to feel like you've lost everything, but life isn't steady. It's cyclical, like the seasons."

A bird flew down and landed on a branch as the snow melted. It pecked at newly exposed grass to find scattered seeds as it waited for the remainder to disappear. "The winter can be long and devastating, but if you survive, summer will always come."

The music continued, and the melting snow became a stream, and as the last of it disappeared, spring winds blew and trees began growing leaves. Flowers sprouted across the increasingly lively landscape where the local wildlife began to awaken.

"Take this bird. It builds a nest and lays eggs that soon hatch. Not all of them survive, but that hardly matters. Spring turns to summer, and the birds flourish. Two birds become six, and with enough winters, these two birds might well make thousands. But for every lucky couple, there are many that didn't make it."

These many winters flashed before his eyes, and he saw few birds become many. He saw the same for rabbits, foxes, deer, and wolves.

"Some animals must change instead. Their personal success is dependent on successfully changing. Those who don't change don't survive."

He saw thousands of caterpillars erupt on trees. Birds scrambled to devour them, but there were too many. Trees died, but the caterpillars flourished. Those who ate enough made cocoons, and soon the land was covered in beautiful butterflies.

"These two ways are how normal animals flourish," the headmistress said. "But some animals are like humans. They change their environment to survive and thrive."

The scenery changed to that of a river. A pair of beavers worked hard to cut down trees, drag them into the river, and build a dam. They weren't safe in the river, so they changed it. The river soon became a small lake thanks to the dam, and the beavers thrived in their artificial sanctuary.

"You have three paths ahead of you. Which will you choose?" The lights faded, and Wang Jun heard the last note of the song he'd barely heard. He felt unusually calm, yet at the same time, excited. It was like a fire was burning in his heart while an icy shell kept it from being damaged. And with it came inexplicable anxiety. His mind raced as he thought of various possibilities he could barely register.

"My apologies," Wang Jun said. "The concert's effect is much more exaggerated than I'd expected."

The headmistress smiled. "It's always that way on your first time. Subsequent experiences are bound to be disappointing."

He blushed at her play on words.

"Make sure you go home and rest," she said. "You can't think properly with so many ideas, and the sleeping mind is best for dreaming. Tomorrow could be the most important day of your life. Don't waste it."

Wang Jun nodded. Then, frazzled, he wandered down the steps, ignoring the red dust as he rejoined his companions. A middle-aged woman in a red dress passed by him on his way down, and soon he left the premises under Wang Tong's guidance. They didn't stay for the after-party, where people mingled, spoke about the performance, and met with the performer and the various mistresses. Only regulars could properly enjoy the event anyhow.

They soon arrived at the Jade Bamboo Headquarters, where they each made their way to their own bedrooms under Wang Tong's careful guidance. Wang Jun fell asleep the moment his head hit his pillow.

Hong Xin's eyes lingered on Wang Jun's familiar figure as he walked out the doors and headed back toward his residence. She yearned to show him her true face and speak with her real voice, but she knew better than to do such a foolish thing. Revealing herself would only hurt him; it would hurt her as well. Besides, she had too much to do in this wretched city.

"You seem perturbed," Mistress Huang said as she walked up behind her. "And he seemed preoccupied. Did everything go well?"

"We'll see," Hong Xin said, licking her lips. Then, she glanced down at the first floor. "I see a person downstairs I wasn't expecting. Did he come alone?"

A green-robed man with a tightly wound topknot held up a glass of red wine in their direction. He was the only person at his table.

"He says he has something important to talk about," Mistress Huang said. "Should I tell him you're busy?"

"No," Hong Xin said, shaking her head. "We do a lot of business with him and his faction. He deserves the attention."

"Then I'll see him up," Mistress Huang said. She bowed slightly and walked down the black and red steps. The man in green came up soon after and walked straight toward her familiar balcony.

"Is something on your mind?" the man said as he approached

her. "You're usually so calm and composed, but you look concerned tonight."

"It's just a wonderful evening," Hong Xin said. "Too wonderful. Even so, Master Mu, it wouldn't be complete without your attendance."

He nodded lightly.

"I heard the Chen family is opening up a shop just opposite yours," she said. "Same business, different prices."

"It shouldn't be the same business," Mu Feilong said, shaking his head. "I have it under good authority that it's spirit clothes, and that he's hired one of the best seamstresses on the continent."

"Perhaps I heard wrong," Hong Xin said with a shrug. "One of my acquaintances overheard some people talking about your best jewelsmith. Apparently the Chen clan patriarch has gone through many troubles over the past few months to procure a supply of iridescent feygems, as well as a peak-core-grade gem hammer. Something about wanting to close a deal. It's a pity I was mistaken."

Mu Feilong licked his lips. "*That* piece of news might have escaped my notice. Now that I think of it, the jewelsmith I have on retainer has a very loose contract. It wouldn't be difficult for her to escape to a competitor given sufficient incentive."

"How fortunate that your contract hasn't dissolved," Hong Xin said. "And that it contains a clause requiring her to disclose any such offers and give you the chance to match them."

"But she's locked herself up to work on a big project, and I'm contractually forbidden from interrupting her work," Mu Feilong said. "Rat bastards, abusing loopholes in our contracts. They almost succeeded too."

"I'd hurry and talk to her if I were you," Hong Xin said. "The hammer apparently arrives the day after tomorrow. No information is perfect, so it's best to act quickly."

"It can wait for now," Mu Feilong said. "I saw you had Wang Jun come up. Any juicy information you might be privy to?"

She smiled lightly. "I've only heard that he's causing a bit of trouble in his family, so I was interested in meeting him. Chaos is cash, after all."

"True, true," Mu Feilong said. "But it doesn't feel like chaos. Only the calm before a storm. As their new auditor general, I heard he's unearthed quite a few juicy mistakes on his main competitor for the family leadership, Wang Ling. Nothing major yet, but he seems out for blood."

"Curious," Hong Xin said. "I thought the Wang family was usually tight-knit. They don't stoop to personal attacks, choosing instead to use the market to do battle."

"That would normally be the case," Mu Feilong said, swishing his wineglass. He sniffed and drank a sip. "However, I have it on good authority that he's got issues with Wang Ling. Serious issues."

Hong Xin raised an eyebrow.

"I know it sounds fresh from the knitting circle," continued Mu Feilong, "and believe me, men have *exquisite* knitting circles, but I did some digging. It seems Wang Jun and Wang Ling had a sister. But no one ever mentions her. She was also retroactively wiped from the family genealogy, and all mention of her since was wiped clean."

"What happened?" Hong Xin asked.

"That would be the million-spirit-stone question now, wouldn't it?" Mu Feilong said. "In any case, it's clear from the moves he's made that it's personal. I've also heard he's been barred from competing with his brother's businesses. Something about conflicts of interest. Everyone knows its all hogwash, though—young Master Jun is a deadly talent, and they're scared. The family leadership's doing its best to keep him on a leash, but no one thinks it'll really hold him."

Hong Xin nodded. "You're usually a busy man, so I doubt you're here for gossip."

Mu Feilong licked his lips and nodded. "We've dealt with each other for around a year and a half now. Things have been going well, of course, but they could be going better."

"They would be better if you made full use of our people," Hong Xin said.

"Right," Mu Feilong said. "But we've been hesitant to do so because of certain rumors. After doing business with you this long and getting to know your character, we've decided to move forward with negotiating a long-term contract."

"That's wonderful news," Hong Xin said.

"It is," Mu Feilong agreed. "We were originally hesitant to take this step. The Mu family, and the four other families that I represent, didn't want to be implicated in your matters."

"Implicated?" Hong Xin said, frowning. "I take it you mean the split with our former members?"

Mu Feilong chuckled. "If it were only that, we wouldn't have hesitated. The competing houses that snagged your old members have been doing well, and as the only major houses left without the Red Dust Pavilion's full services, we've been at a bit of a disadvantage. But that's nothing compared to having the Church of Justice breathing down our necks. Fortunately, that problem has been solved."

Hong Xin's frown deepened. "I'm not sure I understand you. The Church of Justice frowns on our activities, yes, but they aren't illegal. We haven't done anything worth their attention."

"You haven't *recently*, which is why we're willing to work with you," Mu Feilong said. "But the Red Dust Pavilion has committed many crimes in the past." A blue jade slip appeared in his hand. "Please take a look. Bear in mind that it's only a copy."

Hong Xin hesitantly poured her resplendent force into the jade and discovered that it was actually a recording jade. A mistress of the Red Dust Pavilion walked through a small town. People laughed merrily all around her, and she nodded back to those who greeted her.

She did some very mundane things before proceeding to a large living complex. Several guards were posted, and Hong Xin saw several signs warning about a plague. The mistress walked past several sentries until she finally walked into a room filled with horrors.

"How is everything going?" the mistress asked a pale attendant. She ignored the people that lay writhing and moaning on cots in the makeshift dormitory. The few dozen people were chained to their beds, and very few of their limbs had been left intact.

"Number three is ready for extraction," the pale man said.

The mistress nodded and approached a bed. It contained a shivering old man with tears in his eyes.

"Get away, you monster," he growled and recoiled as far as his chains would let him.

The mistress smiled. "You've suffered long enough. It all ends today."

The man paused. "Truly?" he asked, his eyes brightening. "You'll let me die?"

"Of course," the mistress said. "Offer up your soul, and I'll let you leave this wretched world behind."

"I accept!" the man said hastily. "I accept. Please don't take it back."

"I won't," the mistress said. She took out a small black urn and placed it on the bedside table. Then she summoned a cruel black dagger and placed it against his heart. He moved to impale himself with it, but she held him firmly in place. "Repeat after me. I offer my soul of my own free will to Mistress Ling to do with as she will."

"I offer my soul of my own free will to Mistress Ling to do with as she will," the man said, almost panting. "Well? Is that all?"

"That's all," Mistress Ling said. She then plunged the dagger into his heart, and to Hong Xin's surprise, no blood flowed out. A crimson ghost drifted out from his body. As the Yellow River appeared to whisk it away, the soul was quickly sucked up by the urn Mistress Ling had placed beside the bed.

She smiled. "A success. Collecting souls is such hard work." She took away the urn and turned back to the pale man who had been patiently waiting for her to finish. "When is the next one due?"

"It could be either days or a week," the man said. "Why don't we make it a week to be sure?"

"I'll see you then," Mistress Ling said. She handed the man a bag full of what Hong Xin presumed were spirit stones and left the building and the village. The recording ended.

"What have you done?" Hong Xin said with gritted teeth.

"It's not what we've done, but what the Red Dust Pavilion has done. The soul trade is a dreadful thing," Mu Feilong said. "Which is why it's been outlawed for millennia in the North. The Spirit Temple has historically avoided this trade north of the border to avoid the ire of the Church. They do it in the South instead, though it's not as efficient there since you need to accumulate a certain amount of resentment to generate ghosts. People have trouble resenting what they're born into." He cleared his throat. "In any case, we purchased this from the Greenwind Pavilion and obtained exclusive rights to it."

"They didn't give it to the Church?" Hong Xin asked.

"And give away something that could make them a lot of money?" Mu Feilong scoffed. "No, they waited for the right buyer. Now, the Church of Justice won't get a chance to see it."

Hong Xin's eyes narrowed. "Unless you give it to them."

"We hope it won't come to that," Mu Feilong said. "We understand that you need to make a living, but I'm sure you'll take this into account when we negotiate our contract."

Hong Xin trembled. She'd dealt with the man for a year and a half, and she'd never felt a hint of animosity. Yet suddenly, he'd betrayed her. No, it wasn't a betrayal. Betrayal was something you weren't planning to do since the beginning. She thought Mu Feilong and his ilk simply hadn't been able to capture free members of the Red Dust Pavilion. It seemed more accurate to say they'd avoided capturing them so they wouldn't be seen as sheltering monsters if they turned in this information. But disguising their relationship as a client-vendor one, they could insulate themselves from the Red Dust Pavilion.

"This one's on us," Mu Feilong said, handing her another jade slip.

She scanned its contents and discovered that it was data and information. Information on various actions of their members with the Spirit Temple, a record of their secondment to the Hall of Souls, and finally, a record of various locations and travel schedules for said members. The schedule was valid for the next two weeks.

"What you do with that information is up to you. I personally find the soul trade quite distasteful, so I fully encourage you to prevent any further actions by your rogue members."

Hong Xin's head was spinning. She wanted nothing more than to lie down and hide beneath her blankets while hoping the world went on without her. "I'm afraid I'm not feeling well, Master Mu," she said. "It was a pleasure meeting with you, but I'll have to excuse myself."

"I was just leaving," Mu Feilong said. "Our people will be in touch shortly."

As he traveled down the stairs, Mistress Huang came back up. Then, seeing Hong Xin's trembling figure, she used dousing arts to regulate the younger woman's surging emotions. "What happened?" she asked.

"A disaster," Hong Xin said. "Terrible news with dire consequences."

Mistress Huang frowned. "Should I end the party early?"

Hong Xin shook her head. "No, we don't want them seeing us any weaker than they already do," she said. "Finish the party, but I want you, Bai Ling, and Ji Bingxue in my quarters as soon as the last guest leaves. I'll be heading back to my chambers early."

Mistress Huang nodded slowly. "Do you need anything? A scented bath, perhaps, or something to eat?"

"A drink," Hong Xin said. "A strong one at that." She left the stunned Mistress Huang on the balcony and walked listlessly toward her bed.

Hong Xin never drank.

Chapter 15: Changing the World

In a dark room in the Jade Bamboo Headquarters pavilion, Wang Jun stirred in his sleep. His dreams were chaotic and messy, a mixture between wonder and nightmare. He saw his sister's bloody face, smiling and telling him to be safe while his brother smirked in the distance. He saw Elder Bai taking care of him in the numb years that followed. Vengeance burned in his heart. It threatened to engulf him if he didn't let it out.

But how? he thought. Overcoming him financially had become all but impossible. He could kill his brother, yes, but did the man deserve a peaceful death? No. He deserved to suffer a terrible defeat and wallow in self-pity before breathing his last.

Wang Jun saw birds building nests in the spring, laying a steady foundation for when they laid their eggs. He saw humans raising their children, hoping they'd at least be as successful as their parents. Then he saw angels. They taught restraint and kindness to the deaf, while devils encouraged those who listened.

But why? he thought. *Why do they even bother?*

A butterfly emerged from a cocoon, completely transformed. Not all caterpillars could become butterflies, however. It was an unfair situation, much like the cultivation world. *Why is it so unfair?*

Below him, a beaver worked hard to build a dam. Once built, not only were the beavers safe, but all sorts of animals and fish took refuge in the changed habitat. The dam not only benefited them but many others.

I need to make money, not start a zoo, Wang Jun thought.

When he thought of money again, he saw piles of spirit stones he didn't have, a fortune he couldn't reach, and a bottomless pit trying to swallow it all. He saw his brother gloating with all his advantages. No, if he focused on money, his brother would win. His brother had more, and this game was rigged against him. He needed a new idea, something that would flip the board and let him start over on a playing field of his own choosing.

Then back to the birds, what are they doing? he thought, looking back to them. *The birds are building a nest. A foundation for their young.* It wasn't just a safe place for them but a place for their entire family. If their family succeeded, their descendants would succeed as well. Birds who didn't build nests didn't last long, and the smartest birds built their nests with the best materials they could find.

And what of the butterflies? he thought. *Aren't they just living?* Yes, the butterflies were living, but they were also changing. They came from the cocoons they formed as caterpillars. There was only enough food for less than one out of every hundred caterpillars. The others would die without reproducing. Humans were like butterflies in that sense. Only one out of every hundred became cultivators. Perhaps that was due to shortage as well?

And the beavers? he thought. They changed their environment to make it more comfortable. Other species couldn't do this, for as beavers, they were equipped with all three tools—their teeth, their tails, and their knowhow. Without all of these things, changing their environment was impossible. But they had them, and they used them to change their entire ecosystem. Many other species benefited.

All for money, he thought. He saw bloodstained spirit stones and mountains of treasures. He saw jade bamboo sticks protecting his sworn enemy. They used light to expose him in the shadows and chain him, forcing him to work for those he hated.

But do I really hate them? No, he didn't. Elder Bai, Protector Ren, Wang Bing, Wang Tong, among others. There were many family members he liked, and there were many innocent family members who simply existed under the family's leadership. They weren't responsible for what had happened to his sister. Neither were they responsible for what the elders were doing to him now.

Change... change... The order in his dreams disappeared, and the experience became surreal. He was in a different world, one that resembled Quicksilver City. But unlike Quicksilver City, everyone here was weak. So weak that Wang Jun felt they'd get blown over by a stiff wind. None of them were cultivators. Yet these mere mortals somehow moved about as quickly as cultivators, riding in large vehicles propelled by chemistry and mechanisms. They communicated across an entire planet, despite not having an ounce of spiritual energy.

The information they had access to was staggering, and unlike those in his own world, everyone was fed, content, and entertained. They were weak, but together they were strong. This world was completely different than his own, where the weak relied on the strong for just about everything. They'd somehow come together and built marvels that even the strongest on Wang Jun's plane wouldn't dare dream to build.

They didn't use runes either—they couldn't. Instead they used the most basic forces of nature and harnessed them in ingenious ways. They ignored their weaknesses and focused on their strengths— society, intelligence, and something he'd long forgotten: hope.

Hope, he thought. It had died with his sister and had been reborn with Hong Xin. That hope was gone once more. He wasn't confident in finding it a third time. He doubted his heart could take it.

Can you afford not to find it? he asked himself. No, he couldn't. Without hope, his vengeance would be nothing but a pipe dream, forever unattainable and out of reach. He had to find it. He *needed* to find it. That was the last thought he had before his dreams descended into chaos and sweet oblivion took him.

Wang Jun woke in a cold sweat. He looked out the window and realized it was still night. *What time is it?* he thought. He looked to the clock in his room and realized it was three in the morning. His mind was still racing, so instead of going back to sleep, he took a misty shower and put on fresh clothes. Then, after thinking for a moment, he grabbed his core-transmission jade and sent out two messages before heading to his study.

I can't think properly, Wang Jun thought as he leafed through the inky black folio, carefully sifting through its contents for what could have been the dozenth time. It made little sense for him to read it, given his photographic memory, but he couldn't help but scrutinize it carefully. This was the work of an assassin who had nearly killed him, carefully prepared and gift-wrapped in the unlikely event of his demise.

He looked over the key evidence—a list of transactions between the Spirit Temple and various individuals. These individuals had traded in an illicit commodity: souls. In return, the Spirit Temple had eventually funneled the funds back into the Jade Bamboo Conglomerate via various money-laundering channels. The supporting evidence detailed everything. Trading in souls was lucrative, but if they were caught, the Church of Justice would destroy their entire family. It was this sort of unforgivable crime he needed to bring to light if he wanted to destroy Wang Ling.

Wang Jun pondered how to pursue the case. Given his investigative powers and the current laws of the kingdom, the transaction receipts and pictures collected should be enough to prosecute. At the very least, his family would be dragged into a huge investigation that wouldn't die down for decades. But that wasn't good enough for Wang Jun. He wanted to hit hard and fast. Catching his brother in the act would be ideal, but he was also hoping to catch

Wang Ling's most trusted subordinates instead.

He heard a soft knock on the door before it opened. Elder Bai entered, not looking the least bit tired, his robes pressed and his white beard well groomed. He moved to a side cupboard where he retrieved an antique tea set and some of Wang Jun's favorite tea leaves—Jade Rabbit tea from the untamed eastern lands. To his knowledge, the tea grew on a demonic mountain. It was harvested by its demonic residents and sold to them for a very high price. In Wang Jun's mind, however, it was worth every spirit stone.

Elder Bai brewed, and they both drank. A half hour passed in silence as they took the opportunity to relax and let their worries fade away. Finally, once the resilient tea leaves lost the last of their potency, Elder Bai put the tea set away. He returned to Wang Jun's desk, where three piles of paper were waiting for them.

"Exhibit A," Wang Jun said, patting the leftmost pile. "Accounting fraud, middling offense. We discussed the evidence yesterday and its potential fines. What did your research glean?"

"All things considered, the potential fines amount to perhaps ten top-grade spirit stones," Elder Bai said. "The mistakes clearly weren't intentional, so there's no need to mount an aggressive defense. At most, the family lawyers will be in court for a year, and there won't be any substantial fallout."

"Ten top-grade spirit stones," Wang Jun said, shaking his head. "A paltry sum compared to what we need to generate. Did you speak to the disciplinary elder about the reward for this case?"

"He was very understanding," Elder Bai said. "Almost *too* understanding. He stated that any accounting errors found that the family can voluntarily report will be granted to us as a bounty equal to the estimated savings, paid by the offending party. The likelihood of discovery is set at twenty percent by the family, so the find entitles us to two top-grade spirit stones."

Wang Jun sighed. "Exhibit B?" he asked.

"Also seems accidental," Elder Bai said. "Five hundred top-grade spirit stones in potential fines nets us one hundred top-grade spirit stones."

"With that single investigation, we made ten percent of what we worked ourselves to the bone to make in the Song Kingdom," Wang Jun said, gnashing his teeth. He picked up the third pile of paper. "No way this is accidental."

Elder Bai's eyes twinkled. "This case is a rare success. They tried to hide things but botched it badly. We discovered the mistake by combining information from the Greenwind Pavilion, our own documents, and transaction reports from three separate banks. These weren't accounting errors but attempts to hide money laundering. It's not something the family can disclose voluntarily, but in the spirit of spurring competition between members, they decided to award us a fifty-percent bounty for giving them a chance to erase traces of wrongdoing. After swearing a vow of secrecy, that is."

Wang Jun snorted. "It's not like I'll turn in my own family." He took a paper that Elder Bai gave him and reviewed the payment terms—five hundred top-grade spirit stones—before signing it in blood. Elder Bai, his key confidant, also signed it. As much as he hated giving up any dirt he had on Wang Ling, he needed vital seed capital. Taking it from his competitor was ideal.

"It won't be easy to find such things in the future," Elder Bai said. "I noticed that your brother's accounting room is a whirlwind of activity. People are getting fired and hired like there's no tomorrow, and they're going through everything with a fine-toothed comb."

"Then we need to make money some other way," Wang Jun said. "Invest." He looked to the door, to the clock, and to the door again. Then he pressed a rune on his desk and spoke. "You can come in now."

Wang Bing, his cousin from Quicksilver City, walked in with a smile. She kept a jade tablet glued to her chest as she walked, the mark of any good assistant. She could jot down notes whenever the situation arose, and if required, search the database it contained for useful information. Judging by the glow it emanated, it was a core-grade treasure. The brightness of the glow spoke volumes about what it contained.

"Thank you for finally taking me up on my offer," Wang Bing

said, taking a seat beside Elder Bai. "Though I really wish it wasn't so early in the morning."

"I'm happy you could make it," Wang Jun said. "Elder Bai, if you could?"

"Right away, young master," Elder Bai said. He went back to the cupboard and fetched a substantially less expensive—though still high-quality—tea. "This one is a Pu'er tea from True North Country. It was grown alongside rare beans called coffee beans, giving it a unique flavor from sharing the soil. A few of the beans were pressed into the cake, further enhancing the aroma as it aged."

"Thank you," Wang Bing said, accepting her cup. "Now tell me, what are we working on? What's your master plan?"

"You're putting yourself and your entire family branch at risk by helping us," Wang Jun said as he also retrieved his cup and took a sip.

"It's worth it," Wang Bing said unflinchingly. "Your talent is far greater than Eldest Cousin's. He might have a fat stack of money and influence, but how long will it last? How will he be able to resist as we whittle away at his fortune?"

"You know full well that my hands are tied," Wang Jun said. "I can't directly compete with him."

"That's what makes it exciting," Wang Bing said, rolling her eyes. "Otherwise you wouldn't even need my help."

"I can't do without it," Wang Jun said. "The others are just blind, whether due to pedigree or petty politics, but you're different. You're smart and capable. Now, why don't you give us a rundown of industries claimed by Wang Ling?"

"Certainly," she said, drawing a straight line in the air beside them. A green screen appeared, containing dense streams of information. She flicked right three times, and with each flick, loads of information were removed from the original text. "I had the tablet condense and categorize the information, consolidating it into key categories."

"Impressive," Wang Jun said.

"It's just minor data manipulation," Wang Bing said casually. "It can do many better things. I took the time to review Wang Ling's holdings. Unsurprisingly, he owns a minority stake in a lot of industries. Twenty percent, to be exact. Given that the number is even across the board, it seems like an intentional number."

"Likely an arbitrary threshold hashed out by him and the elders," Wang Jun said. "Enough to give him a reason to claim ownership of an entire industry."

"Right," Wang Bing said. "And it seems like his stake in each one was different until six months before your arrival. It was then that he began rebalancing his portfolio, taking a loss in the process. Then he used most of his available capital to purchase up to twenty percent of the family's most profitable industries.

"Alchemy, blacksmithing, farming, and mining, as well as associated distribution channels," Wang Bing said. "Though, for some reason, he doesn't own much real estate."

"Likely because it's too expensive," Wang Jun said. "Real estate is a highly leveraged industry. In addition, the argument that no one can compete in a basic industry like real estate is laughable, since every business depends on owning property. He probably just parked spare money there because it was convenient."

"Some industries are conspicuously lacking," Wang Bing said. "Mercenary and security services, insurance, artificery, wholesale."

"Wholesale's profit margin is much too low," Wang Jun said. "Artificery is still in its budding stages, so it's very speculative. In addition, it's only useful for low-level cultivators at this point. As for mercenary work and insurance…"

"The risk is just too high," Wang Bing said, shaking her head. "The blood price for slain mercenaries and the high risk of failure can bankrupt any investor. It would be far too easy for him to hire a rival company or set up easy-to-botch jobs to make you lose your shirt. Insurance companies are much the same."

Wang Jun leaned back in his chair and tapped a finger on his lips. Wang Bing and Elder Bai remained silent as he thought. Only the sounds of clinking china could be heard in the room as his mind sifted through the endless possibilities.

"Are insurance companies really the same as mercenary

companies?" Wang Jun said. "The risks are similar, but the business model is entirely different." He walked up to her green screen and flicked his fingers a few times, dragging up key characters for her benefit. "Mercenary companies have a blood price, and their jobs are a gambling act. Regardless of how you approach it, your men need to fight to make money."

He swept his fingers and summoned a new diagram. "But insurance is different. We can keep a small pool of working capital to pay out losses, but where we make our money can vary greatly. We can invest the spare capital wherever we like."

"I suppose you have a good idea?" Wang Bing asked.

"Why, all the industries he neglected," Wang Jun said, his mouth widening into a wolfish grin. "Artificery. Real estate. Wholesale. Mercenary work."

Wang Bing massaged her brow. "I'm missing something here. I believe I said investing in those industries was a terrible idea, and you agreed."

"On their own they are, my dear," Wang Jun said. "However, what if there was a sudden influx of low-level cultivators and their associated demands?"

Wang Bing frowned, but suddenly it dawned on her. "You mean Mo Tianshen's cultivation endowment pills?"

"That's right," Wang Jun said. "My brother might have the alchemy market cornered, but this is a pill that isn't sold by any companies he owns. He can't make the argument that I'm infringing on his industry."

"It'll be hard to negotiate with Mo Tianshen," Wang Bing said. "He says his invention is for the good of mankind, and he's even filed patents to protect it."

"My dear, we are *not* in this for the money," Wang Jun said. "We want to protect the North from the Southern invasion. We want to improve people's lives. What good is the profit of the few when faced with the despair of the many? In fact, we should even subsidize his noble goal. We need as many young parents and growing children endowed with cultivation talent as possible. They'll be able to improve their lot in life, defend themselves, and begin a new age of prosperity for the cities we live in. And not just in Gold Leaf City. Imagine *all* major cities in *all* Northern countries. Mo Tianshen might not be able to accomplish this, but with enough venture capital, his dream could be achieved within a few years."

Elder Bai coughed. "I didn't know you were such an idealist," he said. "Perhaps we could work on this *after* you've defeated Wang Ling and wrestled away the family leadership."

"No, he's right," Wang Bing interjected. Her fingers were darting around her tablet, furiously looking through the numbers. She shook her head and continued poring over the information. Wang Jun let her work while Elder Bai sat looking rather confused. Finally, after working furiously for fifteen minutes, she looked back up.

"How much do we need?" Wang Jun asked. "What's the market potential?"

"How long is a piece of string?" Wang Bing said. "It's far too difficult to predict. However, I managed to run some numbers on the base capital we'd need to make this happen. It's a lot lower than I expected."

"That's because the market is skewed toward profitable industries," Wang Jun said. "The businesses and real estate we're interested in are currently unprofitable. Let's start with the pills. How much will it take to supply every child, young adult, and newly married parent in the North?"

"With a population of a hundred billion, roughly fifty percent of the population falls within these parameters," Wang Bing said. "Mo Tianshen worked hard to reduce the cost to about one least-grade spirit stone per pill, but each person is likely to ingest an average of four pills. The material costs aren't an issue, however. For this to work, we need infrastructure, and *fast*. I estimate it would take around one thousand top-grade spirit stones to fully roll out this project in the North in the next six months to a year."

Wang Jun whistled. "No wonder he didn't do it himself."

"It probably wasn't just the money that fazed him," Wang Bing said. "He's not a poor man. But the time and effort required to implement it is astronomical. If we offer to do the heavy lifting, and subsidize the cost of the pills by fifty to eighty percent…"

"He would be on board," Wang Jun completed. "In addition, we'd have full control over the distribution. Let's do it."

Wang Bing nodded. "The real estate market is tough to corner. However, real estate aside, your brother owns nothing in the lowest tier of spirit weapons, herbs, apothecaries, and talismans."

"Then let's snap up everything at grades he isn't interested in, especially mid-level mortal-grade items," Wang Jun said. "I want to invest in the countries of the North as much as they'll allow us to."

"Likely a third of the market," Wang Bing said.

"Let's push and see if we can do better," Wang Jun said. "Now that I've completed the family's task in the Song Kingdom, I've been allocated assets that were previously held in trust. I now have sixty thousand top-grade spirit stones to invest, and I don't want a single stone idle. I want fingers in wholesale distribution for mass market goods. I want to invest money in research and development for artificery, especially low-grade artificer goods. Anything they produce, whether it be useful for combat or just for quality of life like air movers, I want it all."

"I heard someone in Evergreen created an artifice that can clean your house and entertain your pets at the same time," Wang Bing said.

"What?" Wang Jun exclaimed. "That's possible?"

She nodded.

"I want that man hired, no matter the cost. That is the kind of thing that will make us rich."

"We'll need funds, and lots of them," Wang Bing said. "Your current funds aren't enough. I'm estimating we require at least a hundred thousand pinnacle spirit stones."

"I want us to start insurance companies in every city in the North," Wang Jun said. "We'll milk investment capital out of them, and we'll leverage our money through loans."

"I'll get right on it," Wang Bing said.

"Can anyone tell me what the bloody hell is going on?" Elder Bai suddenly shouted, ending their excited conversation.

"So sorry, we got carried away," Wang Jun said. "Can you get started while I explain, Wang Bing? Time is precious."

Wang Bing nodded and walked out of the room, a determined expression on her face. This time, Wang Jun poured tea for Elder Bai, who, for the first time in his life, felt senile and out of touch.

"If we can't win with the cards we're dealt, we need to change the game, Elder Bai. If this plan works, we'll likely make over a thousand percent return in ten years' time."

"But how?" Elder Bai said. "Making money isn't easy. You know that."

"By changing the world," Wang Jun whispered softly. "This world currently revolves around strong cultivators. They keep us safe, and they contain chaos. The lower class is nothing but a machine that pumps out the occasional cultivator. These cultivators grow into meaningful citizens while the others make up the dregs of society." He shook his head. "When I returned home last night, I had a dream. I dreamed of a world with no cultivators, and do you know what I saw?"

Elder Bai shook his head.

"I saw success. I saw power. Tell me, Elder Bai, what would happen if cultivators weren't a minority, but rather the norm?"

The older man's eyes widened. "That's impossible."

"It wasn't possible before, but now it is," Wang Jun said. "Using Mo Tianshen's pills, what used to be the privilege of a few will become the right of the many. With so many weak cultivators popping up, new industries will be born. I can't begin to speculate what will come to pass. One thing I can say for sure, however, is that those newly ascended cultivators, the huge lower class, will no longer be content with their lot in life. They'll work hard to carve out a piece in this world to call their own. They'll aim for a better life, but what will they need to achieve that?"

"Weapons," Elder Bai whispered. "Cheap ones. And cheap herbs, medicines, and potions."

"And artifice to complement their weak abilities," Wang

Jun said. "They'll need jobs, and many of them will likely go to mercenary companies. Farming cheap spirit herbs and making weak concoctions as apothecaries will be their go-to occupations. Fire cultivators will be instrumental in casting the cheap metals they'll need in abundance.

"In Quicksilver, they're operating trains with the weak cultivators who have just started training. What else can they do? The transportation industry will boom because of artifice, and likely many other industries will change as well. Then, with their growing wealth, they'll snap up increasingly expensive plots of land, and the consumption of cheap goods will skyrocket. Demand for lower-ranked goods will spike for decades and only settle once an equilibrium is reached."

"Madness," Elder Bai said, shaking his head. "You'd change the very continent's foundation just to compete with your brother for the family's leadership?"

"No, I would do much, much more," Wang Jun said with teary eyes. "I would overturn kingdoms and shed rivers of blood. I'd trample the heavens if that's what it took. But not just for the family leadership, my friend, my mentor. I want Wang Ling to regret he was ever born. I want him to see what true talent is and how laughable it was for him to envy my sister and me, and how worthless he was for growing jealous of her talent and killing her. I want to show him that he miscalculated and should have killed both of us when he had the chance.

"I had so much more talent than her, Elder Bai, but I was still content to let her lead. Yet a small fry like him dared to do the unthinkable because he wasn't satisfied in serving her? I want to show him that it was *his* actions that motivated me, *his* actions that fueled my desire for vengeance, and *his* actions that caused his fall. Only then will I kill him, Elder Bai. I'll make him watch as the last of his blood seeps out from his lifeless corpse, his soul shackled to rot for all eternity, forever a failure."

Chapter 16: A Night to Remember

The clock in Hong Xin's study ticked away as Bai Ling, Ji Bingxue, and Mistress Huang looked over the two jade slips. Their expressions contorted as they witnessed the grisly footage. Mistress Huang and Bai Ling were able to maintain their composure throughout the entire recording, but Hong Xin wasn't worried about them. She was worried about Ji Bingxue. She used her dousing arts to regulate the woman's mood as she reviewed the contents, and she poured hot drinks for each of them as they finally looked up from the two slips. They accepted the soothing medicinal tea with shaky hands.

"I've seen a lot in my days, but nothing as dark as this," Mistress Huang said. "Not even in my field days."

"Apparently those who perform such deeds are bound by a confidentiality contract with the Spirit Temple," Hong Xin said. "Whatever that means."

"It's likely very strict if even Miss Icicle here never heard a whisper," Bai Ling said.

"Who are you calling an icicle?" Mistress Huang quipped back. "I'd break my fist on your frozen heart."

"Stop it, both of you," Hong Xin said. She didn't want to deal with bickering now of all times. "We've been dealt a bad hand. Unfortunately, this is real life, and we still need to play."

They both nodded and closed their eyes to think.

"How could any of our sisters even do such a thing?" Ji Bingxue said. She'd started crying halfway through the recording.

"I don't know," Hong Xin said softly. "But this is exactly why we're here. They're incapable of empathy, so it only follows that they're ideal for performing such tasks."

"Lack of empathy isn't sufficient," Mistress Huang said. "One also needs proper motivation for committing to such risky, socially unacceptable acts. I'm sure a great deal of profit was involved."

"Or other benefits," Bai Ling said. "I must applaud Mu Feilong and his ilk. This is open intrigue at its finest."

"Open intrigue?" Ji Bingxue asked.

"It means they've laid their cards down on the table, and we're backed into a corner either way," Hong Xin said. "The ball is completely in their court."

Bai Ling nodded. "By giving us this information, we're left with three options, all unfavorable to us but favorable for them. The soul trade is considered a dangerous trade for a reason—if the Church of Justice even suspects someone of carrying it out, they'll uproot their entire organization and punish it severely if anything is found."

"Why is the Spirit Temple even allowed to operate in the Golden Kingdom in the first place?" Ji Bingxue muttered.

"Because their main business isn't the soul trade; it's assassination," Mistress Huang said. "Ironic, isn't it? They promised the Church that they wouldn't engage in any *funny business* North of the border, since killing is so common and assassinations are unavoidable."

"Not to mention the Spirit Temple could assassinate at least a quarter of their high-ranking members in one night if they set their mind to it," Bai Ling added. "Since the Spirit Temple doesn't test their bottom line, they turn a blind eye.

"But back to the three options. Our first one is straightforward: we confess to the Church of Justice and our whole organization pays the price. Mu Feilong and his allies will likely deny our accusations and dispose of the evidence, so they'll be hit very lightly by our allegations of blackmail. Their competitors, on the other hand, will all be subject to a ruthless inquisition for sheltering our old members. The Golden Kingdom will fight with the Spirit Temple, and by the time the red dust settles, we'll all be prisoners despite not having personally committed any crimes. Most of our sisters will likely be executed."

"That doesn't sound like a real option," Ji Bingxue said.

"It's the lower-risk option that locks in our losses but allows some of us a chance at survival," Bai Ling said. "On the bright side, we won't even need to recapture our stray members causing havoc in the kingdom; they'll do that for us."

"But we lose control," Hong Xin said. "I don't know about everyone else, but I like existing on my own terms. Does anyone feel differently?"

No one answered.

"That leaves us two options," Bai Ling said. "In both cases, we make a deal with Mu Feilong and his organization. We'll set up a very favorable contract for them, and while we won't be happy with it, they'll give us enough funds to continue operating. One doesn't buy slaves without feeding and clothing them, after all. How onerous the contract is depends on how we respond to the supplementary information. Do we recapture or eliminate our members, or do we let them continue with their ghastly work?"

"What do you think, Bai Ling?" Hong Xin asked.

"The Spirit Temple is too powerful," Bai Ling said without any hesitation. "We're better off slowly whittling them down via assassinations or ambushes. It'd take decades, but if we played our cards right, we wouldn't have Spectral Assassins breathing down our necks for the rest of our lives. Another benefit is that Mu Feilong would have less leverage on us. We'd be able to make some profit, giving us a chance to repatriate the rest of our members in the city."

"But they're doing horrible things," Ji Bingxue protested. "Our members are very effective at manipulating hearts, and this is exactly what we came here to prevent. We have a chance at stopping a lot of suffering. Why not take it?"

"And for what?" Bai Ling snapped. "We'd eliminate our rogue

membership, but the Spirit Temple's demands for souls won't disappear. They'd find someone else to do it for them. We're here to stop evil, psychopathic members, not throw our lives away."

"Please try to be constructive, you two," Hong Xin said. "Mistress Huang?"

"I'm fine with either approach," Mistress Huang said. "Though I'd like to remind everyone that both options also have benefits. Leaving the Spirit Temple alone gives us safety, but we also lose control over their future actions. The members at the Spirit Temple might be busy with their work for now, but I doubt they'll forget old grudges. Or let a threat like us continue existing. They'd be a problem just waiting to happen."

Bai Ling grunted. "True. Initiative is important, and as long as we're controlling the game, we might be able to find a way to turn it around."

"And it's the right thing to do," Ji Bingxue said.

"And it's the right thing to do," Bai Ling said, rolling her eyes. "In the end, it's the Headmistress's decision."

Hong Xin sighed. "How many core-formation guards have we been able to recruit? How many active members do we have?"

"We have about fifty active members and half as many guards," Mistress Huang said. "We'd only need to leave five or so here to control the grand formation if we want to secure the premises."

"All right," Hong Xin said. "Well, I don't know about you ladies, but I like deciding how I die. At the same time, other rogue members in the city haven't done anything particularly nasty. They aren't the problem we came to fix. If all we did by coming here was eliminate those evil women under the Spirit Temple's control, then I'd call that a win." She turned to Mistress Huang. "Please gather all available sisters—make sure we have equal numbers of oathbound sisters and free members."

"As you command," Mistress Huang said.

"Bai Ling?" Hong Xin said.

"I'll use the data we've gotten to organize strikes for tomorrow night," Bai Ling said. "No sense giving them an opportunity to change plans. All these locations can be reached within twelve hours, and I have confidence that two dozen teams consisting of one free sister, one oathbound sister, and one guard will be sufficient. I'll need enough communication jade to make this work, however. Please make sure I have them."

"I'll take care of it," Hong Xin said. "Ji Bingxue?"

"Don't worry, I know my strengths," Ji Bingxue said, swaying her hips slightly. "I'll go motivate the guards. This is a bit of a departure from their contract, but I'm sure I can… convince them to accept a secret mission."

"Thank you, everyone," Hong Xin said. "We'll be in for a world of hurt after this. Regardless of how tomorrow turns out."

Twenty hours later, Hong Xin found herself hiding near a small village ten hours away from Gold Leaf City. It was a farming community with a few thousand villagers, and their main product was wheat. The fields were filled with green stalks of unripe grain, so to bide their time, the farmers took care of livestock and tended to their massive vegetable gardens.

One month ago, a plague had struck the village. They'd responded quickly with the help of the king's men, quarantining the victims quickly and efficiently. Unfortunately, the disease was a harsh one. Under the stringent care of a good doctor, the plague's many victims had been able to endure. They were still contagious, so no one save the doctor could enter the large dormitory that kept them.

She should be there soon, Bai Ling sent via communication jade. A few minutes passed before a red-robed woman appeared.

I see her, Hong Xin said. It was Mistress Ling, the same she'd seen in the original recording on the jade slip.

Move in as per the plan, Bai Ling instructed.

Hong Xin signaled for Mistress Shan and her assigned guard to follow her as she snuck around the village to the back entrance. She used her water qi to create an optical illusion, allowing her to safely bypass the town's weak guardsmen.

They approached the quarantine building from the back. Hong Xin held up her hand when she sensed a light resistance with her resplendent force. She placed a small jade plate on the ground next to the invisible barrier and poured resplendent force into it. The runes lit up, activating a null field through which they passed the formation. Then they circled around the building to a barricaded back door.

Stop, Hong Xin said. She leaned closer to the window and peered into a familiar room where Mistress Ling and a pale doctor were busy examining a "patient." The person in question wept and trembled, and though she couldn't hear the words exchanged, she saw a smile of delight from Mistress Ling, who took out a small black urn and a wicked black dagger.

Damn it, she thought. She'd wanted to confirm what was happening with her own eyes, and what she saw made her blood boil. *Bai Ling, a soul extraction is in progress. I'll be stopping them.*

Wait for my go-ahead, Bai Ling sent back firmly.

Must we really wait? Hong Xin asked. With someone getting their soul sucked out in front of her, she couldn't just do nothing.

Not everyone is in position yet, Bai Ling sent back. *Since they're tracking moving targets on their way to extraction sites. Even twenty-six simultaneous strikes will result in mishaps. We must complete each one concurrently to minimize the risk of losing targets or having them warn the others.*

Tell me the moment they're ready, Hong Xin sent back, biting her lip hard until it bled.

The person on the bed had just been stabbed in the heart, and their crimson soul was currently being captured by the mistress. After the successful capture of his soul and the death of their prisoner, the mistress exchanged a few words with the supervising "doctor" before proceeding to another bed.

Really? Another one? Please tell me they're ready. It's a child this time.

Twenty more seconds, Bai Ling sent. The mistress spoke to the child crying on the bed. She sat beside her and began explaining something like a mother would to her daughter.

Ten seconds.

The child nodded, and the woman took out the urn and the wicked dagger.

Five seconds.

Screw it, I'm going in, Hong Xin said. She pulled back her palm and blasted through the wall. Mistress Shan and the guard, Li Yigen, rushed at the surprised mistress with weapons drawn. Unfortunately, they were too late. The cruel dagger had already pierced the child's chest. Her ghost was already leaving her body.

"Restrain her!" Hong Xin yelled to her two companions. She formed a hand seal and summoned fire. The pale torturer, who'd been waiting beside the mistress, burst into flames. Four guards rushed into the room, two of them activating devilish transformations. Hong Xin thrust out with a palm of ice that froze them instantly. Then she thrust out with a second palm that reduced their bodies to red snow that fell on the wooden floor.

"She's escaping!" Li Yigen said.

While Hong Xin had been taking care of the trash, Mistress Ling had managed to wound Mistress Shan and escape her and the accompanying guard.

Hong Xin clenched her fist, and icy runes appeared around the escaping red-robed woman. Mistress Ling snorted and summoned an icy serpent that bit into the runes and shattered them. In turn, Hong Xin summoned a fiery mongoose that bit down on the serpent. Mistress Ling coughed up blood from the backlash.

Meanwhile, Li Yigen had not been idle. As Mistress Shan chanted an incantation and summoned an icy prison around Mistress Ling, the fearless guard rushed toward her with several pairs of qi-binding manacles. They spun around his body as he sought for an opening to place them. The clever mistress would have none of it, however. She batted away two of the manacles with her fan and hit him square in the chest with a freezing palm to his heart. He staggered backward and dropped the other two pairs of manacles.

As Mistress Ling bent down to collect them, a freezing prison appeared around her. She then thrust out both her palms, summoning dozens of icy runes in the process. They collided with the glistening prison and broke through nine-tenths of its bars. She bent back down toward the manacles. It was only then that she realized they'd mysteriously disappeared.

Concerned, Mistress Ling kicked out toward the empty air where an icy platform was materializing. As she pushed off it, she realized a cold metallic cuff had been placed around her right wrist. Determination flashed in her eyes as she summoned a blade of ice on her left arm and hacked down with all her might. The blade shattered against a shield of ice Hong Xin had hastily cast as she grabbed the woman's remaining free wrist and fastened another manacle around it, completely sealing off her qi flow. She then placed a soul-binding collar around the woman's neck, completely sealing off all means of communication.

"Li Yigen, are you all right?" Hong Xin asked.

"I'll live," he said. Fortunately, he was one of the few body cultivators in their group.

Hong Xin placed two fingers on his heart and melted the ice, allowing it to beat normally.

Hong Xin finally looked at the patients. "Please, release us," the many patients said.

"Kill us," other said.

So much suffering, so much pain, Hong Xin thought.

Have you neutralized the target? Bai Ling sent.

The target has been apprehended alive, Hong Xin said. *The others?*

Twelve targets were either killed or committed suicide, Bai Ling said. *Fourteen were captured, including yours. Our people are moving in to erase any evidence. Tie up lose ends on your location and move on to the next.*

Right. Loose ends. Capturing or killing offending members

was comparatively easy. Now they had to race against time to avoid getting framed as devil worshipers by the Spirit Temple. They would immediately know of these sisters' deaths and would act swiftly to discover the cause.

"I won't kill you," Hong Xin said to the survivors. "But I can do something else. I can heal most of your wounds. More importantly, I can make you forget." She didn't ask for permission before proceeding.

Hong Xin summoned a multitude of talismans. She poured her resplendent force into them and sent them out to each of the victims, whose many wounds began to heal. Though she couldn't regrow their lost limbs and appendages, she could at least prevent any further complications. Once their wounds healed, and Li Yigen and Mistress Shan left the village, Hong Xin summoned several amnesia talismans. They struck each of the victims in the forehead and caused them to immediately pass out. She used her resplendent force to carry them outside the building just beside the illusory field before coming back into the building.

She wanted nothing more than to show the torture implements, the shackles, and the beds to the inquisitors and let them loose on the vile Spirit Temple. Unfortunately, such a move would only backfire. She could only do the next best thing, which was to destroy them. Flames erupted around her, intense flames that melted metal and evaporated wood. These flames didn't immediately destroy the building because they were contained by an icy shell that prevented them from spreading.

After all the primary evidence was erased, she eased up the flame and allowed the rest of the building to catch fire. To any investigator, it would look like a normal arson of a normal building.

Hong Xin sighed as she walked over to the illusory formation and shattered it, revealing the smoldering husk of a building that remained. She heard shouting from the village, and once they found the villagers who had been mysteriously piled up outside the building, she left. Anyone with half a brain would be able to tell that the hundreds of fires that broke out that night were related. What was important, however, was that nothing concrete was tied back to them. A few well-placed bribes would ensure word never spread out from each respective village.

It was an eventful night for the Red Dust Pavilion, a night where they stained their hands with blood and freed the innocent. It was a night where they covered their tracks through fire and punishment. It was also their last *free* night.

From then on, no members of the Red Dust Pavilion dared travel alone.

Chapter 17: Pushing Past the Peak

"Finally," Cha Ming said, heaving a sigh of relief as he entered his chambers. It had been an exhausting few weeks where he did nothing but teach his new students. Finally, after working for twenty-three days straight, he was allowed to leave.

"Don't pretend you didn't enjoy escaping my dreaded clutches," Sun Wukong said. "Now that we're stocked up on ingredients, you'll be making pills until that's all you see in your dreams."

Cha Ming sighed. "Tell me why we needed time essence again? Those discs are extremely expensive and in very short supply." He summoned a gray portal in the room and stepped into it.

Sun Wukong appeared beside him as he entered. "Follow me," he said.

Cha Ming followed, and to his surprise, they stopped at the edge of Jade Moon Garden. There seemed to be an invisible membrane that surrounded the garden now. On the other side of that barrier, the beautiful garden was the same as ever, but something was off. He willed himself to appear just outside the edge and was aghast when he realized what was different. Everything was moving extremely quickly. Uncertain, he reached into the invisible bubble around the garden. Nothing happened. He then stepped through it and saw everything slow down in an instant. That, or he'd sped up along with it.

"It's time contraction," Sun Wukong said, walking through the bubble behind him. "While you were hard at work these past six months, the Clear Sky Brush was trying its best to integrate the large spatial fragment along with that very powerful time-essence disc the princess gave you. Three days ago, the fusion finally finished. The Clear Sky World can now contract time by a factor of five without using any ambient energy. There's only one drawback."

"I'd imagine that's why you got me to collect time-essence discs," Cha Ming said. "That, and the literal mountain of spirit stone ore and the small ocean of liquified elemental essence you had me buy."

"Bingo," Sun Wukong said. "This is by far the fastest way to advance your alchemist grade. It took you six months to advance to mid grade, and normally, it might take you two years to advanced to high grade, and eight years to advance to peak grade. It should go much faster since you don't lack skills or knowledge, only experience. Unfortunately, your progress is slower than most for obvious reasons."

"I supplement my qi by using my soul," Cha Ming said. "I have much more downtime than most alchemists. I could craft a pill a day just like a peak alchemist, but it would take me a full day to recover. Will our stockpile last that long?"

"Not even close," Sun Wukong muttered. "You can't even conceptualize how fast alchemists burn through money. Fortunately, those Grandmist pills are in high demand. For now. You have a backlog of orders, while many alchemists would be hard-pressed to fill up even a quarter of their time concocting high-level pills. You can attempt to craft about four mid-grade pills per day at a fifty-percent success rate. Since your Grandmist pills sell at triple the list price, that means you can net about 15,000 top-grade spirit stones for a dedicated month of hard labor. But that's only *if* you waste your time making them instead of improving your skills."

Cha Ming groaned. His ability to make money was impressive, but he had much more to do than craft pills. Moreover, a single batch of high-grade alchemy ingredients costed roughly 250 top-grade spirit stones, and he would need one batch every single day to improve his skill, regardless of success or failure. The successes would be so few that a whole month of training would set him back by 7,500 spirit stones.

"It's a good thing we have time contraction," Cha Ming muttered.

"It is," Sun Wukong said. "Though your advancement might seem frightening on the outside, only you will know the truth. Expect to spend a decade or two practicing in solitude."

It was a long time to Cha Ming, but if it was the only way to see Yu Wen again, he'd do it even if it took a thousand times longer.

"Let's get started," he said, summoning his alchemical cauldron.

Large lengths of time passed on the outside as Cha Ming trained. During the first year, the membership in the Alabaster Group grew significantly. Cha Ming only came out occasionally to replenish his herbs, teach, and take pill orders. His skills grew by leaps and bounds, and to everyone's amazement, it only took him a single year to become a high-grade grandmaster alchemist.

Their faction celebrated, but only he knew how much time he'd spent. He wasn't a genius, only someone with a lot of time, funding, and knowledge captured by Yu Wen's Space-Time Camera. His knowledge of herbology helped him greatly as well. Flames interacted with herbs in strange and mysterious ways, and crafting pills slowly became an art rather than a science. Sun Wukong still insisted it was a science, however. It was only due to his limited knowledge and perspective that he thought otherwise. Disagreeing with him only brought pain, so he let it go as he crafted.

A year later, Ling Dong broke through to the middle of core formation, following in the steps of Cha Ming's other disciples. From then on, it would take an exponential amount of effort for them to improve their cultivation. Seeing their master hard at work, however, no one dared relax.

Meanwhile, they had not heard even a whisper from Zhou Li's faction. It was as though they'd vanished and never existed in the first place. In Cha Ming's experience, that was bad news. The eerie quiet was just the calm before the storm, but until he fixed his cultivation, there wasn't much he could do about it.

Finally, three years after he secluded himself—a total of fifteen years for him—Cha Ming finally created his first peak-core-grade pill. It was a healing pill with a Grandmist seal, something that could fully heal almost anyone, even their birth defects. He thought of the man who'd taught him medicine, Li Yin, and resolved to give it to him. Becoming a spirit doctor was, after all, his teacher's dream. He yearned to give him that opportunity.

A few more weeks passed, and soon he could confidently craft every recipe he knew save the Nirvana Pill. A total of three years and three months had come and gone in the outside world. As Cha Ming was sitting in a meadow, enjoying the peaceful contentment that came with success, a small rainbow fish snuggled up to him.

"Yu Gen," Cha Ming said, scratching the small fish. He noticed Yu Gen was missing a few more scales than normal. "Did something happen?"

"We finally finished!" Yu Gen said excitedly, practically pulling Cha Ming over. They zipped through the woods, passed the river, and flew up to the peak of a bare mountain. Or at least, it used to be bare. Now, on the middle of the plateau, at the peak, was a mountain of glittering scales.

Cha Ming gasped when he saw these. He'd known they were up to something for the past decade and a half, but he'd never imagined it was something so huge. Back on Jade Moon Planet, cultivators had fought tooth and nail for only a scale or two. Here, there were millions.

"It took a bit of coaxing, but not too much," Sun Wukong said. "They really like you, and when I told them you wanted to find your girlfriend, they were only too happy to help."

"So many scales," Cha Ming whispered. "But for what?"

"They aren't worth so much in transcendent realms, but in

mortal realms, they're a godsend," Sun Wukong said. "Not only can they serve as a catalyzing agent, greatly increasing your chances of crafting any pill, but they can also supplement pills with transcendent heaven and earth qi. In practice, this usually means an alchemist can promote a peak-grade pill to a half-step transcendent pill. But with such a huge amount..." He shrugged. "It should be easy to craft quite a few transcendent pills in the mortal realm."

Cha Ming bit his lip and asked the question he'd been dreading. "How certain are we of succeeding?"

Sun Wukong remained silent for a moment. He used his staff as a toothpick to remove something from his sharp teeth. "With my soul assisting you in crafting the pill, thirty-three percent per try," he said. "But we'll need to practice, and it will be very harsh on your soul because I'll effectively be possessing you for the duration of the process."

"That's not what's worrying you," Cha Ming said.

"It's not," Sun Wukong replied. "What worries me is the tribulation. This plane isn't the weakest mortal realm in existence, but it isn't the strongest either. Who knows how violently it'll respond when we try crafting a transcendent-grade item? Even you, with your talent in creating poetic talismans, haven't dared to create anything past half-step transcendence, right?"

Cha Ming shuddered. "I just felt an inexplicable foreboding feeling. I felt that if I tried it, it would be the end of me."

"It's the same with this pill," Sun Wukong said. "It won't be my first time fighting a pill tribulation, so I know what to expect if the tribulation is reasonable. *If it's reasonable.* But that's not something we can affect. All we can do now is practice and prepare for the tribulation."

He summoned a long sheet of paper in the air and flung it at Cha Ming. "Here's what I need you to get for me."

Cha Ming's eyes widened when he saw the list. He didn't balk, however; they'd need to stake everything they had on the success of this pill. Still, if Sun Wukong thought all of these were necessary, the tribulation was a greater threat than he'd ever imagined.

Cha Ming emerged from the Clear Sky World a few months later. Huxian was outside playing with his four friends.

Fear me, Mr. Mountain, the greatest mountain in existence! the mountain yelled, appearing and disappearing as it tried to crush them in their clever game of tag.

Cha Ming chuckled every time he saw it. The mountain was childish, temperamental, and rather silly, but it somehow suited the other four demons and their own quirks. Gua had his vanity, Silverwing had his strange wisdom and pride, and Lei Jiang was a little stupid and loved bragging. Huxian didn't have a quirk so much as an obsession with eating, a manic lust for power, and a complete disregard for the rules. Cha Ming considered it a stroke of good fortune that Haijing's laws were so severe that even the small fox was kept in line.

"Big brother!" Huxian yelled, zooming through the yard and up his arm. "How did it go?"

"Just a few more steps and we can begin," Cha Ming said. "But I need a favor. I need to borrow Lei Jiang."

"For the tribulation?" Huxian asked as though he'd been expecting it. "No problem. If he can't handle it, no one on the plane can."

"The lightning isn't my worry," Cha Ming said, "it's what comes after it. The three of you should benefit greatly from this at the very least. You can channel the lightning through your terribly named Greater Friendship Circle and push for a breakthrough into late core formation."

"Great!" Huxian said. "I've already established that tribulation lightning isn't so tasty, but what about pill tribulation lightning? I wonder if it tastes any different?" He thought for a moment before going back to teasing the pet mountain. While it wasn't as strong as Huxian and his three other friends, they'd managed to boost its cultivation to the middle of foundation establishment, a very respectable strength for a three-year-old demon beast.

After greeting his disciples and answering a few questions, he weaved through the winding alleys of Haijing Academy until he arrived at another courtyard much closer to the Alabaster Group. Elder Gan answered the door and looked at him in surprise.

"What a rare guest," Elder Gan said, waving him in. "I haven't seen you in months."

To Cha Ming's surprise, he poured hot water into a brown paste. Once the scent hit him, he knew exactly what it was.

"Jin Huang succeeded," Cha Ming said, taking the cup eagerly. He took a sip of the alchemically enhanced coffee and realized that, despite his extremely strong body, he felt more alert and quick thinking. "This is amazing! This would even affect Haijing royals!"

"That's right," Elder Gan said. "He's making quite the fortune with this invention. Apparently your friend from Gold Leaf City, Wang Jun, caught a whiff of it and splurged venture capital on expanding the business. Thousands of chains are popping up all over the continent as we speak. The producers are under a very strict nondisclosure contract on the recipe, though I doubt that's necessary." He ground the brown grit between two fingers. "I can't, for the life of me, figure it out."

He didn't know the secret, but Cha Ming knew. With his transcendent soul, he could see shimmering runes suffusing the coffee paste. Along with select alchemical additives, many of which he suspected were poisons, the coffee would not only have an enhanced flavor but would also bypass the body's natural resistances.

"I'm sure it's a vital trade secret," Cha Ming said, his eyes glittering as he drank another wonderful sip. He would need to visit Jin Huang for supplies the next time he secluded himself. He was convinced that his results would be much better if he concocted while drinking the beverage. Then he shuddered as he realized he was very close to committing the same cardinal mistake as Mo Tianshen.

No food or drink in the laboratory, he reminded himself.

"I'm sure you didn't come to my room to discuss coffee," Elder Gan said, drinking from his own cup.

"Indeed, I didn't," Cha Ming said. He brought up a barrier of transcendent force to seal off the room, then waved his hand. Fifty vials landed on the table, twenty types of pills in all. All of them were peak grade, and all of them bore a Grandmist seal.

"What a fortune!" Elder Gan said. "You could fetch a quarter million top-grade spirit stones with this!"

"I want you to sell these for me," Cha Ming said. "Then I need you to buy some things for me." He handed Elder Gan a folded sheet of talisman paper.

"What are you up to, exactly?" Elder Gan asked as he unfolded it. "The formation flags, even peak-grade ones, will take months to manufacture. The vast amount of elemental essence and evanescence is difficult to come by, even in Haijing. And this last request..." He flicked the sheet of paper. "One does *not* rent the Heaven Ascension Platform. It is the personal property of the Haijing royal family. We sometimes hold events there at their pleasure, but renting it like a normal facility?" He shook his head.

"I wouldn't ask if I had alternatives," Cha Ming said. "I can always craft my pill in the wilderness, but there's nowhere safer than inside the city. Moreover, I'm concerned about collateral damage. The Heaven Ascension Platform is the only place that can handle it."

"That's where Haijing royals transcend!" Elder Gan exclaimed. "You might be strong, but you're far from transcending as a body cultivator."

"Yes, I'm still far off from that," Cha Ming said. "But the tribulation I'll be facing won't lose out. They can watch if they're interested. A few people from the Alabaster Group can too, but they must all be peak-core-formation experts. I won't even allow my personal disciples to spectate if they don't meet that requirement."

Elder Gan's expression turned grave. "What should I relay to the Sea God Emperor?" he asked.

"Tell him I'm crafting something unlike anything he's ever seen,"

Cha Ming said. "Something that shouldn't be born in this world. If I succeed, I'll make history."

"And if you fail?" Elder Gan asked.

Cha Ming's expression turned cold. "I won't. I can't. Death is acceptable, but failure is not."

Elder Gan trembled as Cha Ming left the room. He recognized the look in his eyes. It wasn't the look of a calm and composed man, which Cha Ming usually had. It was the look of a madman. Cha Ming would stop at nothing to achieve his goals.

Chapter 18:
Creation and Destruction

"Today's the day," Cha Ming said, looking up toward the starry sky. He sat in a hot spring protected by illusory woods. Only he could come here, for Yu Wen had moved on to another life. He lifted his hand and summoned the familiar jade camera. He felt its smooth surface, remembering how cheerful she'd looked whenever she'd taken pictures. Tears ran down his face as he looked through their moments together, remembering nothing but the best as he'd been instructed.

It wasn't enough. It would never be enough. He would find her and give her this camera back so they could take more pictures together. He'd bring back her memories so they could be together again. And this time, he would be stronger. This time, he would protect her.

With a determined look in his eyes, Cha Ming left the hot spring and clothed himself in a new set of robes. This was the first item he'd asked for: peak defensive robes especially resistant to wind, lightning, and fire. Their white surface was covered in gold-and-blue runes. They were bereft of any excessive ornamentation and simple in style, conforming with the latest fashion in Haijing. But at this point, he cared not a wit about fashion, only protection.

"Are you ready?" Sun Wukong asked as Cha Ming appeared on the mountain.

"Ready as I'll ever be," Cha Ming said. "Are you?"

"I'll survive," Sun Wukong said. "I'll lose a great deal of power by doing this, but if it helps you transcend, it'll all be worth it. Unlike last time, there's no way I'm falling unconscious." The Monkey King was apparently still aggrieved and embarrassed by his extended near-death state.

Cha Ming painted a gray circle in the air and exited the Clear Sky World. He walked out of his chamber where his ten disciples were waiting. The moment he walked out, they kneeled solemnly and kowtowed three times.

"Come now," he said, using his transcendent force to bring them back up to their feet. "You're all acting like we'll never see each other again."

"Don't try to hide it," Yue Bing said between tears. "Your focus has been laser sharp these last few years, and you've lost your cheer. You're growing older, much faster than you should. Then you get the Alabaster Group to trade away your entire net worth for some defensive formations and alchemical ingredients? And you won't even let us see what you're doing. What are we supposed to think?"

Cha Ming measured his words before answering. "It's possible that I'll die today," he said. "But it's something I need to do. If I don't do it, I won't be myself. I need to see her, and for that, I need to fix my core."

He summoned an illusory replica of his core before them. His eyes were a little teary, because for the first time, he was showing weakness to them. Something finally clicked, and they realized that while their cultivations had progressed by leaps and bounds, his had not. He'd spent all his time mastering professions, yet his qi cultivation had stagnated. And the core he showed them was nothing more than a mess of colored cracks glued together by some unknown substance. It could never grow, for if it did, it would shatter.

"There must be another way," Yue Bing said. "You could just start over."

"There *is* no other way," Cha Ming said, shaking his head. "Look at this as my last-ditch effort, my last attempt at breaking through these shackles. I can't imagine and I won't accept failure." He wiped his eyes and walked out, not allowing his disciples to follow.

Outside, he was joined by Huxian and his friends. They followed him like an honor guard, friends who would fight with him to the bitter end. Several elders joined them as they left Haijing Academy and congregated before the clock tower.

The clock tolled when they arrived. Once, twice, three times. It was an ominous sound, like a warning not to proceed any further. But proceed he must if he wanted to see her. The doors opened, revealing Gong Shuren. Unknowingly, she'd climbed up all the way to the peak of marrow refining during his absence.

"Please follow me," she said, escorting the small group to an inconspicuous place on the side of the clock tower. She pressed on a blue glyph that lit up and summoned a flight of clear blue steps leading to the top of the nine-mile tower. They began their climb, and as they scaled the mighty tower, they realized the sheer magnitude of Haijing City. Its vehicles, its glowing buildings, and its powerful population. Guards directed their demonic beasts around the tower as they climbed, saluting to the crown princess as she ascended the steps.

Only one person stood at the peak of the tower when they arrived. It was the Sea God Emperor himself.

"Many thanks for allowing me to use the Heaven Ascension Platform," Cha Ming said. "I won't forget this favor."

"You don't owe us a favor," the Sea God Emperor mused. "We simply saw an opportunity and grabbed it. Our family is now thirty Grandmist pills richer. And peak ones at that."

"Many thanks regardless," Cha Ming said. "I'll ask that everyone here not enter the centermost nine hundred feet as I prepare."

Everyone moved out and looked at him expectantly. Cha Ming attuned himself to the heavens and the earth and summoned the Clear Sky Brush. At the same time, he summoned Sun Wukong's soul and superimposed it with his own body. The phantom of a crown appeared on his head, and so did the phantom of a tail on his body. The significance of these things escaped most on this peak.

Huxian was unsurprised, but the Sea God Emperor's eyes widened in realization.

Cha Ming gripped the Clear Sky Brush and summoned a massive amount of Grandmist Essence, the forced product of creation and destruction essence. He painted broad strokes at first, demarcating a boundary nine hundred feet in diameter. He lifted his hand and summoned 5,400 gray flags. They were each inscribed with a variety of five-element characters and formations, subroutines to the greater circle.

One after another, he formed hand seals and jammed the flags into the Heaven Ascension Platform. Everyone but the Sea God Emperor and Cha Ming were surprised to see that there were formation flag holders on the platform specially placed to accept them.

Straight line, hook, curve, dot. Vertical, horizontal. His brush weaved around the flags, using broad strokes at first, then filling the empty spaces with gentler, more detailed ones. Lines that resembled rivers blossomed with extra distribution streams and tributaries. Single trees blossomed into forests that came to life with every stroke of his brush.

Mountains gained stone after stone while metal rusted and crystalized, melted and hardened. Fires raged from a single wisp on a candle, while raging bonfires gained tiny details that most people missed while shielding their eyes.

The brush was wind incarnate, connecting and merging the flowing pattern together.

The brush was lightning, shattering and segmenting the formation into its key functions.

The brush was the beginning and the end.

A day passed while Cha Ming worked, and everyone could barely breathe as he did. Those who knew runic professions felt deep awe as they gazed upon the work of art they could never imitate. Finally, as the last line was drawn, Cha Ming poured a mountain of top-grade spirit stones onto the center. The formation howled as it soaked up the purest energy and glowed with gray light, shooting out lines of black, white, and all five colors of the elements.

Then... it stopped. It halted as though it had never been activated. Yet anyone who looked at it could see its frightening potential.

"Half-step-transcendent formation," the Sea God Emperor finally said as Cha Ming sat down cross-legged to recover. "It looks like we have a new grand elder."

Cha Ming's crown and tail were still there, though they were much less substantial than before. He sat for a full twenty-four hours, recovering his state of mind before finally opening his eyes.

When he stood, he summoned a cauldron. It was a large ancient-looking cauldron made of jade, something he'd acquired on Jade Moon Planet. He seldom used it, for the power it consumed during activation was massive. But over the last few months, he'd seasoned it with medicinal ingredients and rainbow-fish scales.

The cauldron pulsed as Cha Ming fed it a thousand jin of Immortal Jade Core and brought it to life. These two preparations alone, the formation and the cauldron, were greater than anything other craftsmen had done in Haijing for the past ten thousand years.

After feeding the cauldron, Cha Ming summoned dozens of ingredients. He summoned his Grandmist flames to burn away what he didn't need and stuck the rest inside the massive hundred-foot-wide cauldron. The surface was oddly transparent, so everyone could see what was happening within.

Gray flames chopped away mercilessly at the herbs inside it. They burned what they didn't need and melted what they did. Some plants were untouched by the scorching heat, instead growing branches and sprouting as they combined and transformed.

Some places in the cauldron were stagnant, while others were perfectly mixed. Ingredients jumped around at the instruction of the all-purpose gray flame. It broke apart gems as Cha Ming tossed them in, while sometimes freezing and hardening other components. It was a dance of five elements, and the gray flame was leading.

Twelve hours passed before Cha Ming finally paused. He frowned and touched the cauldron, inspecting the ingredients with his transcendent soul. Then he shook his head. In an instant, the ingredients inside were reduced to less than ashes by the gray flame. Cha Ming sat down in meditation and pondered his failure.

Hours passed, and these hours felt like days. His audience was itching to see the outcome of this ferocious display of skill. After a full day passed, Cha Ming opened his eyes again; a faint twinkle of enlightenment lay within them.

He swiftly repeated the process, but this time, everyone could see a subtle change in the current of the flames. Some places were slightly cooler, and others slightly warmer. Everything seemed more tightly knit than before, making everyone wonder how all this was possible with a single flame.

Finally, when he reached the same point as before, he clenched his fist. His crown pulsed, his misty tail twitched, and the contents of the cauldron merged together into a single blob of liquid.

Sweat poured from Cha Ming's body as he maintained his exerted state. He threw a large bone into the cauldron and used the intense heat to sear it and break apart what didn't belong. Gray runic characters popped out from the bone; these were relics, a mutation that appeared on the bones of powerful demons. They were infused with Grandmist Essence, a necessary component for the Nirvana Pill.

He fed the characters into the blob of grayish liquid, and as he did, it began to glow bright red. Then, when the glow reached its peak, he summoned a small golden flask from the Clear Sky World. These were the Waters of Life he'd obtained from the Sea God Emperor.

Three jin of water flew out from the flask and jumped into the cauldron. The Sea God Emperor's eyes grew wide when he realized that this young man hadn't wanted the Waters of Life for the usual purpose of healing injuries. Rather, he was using them as the basis for a more potent medicine. He'd never heard of such an extravagant use.

Cha Ming wrestled with the golden water and red blob for several hours, but five hours into the process, he stopped. He sighed, and the product inside the cauldron dispersed as the gray flame consumed it.

This time, a few days passed as he pondered the several mistakes he'd made.

The demon-bone relic is too strong, Sun Wukong said. *It's too difficult to control.*

We'll need to add the remaining Waters of Life, Cha Ming said in agreement. *It's the only way to control it. That means this is our last chance. We can't fail.*

We won't, Sun Wukong said. *I never make the same mistake twice, and neither do you. We're in perfect sync out there. Just make sure you control those wonderful flames of yours, and everything will be all right.*

Cha Ming opened his eyes, and the next few moments were a blur. He saw torrents of ingredients merging together with gray flames. Hours passed by in a flash as he repeated his actions from before. This time, he threw in one demon bone. Then, four jin of Waters of Life followed. He weighed their potential with the demon-bone relic and discovered that four weren't enough, so he added another. Then, sighing, he added the remainder. He and Sun Wukong did their utmost to concentrate on keeping the clashing ingredients together. They fought with their very souls on the line.

One hour, two hours. Three hours passed. At the three-hour mark, the liquid began to harden and form a lustrous sheen. The pressure intensified, and so did the temperature. Four hours, five hours, then six. The surface melted again, forming a malleable outer shell on which to inscribe the seal.

The next three hours were pure agony. Both Sun Wukong and Cha Ming mobilized everything they had as they carved a seal into the nascent pill with their soul, one strike at a time. Their souls pushed so close together that not only did Cha Ming have a crown and tail, but his teeth grew sharp, and his eyes grew red. His personality began to warp, but he didn't care. One stroke. Just one more stroke.

This continued 10,800 times. Then, on the last stroke, their surroundings pulsed. Cha Ming summoned his trump card, a small mountain of glittering scales. The audience gasped as the scales evaporated. The transcendent qi within them flooded into the pill, causing the lightning clouds that had begun to form above them to retreat slightly.

Most of Cha Ming's stock of scales evaporated, leaving only a small pile from the original mountain. This was the last step, so no reserves were needed. A single gray pill with five colored marks slowly floated out from within the cauldron.

"We did it," Cha Ming said with tears in his eyes. "We made it. It's real. It can be done."

Sun Wukong's soul drifted out from him. He appeared a little faint from all the exertion but nothing more.

"Yes, son, we did it," Sun Wukong said, patting his back as they watched the pill descend. He gazed at the skies warily. The tribulation he'd been expecting hadn't come.

"I'll go grab it," Cha Ming said, pushing himself up. His legs were wobbly but gaining strength with every step. If not for his marrow-refining cultivation, he wouldn't have been able to move.

He took a few steps toward the pill, and his eyes narrowed as he approached. A feeling unlike any other filled Cha Ming. His very soul warned him to stop. He'd done something wrong. Created something wrong. That thing should be destroyed, and it would happen regardless of what he did.

Cha Ming shook that feeling away and glared at the heavens. "I refuse," he said, and the moment he said these words, the skies broke out in a symphony of clouds and lightning. "Huxian, I need to borrow Lei Jiang."

The small purple mouse appeared beside him and zipped up into the clouds. They howled in anger and attacked the mouse. The mouse laughed; he'd fed on such clouds before. The indignant heavens sent strike after strike downward, but every time, the mouse devoured the lightning before it could land and sent it into the runic circle that connected him with Huxian and his friends.

The four demon beasts—Mr. Mountain was excluded for some reason—increased their cultivation through their bond as they pillaged the heavenly energies. The frightening efficiency with which they were doing so left both the Emperor and the elders aghast.

Seeing that the lightning wasn't accomplishing anything, the skies finally dimmed. A piercing wind howled toward the pill instead. The whirling blades of death came down to destroy both Cha Ming and the pill. Cha Ming moved to activate the formation, but before he could, Huxian barked in warning.

Silverwing appeared at that moment. The massive falcon screeched, and the winds, which had been gunning for the pill in Cha Ming's hand, grew frightened. They struggled, but try as they might, they couldn't escape the giant falcon's suppression. Silverwing clenched his armored claw, and the wind surged into their formation just like the lightning had. The mouse had devoured the lightning, and the falcon now devoured the tribulation wind.

The heavens roared in indignation. Tornadoes came crashing down on the Heaven Ascension Platform, threatening to tear it apart. Cha Ming shielded the pill with his body, conserving his energy for when it was needed. His soul's numbness eased with every passing moment.

Seeing that they were accomplishing nothing, the winds dispersed. They left as quickly as they'd come. A sharp sound echoed around them, and everyone realized that Huxian and his three friends had simultaneously broken through to late core formation.

Stay back, everyone. I'm going in alone! Huxian shouted. He jumped into the circle just as Cha Ming activated it.

A man, a ghost, and a fox stood solemnly as fire came raining down from the heavens. Cha Ming summoned his Grandmist flames to fight off the torrent of heavenly fire that managed to sneak through the straining formation. What he didn't catch was devoured by Huxian as it fell. Even Sun Wukong, exhausted as he was, lashed out at the oncoming flames, which eventually crashed into Cha Ming's qi-depleted body.

The Sea God Emperor saw the princess move to charge in, hoping to repay her life debt, but there was nothing that either of them could do to help Cha Ming. He stopped her and tried to shield her eyes from the carnage that would follow, but she refused to look away.

To his surprise, Cha Ming was still standing. His body, which had been scorched until he was completely defaced by the heavenly flames, healed within moments. The process repeated itself again and again, each time more violent than the last. The formation convulsed more and more, and on the eighth blast of fire, the half-step-transcendent formation shattered.

Then, on the ninth and final strike, Huxian grew to phenomenal proportions. He became a massive creature of suppression that spanned a third of the formation circle. His body was a full three hundred feet long, just missing another thirty-three feet to the maximum allowable for mortal bodies. His three tails flailed, and at that moment, everyone on the platform understood that what they'd seen before was only an illusion. Huxian wasn't a normal three-tailed fox, but a Godbeast through and through.

His three black-and-white tails flailed as he became the very definition of savagery. In this case, time acceleration wasn't a benefit, but he'd recently consumed a spatial fragment. A shell of distorted space-time appeared around him, fending off a large part of the heavenly flames before they crashed through. The three stars on his tails, the ones for lightning, wind, and swamp, glowed brightly, significantly eating away at the flame's power. Huxian's light and shadow domains ate away and purified the flames before finally, they crashed into his massive body, which he used to shield his brother.

Then the flames did something unexpected. Despite being mindless agents of heaven, they didn't try their best to reach Cha Ming and the pill. Instead, they continued burrowing into Huxian below his fur. Huxian let out howl after howl of pain as they worked their way through his flesh and toward the most vital part of his body—his demonic core.

Cha Ming cried tears of blood as he realized what they were doing. The heavens were challenging him. He knew, in this moment, that if he so chose, he could save the pill. But the heavens would take away his brother's life, and as a result, his own.

Cha Ming howled in rage. This was too unfair. Time and time again, the heavens had denied his advancement. Time and time again, he'd wanted to advance, only to be stopped at the final step. He gripped the pill, which he'd worked so hard to create. Then, without any hesitation, he crushed it. The moment he did, the flames left Huxian's pain-ridden body and hovered around Cha Ming's fist. They waited, for even the dust in the pill was an affront to the heavens.

"Why?" he yelled out at the skies. "Why do you hate me? I just want to see her again… I just want to see her again."

The powerful man who'd created miracle after miracle kneeled in anguish. He opened his palm and let the gray dust trickle to the ground. The heavenly flames, the final wave of gray flames that had sought to kill his brother, darted out and consumed the dust, allowing none of it to touch the platform. It disappeared with the last of the pill.

The skies stilled. Huxian shrank in size, and his friends rushed over to his side. They poured their demonic qi into his body, trying their best to stabilize his condition. Meanwhile, the elders rushed over to Cha Ming. But he couldn't feel their helping hands, nor could he hear their reassuring words. He could feel nothing, could process nothing.

All he could do was weep in despair. Despite all his efforts, he had failed.

Gong Lan looked around warily as thin violet wisps meandered across Violet Wind Mountain. She stood at the base of the steps to the monastery that had protected the Ling Nan Plane against the forces of evil for countless millennia. Their usual mental attacks didn't trigger as she ascended to the peak, step by step. They were broken, their enchantments dispersed.

What caused this? she wondered as she climbed the last step. The ancient buildings of the monastery no longer radiated their calming presence. Ghosts fled as she traveled toward the tall purple building at the back. Its 999 stone steps were now divided in three broken segments, each one more precarious than the last. The peak of the purple stone tower was a mess of rubble and ruin. Traces of destruction and lightning lingered in the air.

Evil, the bodhi seed on her shoulder replied. It was a simple but accurate judgment. Only corrupted beings like devils and evil spirits could have filled this once-peaceful domain with so much horror and resentment.

Gong Lan didn't waste time on propriety. Rather than scale the steps, she took a single well-calculated one. It tore through space-time, and she arrived in the chamber where she'd once met the Violet Wind Master. Unsurprisingly, the room was a mess of blood and charred flesh. The corpses of dozens of monks littered the floor.

They were strewed about the cross-legged body of a single man in violet robes. She didn't need to check his pulse to know he wasn't meditating. He was dead.

"I predicted this, you know," a voice whispered in her ear.

Startled, Gong Lan turned around and lashed out with her exorcist staff. It halted just millimeters away from the weakest ghost she'd ever seen. Its presence was faded and barely discernable. She only sensed a hint of resentment on the minimalistic specter that she now recognized as that of the Violet Wind Master, who had died in meditation.

"You shouldn't be here," Gong Lan said, stowing her staff. As powerful as he was in his past life, the ghost could do nothing to her. "You should have either transcended karma or entered the cycle of reincarnation. Those who linger are inevitably corrupted."

The fuzzy ghost smiled. "You're right, of course. I stayed to my own detriment. But isn't self-sacrifice often required for the salvation of many? That is the path of a Bodhisattva: staying behind, swearing to leave only once the last of us have escaped the wretched cycle of reincarnation."

"What happened?" Gong Lan asked. She wasn't sure how long the ghost could continue to linger. Ghosts were antithetical to the Buddhist way, and just the fact that he'd managed to maintain this astral shape was impressive to say the least. The karma he'd incurred to do so was likely substantial.

"The Violet Wind Monastery has only ever served one purpose," Master Zi said. "The seer-like powers of every master were just cover. The true purpose of the monastery was to obscure the location of the World Tree Monastery and prevent others from scrying on it. We'd always believed our enemies were clueless about this. We were clearly mistaken."

Gong Lan's eyes narrowed. "Then the fiendish demon attacks, the presence of devil cultivators…?"

"All because the Violet Wind Monastery fell," Master Zi said. "They'd only known the World Tree's approximate whereabouts before. Now they know the exact location. It's only a matter of time before they launch their assault. The tides are shifting, and not in our favor."

We can still fight, Gong Lan thought, grasping the 10,080 beads in her right hand. She flicked through the beads as she prayed for inspiration from her predecessors. They'd recruited many monks over the past years, and the Church of Justice was cooperating. But against the full forces of the South, it wasn't enough. Not nearly enough. The Song Kingdom couldn't repel an all-out invasion from half the continent.

"Fortunately, destroying the Violet Wind Monastery came at a great cost to the enemy," Master Zi continued. "They lost several transcendents during the invasion, while many others were wounded. Due to our remote location, however, they had little choice but to make this sacrifice. They won't launch an all-out offense until their members have fully recovered."

"How long do we have?" Gong Lan asked.

"Who knows? Years?" Master Zi said. "Divination is difficult enough, even more so when transcendents are involved. Especially when you're dead. But that's not what I wanted to talk to you about. They're the least of our problems." The ghost flickered for a moment before recovering its stability. "I don't have much time left. We can always retake the plane if the devils take over, but there's nothing we can do if the plane no longer exists."

"No longer exists?" the bodhi seed cried. "Destroying a plane is difficult enough for transcendents to achieve. They could damage it, yes, but destroy it? Hardly. Moreover, no one would have the motivation. The price for destroying a mortal plane is astronomical. Even devil emperors wouldn't try it."

"That's true for most beings," Master Zi's ghost admitted. "But what about this one?" The ghost strained, and a picture of the starry sky appeared. It wasn't the sky they usually saw, but an unimaginably vast expanse. Several planes were present, thriving like they should. Millions of years passed by in the blink of an eye.

Suddenly, a black spot appeared inside one of the planes. It grew a bit with each passing year, unnoticed by its inhabitants. One year, however, the spot changed. Its growth rate skyrocketed, and the plane that housed it began to fall apart. At first, it was only a piece here and there, but eventually large segments were devoured. Its growth matched the destruction of the plane until finally, the plane realized what was happening. It resisted with all it had. It mobilized all the energy it could, but by then, it was too late.

The devouring continued, and the plane fell. Several neighboring planes followed in its footsteps before angels and devils filled the starry skies. They didn't fight each other as they usually did but cooperated in fighting the monstrosity. Even the Jade Emperor, hosts of demons, and the Curse Sovereign joined hands in eradicating the black spot.

In the end, the spot was purged. But the damage it had done to those planes remained. Aeons later, other celestial bodies migrated to fill the emptiness, but nothing could change the fact that the universe was just a little smaller than it used to be, just a little lighter.

"Guard against the growing darkness," Master Zi said, his form fading fast. "Protect the plane. Do your duty. The creature has a name, but it is hidden. Good and evil, natural and artificial, attached and unfettered, all caught up in the cycle of reincarnation. What lies between these subtle intentions? There is only one truth, so find the eyes that see. The blind can't banish the pressing shadows."

With these final words, the ghost faded. A sliver of golden essence shot out from its forehead and entered the silent cross-legged corpse. It joined a golden soul filled with soft lines of corruption, which floated out briefly before a cloaked figure collected it, easing its way into the Yellow River.

"What does it all mean?" Gong Lan asked.

"It was pretty clear as far as predictions go," the bodhi seed said. "But like all of them, they're not something you can act on until a key moment. Just keep these things on your mind, and when the time comes, you'll know what to do."

Or the world as we know it will cease to exist, Gong Lan thought. What a cheerful notion.

She took a step and appeared at the base of the mountain. Then another to appear in front of the World Tree Monastery. She bathed in its calming presence, suppressing the first sliver of uncertainty she'd felt since her transformation.

Something was coming. If it wasn't stopped in its tracks, everything she'd grown to love and cherish would vanish forever.

Chapter 19:
Market of Souls

G entle zither music sounded through Hong Xin's study as she worked through ledger after ledger. Ji Bingxue was the one who played, for while she couldn't help the headmistress personally, she could calm her frustrated heart and soothe her tense nerves.

"I'm done with this nonsense," Hong Xin said, setting her pen down and placing her face in her hands. She used her middle forefingers to rub the area between her eyes.

Hong Xin was tired. She hadn't slept a wink since their last report. "Three sisters are dead, and our supposed allies haven't even done anything to prevent it. You'd think it would be in their best interests to protect us."

"It's in their best interests to keep us scared," Bai Ling said. She was playing a game of *Angels and Devils* beside the tea table. By herself, of course. "One death here and there won't affect our ability to fulfill our contract. They'll pay us our meager fare and sleep soundly while we don't dare leave the Red Dust Pavilion. A perfect situation if I do say so myself."

"I understand why they're doing it," Hong Xin said. "I'm just frustrated. It doesn't help that the ones we captured still haven't given us a single useful answer. That's all despite a year and a half of both pleasure and pain to get it out of them." She walked over to the tea table and poured three cups of tea.

"I can't blame them," Ji Bingxue said. She'd stopped playing her calming tune. "The first and last one who did had her soul devoured by… What did you call it again?"

"A contract enforcement specter," Bai Ling said, still playing the game. The soft clicking of black and white stones grated on Hong Xin's delicate nerves. "It's a mild possession, mostly brainless, that will activate in key instances. Which, as far as I know, includes anything to do with their activities for the Spirit Temple, the Spirit Temple itself, and the nature of their contract."

"We should ask the Church of Justice to exorcise them," Ji Bingxue said. "Though they'll ask questions, we can give them enough truths to satisfy them."

"They'll never be satisfied," Bai Ling said. "You may not have seen an inquisition in person, but I have. It's not pretty. Besides, I'm sure we'd activate one of the specters' termination clauses even if we *did* find a chaplain. No, we're better off just killing them and tying off loose ends. Those evil women are beyond saving anyway, and they're a huge liability waiting to happen."

Hong Xin sighed. "Our game isn't even close to even. No, it's straight-up terrible for us. What would you do if you were losing so badly at *Angels and Devils*?"

Bai Ling paused. "If it were just a game, I'd concede and start a new one. It's easy to do that with games, but life just doesn't work that way." She grabbed her cup of hot tea and drank deeply. "The closest analogy that's actually applicable to real life is evening the playing field. We need to either take away our opponent's advantage or gain enough advantages to make up for it."

"We'd just get hammered down again if we went after advantages," Hong Xin said. "Don't you remember our attempt at ironing out a contract with the Jade Bamboo Conglomerate?"

"Right," Bai Ling said. "They spiked our workload, making it so we couldn't accept the contract without substantial risk."

Hong Xin sighed once more. They'd agreed to Mu Feilong's terms, but that didn't make it easy to tolerate. "Contracts, contracts, contracts," Hong Xin said. "It's all these bloody contracts. Their contracts stop them from speaking, our contracts stop us from acting. If there was a way to burn all these wretched contracts, I'd pay a fortune!"

Ji Bingxue and Bai Ling looked at her strangely.

"I'm sorry," she said, realizing she'd raised her voice. "I just wish we could take all these contracts and bury them in a pit where they couldn't see the light of day." Then she thought of something. "Bai Ling, those ghosts can't act up in the absence of a trigger mechanism, right?"

Bai Ling thought for a moment. "Contract enforcement specters aren't very smart. They aren't given any *real* intelligence for fear that others could use it to find loopholes in their behavior. Therefore, they obey the letter of the law and not the spirit."

"Then would it be safe to say that," Hong Xin continued, "should nothing trigger the clauses, the specters wouldn't act up no matter what? No matter how much time passed?"

"That's right," Bai Ling said. "What are you planning?"

Hong Xin bit her lip. *It's possible in theory,* she thought. *But would he be willing?* "Bai Ling, could you kindly issue an invitation to Young Master Wang Jun? I want him to speak with us in secret. You have his transmission mark, right?"

"I do," Bai Ling said warily. "But if we're going to ask for his help on something, we'll have to give him more information than I'd advise."

"What do we have to lose?" Hong Xin asked. "Our situation is not just terrible; we're literally dying out there. Meanwhile, we have huge liabilities locked up in the Red Dust Pavilion. I'll tell you what, if we can't get what we want out of them with this idea of mine, I'll do what you want. I'll just kill those wretched women to wash our hands clean of them."

"Fine," Bai Ling said. She took out a core-transmission jade and whispered a message. A short while later, it pulsed as a reply arrived.

"What did he say?" Hong Xin asked.

"He said he'd come over at three in the morning," Bai Ling said, surprised.

"Good," Hong Xin said. She rubbed her hands in anticipation, but the uncertainty in her expression was difficult to hide. "If I'm right, we might just have something to work with."

"What exactly are you hoping for him to do?" Bai Ling asked. "A seer is hardly useful in this muddled situation. Evil spirits are tough to read, even for really good ones."

"Who said anything about reading?" Hong Xin said. "Wang Jun is good at many things, but there's one talent he doesn't advertise: he's good at hiding."

Bai Ling quirked an eyebrow. "You want him to hide us from the Spirit Temple?"

"No," Hong Xin said. "I want him to hide our prisoners. Only then will they be free to speak. Then we'll make them talk."

They'd kill them afterward, of course. There was no saving creatures like them. But she was confident that, given the means at her disposal, they'd be eager for such an ending. They'd work for a swift, painless death.

"Our appointment is coming up soon," Bai Ling said. "I think it's time we had *the talk*."

Hong Xin sighed. "All right, let's walk and talk." They left the cells beneath the pavilion and entered the beautiful red-carpeted halls with golden décor. Wherever they walked, they saw servants and courtesans cleaning up after the evening party.

"I won't bore you with the basics. You know about Wang Jun's fight with his brother, and you know about his financial position," Bai Ling said. "And most importantly, you know about his late sister, Wang Hua."

"She's the reason he's fighting with his brother in the first place," Hong Xin said. "The most talented family member they'd had in three thousand years had somehow gotten killed in a fight between core-formation cultivators. In his rage, the clan patriarch ordered the cultivators executed. But despite the harsh punishment, Wang Jun was never the same."

"His relationship with his brother soured overnight," Bai Ling said. "We've retrieved a dozen firsthand accounts of the incident that showed suspicious behavior during the fight between the cultivators. It's almost guaranteed the fight was instigated so they could use underhanded means to kill her. Anything past these firsthand accounts, however, can't be found. There are no traces of any investigations. The record has been wiped clean. All information about her vanished overnight."

"She was erased from the family genealogy," Hong Xin said. "No one even knows what she looked like."

"No one *did*," Bai Ling corrected. She hesitated before continuing. "I found a picture, Headmistress. I think it's important that you see it before proceeding with the meeting."

"Bring it out," Hong Xin said. She walked up to her vanity mirror and touched up the thin black lines on her eyelashes. Then, after touching up her lip paint, she picked up a talisman brush and began drawing intricate runes on her face, as per her usual practice.

Moments later, the glamour sank in, and the runes disappeared. Those who tried to look at her directly would find it difficult to do so. Those who tried to remember her face would be unable to. Those who heard her voice would have trouble putting their finger on it. She was an enigma, an unknown to all but her closest friends.

She turned, about to check on what was taking Bai Ling so long, but yelped when she saw a life-sized rendition of herself. She was young, perhaps fourteen years old. She wore a green dress and a familiar mauve hairclip.

And then, she realized it *wasn't* her. The face was slightly off, even if her hairstyle and her overall facial structure was the same. Her hair was blonde. She was slightly taller and looked much more confident than Hong Xin had in her younger years. Her eyes were the sharp eyes of a scholar. "Is this…?"

"Wang Hua," Bai Ling said. "A spitting image, if I do say so myself. When you're not wearing your glamour, that is. Now you see why I thought it was pertinent."

Hong Xin closed her eyes and recalled the various moments they'd spent together. Wang Jun's doting expression, his look of unconditional care and the hint of sadness in his eyes. Apparently she'd been a stand-in of sorts. He'd been attracted to her because she looked so much like what he'd lost.

"This changes nothing," Hong Xin said, sweeping her hand over the rendition and reducing it to ashes. "He won't recognize me, not through my glamour and disguise arts."

"I'm not concerned about his motivations; I'm concerned about yours," Bai Ling said sternly. "Remember what you're doing this for. We want to recapture our remaining lost members in Gold Leaf City and put a stop to the atrocious things the Spirit Temple is doing. After that, we're packing up and leaving. End of story."

"You're right," Hong Xin said. "This is purely a business meeting, and once we've achieved our goals, we'll let the sisters who haven't committed any crimes free but make sure they are bound by a strict contract. We'll try our best to treat them and thaw out their hearts if they so wish. We'll kill those that have committed too many sins. As for me, I'll continue helming the Red Dust Pavilion as long as I must. Anyone who wishes to stay can stay. Most of us don't have homes to return to, after all." She smiled wistfully and headed for the door.

"You don't have to, you know," Bai Ling said. "The pavilion could burn, and no one would blame you for it."

"There's a war brewing," Hong Xin said. "Angels and devils are fighting, and everyone must choose a side. These things with the Spirit Temple are just the tip of the iceberg. Besides, where else can I go?" She'd burned far too many bridges to go home.

The two women in red made their way to the audience hall. Hong Xin bypassed the tall chair at the back and walked toward a tea table where a guest in green robes was waiting. She immediately recognized the man with long blond-and-white hair. He looked toward them when they entered the room. No, toward *her*. Her heart skipped a beat, but she regulated her emotions and simply smiled softly as she walked at a slow but comfortable pace. She sat on one of the red cushions facing Wang Jun while Bai Ling kneeled beside them and served tea.

"I still can't get over the familiar feeling I experience whenever I see you," Wang Jun said, accepting the cup that Bai Ling poured. He took a quick sip but didn't comment on the blend or quality as he usually did. A cough from Bai Ling reminded her that he'd asked an implicit question.

"We've never met," Hong Xin said sweetly in her disguised voice. "Truth be told, I disguise myself with glamour arts. Anyone I meet will experience that same feeling." It was a half truth.

Wang Jun chuckled. "I'd guessed as much. My time is precious, but a single conversation with you is unbearably expensive. My curiosity is piqued. What can I do for you today, Headmistress? I take it your business today is much more important than the usual information we purchase?"

"Yes, it's something of a delicate nature," Hong Xin said.

They accepted a second round of tea from Bai Ling, and this time she saw Wang Jun savor it. A good sign. She observed his state of mind, his behavior, and his heart before asking the most important question. "What do you know of the Spirit Temple?"

Anger. Curiosity. Want. Need. The tells that accompanied these emotions flickered briefly before immediately being suppressed. *If there's anger, I can work with that,* she thought. She urged his feelings along, kindling them into something greater.

Then, to her surprise, the feelings vanished. Her kindling powers had nothing to latch on to. He showed no surprise or indignation at her actions, however, and she wondered if it was his self-control that was impressive, or if he could just fight off her powers instinctually.

This might be difficult, she thought. *I'll have to change tactics.*

"I know they run a few businesses," Wang Jun said after drinking another sip. "Their first one is communion with the dead, an ever-popular sham they milk for all its worth. The expense of such a task is naturally proportional to one's ability to pay."

"That's the official business," Hong Xin said. "Along with information-gathering services."

Wang Jun nodded. "Spirits make very good spies. Very few people can detect their intrusion, and it's also a very good lead-in for their third business."

"Assassination," Hong Xin said. "Legal, but barely so."

"No one wants to confront an assassin organization that could kill half the court in less than a day," Wang Jun said. He took another sip.

"You hate them," Hong Xin said. "There's something about them that makes your blood boil."

Wang Jun gave her a surprised look. "Close, but not on the mark."

Truth.

"They're just a business like any other. As a man who sells weapons, who am I to judge them?"

Also truth.

"It's just that their hidden fourth business makes me sick to my stomach."

"You lie," Hong Xin said. Inwardly, she was greatly disappointed. It seemed she'd overestimated Wang Jun's moral compass.

"You're right," Wang Jun said. "I'm not a good person. I care about only two things in life—my friends and my family."

Lie.

"Your knowledge of their fourth trade makes this much easier," Hong Xin said.

Wang Jun shrugged. "The soul trade doesn't especially bother me in and of itself."

Lie. The soul trade might not make him sick, but it still bothered him.

"I'm more concerned about the people they're dealing with."

Truth. That was interesting.

"Well, the soul trade bothers me as well," Hong Xin said. "Both on a personal level and for the same reasons you mentioned. I'd prefer if you didn't speak of what I'm about to tell you after you leave."

"My lips are sealed," Wang Jun said. "Though I expect the same professional courtesy."

Hong Xin nodded. "Many of our ex-members were employed by the Spirit Temple—rogue members that split from the Red Dust Pavilion after I took over. Our rogue members have aligned themselves with various entities since the split, of course. They've engaged in many unsavory activities. But trading souls is where I draw the line—it's unacceptable and immoral."

"Ah," Wang Jun said. "An idealist. I never thought the mysterious headmistress of the Red Dust Pavilion would be an idealist. I'm sure this has nothing to do with the very incriminating nature of their behavior and the threat their involvement with the Spirit Temple poses to your establishment, your members, and yourself."

"Motives aside, I require your services," Hong Xin said. "This service has to do with the Spirit Temple and its soul trade. Are you willing to discuss further?"

"I'm all ears," Wang Jun said.

"Excellent," Hong Xin said. "I've just told you that we had rogue members working for the Spirit Temple in the past, but they don't anymore. They disappeared overnight, and it was our doing."

Wang Jun shrugged. "Ethically dubious, but what's your point?"

"They're still alive," Hong Xin said. "But they won't speak or spill any secrets on the Spirit Temple. They've been possessed by contract enforcement specters, and the moment they utter anything incriminating, the specter devours their souls, killing their hosts."

"Vicious," Wang Jun said. "I've heard of such things before. The possessed must avoid exorcists at all costs, or they'll die just the same."

"Right," Hong Xin said. "Now, I've heard on good authority that you're very skilled at hiding things. I want you to hide the rest of the world away from their contract enforcement specters. To blind them, in a way. I want you to make it so that they're blissfully unaware as their hosts divulge every precious secret."

Wang Jun paused briefly when he heard this. Then he continued to sip tea. "Where did you hear such a rumor?"

"I heard from a friend of a friend that you're a special person who can give up his lifespan to obscure even fate itself," Hong Xin said. "Compared to that, this should be a piece of cake."

"It might work," Wang Jun said. "Though I'm deeply disappointed in whichever close friend divulged this secret of mine."

"Once you've hidden their specters, I'll have them swear other oaths," Hong Xin said. "This way, I'll be assured that they're telling the truth."

Wang Jun rapped his finger on the jade table. "To what end?"

"Excuse me?" Hong Xin asked in surprise.

"I want to know why," Wang Jun said. "Hiding their oath isn't required to eliminate or silence them. The information you get will only be temporally useful and outdated."

Hong Xin's eyes flickered to Bai Ling, her silent advisor. She nodded slightly, giving Hong Xin the go-ahead. "We're planning on using the information to infiltrate the Spirit Temple. We'll use what we discover about the soul trade to catch them in the act and cripple them."

Wang Jun continued tapping his fingers. Bai Ling served tea as he sat, deep in thought. It seemed he could help, but it might be difficult to convince him. While Hong Xin didn't want to reveal herself, she would if she had to.

"This wouldn't be an employer-employee relationship," Wang Jun said finally. "What I'm looking for is a partnership. You may not know this, but our family has also been entangled in the soul trade as well. It isn't worth it to deal with you if we get caught up in whatever you're planning."

Now that was a surprise.

"What did you have in mind?" Hong Xin asked.

"I will hide their specters at my expense, but in return, I want all information you gather from the Spirit Temple," Wang Jun said. "Who works there, what they do, and who they deal with. Everything."

"Anything else?" Hong Xin asked.

"Time," Wang Jun said. "I need time to act on the information. Someone in my family is dealing with them, and I want the opportunity to expose him to our elder council but hide it from those outside our family. Once I've done that, you can do whatever you want to them, and I'll have no other demands, whether it be information or otherwise."

"I can't give you indefinite time," Hong Xin said, shaking her head. "I can give you a year."

"Five," Wang Jun countered.

"Three," Hong Xin said. "That's the most I can give. If this operation fails, it will be very difficult to expose them in the future."

"And who will you expose them to? The Church of Justice?" Wang Jun said, raising an eyebrow. "Fine. Three years it is. But I'll give you some free advice: Don't trust others to do your work for you. If you need to kill someone or stop something, do it yourself, and do it cleanly. Otherwise, you'll just end up being disappointed."

"I'll take your advice under consideration," Hong Xin said. "Do we have a deal?"

"We have a deal," Wang Jun said. They shook hands on it. Only the heavens knew if contracts held any weight with him anyway. "Now let's see what your prisoners have to say."

Chapter 20: Destiny's Strings

The rest of the evening was quite eventful for Wang Jun. The prisoners, he discovered, hadn't been kept in comfort. Their clothes were ragged, and they hadn't bathed in months. He could tell at a glance that their cultivations had been crippled, and their restraints were less to prevent them from escaping and more to prevent them from committing suicide.

They'd had a way out, of course, but that way involved getting their souls consumed by an evil spirit. They'd never taken it, meaning that as desperate as they were, they weren't foolish. Even reincarnating in a lesser realm was preferable to losing your existence.

Once he'd obscured their contracts, they were only too willing to sign a new one. They only had one condition: a painless death. Their cultivations had already been crippled, and the Red Dust Pavilion would never allow their freedom. It was better to simply end their miserable lives and enter the cycle of reincarnation.

The sun had yet to rise as he jumped from shadow to shadow on his return to the Jade Bamboo Headquarters. No one had seen him come or go. As he traveled, he couldn't help but think of the mysterious headmistress. What did she look like under that glamour of hers? Why did she seem so familiar? Fooling his eyes was one thing, but fooling his heart? Very few things could do that. He was half convinced that he knew her, but he dismissed that as wishful thinking. After all, he could count the number of actual friends he had on two hands, and none of them fit her description.

Wang Jun entered his bedroom and walked over to his work desk. He tossed a few black runic coins on the table. Nothing, as always. His divining abilities had greatly deteriorated since his return. Either fate was so muddled it couldn't be predicted, or every one of his targets had found a way to shield themselves from his scrying. That included the headmistress, whose fate he'd just tried to divine.

Since he was unable to sleep, Wang Jun sat at his desk and pored over some documents. Only a few were business documents—Wang Bing and Elder Bai took care of most of it now. These were auditing documents he'd secretly obtained to perform his own inspection. No sense in spooking his target.

He worked for a whole hour, adding finishing touches to three reports he'd worked on for two full years. They included letters recommending corrective actions. Their contents included ironclad proof of gross fraud and misdemeanor, in addition to total incompetence in running these very important business sectors. If the elders ruled in his favor, he could wrest control of these assets from his brother and gain an edge in their feud.

He signed his name and bound the top-secret reports. As he finished, the sun poked its head above the horizon. A courier arrived. The young man picked up the documents reverently before darting out of the office. He passed Wang Bing and Elder Bai on their way into their morning meeting.

"That courier seemed frightened," Elder Bai noted as he walked in. "Was there something important in those bundles?"

"Let's just say he loses his head if he loses them," Wang Jun said. "He's right to be nervous, despite the short distance to the elder council."

"Why not just deliver the documents yourself?" Wang Bing asked.

"If I deliver them, they can't be intercepted," Wang Jun said. "Protector Ren is shadowing him as we speak. The documents will make it to their destination without a hitch, but it wouldn't hurt to catch enemy spies or assassins in the process."

They took their usual seats, with Elder Bai brewing tea. Wang Jun waited for his cup, and after taking a sip, he opened the meeting. "Elder Bai, how are our real-estate holdings?"

"They're doing quite well," Elder Bai said, stroking his beard. "Despite housing prices rising by eighty percent year after year, there are no signs of it slowing. We continue to acquire cheap properties within key cities, though the market has gotten much more... competitive lately."

"Our competition is catching on," Wang Jun said. "Not just within the family."

"It's a hard wave to miss," Elder Bai said. "Large corporations typically exclude these cheaper properties from their portfolios, but the returns are staggering. They're all bitter with regret at having missed the initial surge."

"Then let's fan the flames," Wang Jun said. "I want our men increasing the prices for prime properties by bidding high in upcoming auctions. We should make large offers for personal properties as well. I want these people to sweat. It's all right if we buy overpriced properties in the process—that will give us plausible deniability. We'll make it up when the market shoots up even further."

"Where would you like me to spend the rental revenue we've been generating?" Elder Bai asked.

"It'll soon be time to exit the real-estate market," Wang Jun said. "At least in big cities. Parents want what's best for their children, so they're snapping up properties there like there's no tomorrow. The price is nearing its limit, however, so we need to approach small towns near these cities. No more than a few hours away by magic-grade transport.

"Before we buy up properties, I want you to speak with the city's management. I want us to enter into development agreements wherever we buy. People are migrating from smaller towns to bigger cities, so the mayors in those towns will be looking for a way to make their towns more attractive. In exchange for large swaths of land—no matter if they're inhabited or uninhabited—we'll invest in schools, shops, inns, entertainment, you name it. We'll make the towns beautiful. Then we'll build housing to complement it. People will realize that perhaps it's not so bad to live just outside a big city, especially when the real estate is so much cheaper, and the smaller towns are just as nice if not nicer."

"I'll get right on it," Elder Bai said.

Wang Jun turned to Wang Bing, whose strengths lay outside of real estate. She was the one who'd rolled out the cultivation endowment program two years ago. Now, nearly twenty-five percent of the mortal population had some level of cultivation talent. "How are your businesses doing?"

"I've finally recruited Artificer Bai," Wang Bing said. "With the production assets we've developed, we'll be able to release his urban comfort product lines to every major household in the North within three months."

"Not everyone is a battle maniac," Wang Jun said knowingly. "It's just our society that thinks so."

"Most people just want a comfortable life," Wang Bing said in agreement. "Just the possibility of advancement is enough for them. Moving on, our low-grade blacksmithing, alchemical, and apothecary acquisitions have all reached peak profitability. It can only go down from here, unfortunately."

"The fast cash was what we needed," Wang Jun said. "And what we'll continue to need."

"I recommend against further investment in these sectors," Wang Bing said. "Meanwhile, our most surprising asset is still Nephew Jin's coffee chains. I still can't get over how popular coffee is. His runic alchemy has been very well received as well, so we've been focusing our funds in these two directions. Not only are they our most profitable businesses, we also have no competitors in these markets."

"Do you need help with anything?" Wang Jun asked. "Or should I just sit back and let you do your thing while I brew tea? Or coffee, if you like?" He disapproved of the new beverage, as lucrative as it was.

"I want your permission to get into fashion," Wang Bing said.

Seeing his raised eyebrow, she continued. "You might not be aware, but in most households, men don't call the shots. It's gotten even more skewed now that the most powerful cultivators in many households are, in fact, women."

"Point taken," Wang Jun said. "I trust in your instincts. You have my full support going forward."

"Thank you," she said with a hint of a smile.

Not only had Wang Jun's assets grown quickly, but hers had as well. He was fine with that. If you didn't enrich your followers, they'd abandon you in a heartbeat.

"Then if that's everything, let's call it a day," Wang Jun said.

Wang Bing left, leaving Wang Jun alone to his devices. The day passed by in a blur. Appointment after appointment, stack of paper after stack of paper. Wang Jun resembled less a human and more a custodian. By the time the last letter of the day came, it was sunset. He opened the envelope eagerly but was soon disappointed by what he read.

Auditor General Wang Jun,

We thank you very much for your findings of corruption and incompetence in our family.

Those responsible have been advised to correct their actions and remove those responsible for the breaches. Though it is regrettable that these cases show up, it is inevitable for misdemeanors to worm their way into a large financial organization such as ours.

Your help will no longer be required on these cases. The board has decided to reject your request for reallocation of assets.

Wang Jun breathed deeply. Though he wanted nothing more than to throw a teacup across the room, it wouldn't help his situation. It was unfair, of course; years of work, years of planning had done nothing for him. Though he hadn't expected them to follow through on his request to confiscate assets, he'd expected some sort of reward for meritorious contribution, or a punishment for his opponent. It seemed like the elder council had opted to do nothing. That fact bothered him less than the implication that during the time he'd taken to grow his wealth, the elder council had fallen deeper and deeper into his brother's pocket.

Though these reports had taken two years to write, it wasn't as if he'd spent the entire two years on them. Most of the time, he'd been waiting on more information. He'd used this downtime to feed better information and better opportunities to Wang Bing and Elder Bai for processing. He'd smoothed out their management and supply chains and negotiated on their behalf. That was why, after only two years, they now possessed an astounding half a million top-grade spirit stones in net assets.

Still, what did it all matter? The game was rigged against him. He wagered that his brother would succeed even if he accumulated enough wealth to physically smother the entire Wang family manor. He'd known from the start that it would be difficult, but he'd severely underestimated his opponent.

I can only go in for the kill, Wang Jun thought. These petty squabbles on the side would only result in slaps on the wrist. He needed something big, something irrefutable. Something that, if leaked, would ruin the family. And the contents of his black folio, the document that never left his storage ring, was just the thing. The Red Dust Pavilion's offer happened to coincide with his objectives. It was a godsend that made him reevaluate his own past karma. Had he been virtuous in a previous life after all? No, he decided. If he had been, Wang Hua wouldn't have died.

Disappointed, he casually picked up the black coins on his desk. He tossed them several times but to no avail. The Red Dust Pavilion. The Spirit Temple. His brother. Everything worth divining couldn't be divined in the slightest. It was as though everything he touched no longer fell within the bounds of predictability.

Hours passed as the sky darkened. Finally, Wang Jun got up, brushed himself off, and prepared to see his master. His door creaked shut as it locked with a click, his runic wardings activating as it did. He walked past vacant office desks and desks where people were still quietly working. They didn't have to, of course; working from home was allowed. But some people just couldn't concentrate with their family around, so working at the office was their only option.

Wang Jun entered the large circular hallway in the main family dwelling and made his way toward the dark corridor no one else knew existed. No one save the Patriarch, of course. Just as he was about to enter, he heard a soft voice.

"You never come visit," a man said from behind him.

Wang Jun looked back at the man, who coughed lightly due to his poor health. The man was his father, and Wang Jun had visited him a total of four times since his sister's death.

"I saw no need to visit," Wang Jun replied. "Ling is clearly the only family you recognize." His father was the current Patriarch's brother. Wang Ling and Wang Jun were competing for the family leadership because the Patriarch's wife had died young, and he'd refused to remarry. They'd never borne any children, and the Patriarch preferred to commit himself to running the family.

"There are things that are beyond me," his father said.

"You're the chairman of the family," Wang Jun said blankly. "You can do pretty well anything you like." He got the implication, of course. His father's hands were tied because of the family patriarch. Or quite possibly the grand elder.

His father sighed. "You need to stop competing for the family leadership. You won't succeed, and you never could. It's something no one else wants to tell you, because they fear you. But as a father, I need to say it."

"This is why I don't visit you," Wang Jun said. "You always favored Ling over Hua and me. When Hua died, you swept her death under a rug and erased all traces of her. But I remember. I remember who she was to us. I remember who she was to me. When she died, you hid all the evidence. For a much. Lesser. Man."

A pained expression appeared on his father's face. "I just don't want to lose you too," he said softly. "I've already lost one child, and I don't want to lose another." He broke into a coughing fit and kneeled to recover.

Wang Jun didn't budge to help him. He did, however, wait patiently as the coughing receded.

"Fine, I won't waste my breath. Just be careful. I love you both, so I won't pick sides. But I will tell you this: He doesn't play fair. The game is rigged, and you can't win with their rules. If you continue down the path you've chosen, you'll fail. And judging by your stubborn personality, you'll do something desperate, and losing one or two more children will be the least of my worries."

"Are you done?" Wang Jun asked. His eyes flickered to the darkness.

"I'm done," his father said, nodding. He turned around and walked toward his chambers. When he was finally out of sight, Wang Jun sighed and entered the dark corridor. The usual twist of white and black followed, and soon he was face-to-face with Daoist Obscurus.

"You don't come visit me very often," Daoist Obscurus said, sending a platter Wang Jun's way. "Here, try these."

There was a bunch of grapes on the platter, but unlike their vivid-colored cousins, these radiated pure darkness. Wang Jun frowned but picked one up. He popped it in his mouth, chewed, and swallowed. It was the most dissatisfying fruit he'd ever eaten. It almost seemed like the fruit was eating him instead.

"What a strange fruit," Wang Jun said.

"It's strange indeed," Daoist Obscurus said. "It grows on a vine, and the vine devours everything around it. Living or dead, everything will disappear. Finally, after eating away at reality for long enough, it bears these dark fruits. They can grow extra vines, and any living being who swallows them will die."

Seeing Wang Jun's eyes widen, he broke into a toothy grin. "Except you and I, of course. We're different. Our innate darkness constitutions render us immune to it. By eating these fruits, we can gain inspiration on the essence of darkness and obscurity."

Wang Jun seated himself and served tea for two. After they drank several cups, he finally spoke. "Master, I have questions about fate."

"Ask away," Daoist Obscurus said.

"My divinations don't work anymore," Wang Jun said. "I can't divine anything important. Divining the mundane still works, but only in cases where it doesn't affect me."

Daoist Obscurus seemed unsurprised. "It's our nature, disciple. Our constitutions obscure the tapestry of fate. It all starts with us, but eventually everything around us darkens. You're at a point where you can't divine anything related to yourself. On the bright side, no one else can either."

"Isn't this a useless ability, then?" Wang Jun asked. "The greatest advantage I had growing up was evading others while divining their intentions. It was only through these powers that I was able to survive."

"How is it useless?" Daoist Obscurus asked, leaning forward. "I said your fate is obscured. That means it's hidden, even from the heavens themselves. Your fate is mutable, and every action becomes even more meaningful. That means that whatever fate you'd been shackled with at birth is no more. Isn't that ideal?"

Wang Jun pondered that for a moment. He'd never thought of it that way. And the more he thought about it, the more it sounded like he wanted to have his cake and eat it too.

Everything about what I do is hidden, he thought. Instead of trying to manipulate others' karma, shouldn't he take advantage of this? He was like a hidden player in other people's games.

"I see you've finally realized it," Daoist Obscurus said. "I'm glad. I'm just saddened that you've ignored my warnings, as well as your father's warnings. You're not bound by the rules, but you still want to play by them."

"I have to try," Wang Jun said, closing his eyes. "It's the last thread of hope I'm holding on to."

Daoist Obscurus's eyes glittered. "Then go. I've done all I can for now. Come back when you're willing to think outside your carefully crafted box. Nothing I tell you will matter until then." The man waved his hand. Before Wang Jun knew it, he was outside in the dark corridor.

Wang Jun sighed deeply and headed back to his room. He

looked at his desk where several investigations were pending and tossed them into the garbage. These weren't substantial, so there was no point wasting time on them. Instead, he began to formulate other plans. There were very profitable business activities not amenable to committing daylight hours to think about. To most people, they were high-risk activities. But Daoist Obscurus's words and his clandestine activities at the Red Dust Pavilion had made him realize there was an entire market he hadn't yet tapped: the black market.

Officially, he would play by the rules. And while he wasn't willing to fully commit to the darker side of things, dabbling wouldn't hurt, would it?

Chapter 21: Bounce

Cha Ming looked around half-heartedly as he sat beside a small fire. Not far away, Ling Dong was busy carving a piece of bone. Through his Demon-Subduing Eyes, Cha Ming could see demonic energies accumulating where he worked. It sat there like a gentle pet, waiting for its master to pay attention.

His disciple carved away, and when the last of the markings were finished, the violet mist rushed into the completed weapon. It was a dagger, a peak-magic-grade one.

Having forged the dagger, Ling Dong walked away from his natural forge looking rather pleased with himself. He twirled the dagger around and tossed it over to his master, who grasped the weapon with ease. Despite being made of bone, a soft material, the dagger was sharp. So sharp, in fact, that it managed to cut his finger with only the slightest application of pressure.

"Why a peak-magic-grade weapon?" Cha Ming asked, handing the dagger back to Ling Dong. He'd noticed a large variance in the man's products, despite him having mastered the runic arts and sigils from Fuxi's Library. He was an early formation grandmaster. Surely he could do better.

The larger man shrugged. "Why should I?" Cha Ming wasn't sure how to answer that. Spotting his confusion, Ling Dong continued.

"You think I should have made a better weapon. A stronger weapon. I could have, you know."

Cha Ming shook his head. "Who am I to judge what you've made and why you made it? I reached for the heavens, for all the good it did me. I spent everything I had to make something I couldn't even keep."

Ling Dong said nothing. Instead, he fished around for a piece of metal. It was a chunk of black steel with a slight greenish hue. Then he looked around for something else. He eventually found a piece of dark brown, almost black wood. "You've read everything in my personal library, right?"

"I have," Cha Ming said. He'd been bored, and reading had helped fill a void he hadn't known existed. "Lifegiver steel coupled with ghostwood. With that amount of material, you could make an axe. Or a hammer. Given the quality of the material, you could make an initial-core-grade weapon."

"Theoretically, yes," Ling Dong said. "But I'm not going to make an axe. Or a hammer. You didn't hear it, but these materials spoke to me just now. They asked me to make something completely new and different."

"And what might that be?" Cha Ming asked.

"I'll show you," Ling Dong said. Instead of going to his forge, the large man took out a thin soul-alloy knife. He held the ghostwood over a small fire he summoned. The wood softened but didn't burn.

After the wood reached a certain temperature, Ling Dong retrieved it. The piece was cylindrical, but instead of shaping it for a haft, he sliced it into irregular shapes. Small wooden medallions fell onto the ground between them, and to Cha Ming's surprise, tiny violet lines wriggled around on their wooden surfaces. They looked familiar. He soon realized what they were: natural runes.

"Ghostwood isn't usually used like this," Ling Dong said, shrugging. "It seems like this branch was cut off and kept near a source of natural water energy. It laid there, forgotten, until someone who wasn't sure what to do with it found it and brought it to me. I took it as payment for a peak-magic weapon. A steal of a deal in my opinion."

"If it was normal, it would have been a fair exchange," Cha Ming said.

"But no one could see its true nature," Ling Dong said. "I couldn't either, but I had a feeling it was a worthwhile trade." He picked up one of the pieces and poured demonic energy into his soul-alloy knife. Then he cut into the medallion and added a few choice lines. According to normal runic rules, it was nonsense. But Cha Ming couldn't help but feel there was a method to his madness.

As Cha Ming was busy staring at the single medallion, Ling Dong continued working on the other pieces. He did much of the same, but each time, the lines were different. Finally, he took the bar of lifegiver steel and used his natural qi to heat it. It was a very malleable metal that was only useful in weapons because of its self-restorative abilities. No matter how much it broke, the pieces would always find themselves and return to their original quenched form.

Ling Dong didn't form a blade. Instead he tore off small pieces and forged links. He also tore off strips that wrapped around the wooden medallions. They began joining and linking together, and before Cha Ming knew it, he realized they were surrounded in violet mist. This cloud was much thicker than the one the dagger had attracted. In fact, it was bigger than the hundred others he'd seen before.

Under the larger man's wild guidance, metal and wood interlinked. They came together and formed a sort of puzzle. When the last of the links came together, Ling Dong summoned a torrent of normal seawater. It was the crudest of quenching mediums, and even mortal blacksmiths would scorn it. But Cha Ming knew there must be a reason for using it. As wild as his creations often were, Ling Dong always knew what he was doing.

The metal cooled, and the violet mist rushed in. Like all demonic treasures he'd crafted, the ambient natural energy imbued his new creation with special properties. It let out a hum, and to Cha Ming's surprise, it was a late-grade core weapon, two ranks higher than the man's demonic blacksmith rank.

"This, Teacher, is why I made the dagger a top-grade weapon," Ling Dong said. He passed the puzzle over to Cha Ming. "I made this for you. I'm not sure what it is, but I'm sure it's what you need."

Cha Ming accepted the puzzle but remained confused. Ling Dong continued speaking as he looked over each of the treasure's rune-covered medallions.

"The way of a demonic smith isn't to create artificially powerful weapons, but rather to unearth natural potential," Ling Dong said. "These two materials were made for each other, which is why they joined so perfectly. The result is something several levels above what I'm normally capable of. I could never repeat the process. Seven hells, I don't even know how I made it. The material guided me. It showed me what it wanted to be, just like the dagger did. I'm not a craftsman, Master—I'm a medium. Some things should be made simple instead of strong, end of story. Normal people may not understand, but I do."

Ling Dong returned to the forge, crafting one masterpiece after another. Cha Ming simply sat there, entranced at the assortment of links, chains, and wooden medallions. Despite his transcendent soul, the runic lines were confusing. They made him question why they were there in the first place, but when he thought about it, he realized that it didn't matter. The simple complexity of it was marvelous to behold.

If crafting a weapon was discovering the truth of the materials, did such a truth apply to other things? He pondered this question in silence, and days passed by as he did. Customers came to visit Ling Dong, and he would often craft them exactly what they asked for. Other times, however, he would take their order and make something completely different. They would argue with him, but in the end, he always convinced them he'd crafted them what they needed. He was right every time.

Every material has an ideal shape, and every person has a weapon that suits them, Cha Ming thought, looking at the wooden medallions in a daze. *Then what about actions? Weapons shouldn't change a person but enhance them. Actions shouldn't change a person but enhance them. A person shouldn't force a path but uncover the path that leads to where they need to be.*

It was a simple but powerful truth that made him realize how pitiful he looked. He'd given up and was simply wallowing in self-pity. His disciple had allowed him to stay, so he did. He felt more at ease with Ling Dong's easygoing personality, as well as the fact that the younger man never made any demands of him. He always seemed to know what to do, and why.

I might still find Water Source Marrow and Gold Source Marrow, Cha Ming thought. *But that doesn't mean I should just drop everything else. I'm a craftsman, a creator. Perhaps by making things, I'll find a turning point or opportunity.* Having made this decision, he felt his affinity for the water around him grow.

"Thank you," Cha Ming whispered. He thought about leaving the chain-link puzzle but ultimately decided to keep it. It was a precious gift, and he guessed its properties were mental rather than physical. Examining it had been very beneficial to his state of mind, like a rebirth of sorts. It wouldn't hurt to keep it a while longer.

When Cha Ming returned, he wasn't in the mood to craft pills like he had in the past. Therefore, he turned his attention to the Clear Sky Brush and used it for its intended purpose: painting. But instead of painting talismans, he decided to paint pictures. His creations were mediocre at best, but his endurance made it so he could paint nonstop.

A month passed by, and during this month, he painted the major moments of his life. His near-death experience near Greatwood Bridge, then fighting the lightning tribulation. His paintings changed when he washed up from the river. Like Jun Xiezi's painting, *Samsara,* they were filled with the essence of duality and contradiction. Flowing and resisting, hardening and crumbling, sharpening and dulling, kindling and dousing. Though he didn't know much about living and dying, he gave it a shot anyway. These were crude paintings without much feeling, but by creating them, he felt like the mysteries of wood were shedding a thin skin, allowing him to grasp them even further.

Cha Ming heard soft footsteps behind him as he added the finishing touches to a rendition of Yu Wen. He could never do her justice every time he painted her, but he poured his heart and soul into it regardless.

"You must love her very dearly," a voice said from behind him. He recognized the voice as Gong Shuren, the Sea God crown princess.

"More than you can imagine," Cha Ming said, touching up Yu Wen's hair. Her surroundings were fiery and serene, his own interpretation of the volcano. "When you love someone, it's difficult to stop thinking about them even for a day."

Gong Shuren took a seat at one of the stone tables in the courtyard. Her long flowing white hair and the blue runes covering her pale skin caused her to stand out in the small space where he'd been painting. "Where is she now?"

"In another life, another world," Cha Ming whispered, touching up her eyes. Those bright, caring eyes he could get lost in for hours. "She died."

"I'm sorry," Gong Shuren said. "I shouldn't have pried."

Cha Ming sighed. He added a few other strokes and finished his creation. Then, he summoned his Grandmist flames and burned it. Even the Space-Time Camera in his possession couldn't do her justice, and a poor imitation didn't deserve to stay in this world.

"What can I do for you, Crown Princess?" Cha Ming asked.

"You can start by calling me Sister Shuren," the princess said. "You're my savior, and even Royal Father calls you Nephew Cha Ming."

"As you wish, Sister Shuren," Cha Ming said. He took a seat at the table where she was. "We last met on the Heaven Ascension Platform. My apologies for the embarrassing display."

Gong Shuren chuckled. "No other alchemist on this plane, save transcendents, of course, are capable of summoning a tribulation through their arts. To do so and fight until the end of the fire tribulation was impressive. Alas, some things are not permitted inside the Ling Nan Plane. Even gods and immortals can't change that." She cleared her throat. "I came here to ask a favor."

"I'm not sure what sort of favor I can do for Sister Shuren, but I'll try my utmost to help," Cha Ming said. "Do you require a pill or talisman? Perhaps a formation?"

"I require a teacher," Gong Shuren said.

Cha Ming raised an eyebrow.

"I wish to learn runic arts from you, time permitting."

"I was under the impression that the royal court employed two formation artists and one talisman artist at the elder level," Cha Ming said. "Perhaps they might be better equipped to help someone of your station and lineage."

"There are no better runic art teachers than you in Haijing City," Gong Shuren said. "Your students are proof of that. Two of them have even reached the elder level since your arrival."

"My direct disciples weren't so successful in comparison," Cha Ming said.

"Only because their cultivation is limited," Gong Shuren said. "Please don't refuse me. I can ensure you'd be adequately compensated. Besides, I have elder-level teachers, but none of them are *grand* elders."

Cha Ming chuckled and flicked the violet-gold medallion on his robes. It was his formation master medallion, the one the Formation Master Guild had bestowed on him at the Emperor's instruction. "It's not about money, Sister Shuren. I just want to be left alone. I suffered a great setback when I crafted that pill. I need to reorganize my thoughts and reassert my motivations. Then I'll pursue a different path to transcendence."

Gong Shuren looked him up and down. Her clear blue eyes peered into his, and he looked back into hers. He saw purity but not innocence. He saw calm, but there was also panic hidden deep within. He wasn't sure how he knew these things; he simply did.

"Your situation isn't as rosy as it seems," Cha Ming said. "Despite being the crown princess."

Gong Shuren nodded. "Crown Princess is just the title borne by the most promising child. It gave me the best resources and the best grooming. But that alone is insufficient to claim the throne when my father transcends. And make no mistake, he *will* transcend. Without fail, every Sea God Emperor or Empress has transcended after ruling for one thousand years."

Cha Ming whistled. "I didn't realize your lifespans were so long."

"It's the benefit of descending from a god," Gong Shuren said. "The Sea God has blessed our family in perpetuity, and his gifts have granted us unshakable power on this plane."

"Thus, Haijing's neutrality," Cha Ming said. "There's no need to involve yourselves in the petty squabbles of good and evil. While children die and mothers weep, you can remain comfortable in your underwater paradise."

Gong Shuren's expression darkened. "That was uncalled for. We have our reasons for remaining neutral. Besides, the plane's karmic destiny is anchored by the World Tree. There's no need for us to interfere. Eventually, good will prevail."

"Anchored by the World Tree?" Cha Ming asked.

"It's not something you should worry about," Gong Shuren said. "The angelic transcendents who watch over the plane know about it. You'll find out more if you join their ranks."

Cha Ming pondered for a moment. "Back to inheriting the throne, then. Are runic arts involved somehow?"

Gong Shuren nodded. "There's an event every thousand years called the Sea God Trials. One of the tests is a test of runic knowledge. It's not that I'm ungifted in runic arts, but that my brother is far too talented. That, and he's older and has more experience."

"Then why shouldn't your brother inherit the throne?" Cha Ming asked.

"Yes, why shouldn't the man who's so friendly with Zhou Li, envoy of the Southern Alliance, inherit the throne?" Gong Shuren said sarcastically.

"I thought Haijing was neutral," Cha Ming said.

"That's something the Emperor enforces," Gong Shuren said.

"You have a point," Cha Ming said. "Well, if it's something Zhou Li wants, it's my obligation to prevent him from getting it."

Gong Shuren beamed. "Then you'll teach me?"

"Starting this week." Cha Ming nodded. "Who knows? Perhaps teaching runic arts once more will give me the change of pace I need." He looked to the south as he heard soft footsteps running toward them. Jin Huang appeared inside the courtyard, covered in sweat and soot and panting deeply.

Jin Huang stood catching his breath for a bit. "I didn't interrupt anything, did I, Master?"

"No, the princess was just leaving," Cha Ming said. He turned back to her. "Let's start in a week, Sister Shuren."

"I'm looking forward to learning," Gong Shuren said. She bowed lightly and excused herself. Jin Huang looked a little guilty as the woman left.

"Relax," Cha Ming said, putting his hand on Jin Huang's shoulder and using his soul force and qi to help him recover. How in the heavens did an early-core-formation cultivator manage to exhaust himself so thoroughly?

"Master, I was on the cusp of a discovery," Jin Huang said. "Unfortunately, it seems my cultivation can't keep up with my profession. I need help, or it'll take another half month to figure this out. It's unbearable."

"All right, all right, relax," Cha Ming said. "I'll do what I can. Do we need a workshop?" This was the first time Jin Huang had ever come asking him for anything, so he didn't want to disappoint. Seeing the younger man's nod, Cha Ming took him to the alchemical lab he sometimes used. He activated the various flame focuses and summoned his transcendent cauldron.

"Tell me, what's the problem?" Cha Ming asked. He assumed the problem was alchemy related, as that was what his disciple spent virtually all his time on. That and poisons, but he couldn't possibly help in that regard.

"Follow my resplendent force," Jin Huang said. Their spirits entered the cauldron together, and as expected, Jin Huang threw in a massive number of ingredients.

Cha Ming was amazed the man could manage so many ingredients and five separate flames despite his limited resplendent force. *It looks like an early-grade effervescence pill,* he thought. *Ideal for boosting resplendent-force growth in core-formation cultivators. Ceases to be effective past early-grade resplendent soul, though, so it's likely not for himself.* His train of thought was interrupted when the familiar recipe suddenly deviated. He moved in to help, as he thought it was a mistake, but his attempt was quickly rebuffed by his disciple.

You're not familiar with my research, so please keep your soul to yourself until I ask for help, Jin Huang said bluntly.

Unsure of what to say, Cha Ming remained silent. He knew obsession when he saw it. Puddles of melted reagents wriggled under his watch, and before he knew it, they formed runes. Jin Huang wasn't performing normal alchemy; this was runic alchemy.

Cha Ming watched in awe and wonder as the runes joined together like tightly knit puzzles, reacting in ways moderated by the shape and nature of the runes. Some runes drank reagent puddles, while others combined and formed others. It was a shifting mosaic of runic structures unlike anything he'd ever seen.

Everything was joining perfectly, and then he saw it: a strain. Something wasn't linking together properly, and he felt a dissonance in the reagents and the runes.

Do you see the problem? Jin Huang asked. *Every step prior to this is perfect, and my intuition tells me this is the right rune, but it won't come together. It's unstable.*

Yes, it's unstable, Cha Ming said as he inspected the rune. He didn't know much about runic alchemy, but he knew a lot about runic arts and alchemy as separate subjects. The rune before him seemed slightly unnatural, like there was too much packed in too small a character. *May I?*

Jin Huang's soul force allowed him through. Perplexed, Cha Ming prodded at the rune with his transcendent force, looking for where the flaw might lay. *There,* he thought, using his transcendent force to expand a section of the sigil. *Here as well,* he thought. He moved to several dozen locations on the alchemical sigil, and with every modification he made to the character, some of the pressure was released. It was a strange process, as he'd never dealt with alchemical runes before. However, based on his knowledge, it felt right. The reagents were in harmony, and the rune conformed to them.

Time passed, and as it did, the reaction continued. Several runic components dissolved and merged into the greater one. With the initial deficiencies resolved, the runic structure evolved as it reacted, until finally, it became one final rune.

Jin Huang increased the temperature and melted it into a small blob. Then, after shock-hardening it, he melted the outer layer and began inscribing runes with the golden power that rushed into the pill from their surroundings. The runic exterior was branded with the character "Mystic," Jin Huang's mark.

Their senses exited the cauldron as the pill popped out. Jin Huang caught their joint creation in a small bottle.

"Success!" Jin Huang said, a giddy smile on his face.

"An interesting pill," Cha Ming said. "How will this differ from a normal effervescence pill?"

"It should be about one grade more powerful compared to a normal effervescence pill," Jin Huang said, still grinning. "In other words, it can still reinforce my soul despite being at a lower grade than necessary."

Cha Ming's brain short-circuited. "Say that again?"

Jin Huang looked at him strangely. "Don't you know why I was so unpopular in Evergreen City?"

Cha Ming shook his head. "I assumed it was the poison master thing."

"No, being a poison master was how I managed to *stay,*" Jin Huang said. "The reason they didn't like me was because, through my runic alchemy, I could create more powerful pills with the same reagents. Their actual grade didn't change. This caused normal pills to devalue because I'd tarnished the reputation of normal alchemists.

"Virtually any pill can be made a step stronger if the proper runic formula is incorporated while crafting it. The thing is, it's difficult, and I refused to teach anyone. Even now, I've only been teaching select people, including some from Gold Leaf City who report directly to Uncle Wang Jun."

Cha Ming's mind wandered chaotically. He wasn't sure why, but he suddenly couldn't focus. "I'm very interested in this runic alchemy of yours. Would you mind if we studied it together?" It was a big ask, especially since he should be the one doing the teaching.

"Would you?" Jin Huang said excitedly. He tossed out dozens of storage jades onto the desk. "Quick, take these and learn as quickly as possible. There's no time to waste!"

"What do you mean, no time to waste?" Cha Ming asked.

"It's just been me, trailblazing all alone," Jin Huang said. "Research is exhausting, so I've been delaying my cultivation just to develop the profession. But with you sharing the burden, I'll be able to advance by leaps and bounds!"

"Oh." Cha Ming had never thought about it that way. If he could save his disciple time while simultaneously merging runic arts and alchemy, it would be time well spent. Besides, he'd finally have a good reason for the young man to call him master if he worked fast enough. He felt he'd already lost enough face by teaching him nothing. He swept up the jades and nodded. "I'll get right on it. You can count me in."

"Great!" Jin Huang said.

"How far have you developed the art?" Cha Ming asked.

"I have a full system to early core formation," Jin Huang said casually.

Cha Ming almost coughed up blood.

"Yes, I know it's disappointing. You and teacher Mo probably only spent a few days developing the first few mortal grades, and here I am developing the rest of it so slowly. I'm truly ashamed. Master, are you all right?"

Cha Ming was not all right. In fact, he felt like killing himself on the spot. Despite all the blood, sweat, and tears he and Mo Tianshen, a grandmaster alchemist, had poured into the art, they'd only managed to raise the concept of runic alchemy to the middle mortal grades over the course of a year. They'd thought that was pretty good too. Now, however, his disciple had developed the profession to grandmaster level in only a few years! If Mo Tianshen knew, the older man might just die of shock.

"I'm fine, I'm fine," Cha Ming lied. "This day has just been too exhausting. Go on ahead without me, and I'll come see you soon."

"I'm looking forward to it, Master," Jin Huang said, giving him a thumbs-up. When the young man left, Cha Ming collapsed in a chair. Sun Wukong appeared out of the brush, cackling madly.

"It's truly a story of the young outdoing the old," Sun Wukong said.

"I'm not old," Cha Ming said with his face in his hands. "Just overwhelmed. Tell me, where did I go wrong? When did I err?"

Sun Wukong laughed. "You didn't. Some people are just talented in certain areas. Given that alchemy concerns your two weakest elements, wood and fire, it's not surprising at all that you're so bad at it." He looked pensive. "Still, you *do* have the Myriad Truths Diagram, a transcendent soul, and peak skills in two runic arts and alchemy. If you can't succeed, I don't think anyone else can. Except that little freak, that is. Now tell me, what's got you so flustered?"

Cha Ming's eyes, which had been dull and uncaring earlier that day, were now burning with excitement. "Tell me, Teacher: if it's possible for us to make a pill more potent by making the ingredients conform to their runic nature, could the opposite be true? Would it be possible to craft a lower-tier pill with the same effects as a higher-tier one through reverse-engineering?"

Sun Wukong thought about it for a while before nodding slowly. "In theory, it's possible. Though be warned that some ingredients are transcendent grade. We won't be able to use those."

"Then we'll need to find substitutes," Cha Ming said. "If this plane won't accept a transcendent Nirvana Pill, then we'll need to modify it. Instead of a transcendent pill, I'll settle for a half-step transcendent one with the same effects." It was a bold plan, he admitted, but one he couldn't let slip through his fingers.

Without a second thought, he painted a portal and entered the Clear Sky World. He had a plan, but this plan required a lot of study, thinking, and trial and error. What he needed now was the scarcest resource: time.

Chapter 22: The Scarcest Resource

One week later, as promised, he began teaching Gong Shuren. She was a middle-grandmaster talisman and formation artist, which gave Cha Ming something to work with. Many core-formation cultivators would struggle for hundreds of years to reach such heights, so the young woman's progress was impressive. Still, she advanced by leaps and bounds under his instruction.

Following their half-day session, he busied himself studying runic alchemy. He didn't have to reinvent the wheel, since Jin Huang had properly documented everything. The basics took one week to memorize, after which he confirmed everything using his own experiments for the next three weeks. In total, it took him eighteen time-accelerated weeks to catch up. After making his own corrections to their shared knowledge base, he dove straight into forging his own path.

He followed the same routine every week: one half day he spent with Gong Shuren, and another with Jin Huang. He spent the rest of his time in the Clear Sky World. One month later, he and Jin Huang completed the framework for mid-grade grandmaster runic alchemy. Their progress slowed afterward. It took them a full year to build a high-grade framework. Gong Shuren also advanced one grade in her formation arts and talisman arts.

Time was a river. Time was water. He followed the stream where it took him, and soon a full two and a half years had passed since his failure. He finished runic alchemy's peak grandmaster framework in that time, meaning that he could finally focus on the most important part—reworking the Nirvana Pill recipe.

Cha Ming coughed up blood as he recovered from a powerful blast from his transcendent pill cauldron. Not in a metaphorical sense either, as damage to one's lungs was harsh that way. Tweaking the Nirvana Pill was a dangerous process, he'd discovered. His clothes were tattered, and his bones showed, but he recovered in only a second. He held the remnants of a runic component in his hand. "If this one was wrong, the other must be correct."

"Try it, but don't be too stubborn," Sun Wukong said. "You almost died the time before last, and I'd hate to be stuck here all alone. Even *with* the pleasant company of rainbow fish and dryads. Besides, the smell in here when you get smashed to a bloody pulp is *unbearable.*"

"Can you even smell anything in your spirit form?" Cha Ming grumbled. He did some brief calculations in his mind and got back to work. His transcendent soul reentered the transcendent-grade cauldron and summoned dozens of ingredients. At lower grades, runic alchemy was all about creating runes out of reagents. At higher grades, it was about crafting elaborate three-dimensional formations.

His surroundings lit up with gray flames, and each region heated, sliced, separated, broke, and grew as he willed it. Simultaneously, the reagents were reduced to liquids, their various impurities removed at the requisite temperatures. They formed runic circles instead of formations. Then Cha Ming joined the runic circles with lines of elemental essence, creating the complicated web of a grand formation.

Reactions occurred within the web, which he supervised and interfered with as required. Runic alchemy was less hands-on than normal alchemy, with most of the work being done in the beginning by setting up the problem. In a sense, it was like a giant mathematical puzzle; once the right equations, assumptions, and laws were in place, the problem solved itself.

The runes morphed together, and the web collapsed little by little. It shrank and shrank until finally, only a single sigil remained. The sigil was hard and stable, one of the four key reagents he needed to form the final pill. While it was much weaker than the original he'd created, it was exactly what he needed. At most, it would be capable of supporting a half-step transcendent pill, just skirting the limits set by the plane.

He stored the sigil in a jade vial right next to another two vials. One of them contained a sigil made of peak-core-grade bone relic. Now that he was able to melt and remold the bone relic, the resulting one was a tenth of the original size. Which was fortunate, given that he'd failed seven times in creating it. The bone sigil was the second piece of the four-piece puzzle.

Right beside it was a disappointingly small sigil which Sun Wukong insisted was as much as the pill could handle. It was tiny, the size of Cha Ming's thumb. The sigil contained the concentrated power of rainbow-fish scales. The iridescent sigil shimmered through the jade vial, distorting the air around it. It was a catalyst, something that sped up reactions. He now knew it contained the essence of time, something a mortal plane could only accommodate so much of. If it contained any more, the pill would break through the shackles of half-transcendence and become a transcendent pill. All he was missing now was Waters of Life.

"Let's go pay the lady a visit," Cha Ming said. He changed his robes, opting for something a little more ceremonial, with violet, blue, and gold runes covering the otherwise gray cloth. He liked gray now. It was plain, simple, and all-encompassing. After dressing, he walked out of Haijing Academy, receiving quite a few courteous nods in the process. He was, after all, the only grand elder in the academy. His runic alchemy had also done loads to bolster his reputation, not to mention his failed but rather impressive attempt at pill concoction on the Heaven Ascension Platform. The city had not been affected by the tribulation, but they'd felt the aftershock of his confrontation with the plane's will.

Cha Ming arrived at the palace moments later. The guards, now familiar with his identity, allowed him through and directed him to the princess's palace. He waited in a lovely study filled with marvelous paintings before she finally appeared. Seeing Cha Ming's attire, she raised an eyebrow. "I wasn't aware we were going somewhere."

Cha Ming smiled. "I have a favor to ask, and I hope you won't reject me."

She smiled back. "You've been teaching me for three years and have yet to ask for anything in return. I was wondering when you'd ask."

"Unfortunately, it's not you that I need a favor from, but your father," Cha Ming said. "I need Waters of Life, and for that, I can only ask the Sea God Emperor. As for the favor, all I ask is that you get me an audience. I'll negotiate something with your father myself."

Gong Shuren winced. "I can't say I'm too surprised by your request. Unfortunately, the surplus in our stock was exhausted, along with three spatial fragments, to create this potential gathering necklace I wear." She brought her fingers to her neck where a gold necklace inlaid with a single gray gem lay. An iridescent mist floated inside it.

"The Sea God royal family is the only supplier of Waters of Life on the continent," Cha Ming said helplessly. "You and your royal father are the only members I'm on good terms with. On the bright side, I only need a third as much as before. Three jin to complete my creation."

Gong Shuren's eyes narrowed. "You're not going to try making *that* again, are you?"

"Nothing like that," Cha Ming said, holding up his hands. "My creation is something more modest. A half-step transcendent creation. The plane shouldn't react so strongly this time."

Gong Shuren let out a sigh of relief. "Thank the heavens. My royal father would never admit it, but even *he* was frightened by the commotion you caused. Though if you can manage to craft a half-step transcendent pill, I'm sure he'd be very impressed. It's been a long time since Haijing Academy had a grand elder in alchemy."

"I keep hearing about that title," Cha Ming said. He was a grand elder already. "Is it that big of a deal?"

"It is," Gong Shuren said. "Haijing Academy operates by the grace of the Sea God Emperor, and its headmaster is appointed by the holder of the Sea God Scales. Historically, grand elders would be the first ones considered for the appointment. It's not a guaranteed appointment, but grand elders are held in high esteem by their peers. I'm sure you've noticed the respectful glances from everyone else at the academy."

Cha Ming shrugged. "I'm more concerned with crafting this pill. For that, I need Waters of Life."

"All right," Gong Shuren said with a sigh. "I'll ask my father. Elder alchemists appear every generation or so, but grand elders would be very useful to the royal family."

They walked from her audience hall through gold-and-blue corridors. The wavy pattern was mesmerizing. It caused odd fluctuations in the air that reminded Cha Ming of Huxian's temporal abilities. He waited outside the door as she entered the king's audience hall through a side door. He followed at her signal.

Cha Ming walked toward the throne with his gaze downward. When he neared the throne, he bent down in a low bow. To his surprise, his bow was cut short by a firm hand. He looked up and saw the Emperor standing before him, stopping him.

"You saved my daughter and have helped her for many years. You don't need to bow to me, not when we're alone."

Cha Ming looked around and noticed they were indeed alone. The princess was there, but the Empress was absent. Cha Ming also noticed the absence of the royal "our" the Emperor liked to use.

"Your Highness has my utmost gratitude for meeting me," Cha Ming said. "I'm sure you're already aware of my request."

The Emperor nodded slowly. He walked back to his throne and sat on the large chair. He tapped his fingers, looking between him and his daughter thoughtfully. "I have some Waters of Life remaining in my personal stock. Hidden from the treasury, of course, so my family is unaware of its existence. But it's difficult for me to give it out on a whim. As an emperor, I must always look out for the good of my people."

"If there's anything I can do to change your mind, anything at all, just say the word," Cha Ming said. He wasn't sure what he could offer that could move the monarch, but he had to try, at least.

"There's one thing you can do," the Emperor said. "As you might already know, the Sea God Trials will be taking place a short time from now. Originally, I was planning on sending my most powerful subordinate, Gong Fa, to accompany my daughter as her champion. Given his power, she would normally have a huge edge in the competition. That is, she would have if her third brother had chosen the second strongest, as is custom."

Cha Ming's eyes narrowed. "He picked Zhou Li, didn't he?"

"He picked Zhou Li," the Emperor confirmed. "As such, I'm concerned about the result of the competition. Now, don't get me wrong, I wouldn't be so concerned about the success of one specific child over another under normal circumstances. I teach neutrality and balance, so I'm only willing to go so far.

"Unfortunately, these teachings have fallen on deaf ears with my third child, Gong Xuandi. He's been too friendly with Zhou Li, and I'm concerned about what will happen should he become emperor. There's a war brewing on the continent, and we must *not* get dragged into it. It's not impossible for me to give you three jin of Waters of Life. However, I ask in return that you participate in the trials as Gong Shuren's champion."

"What do the trials entail?" Cha Ming asked.

The Emperor waved his hand, and a model of the palace and the Sea God Clock Tower appeared. Cha Ming noticed that the palace only took up a small portion of the clock tower. Between the palace and the Heaven Ascension Platform, three massive floors consisting of dozens of hallways wound down the tower.

"This is the Sea God Clock Tower. Above the palace is an area that only gets used every thousand years. It is a separate dimension used for the selection of each ruler via a competition. This competition is called the Sea God Trials.

"The tests are there to assess each candidate's capabilities. The first is the Trial of Adventure, where the competitors must fight a sea of illusory demons. Its purpose is to assess the candidates' strength. The second trial is the Trial of Puzzles, meant to assess the candidates' intelligence. That is why Shuren requested that you teach her runic arts. She is deficient in this regard. Finally, those who make it through can compete in the Trial of Inheritance. That is where they'll compete for the three Sea God Artifacts."

He pointed at his head. "I, the Sea God Emperor, inherited the Sea God Crown. My prime minister holds the Sea God Scales, and my grand marshal, the second in command, holds the Sea God Shell. The candidates who make it through the first two trials can use their bloodline to attune themselves to these artifacts. It's a race, and the first to attune to the crown becomes the Sea God Emperor—or Empress—while the others become the Emperor's capable assistants. It has been this way for time beyond memory, regardless of anything else that happens in the lands above.

"Shuren will not be in danger when attuning to the Sea God Crown, her target," the Emperor said. "However, she might still have trouble racing through the first two trials. I want you to help her through the Trial of Adventure and the Trial of Puzzles."

"Very well, I accept," Cha Ming said.

The Emperor nodded. "Then please accept this personal, unofficial gift from me, the Sea God Emperor." A much smaller flask than last time appeared.

"When are the Sea God Trials?" Cha Ming asked.

"Three months from now," the Emperor said. "I know your time is precious, but I'd appreciate it if you coordinated with my daughter to strategize before going."

"I'll do my utmost," Cha Ming said. "I'll be done concocting my pill within a week."

"Good," the Emperor said. "Now, hold still. This will only take a second." He held out his hand, and two blue phantoms of a three-pronged crown appeared on his palm. They both bore the number one. The two crowns shot into Cha Ming and Gong Shuren's foreheads and left a pale-blue imprint. "These marks brand you as contender and champion. Be sure to return in time for the trials."

"Thank you so much for Your Grace," Cha Ming said, bowing. Then he heard a mental message from Huxian that caused him to frown. "Your Highness, might I be able to summon my brother, the contracted demon fox you saw on the Heaven Ascension Platform?"

"Is there a problem?" the Sea God Emperor asked.

"I just want to confirm something," Cha Ming said.

The Emperor nodded, and soon Cha Ming's shadow grew. It sprouted three tails as Huxian entered the chamber with as much flare and fanfare as he could muster. The small three-tailed fox popped onto Cha Ming's shoulder. The pale-blue mark of a crown shone on his forehead—the same one Cha Ming bore.

"I've never seen such a thing before in my life," the Sea God Emperor said, looking astonished. "It's never been possible for a contestant to have more than one champion."

"There's more," Cha Ming said. "Huxian?"

Huxian's three tails glowed, and his four demonic friends appeared. The falcon, the mouse, the frog, and the mountain each had a pale mark.

The Emperor grinned when he saw this, and then he laughed heartily. "I knew I didn't make a mistake. Who would have thought I'd get six for the price of one?"

"Father, is this really all right?" Gong Shuren asked uncertainly. "Won't it raise some eyebrows?"

He shrugged. "This is Cha Ming's strength. His bond of equals. It's not my fault my daughter is friends with the contracted partner of a Godbeast."

"Then we'll do our best to see her through as swiftly as possible," Cha Ming said.

"That's all I ask," the Emperor said. "Now, please excuse me, I have words to exchange with my daughter."

For the first time since their meeting, Cha Ming saw fatigue on the man's face. He nodded and left the palace, returning to his workshop, where he took out the flask of Waters of Life.

He summoned a single jin of Waters of Life. Fortunately, the amount required was very strict due to the runes involved in concocting the pill. Cha Ming tried to form the requisite rune a few times but to no avail. The fourth time, the rune disintegrated, and the Waters of Life evaporated.

Not discouraged in the slightest, Cha Ming summoned the second jin of Waters of Life and continued his attempts. This time, he created a formation network and had the energies in the water circulate as they collapsed into their form. The process was extremely slow, and by the time it finally failed, a half day had passed.

Having obtained the data he required, Cha Ming began his third attempt. The third jin of Waters of Life flowed over his palm and began taking shape. He guided it with his Clear Sky Brush, painting an intricate web that was three times as detailed as the last. It collapsed, but unlike last time, he guided the process slightly with his Grandmist flame and his brush. Soon, the Waters of Life condensed into a sigil that was perfectly suited to its nature, just like the other three.

Cha Ming then summoned the three other sigils and his transcendent cauldron. He threw all four components inside along with his Grandmist flame. The four components interlocked, and the gray flames hastened their excruciatingly slow reaction. One hour. Two hours. One day. Two days. Soon, six days had passed.

Finally, as the last of the runic components vanished, all semblance of structure disappeared. The components had merged into a smooth red pill. The pill pulsed, and ambient energy slowly began to trickle into the pill as it formed its pill seal. A minute passed, and the seal still wasn't complete. But Cha Ming was patient. He grew anxious, however, after a few hours passed.

"I was afraid this might happen," Sun Wukong said, appearing beside him.

Cha Ming sighed. "Tell me what's the matter. Break it to me gently."

"There's good news and bad news," Sun Wukong said. "The good news is that the pill was a success!"

"And the bad news?" Cha Ming asked.

"The bad news is that the pill needs time. Lots of it. The pill would normally take a day to form, but you couldn't use more rainbow-fish scales without promoting its grade. As a result, the pill is stuck forming its seal."

"How long will it take?" Cha Ming asked, dreading the answer.

"Ten thousand years? Twenty?" Sun Wukong said, shrugging. "It's tough to say. We can use the Clear Sky World to cut it down, but remember that both you and Huxian only have 2,500 years remaining in the mortal realm. Less, if you consider that he'll have trouble suppressing a breakthrough."

Cha Ming sighed. Though he'd almost grown numb to failure, the result was still disappointing. "The time acceleration in the Clear Sky World isn't quick enough, but it can at least help a little, right?"

"It can't hurt," Sun Wukong said.

Cha Ming nodded and stored the pill away inside it. He would need to try something else, but for now, the best use of his time was making talismans, pills, and preparing formation flags. Anything that could increase their chances in the Sea God Trials.

Chapter 23:
Heaven Ascension

The next few months were a blur. Cha Ming crafted talismans and pills while Huxian took care of some last-minute business before finally returning to the courtyard. When the demons arrived, Cha Ming was busy giving some last-minute lessons to his ten disciples.

"Be careful when I'm gone," Cha Ming said. "Though the Sea God Trials have historically only taken three months at most, it doesn't hurt to be careful, especially since Zhou Li's spent the past half dozen years stirring up trouble we don't even know about."

Ling Dong nodded. "Don't worry, Master. We might be weak, but we have a decent amount of influence in the city."

"Ling Dong is on great terms with most of the City Guard, while I've been teaching many budding formation masters in the city," Zi Long said. "Yue Bing has also been accumulating quite a few favors."

Yue Bing blushed. "It seems the city's warmed up to the concept of blood doctors, especially given how good they are at treating Haijing nobles. I've obtained quite a few students of my own as well. We shouldn't have any problems staying safe if anything happens in your absence."

Jin Huang hadn't said much. He simply twitched his fingers impatiently.

"I take it you'll be studying?" Cha Ming asked. The younger man nodded. "All right. I just hope I'm being paranoid. With any luck, nothing bad will happen. If there are any emergencies, don't hesitate to seek help from the Alabaster Group or Quicksilver's Alabaster Group. You can ask Feng Ming and Wang Jun as well, but I think they have their own problems to take care of." He then looked to Huxian. "Are you ready?"

Born ready, Huxian said, giving him a toothy grin. His four friends were hiding in his tail space, which had been augmented courtesy of the spatial fragment.

Cha Ming noticed the small fox now wore purple goggles above his eyes. *I wonder what he needs them for?* he thought.

Cha Ming and Huxian made their way over to the royal palace after a few more goodbyes. The guards were extremely respectful when they welcomed the duo, likely due to the soft blue marks on their foreheads. They traveled through the golden hallways before arriving inside the throne room. To their surprise, it was literally bursting with people.

Huxian jumped on Cha Ming's shoulder as they looked around for the princess. After a few moments of looking, Shuren's slender fingers grabbed his arm from behind and pulled him off to the side, where she and her brothers and sisters were waiting. Each one was accompanied by an older man or woman who had reached the peak of qi condensation. The only exceptions to this were herself and the third prince. Zhou Li smiled slightly as they joined the crowd.

There are so many important guests here today, Cha Ming sent to Gong Shuren. *Grand Elder Dai and several elders from Haijing Academy are here as well. So are most of the high-ranking nobles in the city.*

Today is a grand event that happens only once every thousand years, Gong Shuren replied. *Everyone in this room will be affected by the power shuffle.* She looked toward a group of women. *Especially the Empress and father's concubines. They'll be at the mercy of the new emperor or empress.*

Would anyone dare do anything to them with the old emperor still around? Cha Ming sent.

Shuren looked at him strangely. *The old emperor won't be around.*

Didn't anyone tell you? Seeing his confusion, she continued. *To open the Sea God Trials, those possessing the Sea God Artifacts must abdicate their positions. There are only two ways to abdicate: death or transcending.*

Cha Ming's eyes widened. *What you mean is that the Emperor...*

Not only the Emperor. His prime minister and grand marshal must also transcend, Gong Shuren explained. *Unlike the tribulation you witnessed a few years ago, however, there is no risk of failure. Space will not be damaged, as the Heaven Ascension Platform will guard the stability of the plane. Once they transcend, they will directly ascend to the Sea God Plane, and their artifacts will return to the Sea God Clock Tower. Everyone possessing the Sea God bloodline on the Heaven Ascension Platform will be sent into the trial along with their champion.*

Then the position of Emperor, grand marshal, and prime minister will be empty for three whole months? Cha Ming asked, worried.

The Empress Dowager will rule until the successor is chosen, Gong Shuren answered. *Conveniently, all participants are either her natural children or naturalized children. As for the roles of the prime minister and grand marshal, these roles shall be presided over by their appointed deputies.*

Cha Ming nodded, but he was still worried. The city could turn very chaotic if Zhou Li had arranged for some surprises in their absence. Before he could think to warn his disciples, however, the crowd grew still. The Sea God Emperor, who'd been sitting this whole time, stood up, and the entire hall grew silent as a graveyard.

"Thank you, everyone, for coming to see us brothers off," the Emperor said. Two other men stood beside him, seeming every bit his equal. While the Emperor wore a golden crown, the one on his left was large and wore a shell-like buckler on his arm. The one on his right held a set of golden weighing scales in his right hand. The two platforms resembled two translucent blue fish scales. All three artifacts emanated transcendent pressures much stronger than anything Cha Ming had ever felt.

"We would like to thank the Empress and our wives for delivering children to succeed us and enrich our lives," the Emperor continued. "We would like to thank our children, both those participating in the succession and not participating, for bringing much happiness to our long reign. Finally, we would like to thank Haijing Academy for continuing our long tradition of research and education for the plane. We ask that the headmaster continue to serve Haijing Academy during the transition until a replacement is appointed."

This development also surprised Cha Ming; he hadn't thought so much upheaval would occur during the selection of the next emperor. Haijing Academy had never taken sides, but if the new emperor and prime minister were so inclined, they could marginalize the Alabaster Group without much effort and allow the South to thrive. Moreover, Haijing's City Guard was far stronger than any army on the continent. He couldn't help but feel a noose being tightened around his throat.

There's no way Zhou Li being here during such a sensitive time is a coincidence, he thought. The upcoming trial was too important. Failure was not an option.

"Finally, I would personally like to thank everyone present," the Emperor said. "What I said before was in my capacity as emperor. But now, I thank everyone from the bottom of my heart."

"As do I," the grand marshal said.

"And I," the prime minister said.

"Please accept our bow of thanks," the Emperor said. They only bowed down forty-five degrees, but the gesture was as heavy as a mountain.

Cha Ming noticed many others were moved. Children and adults cried, and Gong Shuren was no exception.

"If you would be so kind, brother," the Emperor said as they straightened up. The man beside him nodded and held up the scales. They shimmered with gray light, and a large portal appeared behind the throne. "This dynasty is over, and a new one is just beginning. I invite all members of the younger generation to step forward with their champions to witness the end of the era and usher in the next. No matter what happens in the Sea God Trials, I hope you all remember that you are children of the Sea God, and above all else, you are family. You must stay united under the leadership of your new emperor."

"As the Emperor commands," the princes and princesses near Cha Ming shouted. That included Gong Shuren.

They followed the Emperor and his two brothers through the gray portal and appeared directly on the Heaven Ascension Platform. When the last person walked through, the portal closed, and the pressure coming from the Emperor and his brothers increased.

Thump. Thump. Thump.

Where three men once were now stood three completely different individuals. They seemed untouchable, unreachable. Their skin took on a gold-and-blue luster, and Cha Ming felt a mounting pressure crashing down on him in waves.

Thump. Thump. Thump.

He soon realized what that thumping sound was. It was the sound of a beating heart. The blood in his body urged him to bow in worship. He sensed a trickle of divinity in those three men, a drop of kingly might. The three men gathered their potential, and with a loud crash, they broke through to demigodhood and the initial stage of the Blood Awakening Realm.

The moment they did, the heavens roared. Lightning crackled in the skies as a tribulation unlike anything Cha Ming had ever seen appeared over their location. Unlike before, the heavens didn't take their time accumulating clouds and lightning. They sent their entire army upon the three men like desperate generals.

There were no white bolts or colored bolts. There were no black bolts like before. Instead, the clouds immediately produced gray strikes that threatened to tear the world asunder. Whether it was the nature of their ascension or the fact that three people were undergoing tribulations simultaneously, the heavens were angry. They wanted nothing more than to wipe these men from existence.

As the storm grew more violent, the prime minister was the first to act. He calmly took out his scales and summoned a gray spatial barrier. The dome surrounded them, and though it shuddered with every strike of gray lightning, it stood strong. The storm intensified, and the number of bolts doubled and caused the barrier to shake.

"Looks like it's my turn," the grand marshal said. He lifted his arm, and the golden shell-like shield glowed. As it did, a golden field superimposed itself on the gray one, tightening their defenses. Enraged, the heavens intensified their assault. The number of bolts doubled once more, and soon their combined defenses began to waver.

"Cease your struggles," the Sea God Emperor intoned. "You cannot stop us. Just stop trying and let it happen." He knew his words fell on deaf ears; the heavens spoke but didn't listen. As the heavens continued their assault, the Emperor's crown glowed blue. Cha Ming felt pure awe as the bodies of the three initial-blood-awakening cultivators grew even stronger. The crown resonated with the blue runes on their skin, which shifted to form familiar runic patterns: lightning attraction runes. Then, a small opening formed in the shield above them and allowed lightning through in a controlled manner.

"As per the decree of our ancestors, this is the final reward for our thousand years of service," the Sea God Emperor said. "We've looked over the juniors of our clan and protected the Sea God's lineage. All three of us have survived, so we are given a final cleansing of lightning. The plane's judgment will enhance our bloodlines before we are sent to the Sea God Plane."

The gray bolts struck down on the three and spread throughout their flesh. Their rune-covered skin cracked and sizzled, but any damage caused by the lightning was instantly repaired by their fierce blood vitality.

"Such treatment is not an entitlement but a privilege," the Emperor continued. "Such treatment can only be endured by combining the might of the three Sea God Artifacts and drawing upon the assistance of the Sea God Clock Tower beneath us. Therefore, to be worthy of this final boon, all three of the Sea God's inheritors must cooperate. All three must survive, and they must control the Sea God's Clock Tower. There have been many instances where this was not the case, so I hope you take this lesson to heart."

The lightning strikes intensified, and the Emperor was forced to stop speaking. Gray lightning funneled down on them like a stream, and soon it became a fierce waterfall. Their blood glowed brighter as the gray lightning washed over them. It soon shone like the concentrated light of a thousand suns.

Then, suddenly, the gold and gray shields vanished. The lightning in the sky came crashing down on them, forming a gray sea of lightning nine hundred feet in diameter. Their three glowing blue silhouettes could barely be seen, but little by little, the sea receded. So, too, did the blue glow.

The massive clock below them ticked off the seconds. Before long, all that was left was a small lake of lightning thirty feet wide. By then, the blue glow had faded, and the Sea God Emperor's crown had lost its luster. But despite being surrounded by gray lightning, the three men stood tall and strong. Their bodies could no longer be harmed by the plane in the slightest.

Seeing that it had failed in destroying them, the remaining lightning in the pool roared indignantly and leaped back into the skies. Then, space distorted, and the three men disappeared. Only three golden artifacts remained where they once stood, and those three tools sank into the Heaven Ascension Platform below them.

Cha Ming blinked, and when he opened his eyes, he was in another world. The world was filled with bright seawater, and despite being so far away, he could see a doorway in the distance.

"And now the Sea God Trials begin," Gong Shuren said, summoning a thin layer of armor and a golden trident. Combined with her long white hair floating in the clear waters, she resembled every bit a goddess of the sea.

Chapter 24: Transcendent Ocean

For a moment, the sea was calm. Then, suddenly, a violet mist appeared around them. Demons began materializing one after another, and when the demons saw them, they charged. Whirling waters and vicious demons came quickly, giving them no time to breathe. Cha Ming's staff crashed into a hundred-foot-long illusory carp that swam toward him. Though the demonic fish was small compared to many of the demons he'd fought, it used the water to its full advantage. The powerful force of his staff rolled off its slimy skin, leaving only a flesh wound as it jerked around to bite him. It bit a chunk out of his arm before he punched it with a metallic fist and sent it flying toward Gong Shuren, who impaled it with her trident. Then it broke and disintegrated into a puff of violet smoke.

Your staff is completely ineffective underwater, Gong Shuren sent. *It might work fine in mortal oceans, but here, it won't. Haven't you noticed it yet?*

He had, of course. The waters around him were far heavier and more viscous than the waters he'd traveled in before. They were even more difficult to swim through than the lava on Jade Moon Planet. That could only mean one thing: they were not in a mortal world, but a transcendent one that was hidden within the Sea God's Clock Tower itself.

Staves are ineffective because they can't cut through water, Cha

Ming thought. *But blades are too easy to divert due to currents in the water. Stabbing is preferred.* He poured creation qi and creation essence into the tip of the Clear Sky Staff and extended it. The white ink pooled at the tip of his weapon and solidified under his direction, forming a sharp set of three blades. It wasn't a trident but something else entirely.

The Clear Sky Staff now resembled a sky-scorching halberd, which consisted of a long spear with two crescent moons facing outward, making it an effective piercing weapon while retaining the slashing abilities of a halberd. Moreover, its clear shaft was a perfect conduit for five-element qi. Its two blades were attuned to creation and destruction while the gray tip was perfectly suited to executing Origin Strike.

Interesting weapon, Gong Shuren said as she impaled another demon. The creature dissipated in a puff of violet smoke.

It's more useful than a staff underwater and better suited to me than a trident, Cha Ming replied. Weapon situation remedied, he helped her dispatch a few other demons along with Huxian and his four friends' help. Each defeated enemy disappeared in a puff of violet smoke. Once the last of their opponents were defeated, they headed toward the doorway in the distance.

Illusory demons continued attacking them as they traveled. They attacked in groups, and every time they struck, they managed to bite pieces off Cha Ming, Gong Shuren, and Huxian and his friends. It was only a small loss, but judging by the speed at which they were approaching the portal, it would take months to get there. Every piece of lost energy took time to recuperate, time they didn't have.

After the seventh wave, Gong Shuren sank into a deep silence. It was only once the eighth wave finally reached them that she spoke up. *Something's wrong. They're much stronger than they should be. You, your five friends, and I should have been able to blaze through this trial in less than a week. But here we are at the eighth wave, and we're suffering wounds. Wounds! Even a late-marrow-refining noble and his champion should be able to survive easily at this point.*

Cha Ming struck out with Crushing Chaos, destroying four

demonic carps in the oncoming wave while Huxian and the others fought with tooth and claw. Gong Shuren erupted in a whirlwind of watery blades as they attacked her. She was their primary target, after all. Cha Ming rushed through the water and plunged his hand into a carp's head, and it burst into violet mist. To his surprise, Huxian came floating by and *absorbed* the violet mist.

You can do that? Cha Ming asked.

I guess, Huxian said. *This place is scary, but the demonic energy is thick.* His actions, though unusual, bought them time. The demonic attacks became less frequent, as the violet mist didn't return to the pool that surrounded them. But despite the less frequent attacks, their intensity increased. The carps grew larger and larger, and soon they became tiny flood dragons.

The mists come from a transcendent demon called the Dreamweaver Kraken, Gong Shuren said. *The demons in the first trial are manifestations of his illusory powers.*

More like manifestations of delicious demonic energy, Lei Jiang said as he finished swallowing another bundle of mist in his area. *With enough of this mist, we might just break through to peak core formation.*

Like Huxian, the little mouse was a glutton. His small round shape managed to put away enormous amounts of violet mist in every fight.

We might need them to break through if we want to get through this first trial, Cha Ming said. *Why is it so different than described? Is it because we brought in more champions to support you?*

Gong Shuren shook her head. *I don't know. In the past, this trial would just slow competitors down. It wouldn't be lethal like it is now. If we don't fight with everything we have, we could die. And that's not even counting how difficult it gets near the portal.*

Another wave of tiny flood dragons appeared. They spouted flames that mixed in with the transcendent waters and ate away at their skin. The difficulty had increased substantially in this wave. Cha Ming could feel that both his qi and vital energy stores were being depleted faster than he could regenerate them. A casual inspection of Gong Shuren revealed this was also the case for her.

Sister Shuren, come here, Cha Ming said. *Hold still while I work.*

What are you doing? she asked as he summoned his Clear Sky Brush and began painting blue-and-white runes on her skin. He painted until her face, arms, and legs were fully covered before moving to the rest of her body. There, he painted on her clothes; the runes sank through her clothes and latched on to her body. Huxian and his friends defended them as he worked. One hour and fifteen waves later, he finished the formation. It pulsed and began drinking in energy from the transcendent ocean. He repeated the process for himself as Huxian and Gong Shuren protected him.

Cha Ming sighed in relief as he finally felt his energy stores increasing and his blood vitality replenishing. *At least now we'll be able to fight nonstop,* he said. *How long until you gain enough energy to break through?*

A breakthrough is difficult to achieve at this point, Huxian said. *We need to consume enough demonic energy for all four of us at once, since we're linked. Fortunately, we haven't added Mr. Mountain to the formation yet. Otherwise we'd have to split the energy five ways. Since we don't need to feed him, it should only take two weeks. Lucky.*

Their group proceeded at a slow but steady pace. The waves came once every hour as dictated by a large ticking sound that permeated their surroundings. It echoed through the dark waters as though trying to drive them mad. Each wave grew increasingly large and powerful. Fortunately, they had Huxian on their side. His devouring and purifying powers roamed the battlefield like locusts as they swam.

After one more week, the flood dragons changed into violet ones twice the size of the originals. They spewed not fire but golden acid that passed through their skin and attacked their bones. After the second week, they changed to violet-gold ones. These violet-gold flood dragons didn't dissipate as easily as the first ones, requiring direct strikes to their heads to break apart. They inevitably bit through skin and bit off limbs using their razor-sharp teeth, making all participants thankful they'd cultivated their bodies—any qi cultivator would have been doomed to a violent and painful death.

Thousands upon thousands of illusory demons perished every day. At the two-week mark, once Huxian and his friends had consumed over five hundred thousand illusory demons, their cores finally reached their limits and broke through. Lei Jiang stayed the same size, though his weight and the density of his lightning increased. The four other demons, however, grew from their initial size of 300 feet to a healthy size of 330 feet. It was only three feet from mortal limits, but these three feet made a huge difference. To grow them, they would need to increase the purity of the demonic qi in their core. Once they reached this hard limit, the only way to grow was to transcend.

With Huxian and friends breaking through, their pace quickened greatly. The waters around them grew dark and murky as the four summoned an imitation domain suffused with Demon-Subduing Intent. They glowed like beacons in the transcendent ocean that drew the violet mists toward them from every corner.

Cha Ming and Gong Shuren were forced to constantly stab and slash at those that snuck through their defenses, but they didn't mind the light exercise, as Huxian and his friends did the heavy lifting.

Finally, they were only ten miles away from the golden gates. Cha Ming swept out with his sky-scorching halberd and hacked through an illusory eel and swam forward, plunging his bare fist into another one's neck and snatching its demonic core, causing it to disappear.

Just as he was about to continue forward, Gon Shuren stopped him.

Well, we got here, Cha Ming said as he held his hand out to the golden gates. *It took us a month, but isn't that how much time it usually takes?*

Gong Shuren shook her head. *The trial has been incredibly difficult thus far, but the final push to the gateway is always on another level entirely. I'm dreading what we'll have to face. What will it be? Thousands upon thousands of half-step transcendents?*

What will be, will be, Cha Ming said. *We can only try.*

Hack. Slash. Stab. Hack. Slash. Stab.

They closed the distance to the portal in a day, and the waves of illusory demons intensified as they approached. One wave came every minute instead of every hour now, so when they managed to fight one off, another was there to meet them. They began sustaining wounds that wouldn't heal in time, and everyone's energy stores began to plummet. But they pushed on.

Finally, after one final messy battle that took Cha Ming's right foot, the fighting ended. No more waves came to reinforce the one they'd just defeated. Instead, the clock simply ticked. Cha Ming looked around uncertainly at the pure gold gate surrounded by darkness. Even Huxian and the others were a little apprehensive.

Is this it? Huxian said. *Won't there be more of them?*

I don't know, Gong Shuren said. *I just don't know. We can make a run for it and enter the portal, but I'm scared, Cha Ming. I'm scared of that darkness. There's something dreadful there; I feel it in my bones.*

Should we split up? Huxian asked. He was scared too, which was unusual given his fearless disposition.

Gong Shuren shook her head. *We don't know what's inside that darkness.*

I'll send a clone up, Huxian said. A small black-and-white fox split out from his main body and swam toward the golden gates. It yipped underwater as though taunting the darkness to attack it. Then, seeing it not respond, it darted toward the gate. When it was only a hundred feet away, a giant black cable whipped out of the darkness and smashed down on it, reducing it to a puff of black-and-white smoke that vanished in the transcendent ocean.

YOU DARE TEST THIS GUARDIAN WITH AN APPARITION? a voice said from all around them. ARE YOU NOT WORRIED YOU'LL INCUR MY WRATH?

Strong, too strong, Huxian said. He shivered under the voice's pressure.

Might sir be the overseer of the Trial of Adventure, the Dreamweaver Kraken? Gong Shuren said toward the darkness. Four violet eyes appeared from within the shadows. The massive eyes blinked as they looked over their small group. *Might I ask if you've been angered by our many participants? If so, I apologize.*

HA! the Dreamweaver Kraken said. *HA-HA-HA. IF IT WERE ONLY NUMBERS, THIS ONE WOULDN'T INCREASE THE DIFFICULTY OF THE TRIAL TO THIS EXTENT. NO, THE DIFFICULTY IS A PUNISHMENT FOR YOUR BREACH OF THE RULES.*

Gong Shuren looked around uncertainly. *Esteemed Guardian, might we know the breach you speak of? I, a descendant of the Sea God, have come with those bearing my champion mark. It is through my champion's good fortune that his bonded companion gained the champion mark, along with its bonded friends. This seemed like permission to bring them all in.*

IT WAS, the Kraken said.

Then why? Gong Shuren asked.

THE RULES STATE THAT ONE LESSER TRANSCENDENT WEAPON AND ONE TRANSCENDENT ARMOR PER PARTICIPANT MAY BE BROUGHT IN TO FACILITATE THE SURVIVAL OF THE COMPETITORS, the Kraken said. It sent a tentacle forth from the darkness. The giant appendage traveled toward their group with inhuman speed. Before any of them could react, the tentacle stopped right before Cha Ming's body. *IT IS THIS ONE WHO HAS FLOUTED THE RULES. SOUL-BOUND TREASURES ARE EXCEEDINGLY POWERFUL, AND HE HAS NOT ONE, BUT TWO OF THEM. TO MAKE MATTERS WORSE, HIS COMPANION IS A GODBEAST.*

There were no rules against soul-bound weapons, and no instructions on Godbeasts, Gong Shuren protested.

CHAMPIONS ARE MEANT TO MAKE UP FOR DEFICIENCIES IN EXPERIENCE OR SKILLS, the Kraken said. *BUT WITH ALL HIS ADVANTAGES, ARE THE SEA GOD TRIALS EVEN MEANINGFUL? DO THEY ACCOMPLISH THEIR AIM OF SELECTING THE MOST OUSTANDING TALENTS FROM EACH GENERATION? NO! THEREFORE, I HAVE TAKEN IT UPON MYSELF TO PUSH YOU ALL TO YOUR LIMITS. I FOLLOW THE SPIRIT OF THE RULES, NOT THEIR CHEAP MORTAL WRITINGS.*

IF YOU CAN'T AT LEAST EXCEED THIS NEW STANDARD WITH YOUR POWERFUL HELPERS, I CAN ONLY SHAKE MY HEAD IN DISAPPOINTMENT.

Unfortunate. That was the only word that could describe the situation. If Cha Ming had known this rule, he would have refused the Sea God Emperor's request. He bowed to Gong Shuren in apology. But Gong Shuren wasn't looking at him. She was frowning at the Kraken.

This rule was never explicitly stated, Gong Shuren said.

IT SHOULD BE OBVIOUS, the Kraken replied.

But it wasn't, Gong Shuren insisted. *Now, instead of ensuring that the most capable descendant is chosen, you're eliminating the most promising one.*

Silence.

I demand to know what level of strength you'll use to guard this gate, Gong Shuren continued. *With everything you've summoned against us, we might simply die trying to get through. How would this further the Sea God's goal in grooming his descendants and preserving his homeland?*

Silence.

Dying is one thing. I can risk my life to continue the trial if the risk is worth it, but for now, we're going in blind. I can't ask my companions to accompany me, because from what I can tell, advancing means certain death.

This time, a pause. *WHAT YOU SAY IS REASONABLE,* the Kraken said. *AS AN ILLUSORY DEMON, I'VE LIVED LONG AND EXPERIENCED MUCH. IF I WERE TO BRING MY FULL STRENGTH TO BEAR, YOU JUNIORS WOULD BE REDUCED TO NOTHING BUT FISH FOOD IN AN INSTANT. THEREFORE, I PROMISE TO LIMIT MY STRENGTH TO THE INITIATION REALM. THE VERY LOWEST LEVEL OF THE INITIATION REALM. IN HUMAN STANDARDS, THIS IS THE EQUIVALENT OF AN ARMED INITIAL-BLOOD-AWAKENING CULTIVATOR.*

BEFORE YOU PROTEST AGAIN, LET ME BE CLEAR: YOU MUST ONLY EVADE AND SURVIVE MY ATTACKS LONG

ENOUGH TO PASS THROUGH THE GATE. I KNOW ALL YOUR MEANS, SO ANYTHING YOU USE IS APPROPRIATE. PROCEED AS YOU PLEASE.

The Kraken shut its violet eyes, leaving them just outside the darkness with only the golden gate to illuminate their way forward.

Well, that went well, Huxian said. *I no longer feel like prostrating, so I take it he's already reduced his strength.*

But he's still quite dangerous, Cha Ming said. *I've never clashed with transcendents before, but from what I know, they're not just stronger by a single level. They're at least an order of magnitude stronger.*

Not just an order of magnitude, Gong Shuren said. *They hold dominion over natural forces. In the Ling Nan Plane proper, the moment a transcendent even tries using this power, whether intentional or not, the plane revolts and attacks them. Very few people can perfectly restrain their powers when exerting themselves, which is why transcendents tend not to fight or craft treasures on the Ling Nan Plane if they can help it.*

But this isn't the Ling Nan Plane, Cha Ming said. *He can use his powers fully. Given that we're now familiar with each other's abilities, we can only use treasures and formations to tilt the odds in our favor.* He summoned a few dozen talismans, a full set of 1,080 formation flags, the same amount of combat sigils, and a dozen pills. *The talismans are mostly restrictive, suppressing, and group-healing talismans. I have nothing with much offense save one fire-based talisman, which isn't terribly useful here anyway. These dozen pills can replenish vital energy, and some can even boost our cultivation for a short time.*

At a high cost, Gong Shuren said.

At a high cost, Cha Ming agreed. *We'd obtain about a one-minute boost to our body's strength, but it will take days to recover. I tailored some to Huxian and his friends, and two of them are suitable for humans. Will we be physically safe after this trial?*

The next trial is the Trial of Puzzles, so we need not worry once we get to the other side, Gong Shuren said. She summoned five objects, the first one being a small gourd. *I have ten drops of Waters of Life in case of serious injuries. If we all take one just before charging over, it might save us from otherwise lethal blows. The second and third ones* were a brush and a compass. *These two are reserved for the next trial. I'll put them away if you don't have a use for them.*

We shouldn't need them, Cha Ming said. He motioned to the last two objects. *What are those two talismans? I've never seen anything quite like them.*

Every participant is given two transcendent-grade talismans from the Sea God Plane, Gong Shuren said. *They greatly increase the speed of the user underwater for a short time. It's another reason why this trial usually isn't lethal.*

But our situation is different, Cha Ming said. *We don't have two people; we have seven. Even if Huxian can use spatial powers to manipulate the location of his friends, and even store them inside an independent space, that still makes three of us.*

She nodded and flicked out a blue talisman to Cha Ming. "You're the slowest among us underwater, so you should have one." She then looked to Huxian. "I'd offer you one, but it seems you're even faster than I am."

Huxian snorted in response but looked at the darkness gravely. "Cha Ming?"

Cha Ming, who'd just received her talisman, couldn't help but gaze at it in awe. He was a talisman artist, an elder-level one at that, but he'd never seen anything like this before. It was a simple piece of white parchment painted with blue ink, but the depth and intensity of the lines weren't like anything he'd ever seen.

"Cha Ming? Cha Ming?" Gon Shuren said.

He heard nothing. He saw nothing. He felt nothing as he was floating in a sea of blue runes that surrounded and shackled him. These tiny restrictions were the essence of resistance inherent to water and all liquids. His Flow Talisman could greatly reduce the effect of these runes, though in these transcendent oceans, his Flow Talisman wasn't very effective.

But from the talisman in his hands, he could sense a deeper purpose. The characters wouldn't just influence the runes around them but connect to them, forcing them to change. It was like a law or a commandment that demanded that they budge. He realized that this was what he'd been missing; this was the difference between a transcendent and a mortal talisman.

Cha Ming sat cross-legged and sank to the bottom of the transcendent sea. No demons dared wander so close to the gate, so all that surrounded him were dark and heavy waters. They pressed down on him like chains, as though they were aided by something more powerful, something intangible. He sensed tiny shackles coming from each droplet of water. Each one was nearly insignificant. The shackles were karma, and it was through these karmic connections to something greater that the waters slowed and suppressed him. Given enough time, he could escape them, but time was exactly what he lacked.

Friction slowed him down. Speed was covering distance in a set amount of time. It all came down to time. Given enough time, he could dive through his surroundings and reach the gate. Life was also that way. Attachments and relationships, the sheer physical reality of everything around you. They kept you back, and while you could change your surroundings, you could never slip away from the undeniable reality that living took time. That inescapable drag suffused the transcendent waters around him, the air above the water, and even the earth beneath him.

He thought of the Flow Talisman.

The ocean cares not for drowning children;
Man is a slave to the sea of fate.
Flowing down from high to low;
Never questioning his direction.

Before, he'd felt the truth of these words. They reflected his deep emotions, his frustration with how things were. He was tired of the struggle, tired of fighting against the current. So, he changed it. He built up his own momentum that enabled him to continue without slowing in the slightest. It was what kept him going in his struggle toward immortality. It was what he needed to find Yu Wen again.

But in that moment, he saw the tiny tethers that connected him to the ocean waves and threatened to stop him. It wasn't just the relationship he noticed, but the power they drew on. They didn't restrict him because they wanted to, but because they had to. It was a law of the world.

Could he change that if he wanted to? It was a thought, and a silly one at that. Yet the talisman in his hands made him feel it wasn't. He poured his soul force into it, and a fierce watery power soared within him. He recognized this power as the essence of currents, and it filled him with strength that defied his surroundings. It held a command: The waters would *not* interfere. Moreover, they would help. The waters would help them cross the threshold and enter the portal.

He felt the command, and in that moment, it matched the frustration in his heart. The frustration at all the obstacles around him, the constant setbacks. His shattered core; Zhou Li destroying the Water Source Marrow; the heavens destroying the Nirvana Pill. He loathed these things that stopped him from moving forward.

At the same time, the command faintly matched the emotions driving him in the first place. Despite these setbacks, he'd kept on going. His core had been shattered, so he'd wandered to Jade Moon Planet for a solution. He'd needed to learn alchemy to make the Nirvana Pill, so he'd spent almost twenty years doing just that. He'd failed at making the Nirvana Pill, so he'd tried to craft an ambitious replacement. Even now, he was grasping at straws to advance, not giving up when something held him back. This wasn't just a hope on his part, but a weak command of sorts. He was *telling* everything around him that he would succeed.

He realized what he needed to do. He summoned creation essence at the tip of his brush and infused the white ink with a rush of emotions. Then he painted the first stroke. He knew that by making this talisman, he was defying the heavens, but if a transcendent demon could fight here, could he not make a transcendent treasure of his own?

Each stroke was agonizingly slow and painful. He wasn't just infusing emotions and will into his creation; he was forcing his qi up to another level: transcendence. The first two compressions brought his qi to the peak of core formation, and another compression brought it to half-step transcendence. That was easy. What was difficult was taking that small trickle of qi an eighth the size of the original and compressing it even further. He needed this qi to not only obey his commands, but to spread throughout the heavens and the earth and muster it like an army. He needed it to control the heavens and the earth as though they were his own domain.

Cha Ming coughed up blood as he struggled. Huxian appeared behind him and pressed his large paw against his back, lending him what power he could. The brush moved slowly, and by the time he formed the first character, a full half hour had passed. He grinned when he saw it, however, and he recovered his strength.

Character after character, he wrote down his emotions. They were words he'd used before, but different. This time, the words were forceful. They were filled with a commanding presence he hadn't known was possible. The words were no longer an observation, no longer an ethereal feeling, but an expression of frustration. The world might be the way it was, but it *would* change for him. Flow would change for him.

Three days passed as he wrote, and on the third day, the transcendent waters pulsed, and an unfamiliar energy rushed into the writing. The talisman required no paper; paper formed as the writing finally took shape. The runic structure flatted into his first transcendent-grade talisman.

He held the paper up and opened his eyes. He uncrossed his legs and swam up to Gon Shuren with Huxian following behind him. Lei Jiang, Silverwing, and Gua had assembled after sensing the commotion. Cha Ming poured his transcendent soul into the talisman, and everything thirty feet around him changed. Huxian retrieved his friends and shrank down, hopping onto Cha Ming's shoulder. Cha Ming popped a cultivation-boosting pill, popped a drop of Waters of Life, and held his hand out. Gong Shuren did the same and took it.

Their potential surged as they floated out calmly toward the gate in the darkness, and tentacles flew out to stop them. Deep-violet eyes stared at them from behind the portal. They had entered its domain, so it would attack them. They were ants, and ants should be crushed with impunity.

Gong Shuren flinched as the tentacle whipped down, but Cha Ming was unconcerned. The nearest thirty feet were *his* territory, and flow worked how *he* willed it. The tentacle struck his bubble and encountered an undeniably strong resistance. It tried to shove them down but could only slip around the thirty-foot bubble as it floated toward the portal.

Angered, hundreds of tentacles whipped down toward them. Waves battered the bubble but to no avail. Tentacles struck the sphere but slid off harmlessly. Then, when they were only a hundred feet away from the portal, the Kraken changed tactics. It surrounded their bubble in a net of tentacles that squeezed shut.

The pressure mounted around them, but Cha Ming felt strangely confident. He simply smiled and spoke from his heart. "You cannot stop me. This domain is mine, and I *will* move forward."

The tentacles, which had previously been tightly wound around the bubble, suddenly seemed to move. No, that wasn't right. The space around them was distorted. But it wasn't enough to escape, so all six of them pushed like they'd never done before. Four peak-core-formation demon beasts, one of them a Godbeast, and all with their cultivation boosted, pushed apart the tentacles with their paws. Gong Shuren and Cha Ming, the former with her trident and the latter with his staff, pried apart the tentacles with all their might as their potential burned away.

They struggled for endless moments as the tentacles, their domain, and their strength clashed against each other. Then, little by little, the bubble began making its way forward. Slowly at first, but then at a steady pace. Finally, the bubble forced its way through the tiny gap formed in the net of appendages. As it did, it accelerated through the gap like a bullet through a rifle barrel and shot toward the golden gates.

Then all went black.

Chapter 25: Sea God's Puzzle

Tick. Tick. Tick.

The first thing Cha Ming noticed was the ever-present ticking of a giant clock. As he opened his eyes, he noticed they were no longer surrounded by endless oceans but by walls. The room was massive, several miles long by several miles wide. A large clock stood affixed to the wall, and beneath it was a door. According to the Sea God royal family, the door could only be opened by solving a puzzle.

Tick. Tick. Tick.

Cha Ming stood up as he took in his surroundings. "How long was I out?" he asked.

Gong Shuren was seated in front of a small object at the center of the room, observing it intently. Here and there, he saw small notations written on the floor.

"The Sea God's Puzzle," Cha Ming said, scanning the object in the center with his transcendent force. "Supposedly very difficult to solve in a short amount of time."

"Completing it quickly usually takes one month," Gon Shuren said. "But now that the difficulty has increased, it's hard to say."

Cha Ming nodded. He flew up above the object and saw that it was composed of interlocking pieces. They were each covered in runes and lines that restricted movement when joined. Some could be moved on their own, but others could only be moved simultaneously.

It was a formation puzzle, much like those commonly used by junior formation masters to train their formation skills.

"It doesn't look that difficult," Cha Ming said as he came back down. "It's a water-oriented puzzle. Nothing unexpected." The words were meant to reassure, but Gong Shuren turned solemn as he confirmed it.

"That's what worries me," Gon Shuren said. "Why would the puzzle be easy when the Trial of Adventure was so difficult?"

Cha Ming shrugged. "Maybe because my soul-bound weapons won't be too big an advantage in this trial?"

Gong Shuren seemed unconvinced. "We'll see. Let's solve this puzzle first and see what happens."

The clock on the wall continued ticking as they walked to separate ends of the puzzle. Cha Ming took the lead and issued instructions to Gong Shuren.

"Pour your qi into the 'mai' rune and twist the 'kou' rune," he said, pouring his qi into twelve other positions. He twisted the runic blocks until the puzzle locked into position.

"Channel power down to every odd diagonal formation line and work with me to rotate the qi flow counterclockwise," he then said. They used their qi and soul force in unison, and the puzzle moved again.

This process continued for three days. Fortunately, Cha Ming had been teaching Gong Shuren for years now, so they'd developed a good working relationship. She might not be capable of as much as he was, but she could at least follow instructions to lessen his burden and speed up the process. On the third day, they heard a click, and to their surprise, the puzzle sank into the floor.

"That can't be it," Cha Ming said, frowning.

"This was what I was afraid of," Gong Shuren said.

A sliding sound filled the air as a massive object began to rise out of the stone floor. Cha Ming soon realized it was a giant gear. It was fully cast in bronze and covered in complex runic patterns. Once it completed its vertical journey, the floor glowed and vanished beneath their feet. Thousands of tiny gears rose up and set themselves in midair. Some were connected by thick rods that forced them to turn in tandem, while others formed a strange connection with each other with runic lines.

At the center of the room, where the original runic puzzle had once been, a large pillar rose up. Its grooved surface wasn't covered in any runes. It continued rising until it reached the level of the first gear, bringing up an entirely new floor with it. Everything froze in place for an infinitesimal moment, then started moving again.

Tick. Tick. Tick. Tick. Tick.

The ticking again. The newly formed puzzle of gears, rods, and runes began ticking to the same rhythm as the clock on the wall. And the sound was deafening. Try as they might, even with their powerful bodies and strong souls, they could do nothing to block it out. As the clock ticked, the gears began to glow in multiple colors as their runes lit up.

"This is… completely unfair," Cha Ming said. "I understand that despite being primarily body cultivators, the Sea God royal family can practice qi. But it's invariably water qi. They should *not* have to deal with five-element puzzles." He looked around. "And light and darkness, it seems. Seven elements. Great."

"And *you* should not have brought soul-bound treasures here," a voice said. A glowing figure appeared just in front of the clock on the wall. The transparent woman, who looked every bit an immortal fairy, scowled at them and tapped her foot. "Rest assured, I've determined your capabilities. Whether you can live up to my expectations is another matter."

Cha Ming coughed lightly. "Isn't the purpose of the Sea God Trial to test descendants?"

"Yes, but because of your presence, we can't even test her," the fairy said. "Therefore, we can only evaluate the worthiness of her friends. Any other questions?" Her smile was neither encouraging nor reassuring. He had no doubt that she'd be happy to dance around the subject until they ran out of time.

"None, esteemed guardian of the second stage," Gong Shuren said, pulling Cha Ming back. "Arguing with her will do us no good, so let's just try and solve this. I'm less concerned about the five elements and more about light and darkness."

Cha Ming nodded. "Luckily, Huxian can help out with that. Though it seems we'll have to pull out all the stops for this. Are you ready?"

She nodded.

"Then let's get to work." Cha Ming grabbed his brush and began solving some of the smaller puzzles, sliding them into position. The clock's constant ticking and moving made this especially difficult. As Gong Shuren focused on water-based runes, Cha Ming focused on the other four, as well as light and shadow, with Huxian's help.

Every piece of the puzzle they solved allowed them to shift one of the gears. They soon realized the eventual goal: an exposed gear just above the main clock. Only by using the turning gears to energize the clock could they open the door.

But how to get there? Cha Ming thought. They moved gear after gear, but whenever they moved one component, the others would move to compensate, undoing any progress they made toward the clock.

Soon, three weeks had passed. They'd activated all the formations in the gear box, but no matter how they moved the gears, they couldn't reach the clock near the wall. To make matters worse, the incessant ticking was making it difficult to concentrate. Huxian's friends had come out to play for only a short while before being forced to return to his tail space. They were running out of time.

Tick. Tick. Tick. Tick.

"Huxian, can you look at the pieces again?" Cha Ming asked.

The small fox sighed and slipped on his goggles. He used it to survey the strings of karma in the room as he attempted to figure out an optimal order in which to manipulate the gears. He'd repeated the process every day since they'd come.

Nothing, Huxian said. *Like I said, it only takes half of these gears to open the door, but the problem is they keep rearranging themselves. One gear moving over is fine, but it moves some key ones out of position. They get affected a few moves down the road, undoing our progress.*

"Can't you stop them with that time trap of yours?" Cha Ming asked.

I could, Huxian said. *For a few seconds. But that won't buy us enough time.*

Time. It was always about time and how he didn't have enough of it. In the first trial, he'd used a talisman to free them from the shackles of time, and in this one, he needed a way to do the opposite.

Let's go over our assets again, Cha Ming thought. *Flow Talisman—I can't make another one anytime soon. The last time practically killed me. Other poetic talismans don't align very well with time, though I suppose I could try making a Shape Talisman and try to destroy the clock.* He shook his head. *Not a good idea, and it'll waste too much time if it fails.*

I've used all the formation flags and sigils I have at my disposal. My pills have no effect here, and the transcendent talisman Gong Shuren has is meant to speed someone up underwater. It would probably work in the air to some extent, but that's not exactly helpful. Cauldron? Not useful. Hammer focus? Not useful. Clear Sky Staff? Been using it all along, and I suppose I can try to smash the puzzle if all things fail. Hm... wait, what about this thing?

He summoned the Space-Time Camera.

"What's that?" Gong Shuren asked, floating over.

"A repository of memories," Cha Ming said, his voice laced with emotion. "It contains images that are very dear to me. When it seems too hard to keep going, I take it out and look at the pictures inside, and I find the strength to move on." Aside from its ability to take pictures, he'd mostly ignored the mystical artifact. But it *was* a soul-bound treasure, wasn't it? It should have other uses. Besides, he remembered Yu Wen using it to hold off a devil emperor outside Jade Moon Garden. The small camera had taken a picture of those black spikes threatening to break apart the shield and frozen them in space-time. Could he do the same here?

Yes, he could, he realized as his spirit exchanged information with the camera. While it would be very difficult to use it on animate objects or living beings, he could use his qi, spirit stones, and other energy sources to power a time-stilling shot. It would last as long as the camera still contained energy.

"I've figured it out," Cha Ming said. "But I need some help. Sister Shuren, how many top-grade spirit stones do you have?"

"I brought quite a few in case we needed them," Gon Shuren said, tossing a bag to him. His eyes widened when he looked at the contents.

"Huxian, find out which gears we need to freeze to make sure everything is in position," Cha Ming said.

On it, Huxian said. He slipped his goggles on and ran through the air, inspecting the various components as he saw what they couldn't. *I have a plan. Are you ready?*

"Born ready," Cha Ming said.

All right, freeze this gear and activate these two in succession, Huxian said. Cha Ming did so, and two gears moved—save the one he'd taken a picture of. *Now immobilize these two and activate these five as I tell you.*

Snap. Snap. They moved as he directed. The more pictures he snapped, Cha Ming realized that, like his Clear Sky Brush, the Space-Time Camera was a glutton. It burned through top-grade spirit stones as though they were simple firewood. He hoped they had enough.

Now immobilize that big gear, Huxian said.

Cha Ming snapped a picture, and suddenly he heard a screeching noise that threatened to pierce his eardrums. The ticking of the clock slowed.

Tick... Tick... Tick... Tick...

Um, it should be fine? Huxian said.

Worry began to mount in Cha Ming's heart as they continued their work. The gears moved from the center of the room toward the clock on the wall, and the further they went, the slower the clock ticked. Finally, as they put the last gear in place, the clock ticked its last. What should have been a simple turn of the massive central gear to open the door didn't happen.

Well, fudge nuggets, Huxian said. *I did not see that coming.*

"What happened?" Gong Shuren asked.

"It seems we killed the clock," Cha Ming said. "It's not turning like it should."

"Should we remove the time locks on the other gears?" Gong Shuren asked Huxian, who nodded.

They'll move about, but the others are locked in place, Huxian said. Cha Ming erased one of the pictures he'd taken, and the moment he did, a small gear flew across the room and crashed into a wall. It fell on the floor, useless. Seeing that it didn't affect their chain of gears, Cha Ming released them one after another. Soon, they were left with a pile of broken gears above the main one. It stood still like before, not ticking in the slightest.

"Could it be stuck?" Cha Ming asked. "Do we need to wind it somehow?"

With what? Huxian said. *Everything's connected, and even if we used all our strength, we wouldn't be able to move that gear.* He shook his head. *Besides, it hasn't exactly stopped, you know. It's still ticking, just very slowly.*

"Oh? You mean if we wait long enough, it'll tick?" Cha Ming asked.

It could take a month or two, but yes, it'll tick, Huxian said.

"That's not quick enough," Cha Ming said. "By then, they'll have attuned the Sea God Artifacts."

"What if we had these?" Gong Shuren asked. She summoned a few golden discs that Cha Ming recognized. They were time-essence discs. "Could we use these to speed up the process?"

Cha Ming thought for a bit and even consulted with Sun Wukong. "I don't have any way to use them," he said finally. "How about you?"

Huxian, to whom he'd just spoken, had his eyes glued on the time discs. A dribble of saliva was dripping down on the stone floor.

"Huxian…" he warned, but it was too late. The fox zipped toward the discs and crunched down on them like a child would candy. Before they could even scold him, he became a blur in the room. To their surprise, this blur extended around him as a field, and Gua, Lei Jiang, Silverwing, and even Mr. Mountain came out from his tail space. The fourth point, to which Mr. Mountain had yet to be connected, suddenly snapped into place. The space between them shuddered.

They flew up around the central gear, keeping the formation active at all times, but the occasional flicker hinted at instability. For the most part, however, they seemed to be standing still in the air, unmoving. Cha Ming soon realized that it wasn't that they weren't moving, but they were moving too *fast*. The small mountain stood still, which was expected, but Silverwing seemed like he had four pairs of wings, and Lei Jiang's paws were a blurred mess. Gua held three mirrors in his three pairs of hands, and Huxian no longer had three tails but nine.

Little by little, the gear started to move. It creaked slowly at first as it fought against the initial friction, but soon it moved a little, and the clock ticked with it. Then another. And another. The ticking sped up, and soon, the gear was turning along with the other gears, spinning against the lone gear above the clock.

Tick, tick, tick, tick, tick.

The ticking wasn't maddening like before; it was more like music to their ears. The turning gear didn't seem to have any effect, but they could feel some sort of potential building behind the ticking clock. It continued this way for a full minute until finally, it stopped. Then the central gear split in two and fell to the ground, and as it did, the clock sounded.

Gong. Cha Ming felt his bones vibrate as the chime rang through his body.

Gong. He felt his soul tremble as the chime resonated with his spirit.

Gong. His qi fluctuated as the chime caused his cultivation to quicken.

After three gongs, the door opened. Everyone sighed in relief as the small fox flew down to them, panting.

Did I do good? Huxian asked.

Cha Ming smiled and scratched between his ears. "You did good, my friend. Very good." He turned to Gong Shuren, whose face had now turned solemn. "Well?"

"Let's go," Gong Shuren said. "We have no time to waste."

The woman, the man, and the fox walked through the small doors. The Sea God's Puzzle disappeared behind them as another room appeared in front. There, they saw a large clock and three daises. On each platform was a single youngster. Four other youngsters stood guard in front of them, along with seven other champions.

Zhou Li stood in front of them, grinning from ear to ear.

Chapter 26: Sea God's Inheritance

Cha Ming couldn't help but gape when he saw Zhou Li. He looked to Gong Shuren, who wore an extremely concerned expression. The three artifacts were already pulsing with power, and a tide of blue light had worked its way up from their bottoms, washing away all but a bit of gold on each one. Just a small push, and the blue light would completely cover the artifacts, attuning them to their respective inheritors.

The runes on each of the three Haijing royals glowed with the same light as the artifacts. The third prince, Gong Xuandi, hadn't noticed their presence. He was seated in front of the crown, while two of his brothers were seated in front of the shell and scales.

"They've almost completed their attunement," Gong Shuren said with a quavering voice. "Their bloodlines are poor, but they've been here for a long time. We can't win." Her fists were shaking, and her teeth were clenched. She wanted to fight but didn't know how.

Zhou Li clapped as they walked toward the daises. "What a stunning performance. You've gotten here so fast, despite your handicap. I confess myself impressed."

"You knew?" Cha Ming asked coldly. No wonder Zhou Li had been so confident at the outset.

Zhou Li grinned. "Of course I knew. These trials are meant for fair competition amongst juniors. They won't tolerate the presence of an anomaly like you." He pointed to his eyes with two fingers. "Besides, I'm a seer. Even though I can't see through you directly, I can always guess at hypothetical outcomes. I had originally thought your participation was set in stone, but you just had to hole yourself up in research. I had to… encourage your participation through various means. Thank you for guaranteeing our victory, Cha Ming."

How long do you need to attune the crown? Cha Ming sent.

I'm not sure, Gong Shuren sent back. *Based on what my father told me, it should only take me one hour. They've probably been at it for days.*

Cha Ming was surprised by this revelation. He hadn't thought there would be so much difference in bloodline power between siblings. Licking his lips, he summoned the Space-Time Camera once more. Then he infused all the top-grade spirit stones he had left into it. The jade artifact glowed with a faint gray halo and floated up.

I don't know if I can buy you an hour, but I'll get you what I can. Huxian? Cha Ming asked.

Big brother? Huxian said. Three of his four friends had already appeared beside him.

"Clear a path," Cha Ming instructed. He began walking forward, and the Space-Time Camera floated up in the air. The area around the third prince distorted as everyone heard a snap, and a picture appeared on the camera. It was a picture of the third prince, and the moment it appeared, the third prince's progress halted. There was no distortion, no humming, and no pulsing. The area directly around him appeared to have been cleaved away from this reality and frozen inside a perfect picture. The picture on the camera solidified, and the moment it did, Cha Ming retrieved it and placed it in his Clear Sky World.

The third prince cannot progress in attuning the artifact for now, Cha Ming sent to Gong Shuren. *Can you only attune one artifact?*

One royal can only attune a single artifact, Gong Shuren said. *The most important one is the crown, as the bearer of the crown is the new emperor. It is strongest because it can bolster or strip strength from body cultivators.*

Then go claim it, Cha Ming said. *We'll clear a path for you.*

Huxian and the others had already rushed past them and started clashing with the eleven body cultivators. Five cultivators surrounded the black-and-white fox, whose three tails lashed out around him and superimposed five suppressing domains. His teeth, claws, and tails were so powerful that it took all five of them combined to hold him off. Their tridents were glowing with a similar light, and judging by the runic light between them, they were using a collaborative formation.

Unfortunately for them, Huxian and the rest were as well. The squad of demons was connected by runic light that couldn't be seen by most people. But Huxian could see. His violet goggles saw not only these tethers connecting them but the flow of battle as well. They had the advantage.

Off to the side, Silverwing was up in the air. He fought two older protectors and a younger Haijing royal with blades of wind. His wings alternated between attack and defense, and whenever they managed to launch a combined attack, he turtled behind his large feathered limbs. Despite them wielding half-step transcendent treasures, his metallic wings were like impenetrable armor. Cha Ming even wondered which would be first to break—his wings or their weapons?

While Silverwing and Huxian were holding off their own individual groups, Lei Jiang and Gua were attacking three cultivators in tandem. Gua used his fan to restrain their movements and buffet them with turbulent eddies while Lei Jiang simply bounced between them like a rogue bolt of lightning. These cultivators had strong bodies, so his individual strikes didn't accomplish much. They did, however, make easy conduits for lightning. The lightning the Calamity-Swallowing Mouse released from his body funneled through each strike of his gauntleted claws. Despite him being only a single demon, they had no choice but to go all out on defense, leaving Gua to hamper them even further.

Cha Ming summoned the Clear Sky Pillar as he walked up to Zhou Li. He also summoned a sea of 1,080 combat sigils that formed three separate combat formations. This was the most efficient use of his qi and soul force. While three combat formations didn't grant him the power of a top-grade one, they gave him unparalleled flexibility in battle. Two of the formations were freezing and entangling the black-robed man while a shield of fiery energy surrounded Cha Ming. Sparks flew between them as Cha Ming's staff collided with Zhou Li's black sword. Both of them had yet to make any serious moves. They were both coiled springs, waiting for the opportune moment to attack.

The moment Gong Shuren tried to push through toward the dais, Zhou Li darted out like lightning with a flaming black sword. Concurrently, he pushed Cha Ming away with a dragon of flame. Unfortunately for him, Cha Ming had expected this. His combat formations shifted and turned into a maze consisting of metal and ice spikes and poisonous miasma.

Zhou Li was forced to adjust his trajectory, which bought enough time for Gong Shuren, who was a fierce cultivator herself, to push through. Her trident deflected his sword, and her powerful legs pushed off a freshly frozen platform that appeared out of thin air. When Zhou Li tried to chase after her, Cha Ming swung down at him with a well-timed Crushing Chaos, forcing him to turn around and deflect with his black blade.

To Cha Ming's surprise, the sword held its own against the Clear Sky Staff and didn't shatter as expected. They grated against each other, and in that instant, he realized that the pale man's sword was much more powerful than he'd originally thought. It was a transcendent treasure, not a half-step transcendent one. Moreover, it was stronger than most transcendent treasures he'd seen before.

Zhou Li slashed out at him, taking advantage of their close distance to attack him with impunity. Cha Ming shrank his staff and used several instances of Splitting Heaven and Earth to deflect his many strikes. Despite his best efforts, however, several trickles of black flames landed on his body. They burned away at his flesh at an alarming rate, but fortunately, his regeneration could keep up with the flame's potent energies. Barely. They retreated after the exchange to reevaluate their opponent.

"Do you like it?" Zhou Li asked, flicking his black sword with a slender white finger. It let out a dissonant sound. "The sword's name is Sin Eater, the karma-severing blade. It's always the first thing I retrieve whenever I reincarnate, and I've possessed it twelve times. It's a sword that can be used for more than killing, if you know how to use it."

Cha Ming's eyes narrowed. "Twelve times? You mean to tell me that you remember twelve lifetimes?" They exchanged a few more blows. Black chains appeared and threatened to entangle Cha Ming. In response, he retracted a combat formation and summoned a shield of ice to hold it back. The two cancelled each other out, but withdrawing the ice formation gave Zhou Li room to breathe and press the attack. He cut a shallow gash on Cha Ming's chest. Though it wasn't deep, the cut took much longer to heal than normal, even with Cha Ming's late-marrow-refining cultivation. He'd need to be careful and take as little damage as possible.

"Heavens, no," Zhou Li said, content to chat mid-clash. "The memories of twelve lifetimes would be too much to bear. No, I remember snippets, important ones. It's important to pick and choose when you manipulate samsara like I do."

By now, Gong Shuren had reached the dais, and the aura around the crown was shifting. On top of the blue-covered artifact, a new blue film was beginning to overlay with the previous one. It wasn't converting Gong Xuandi's attunement, but rather both attunements were happening concurrently. If she didn't at least catch up before the Space-Time Camera's power ran out, she would still lose the race.

"Since this battle will go on for a while, why don't we have a nice chat?" Zhou Li asked. "I've been dying to have one for a while now, and whenever I try to talk, you ignore me."

They exchanged several more blows, and though Cha Ming's were technically more powerful, Zhou Li's strikes were more precise and well-timed.

By now, Cha Ming's curiosity was piqued. "I'm all ears," he said, executing Crushing Chaos once more. This time, he infused water qi into the attack. The destructive water caused Zhou Li to yelp and dodge. He executed a fierce counter-lunge that forced Cha Ming to divert his strike and roll against the man before pushing him away to a safer distance, just in time to avoid a swift upward slice.

"I just thought it would help if you understood our situation," Zhou Li said. "Our people are suffering, Cha Ming. This world, and all the other worlds out there, are unfair to our kind. Karma is skewed against us. It judges our very reasonable actions as sin, forcing us down to the dregs of society. We can't rise from our stations. Meanwhile, the angels lord it over us, acting all high and mighty. But they're hypocrites. I've died to their hypocrisy many times."

Cha Ming had heard this argument before. "Have you considered not doing bad things? Not trying to assassinate kings, not trying to corrupt the destiny of a nation?" Their weapons were tangled together, so he kicked out at Zhou Li. The physical blow was deflected by a shield of flame. Both leg and shield regenerated as he pulled away.

"I've considered *everything*," Zhou Li said. "But tell me, Cha Ming. The angels believe in self-sacrifice, and we believe in self-interest. Wouldn't it make us hypocrites if we followed a code we don't believe in?"

Cha Ming shrugged. "Hypocrisy is better than wrongdoing." They broke off from each other, panting.

"Is it wrong to seek to better yourself?" Zhou Li said. "Is it wrong to try to benefit your family, to strive for a better life? Those who don't do so are just asking to be punished. The heavens help those who help themselves, Cha Ming. You know that."

"An interesting philosophy," Cha Ming said. A few exchanges later, they retreated once more.

"Since I know I can't overpower you right now, I'll offer a trade," Zhou Li said. "You release the space-time lock on Xuandi, and I'll give you a way to further your body cultivation and transcend. Such a thing is expensive, but that's what you want, isn't it? To transcend this plane and find your true love? After the new emperor gains his crown, we'll return to Haijing City, and I'll give everyone a single week to clear out of Haijing as we take control. I'll sign a death contract to guarantee it. This should give the North a fighting chance and allow you to save as many people as you can from this very unfavorable situation."

Cha Ming glared but looked at the black document that floated his way. To his surprise, it even had a clause to prevent Zhou Li from cancelling the contract via his abilities. "I don't see why I should listen to you," he said, shrugging. "If you're offering me this contract, it means you know you're going to lose."

Unexpectedly, Zhou Li laughed out loud. Then, seeing Cha Ming's confused expression, he shook his head. "You seem to misunderstand what you are."

"What I am?" Cha Ming asked.

"You," Zhou Li said, pointing, "are a karmic anomaly. Your fate is undetermined, under your own control. As such, wherever you go, there will always be uncertainty. I'm not a gambling man, so I'd rather take a guaranteed victory. But believe me when I tell you that your situation is far from promising. Nine times out of ten, I will win. I'm giving you this opportunity to prevent that ten percent from materializing. It's a tempting offer, no? With this, your greatest wish might even come true. You'll get to see the love of your dreams regardless of what happens to this plane. We can *both* be happy."

Cha Ming couldn't deny he was tempted by the offer. So many paths had been closed off to him, and it was increasingly unlikely that he'd ever push past core formation. Recultivating was also out of the question; his core was coiled up like a spring, and if he moved to relieve it, he would never be able to cultivate again even if he survived.

Huxian, you've been holding back, Cha Ming sent, glancing briefly at the fighting demons. Battles with body cultivators were long and protracted affairs, but with enough power, they could achieve a swift victory. *What are our odds if you go all out?*

We'll win nine times out of ten, Huxian said. *There are eleven*

*humans, but remember that you can take care of Zhou Li, and we're
not just ordinary demons. We could even take a few more of them on.*

Then do it, Cha Ming said. Then he smiled at Zhou Li. "Thank
you so much for the kind offer, but I think I'll refuse. If you're dead,
so many of our problems will go away. I'll find the right path myself."

"A pity," Zhou Li said. Then, sensing something, he rushed
toward the group fighting Silverwing. At the same time, the giant
falcon's claws glowed with violet light as he reached for one of the
cultivators. The cultivator tried to evade, but the wind pushed him
back into the bird's claws.

Just as he moved to crush the cultivator, however, a black chain
wrapped around the Haijing royal and pulled him back. Silverwing
cawed in frustration. His wings blurred to attack the escaping
cultivator, but just as he was about to flap them, a black sword
thrust toward his throat. It was too fast, and too close. There was no
escaping the strike.

When the sword was only twenty feet away from hitting its mark,
Cha Ming appeared in front of the falcon and deflected Zhou Li's
sword. Meanwhile, the water around Gua and Lei Jiang darkened. The
darkness expanded, and before anyone knew what had happened, Lei
Jiang and Gua appeared near Cha Ming and Silverwing. Gua swung
his fan to entrap the champions and Haijing royals while Lei Jiang
attacked Zhou Li with peals of lightning. Meanwhile, Cha Ming dove
into the crowd of royals with his Clear Sky Staff, striking down with
Crushing Chaos while Silverwing sent feathers of wind tearing down
toward them.

Just as their attacks were about to hit, however, they bounced
off a shield in midair. Cha Ming frowned as he realized that these
shields were not black, like Zhou Li's usual attacks, but gray. He then
noticed another Haijing royal had joined the battle. He carried a set
of gold-blue scales that caused space to fluctuate.

"Seventh prince, just in time," Zhou Li said. "It will be difficult
for them to eliminate us with the protection of your Sea God Scales."

"It was naturally all thanks to Brother Zhou's help," the seventh
prince said, bowing. "Besides—"

His voice cut off as everyone simultaneously looked toward Huxian. The air around him distorted as he began to move with otherworldly speed. His claws raked the surprised champions and Haijing royals. Two of them crashed down to the floor as blood seeped from their chests.

Meanwhile, Huxian grew, and massive jaws of light and darkness enveloped the remaining three. The seventh prince moved to direct his Sea God Scales, but Cha Ming was on him, rushing toward him with an Origin Strike. Just as it seemed like Huxian would succeed in devouring the three, however, a golden light shone.

It was from the third dais, where the Sea God Shell was located. The three cultivators Huxian tried to bite into glowed with a golden light. That light fended off his teeth long enough for them to regenerate and pull themselves out. Huxian glared as the fourth prince appeared in front of him with the shell-like shield on his left arm. The game had changed.

Six glowing gold cultivators rushed at Huxian, so the massive three-tailed fox blinked out of existence and appeared next to Cha Ming. He joined with Gua, Lei Jiang, and Silverwing and unleashed a massive suppressive domain. Sensing an opportunity, Cha Ming joined in with another Origin Strike toward Zhou Li.

However, in the time that had passed, he noticed the man had taken out a large painting. It was a painting of a black crow, and the crow spread out its wings to shield them from the surprise attack before toppling to the ground and curling up like a piece of burning paper.

The two sides retreated, and once again, they were at an impasse.

"Very good," Zhou Li said. "Now, we have the advantage. There's no need to bargain with you any longer. Kill them."

To Cha Ming's surprise, however, one of the princes hesitated.

"They're too strong," the fourth prince, the bearer of the Sea God Shell, said. "Even *with* these Sea God Artifacts. If we fight, we'll lose many Haijing royals. This is *not* in the best interest of Haijing City."

"Come now, brother, surely we can do something about these pests," the seventh prince said.

"We do not serve Zhou Li. We serve Haijing City," the fourth prince said, cutting him off. "You'd best remember that."

Cha Ming raised an eyebrow at those words. He'd thought they were united behind Zhou Li, but it seemed things weren't so simple. Rather than a solid alliance, it looked like the South and some Haijing royals were simply using each other.

Zhou Li rolled his eyes. "I knew you would say that. Well, then, let me try to reason with your leader." He swung out with his sword.

Cha Ming blinked as he realized that it was headed toward the dais with the crown. It was fast, too fast for him to stop, and before he knew it, a rift had appeared. But it hadn't cut space—it severed karma. Gong Shuren, who had been busy attuning to the crown, suddenly stood up. Her face was pale, and her eyes wide.

"What have you done?" she asked, trembling.

"I severed your karma with the crown," Zhou Li said impassively. "You can no longer attune with it, and the other two artifacts have been claimed. Accept your fate."

Gong Shuren, not daring to believe what she'd heard, reached out to the Sea God Crown, only to be rebuffed by it. "Impossible," she said, sinking down to her knees. Before they even hit the floor, however, Zhou Li struck out again. This time, he slashed toward Cha Ming, who felt a jolting pain as his Space-Time Camera, which had been humming along without any issues, stopped feeding the space-time lock on the third prince.

"Relax," Zhou Li said to Cha Ming. "I could never cut your karma with the camera itself. I just severed its karma with the picture it took. With this, you can no longer stop the prince. If you try, I'll repeat the process. Besides…" The golden crown, which had been almost completely overtaken by the blue tide of bloodline energy, suddenly glowed blue. "He's done attuning. You can't stop him now even if you wanted to."

The glow was blinding, and Cha Ming resisted it with all his strength. It soon faded, revealing the third prince, who picked up the crown and placed it on his head. The moment he did, all the

Haijing royals in the room quivered. They dropped to the floor in prostration.

"I don't suppose I can trouble you to help me kill them?" Zhou Li asked, pointing to Cha Ming and the rest.

The third prince raised an eyebrow. "I don't see why I should. Haijing is neutral. We've simply engaged in a facilitating relationship between our two factions, nothing more."

He looked to Gong Shuren, who was still kneeling in disbelief. "Moreover, they are friends with my sister. According to tradition, she is my future empress, the one with the purest bloodline. It would be wrong to antagonize her by killing her friends, no?"

Zhou Li sighed and shook his head. "What a bittersweet victory."

A soft gray light enveloped the third prince and the others as they left the chamber. They then heard a chime in their heads announcing the name of the new Sea God Emperor. Anyone who wanted to leave the Sea God Trials could now do so. Despite this freedom, Cha Ming and his friends remained to console the weeping princess.

They'd lost. Again.

Chapter 27: Frustration

Breathe, Cha Ming thought, trying his best to calm his tense nerves. *Breathe,* he thought again as he struggled to hold back his frustration. As he did, the events over the past six years replayed in his mind. The endless cycle of failure after failure cut at the meager thread of determination he still possessed.

Huxian looked at him, uncertain of what to do. The fox's friends knew even less; they avoided Cha Ming and Huxian by keeping themselves entertained in a corner of the large room. Most of the light in the room had already faded, and all that remained was the soft golden glow from the face of the large clock behind the three daises.

Don't dwell on what happened. Think of a way forward, Cha Ming thought. But he couldn't help but think back. Ever since crippling his cultivation, his path to advancement had been blocked off repeatedly. But this latest defeat ate away at him like nothing before, as it affected not just himself but many people he cared about. An alliance between Haijing and the South would mean millions if not billions of lives would be lost.

Sure, he'd achieved many things in the process. Becoming an elder-level figure in five professions was praiseworthy. He was even a grand elder in one of them. Creating the Nirvana Pill, if but for a moment before the heavens destroyed it, was nothing short of a miracle. He'd even created a transcendent talisman, something that should never have been possible for someone at his level. But despite these small successes, he'd still failed.

He'd failed in protecting the Nirvana Pill. Further, the runic replacement for it would not be completed before he died. He didn't have enough *time*. To make matters worse, the single portion of Water Source Marrow on this plane had been destroyed by the same spiteful man that had caused his predicament in the first place. No, he wasn't a man, but a devil. He had to be a devil, for no one else could be so hateful. Both body cultivation and qi cultivation were now distant dreams to Cha Ming. And now, he'd failed in preventing an alliance with the South and Haijing. These three failures were far too much for him to bear.

He glanced at Gong Shuren, who still lay kneeling down before where the Sea God Crown had been. If anyone felt worse than he did, it was her. The crown princess had failed in securing the Sea God Crown and could no longer become empress. Moreover, it seemed like she would have succeeded if any other champion had accompanied her. Zhou Li had known all along and encouraged her to invite him. He'd manipulated her judgment, and as a result, ruined her.

"It seems meeting Yu Wen in this life is hopeless," Cha Ming said with a weak, desperate laugh. Sun Wukong's soul materialized near him and patted him on the back. Cha Ming flinched but soon relaxed. "Why are the heavens so spiteful?"

Sun Wukong closed his eyes and sighed. "Indeed, why are the heavens so spiteful? They gave you a brush to change your life only to bar your path repeatedly. Your life would have been peaceful without it."

The Monkey King walked around and felt one of the soft pillars in the room. Though it looked brand new, its aura was ancient. Was it fifty thousand years old? Five hundred thousand? Five million?

"I, too, once obtained the Clear Sky Brush," Sun Wukong continued. "I was a lot luckier in my journey than you were. I was born in a transcendent realm, and I used that brush to become a king among my people. Unlike most of my kin, I didn't follow the path of a demon, but that of an immortal. I ascended to the heavens, and do you know what I found?"

"Disappointment, I'd imagine," Cha Ming said. He'd heard a rendition of the story before.

"They looked down on me," Sun Wukong said. "They tried to put me in charge of a stable. Then a universe war broke out. Devils scrambled out from every corner of the universe, attacking the seven heavens, transcendent planes, and mortal planes alike. I fought with everything I had, and I even killed a devil emperor. But despite my best efforts, the heavens still hated me. When I complained, Guanyin herself sealed me inside the staff as its 'treasure spirit.' Huh. As if I qualified to be this treasure's spirit. So, I understand how you feel more than anyone. It's a feeling that gnaws away at you and makes you yearn to turn over a darker leaf, if just to spit in heaven's eye."

"Why didn't you?" Cha Ming asked softly.

"Because the heavens aren't spiteful," Sun Wukong said. "And they don't coddle us either. They simply are. One aeon, they favor the righteous. Another, they favor the wicked. It's a cycle that keeps the world going, and all of us that suffer are just caught up in the collateral damage. The heavens are doing their job. They keep us on our toes, and when we get soft, they throw something at us to sharpen us and change us."

"Just doing their job," Cha Ming said, chuckling softly. Then he began laughing hysterically with tears streaming down his face. "Well, it could always be worse."

"That's right," Sun Wukong said. "You have friends, a brother to rely on. And, might I add, an overprotective teacher."

Cha Ming smiled at that one.

Sun Wukong motioned to the woman still kneeling on the dais. "She's got it worse. Not only did she lose the throne, but she'll have to marry the one who defeated her, someone she doesn't like, and give him as many children as possible. And she'll have no choice in the matter. Those from Haijing can't disobey their Emperor, at least not easily."

Cha Ming looked at her pityingly. He didn't know what to say. Likely, anything he said would just make matters worse. Still, he cursed his wretched luck. Karma was clearly not looking out for him like it should. But then again, he should have known better than to expect the best because of something silly like good karma. Fate favored the righteous, but it couldn't always do that. Bad things happened to good people too, just like good things happened to bad people. It was the way of the world, and without this basic fact, people wouldn't have a chance to be people. There would be no difficult choices to make.

Sighing, Cha Ming closed his eyes again. He sat in the pool of blood that had dripped from his own clenched fists and closed his eyes to rest.

Huxian was sad. He could feel his brother's pain and suffering, and there was nothing he could do about it. He couldn't feel the princess's suffering, but he could smell it. Sadness was thick in the air. He didn't like sadness; happiness and playfulness were much better options. He also didn't like losing. Winning was much better. They were experiencing both these bad things, and he was keen on rectifying it.

He sighed as he looked about the room. They hadn't left since the battle, as they were still recovering, both physically and mentally. Their opponents had gone, and the room, which had suffered a substantial amount of collateral damage, was repairing itself. It regenerated with every tick of the clock that loomed over them and the three daises.

He growled at the clock. He didn't like it, as it made him feel powerless. The clock was the most powerful object in the room, and he was certain it was responsible for the structure repairing itself. Moreover, he felt that it wasn't a miniature version of the clock tower on the outside, but an incarnation of it. It and its large version were one and the same. One loomed over the outside world while the other loomed over the inside. Laughing at them.

This whole mess was the clock's fault. He knew that, and his friends knew that. Cha Ming didn't know, but he figured his friend wouldn't believe him in any case. Clocks were inanimate objects, or so humans thought. Well, most of them were, he admitted. But this clock was different. *It* had set the tests and administered them. *It* had increased the difficulty of their two original trials at its own discretion, directly leading to their loss. It even had the gall to blame its subordinate treasure spirits. More unforgivable, however, was that even though they were clearly better than the other party, the clock had the audacity to hand the throne over to someone who allied himself to the jerk Zhou Li.

Zhou Li. He spat the name mentally. Whenever he thought of that sad excuse for a man, he felt like destroying something beautiful. He was ruining his brother's good mood at every turn like it was all a game to him. But that was to be expected. Seers were always like this, playing around with people's lives. Perhaps only Wang Jun was tolerable, but barely so.

The clock, he thought. *I should really teach it a lesson. I refuse to believe we can't win against it.* He looked to his friends and shook his head. The clock was part of these wretched walls, connected by both karma and other runic lines. Therefore, he slipped on his goggles and did what Cha Ming should have been doing. He hit them.

He traveled along the walls with frightening speed, carving them up with strokes of his tail. The clock moved to regenerate them, so he continued his work.

You want to fix these walls? Fine. I'm going to break them. I'll break them repeatedly and force you to remake them. Consider this punishment for interfering in our matters.

The more he broke, the faster the clock ticked. Seeing his efforts were paying off, he split into three clones and tripled down on the destruction. Silverwing, seeing him rip up the surrounding walls, decided to join in. His two other bored friends joined in as well. Gua sliced them with currents of water, and Lei Jiang blasted them with heavenly lightning. The clock ticked faster, and the walls fixed themselves even more quickly. Destroying things also helped everyone feel better. Win, win, win.

You think you can outrepair us? Huxian scoffed. His aura of light and shadow oozed out from him and his three clones. His friends unleashed more and more attacks. The walls crumbled around them, raining down on the humans below. The clock ticked faster, and for a moment, Huxian caught a flicker in his violet lenses.

Brother, attack with us! Huxian yelled.

No reply.

Come, brother, help me! he yelled again.

Cha Ming, who'd been sitting in his tiny blood pool—a strange occurrence, but who was he to judge—looked up. His glazed look faded slightly, and he frowned in reprimand.

Huxian scowled and called again. *Help me fight the walls, dammit. I think I see something.*

Confused, Cha Ming summoned his staff, which became a sky-scorching halberd and crushed a chunk of wall off.

Huxian rolled his eyes. *Faster and more perfectly.*

Cha Ming sighed in his usual fashion but decided to play along. He was nice that way. No matter how unreasonable Huxian was, he would eventually give in. Fortunately, Huxian wasn't being unreasonable. Not this time.

With Cha Ming added to the equation, their destruction mounted. It wasn't that he was very strong, but his Clear Sky Staff was just *really good* at destroying things. Or Clear Sky Halberd. Or whatever he called it now.

The destruction mounted, and the ticking intensified. As it did, Huxian saw a distortion out of the corner of his eye. He traced it back to its origins, allowing his eyes to focus as he worked his way toward it.

The destruction continued for a while, and then he saw it. It was a nigh-imperceptible bubble next to the clock tower. The bubble was only an inch thick, clinging closely to the clock face like its life depended on it. Though this invisible bubble didn't seem like much—

he normally wouldn't have seen a difference without his goggles—he could tell it was far more important than that. It was a result of the clock, a by-product of it. And it was exactly what they needed.

Huxian rushed toward the bubble as he barked at them to not stop destroying. Then, using the spatial power he'd harvested from the spatial fragment and the keen insights into time laws he'd gained on Jade Moon Planet, he connected to the invisible bubble. It didn't resist.

Overjoyed, he caused it to expand and stepped back as it did. He continued until it expanded a full hundred feet out from the clock. Then, after hitting a snag, he burned his blood essence and forced it out another two hundred feet. Then, another three hundred. Then finally, nine hundred. Yes, that would be more than enough for his needs.

Huxian frowned as he saw black and white strings dancing within the invisible bubble. The clock was ticking quickly as the others destroyed the building. Perhaps five times faster than normal.

Since the ticking increases the regeneration speed of the walls, I should be able to affect this bubble by affecting the ticking. He glared at the needle that represented seconds and willed it to move. And move it did. It ticked faster and faster, until the sound became a constant droning to everyone around it.

Cha Ming was the first to yelp in shock as he almost failed to retrieve his staff in time as the wall fixed itself around it. That didn't surprise Huxian, as he'd sped up the ticking to thirty times faster than normal. Not nearly enough. Seeing that Cha Ming and the others were no longer attacking the wall, he felt comfortable in accelerating the flow of time. One hundred ticks per second. Two hundred. Three hundred. He kept increasing the flow of time until he could no longer tell how fast it was ticking. Then, satisfied, he summoned Mr. Mountain.

Go in there and cultivate, he instructed. *Sit. Stand.* He sighed. *Just do your thing.*

The mountain hesitated but followed orders. If there was anything good about Mr. Mountain, it was that while he was dumb as a rock, he listened. The violet mist floated inside the bubble in uncertainty. Its pace quickened as it stepped inside, and before Huxian could register what it was doing, it had transformed into a hundred-foot-tall mountain inside the bubble.

Good. Good. He'd use that wretched clock to speed level Mr. Mountain. Plus, he would do it for free, as the clock would draw its power from the nearby oceans to do it. The clock was a near-limitless source of energy. On that note, he willed the bubble to compress even further, and soon a small trickle formed. It was condensed time essence, which he lapped up greedily.

Yes, revenge was a dish best served quickly. Another plan, perfectly executed.

Cha Ming stared wide-eyed at the mountain. He'd seen the purple mist drift slowly toward the clock, but before he knew it, it had zipped in front of it and materialized as a mountain. Further, it seemed to be growing at a rate detectable to the naked eye.

"What's going on?" he asked Huxian.

What's going on is I'm a genius, Huxian said. *See that clock there? It's had it out for us this entire time. It made this challenge way too difficult for us.*

"The clock," Cha Ming said in a deadpan voice.

That's right, Huxian said. *So I decided to get revenge. I saw that it could generate a time field. That made me think of Mr. Mountain, who's very different from Lei Jiang, Silverwing, Gua, and me. He's an illusory mountain, and while illusory demons grow much more slowly than normal demons, mountains do too. It needs time more than it needs energy. That's why I decided to exact the most perfect revenge on the clock. It destroyed your choices for advancing, so I'm stealing its time-altering powers and diverting it for our personal use. Mr. Mountain is going to be awesome because of this. Give him three months tops, and he'll be a god amongst ants on this plane.*

Cha Ming's head hurt. Huxian wanted revenge, so he bent time itself to do it? Then, a thought struck him. *How much faster is time in that area?*

I dunno, ten times near the outside, an average of six hundred times where Mr. Mountain is. Closer to the clock, I have no idea.

"Huxian, you're a genius," Cha Ming said.

"I said that," Huxian huffed. "My revenge is perfect. I'll teach that clock a lesson it'll never—"

"Teacher Sun, what do you think the time flow is like near the center of the time-contraction field?" Cha Ming asked.

Sun Wukong's spirit appeared beside him. "I'm not sure. Maybe a few hundred thousand times? It's tough to say because the time field distorts spiritual perception."

Cha Ming smiled when he heard this. He summoned two objects. One was the Water Essence Core, while another was the Runic Nirvana Pill. "Do you think three months on the outside is enough to mature at least one of these?"

Sun Wukong closed his mouth and opened it several times. He raised his finger, then put it down. "Maybe failing was a blessing in disguise? It's tough to say for sure, but toss 'em in. A mortal body would get torn to shreds near the clock by the space-time distortions, but those inanimate objects are different. Both the Runic Nirvana Pill and the Water Essence Core should be able to withstand the strain. If we're successful, we'll solve both your body-cultivating problem and your core at the same time."

Cha Ming's eyes gleamed. He used his transcendent force and threw them both toward the base of the tower.

At that moment, Gong Shuren walked up beside them. She looked quizzically at Sun Wukong and then at Cha Ming. "What's going on?" she asked.

Cha Ming bowed apologetically. "My apologies, Sister Shuren. While I was sulking over my failure, Huxian discovered something interesting: a time-contraction field. So, while we've failed in our struggle for the Sea God Crown, we've found a silver lining. Huxian can help his friend gain strength, and I may be able to use the extra time acceleration to resolve the problem with my core and body cultivation." He averted his gaze. "I'm sorry about your loss. If there's anything I can do for you in the future, anything at all, I will. This was my fault."

His words didn't seem to register, however. Gong Shuren stared at the miniature Sea God Clock Tower and put her hand to her chin. Her body language shifted. One moment, she was unhappy, resigned to her fate. The next, her back straightened. Then she chuckled. Her laugh intensified, then peals of laughter filled the room as a determined glint appeared in her eyes.

"Who would have thought that this loss was actually a blessing in disguise?" she mused.

"Pardon?" Cha Ming asked.

"We have many records of the trials," Gong Shuren said. "Every trial, three artifacts are claimed. Most parties clear the other two trials in roughly the same amount of time. The first two tests are just screens for worthiness, but the third test is the real one—a test for bloodline."

Cha Ming nodded slowly. "You were able to attune much faster than your brother."

"The disparity in bloodline concentration can be frustrating," Gong Shuren said. "To try and bridge this gap, they tried something daring. They tried to attune to this." She pointed up. "The Sea God Clock Tower."

Cha Ming's eyes lit up in surprise. "You mean it's possible?"

She shook her head. "Theoretically, it is, but the process is far too slow. Based on the attunement rates, an average family member would need over a hundred years to attune with the clock. Not at all achievable in the time we have available. But if time were accelerated somehow…" Her eyes gleamed. "I estimate I only need a few years to attune the clock with my strong bloodline. We normally only have a few months, but Huxian may have just made this possible."

Cha Ming hesitated. "Will getting the clock make a difference? Won't your brother still be emperor?"

"Emperor?" Gong Shuren said. She thought for a while and nodded. "Yes, he would be. But does an emperor matter before a god?"

Before he could say anything, she walked into the time-contraction field. She swiftly sat down, and the blue light of attunement began to wash over the clock tower at the back.

"Well, then," Cha Ming said to Sun Wukong. "What's next?"

The Monkey King shrugged. "Wanna play *Angels and Devils*?"

"Yeah," Cha Ming said. "*Angels and Devils* sounds wonderful." He had many preparations to make before their exit from the Sea God Trials, but that could wait. He'd switched from hopefulness to rage to heartrending disappointment and back to hope again. He had much to do, for sure, but much time to do it in. For now, he needed to rest his weary mind.

They summoned an old board, an incomplete game. They'd been playing it for days, but neither wanted to give in. Sun Wukong had had the initiative most of the game, but his play was hampered by two stones Cha Ming had stuck in the center during the game. The earlier moves he'd allowed Cha Ming to make had set him up for a comeback. They were now the cornerstone of a new offensive, and if he grasped it, Cha Ming would win.

As they played, Cha Ming glanced at the blue stone and the medicinal pill near the Sea God Clock Tower many times. If either of them matured, he could transcend. And regardless of whether they worked or not, it seemed like he'd have a Sea God Clock Tower-wielding goddess with a belly full of rage on his side.

They weren't just continuing their old game with Zhou Li; they were flipping the board.

Chapter 28:
Changes in Haijing

Violet light danced around Zi Long as the specters of his past, present, and future roamed around him. They taunted his hopes and tugged at his dreams. Real and unreal alike, they attacked their creator, furiously ripping into his beliefs with mindless purpose. And by doing so, they made him stronger. Illusions were born of the heart; increasing their power required constantly testing it, bringing it ever closer to the violet gemstone it was close to becoming.

Zi Long appeared helpless to external observers. His body seemed weak, and his mental state distraught. But beneath this fragile exterior was a will of iron. Yet at this moment, the iron wavered. His brow twitched in consternation as he opened his eyes. Simultaneously, a violet mist emerged from his spiritual sea and appeared before him. "Something's wrong. Something's changed."

The holy spirit nodded slowly. "The mood of the people has shifted. It must have something to do with their new emperor."

The new emperor. He had emerged from the Sea God Clock Tower while his master hadn't. Though the Alabaster Group had confirmed that Cha Ming wasn't dead, that didn't mean he was doing well. To make matters worse, the Emperor seemed to favor Zhou Li, and their return had come with many unfavorable policies for their dwindling membership.

Sighing, Zi Long stretched out his stiff limbs and walked out of his residence—one of many reserved for normal members—and into the courtyard. On the opposite side of the courtyard, he saw a small commotion breaking out. A short man whose name he couldn't quite remember was yelling at two men. One of them was an elder. He picked up snippets of their conversation as he approached.

"This is my residence!" the man shouted. "You can't take it from me. I earned it by applying fair and square. My lease isn't due until the end of the year, and even then, I have a perpetual renewal clause."

"Yes, I understand that," the elder said. It was Elder Gan, the leader of all the elders. He, of all people, was the least likely to be arguing with a normal member. "Unfortunately, the newly appointed headmaster has decreed that our faction isn't contributing enough to the general knowledge pool. Since we've refused to supply more, they've reduced our quota for residences and time-essence discs. All we can do now is move some of our members outside of Haijing Academy. I assure you that it will only be a slight inconvenience."

"But it's my *home*," the man said, quivering. "I've been studying quietly here for sixty years. Sixty years! Moreover, you're not just taking away my residence, you're taking away most of my laboratory time. Most of my library time."

Elder Gan sighed. He was tired and worn out, the dark patches under his eyes a testament to his fatigue. He glanced at Zi Long briefly before continuing. "We're all suffering. Not just you, but every single member of our faction. Even the elders are suffering, and I've taken on a lion's share of the cuts. It's a new reality that we have to adapt to."

Suddenly, the man's eyes lit up. "I could leave the faction," he said excitedly. "All I'd need to do is forget. If I forget what I learned from the Alabaster Group, I could stay."

Elder Gan's eyes narrowed. "You can. Many have. But we'll never take you back if you do. I'd suggest you think about it carefully."

Sensing that the man was about to do something desperate, Zi Long stepped in. He used the softest illusions he knew to alter the man's state of mind. His anger lessened, and so too did his sense of attachment. It was a slight change, just enough for him to think through it rationally.

"Why don't you take some time to think about it?" Zi Long said. "It's never too late to consider leaving, but with a single misstep, you'll be falling out with our entire organization. No one wants that."

The man gulped, nodded, and hung his head. "I'll think about it. I'm just so…"

"Confused," Zi Long finished. "You don't know the right way forward. That's fine. No one does. You're suffering right now, but so is everyone. We're a team, so we'll get through this together. Elder Gan will help us get through this."

The man gave him one final nod, then walked into his chambers to pack up.

"Mind explaining what's going on?" Zi Long asked Elder Gan once the man was out of earshot.

"I'd forgotten how powerful your control over emotions was," Elder Gan said. "Maybe it'll come in handy in the coming days."

Zi Long waved his hand dismissively. "It's nothing much. I can't affect very strong people since emotions aren't my focus. I major in illusions, not charms. Now tell me, what's going on?"

"It's the new headmaster, Yao Lan," Elder Gan said.

"New headmaster?" Zi Long asked, perplexed. He'd never heard of such a change.

"He was appointed three days ago with not much pomp and ceremony," Elder Gan explained. "The holder of the Sea God Scales manages the leadership of Haijing Academy, which exists under the good graces of the Sea God Emperor. Unfortunately, Yao Lan is the leader of the Obsidian Syndicate faction. He's enacted many aggressive policies since he took over, so we've been forced to evict many of our own people."

"But why? Isn't Haijing Academy always neutral?" Zi Long asked.

"It still is, according to them," Elder Gan said scornfully. "But there are never enough workshops, whether high quality or lower quality, to go around. The same applies to time-essence discs and library time. While elder votes have typically decided much in the past, there's no obligation for the headmaster to listen. He is well within his rights to use certain parameters to guide his decisions, such as meritorious contributions to the knowledge base, the potential of a member's research objectives, and the like.

"As you can see, Yao Lan has chosen to ostracize our faction. Your master's restrictions on the dissemination of knowledge irked the Obsidian Syndicate faction, so now they're taking revenge. They're arguing that everything they're doing is for science, while we're holding on to knowledge for political gain. They're not wrong, certainly, which is what makes this so frustrating.

"As a result, we've had to cut research budgets and workshop allocations across the board. And ever since Headmaster Yao was appointed, the academy has had an influx of new members, making residences in short supply."

"What a coincidence," Zi Long said wryly.

"Indeed," Elder Gan said. "Many of our newly recruited members have already left, choosing to forget what they've learned so they can keep studying. Meanwhile, many of us are being forced out of Haijing Academy. We can still study here, but it's inconvenient to say the least."

Zi Long frowned. "You say we're being forced out of Haijing Academy?"

"That's right," Elder Gan said. "We can only prioritize lodgings for our strongest and most senior members. Your master's status is high, so you'll retain your lodging."

Zi Long fondled his chin and thought for a moment. "I volunteer myself for eviction."

Elder Gan looked at him in surprise. "*What?* Why?"

"You seem to think they're playing the long game," Zi Long said. "They want to choke out our stream of professionals in the North while diminishing our knowledge base. But that's something that could easily be done by other means. For example, by banning knowledge hoarding entirely."

"So their goal isn't eviction..." Elder Gan said. "Since we still maintain a foothold, and Haijing is very strong on its own, our transcendents don't dare interfere."

"What they are doing is upsetting but still within the bounds of what's acceptable," Zi Long said. "But the short-term consequences are probably what they're after: they're dividing our forces."

"This isn't a battlefield," Elder Gan protested.

"This *wasn't* a battlefield," Zi Long corrected. "Violence is still prohibited in the academy, and the same applies to Haijing City. But the peace in Haijing City is kept by the City Guard. I take it the head of the City Guard has changed as well?"

Elder Gan blanched. "Yes, it has."

"Then it's important I be evicted as soon as possible," Zi Long said. "It's also equally important for us to purchase properties in a compact location where we can look out for each other. I might not be the strongest, but with respect to protective and illusory formations, I'm top notch. We should be able to hold up against enemies even when the City Guard chooses to turn a blind eye to our persecution."

"Shouldn't we just leave the city?" Elder Gan said.

Zi Long shook his head. "It's already too late for that. To leave Haijing, we'll need to cross several continent widths through treacherous waters. Anything could happen out there."

"I'll meet with the elders and make preparations," Elder Gan said gravely.

"Then I'll go find our blood doctor," Zi Long said. "I suspect many of us are going to need her soon."

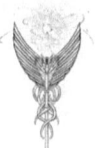

Yue Bing knew something was wrong well before the knock on her door. Her blood vitality twitched and writhed as it sensed the presence of an equal—no, a superior. That wasn't surprising. She hadn't cultivated her blood arts much, as the vitality she could absorb from medicinal herbs was limited. What *was* surprising was that they'd finally come to see her. It was common knowledge that she loathed blood masters, those who'd corrupted blood arts and brought them over to the Southern Alliance.

She hesitated to open the door, but before she could decide on a course of action, the door burst open. Three red-robed men walked in leisurely. None of them were large, but all of them were strong. One was a peak blood grandmaster and the others were high-grade ones.

"Blood Doctor Yue," the man said. "My name is Xue Long. I'm pleased to finally make your acquaintance." He gave her a deep, mocking bow. The type you'd see a jester give in a king's court.

"The pleasure is all mine," Yue Bing said. "How can I help you three? I take it you have a good reason to break down my door?"

"*Our door*," Xue Long corrected.

Yue Bing raised an eyebrow.

"The council has decreed that it's a waste to have a single blood artist form her own school. As such, the Blood Doctor School has been merged with the Blood Artist School. This way, we can all work together at improving our very similar arts."

"Our arts are night and day, unmixable," Yue Bing said. "There's a reason we've been assigned different professions. I'm no more a blood artist than you are a spirit doctor."

"The academy's leadership disagrees," Xue Long said with a grin. "That's why we're here to invite you to our headquarters."

"I'm afraid I'll be declining your invitation," Yue Bing said.

"And I'm afraid that's nonnegotiable," Xue Long said.

A bloody aura filled the air as all three blood masters released their vitality in a sickening cloud. Yue Bing felt her blood try to tug free and escape, but she held it firmly in place.

"You don't want to make an enemy out of me," Yue Bing said.

"If you don't come, we've been told it's acceptable to incapacitate you," Xue Long said. "Very few things are lethal to a blood doctor, so we won't be showing restraint. Given enough time, I'm sure we can make you agree to work with us."

The three men blurred as they lunged toward her. Yue Bing's eyes turned bloodred as she summoned her staff affixed with a golden ankh. Wings of blood sprouted from her back; they flapped, bringing her to safety just before a sword cleaved through the air where she'd once stood.

Yue Bing waved her staff, and a shield of blood appeared just in time to deflect lances of blood that sought to impale her. She tightened her hand, and one of the high-grade blood artist's arms evaporated in a fog of blood. It shot into her bloody shield and reinforced it.

The man didn't even flinch. His hand regrew in the blink of an eye, and before she knew it, he'd disappeared. *Left? Right?* No, he was above her. She summoned six swords and pierced upward. They cut into the blood artist, who ignored the pain and grinned as he landed on top of her. He clawed at her face, only to realize, in horror, that his entire blood vitality was leaching out from him and into her. Then, gritting his teeth, he leaped off. His foot remained on the ground, only to transform into blood that was absorbed by Yue Bing.

"Her blood art is on par with our top cultivation scriptures," the man said. "She's weak, but she can control our blood vitality as though she were a head abbot."

"It's as we thought," Xue Long said. "Change of plans: Strike at her from a distance. Refrain from using blood arts."

The other two nodded, and hundreds of swords shot out from around them. They cut into her shield, but to their surprise, the shield regenerated after every powerful strike. Very few people at her level would have been able to resist, but Yue Bing's blood reserves ran deep. She was a blood doctor, not a blood cultivator, and any self-respecting blood doctor carried their own portable blood bank. Unfortunately, they were far superior cultivators. Her shield wouldn't last more than half a minute, and by then, she would be helpless.

I have a few talismans, including some that Master left me, she thought. *I also know a few combat formations, even if I'm not very good at them. If I can pierce through those swords and impale them with blood spikes, I'll be able to extract their source blood. That should weaken them enough that I can run away.*

It was a plan. A bad plan. She was just a late-core-formation cultivator and a middle-marrow-refining cultivator with a weak body. All she had going for her was her tough, nigh-indestructible flesh. She wasn't afraid of losing arms, legs, or even getting half her body blown to bits. The fact that she'd survive anything they threw at her was equally as frightening as it was reassuring. She shuddered at the thought of what they'd do to her if they caught her.

Suddenly, she saw a glimmer of light behind them. Zi Long appeared in the room. He walked around the three blood masters and danced around their swords. They continued as though nothing had happened.

He's invisible, she realized. He didn't stop until he reached her side. He grasped her arm and then pulled her away from her body. No, she was still in her body. She'd been pulled away from an illusory double who lay on her knees, cowering before their onslaught.

As Zi Long cut through the wall with a soul-alloy knife and pushed it open, she frowned. *You could at least make me look a little more heroic or dignified,* Yue Bing sent. She resented the helpless maiden he'd projected her as.

They're seeing what they want to see, Zi Long sent back. *We need to hurry out of the academy. It's not safe for you here, despite the nonaggression pact they've clearly violated.*

Blood artists are a violent bunch, Yue Bing said. *And now that they've merged our departments, they can call it an internal dispute.*

He nodded and pulled her away. Before long, they found themselves at Haijing Academy's gates. They appeared, showed their identifications, and walked out into the city's streets. They were strange streets they'd only occasionally frequented over the years. Streets where powerful cultivators hid, and even demons roamed. But the academy they'd thought safe was now hostile to them. At least out here, they stood a chance.

What about Jin Huang? Yue Bing asked. Ling Dong always spent all his time outside the city, so they didn't need to worry about him right away.

What about him? Zi Long said sarcastically. *Do you think they'd dare attack the most talented poison master on the plane in the middle of a crowded academy? One wrong move, and they'd be swimming in corpses. No, I think Jin Huang will be just fine.*

Yue Bing nodded and allowed him to lead the way. In the distance, she saw cultivators in white running through the streets toward a poorer part of town. Judging by the red stains that covered their clothing, she'd have her work cut out for her when they arrived.

The transition was proceeding a lot more smoothly than Jin Huang had expected. Instead of a kick in the pants and some pleasantries, several elder-level figures were obediently escorting him outside the premises. They'd obliged his every request to see various workshops he would miss, as well as to collect many books he'd forgotten to read before he had to leave. They'd even allowed him to take many ingredients that might not be available on the outside. Unlike his brothers and sisters, he wasn't being evicted. No, he was being relocated to a remote workshop with top-notch facilities. Anything to keep him happy.

And happy he was. He took the opportunity to visit all the places he liked most. The best workshops. The mess hall. The library. The observatory. In fact, he visited many places he'd never seen before. It was like a massive tour of the facility that continued for a full four hours. Their patience eventually thinned, and now they were pressing for him to leave.

Reluctantly, he left with them. He sighed as he looked back to the academy, to the many friends he'd left behind. Too many friends to count.

"You don't need to see me off," Jin Huang said to the elders who stood around him nervously. "I'm perfectly aware of what's going on. I'll set up my own workshop in the city."

"Are you sure?" one of the elders said. "We hate to inconvenience you, but due to budget cuts, we've been forced to relocate your workshop. But I promise you, the one that's waiting for you is a good one. It would put the best workshop in the academy to shame."

"No need," Jin Huang said. "I can support myself without any problems. Unless... you want to accompany me while I look for a place to rent?" His eyes brightened as their eyes dimmed.

"We'd love to, but the academy is very busy right now due to the influx of new members," one of the elders said hurriedly.

"These are very trying times," another said. "I'm sure someone with a reputation like yours will have no trouble settling himself in. But these new members are young and inexperienced. It'll be like herding cats."

"I understand," Jin Huang said, sighing. "I'll miss my friends. They're all very dear to me."

The third elder's eye twitched. All the young man's friends had already left the academy. He didn't have many of them, since aside from his disciple brothers and sisters, no one dared talk to him. He was a dangerous individual with a fierce reputation, as innocent as he looked.

"I'm sure they'll be fine without you," the elder said. "Perhaps they'll come visit you in the future."

Jin Huang's eyes brightened. "That's right. Once they've grown strong enough, they'll be able to travel outside to see me. Why didn't I think of that before?"

The elder smiled. "It's been great working with you. I'd shake your hand, but I have a cold."

"So do I," another said.

"As do I," the last one said. "It's been going around. Terrible thing."

"Not a problem," Jin Huang said. "See you soon!" He skipped off merrily and began his search for his brothers and sisters. A few minutes later, he felt something squirming in his blood.

I miss them, a voice said.

As do I, another said. *It'll be lonely without them.*

"It'll be fine," Jin Huang said out loud, causing people on the streets to look at him as though he were crazy. "They're young, inexperienced. This will be a good opportunity for them to experience life and all its wonders. I left them in all the best places in the academy, so there will be countless cultivators for them to interact with, as well as an ample supply of medicinal herbs."

I hope so, another voice said. Like the others that had spoken, it was a living poison that lived inside his body. Jin Huang had been creating and raising a brood of them for the past five years, and coincidentally, they'd just gained the capacity for independent thought. Well, as independent as possible with Jin Huang as their master. Without him, they would wander about, looking for hosts to infect, things to consume, and energy to draw on. Nothing too big, or they'd certainly be detected and destroyed.

It was a good day. A new beginning. Jin Huang smiled as he saw Zi Long and Yue Bing in the distance and waved at them. He'd been spending a lot of time crafting poisons, so it was probably time to focus on something he'd neglected. Like alchemy or his cultivation. There were too many things to do, and so little time. That would all change once his helpers grew strong enough to help him.

Fortunately, living poisons grew quickly.

Ling Dong wiped sweat off his brow as he examined his latest piece of work. It was a small red medallion crafted from a strange ore he'd found in the fissure. He'd made it for the dragon turtle, and it had taken him a long time to figure out what to make for it. With his new artifact, the dragon turtle would soon be breathing fire, just like any self-respecting dragon should.

Small violet runes were tightly interlinked with fiery red ones. He had to admit that finally learning formal runic arts had helped his demonic smithing. Intuition could only go so far without knowledge, he realized. With this new runic knowledge, his abilities had increased by leaps and bounds.

As he stored the medallion, Ling Dong heard a soft knock on the door. *That's odd,* he thought. People didn't usually come so late. Most guards came at dawn at the end of their night shift, or at dusk at the end of their day shift. It wasn't a real dawn and dusk, but the artificial dawn and dusk projected by the giant clock tower in the middle of the city. Still, it was the middle of Haijing's night, a time visitors rarely came.

Ling Dong opened the door and was surprised to see a white-haired figure in golden armor. "Please come in," he said, ushering the man inside. The white hair meant he was a Haijing noble. Haijing nobles were normally figures of authority, which he'd already deduced from the man's City Guard epaulettes. He'd never seen a marshal before, but he'd learned enough about ranks from the many guardsmen he'd spoken to. Marshals reported directly to the grand marshal, who in turn reported to the Sea God Emperor.

"What can I do for you today?" Ling Dong asked. His words were polite, but he was wary. His eyes shone with jade light, and he didn't like what he was seeing. Deep ochre coloring surrounded the Haijing noble. The man was a devil, and a strong one at that.

"I won't take much of your time," the marshal said. "You can call me Marshal Ye, and I've just been appointed along with three other marshals by the authority of the new grand marshal. We've been given a strict mandate to improve the fighting capabilities of our armed forces. I've heard from my men that you're a renowned demonic smith, able to improve the ability of our mounts and tamed aquatic demons."

"I've been doing piecemeal work here and there," Ling Dong admitted. "I usually work with individuals who seek me out. The Guard has never approached me directly for weapon smithing, only demon taming."

"Then it's your lucky day," Marshal Ye said, grinning. "I'm here to offer you a lucrative army contract. Anything you'll make for us, we'll buy, with price commensurate to quality. You've struck it rich, my friend."

Ling Dong hesitated, carefully measuring his words. "Your offer is definitely tempting, but I prefer to deal with my clients on a case-by-case basis," he said. "I like to get to know them and their mount's special needs. As an artist, it's vital to find special inspiration in every case."

Marshal Ye's eyes flickered. "I see. Then it just so happens that I have a special commission I'd like to request, if you could follow me." He walked over to the door.

Ling Dong ignored the pounding in his heart as he followed. His smithy was in a small bubble near the outskirts of the city, a convenient place for soldiers to bring their demonic mounts.

Just like before, guards swam around the area as they inspected and patrolled while off-duty guards relaxed. There was a certain edge in their behavior, however. They were uncomfortable, and for good reason. Just outside the bubble, a massive fiendish shark was swimming around. The fiendish shark had somehow been tamed and restrained, yet it still emanated a frightening and evil pressure.

"I'd like you to build armor for my new mount," Marshal Ye said. "I trust that won't be an issue?"

Ling Dong chuckled, then shook his head. "I'm afraid I'll have to decline."

"Is there a special reason that you're turning me down?" Marshal Ye asked.

Ling Dong hesitated, for he knew the marshal would already know his code of conduct. It didn't matter if he said it or not. "The creature's nature is incompatible with my own. I can't in good conscience craft anything for it."

"I see," Marshal Ye said, shaking his head in disappointment. "That's regrettable. I take it my nature is also incompatible with yours?"

Ling Dong didn't need to reply. The man simply walked off. Ling Dong turned to return to his forge, but before he could reach the door, a few dozen City Guardsmen had entered the bubble. He sighed.

"The charges?" he asked, turning toward them. They held shackles that inhibited both qi and body cultivation, as well as a collar usually reserved for beasts. The marshal had clearly done his homework.

"Unlawful refusal to engage in commerce with the City Guard," the leader of the guards said. "The City Guard has offered you a legitimate business opportunity with very reasonable compensation, and you have rejected it. Marshal Ye has concluded that your actions are politically motivated and that you likely oppose the new emperor's ascent. You will be held while the case is investigated and released if your innocence is proven."

"And my forge?" Ling Dong asked.

"Confiscated until your innocence or guilt is confirmed," the guard captain said. "Please come along peacefully, and you will not be harmed."

Ling Dong's instincts told him to fight, but he knew resistance was futile. While he lost no small amount of honor by surrendering, survival was paramount. "Lead the way," he said, holding out his hands. The shackles cut off his qi, his strength, and his resplendent force, while the collar they fastened around his neck cut off the demonic essence floating in the sea around him. He felt blind and powerless.

He looked around as they escorted him toward the city. Many of the guardsmen he'd worked for and befriended looked at him with conflicted expressions. He knew they wanted to help him but were powerless to do so. Such was life. He looked toward the clock tower his master had entered three months ago as they led him to the city..

When would Cha Ming return? He'd need a miracle to get out of this situation, but fortunately, his master was an expert at creating them.

Interlude: Tides of War

*J*ust let it stop, Feng Ming thought, holding his hands to his head as others argued around him. The deceptively large room he sat in was filled with a few dozen chairs placed around a circular table. An important political figure sat in every chair, each one posing as an equal to the others. Some spoke softly, others loudly. But they all had something in common: none of them listened.

Regardless of how loud they spoke, they were arguing instead of working together. Such was the nature of the Northern Alliance. Despite the very dire news they'd received, the assembled kingdoms still couldn't come to a decision.

You'd think a few hundred war vessels mobilizing from a harbor in Southern waters would snap some sense into them, he thought. He knew it was wishful thinking. The small hope he'd held at the beginning of the meeting had disappeared along with the decorum in the room. And now, they were arguing. Again.

"Order, order," a tired old man mumbled as he smacked a hammer on the table four times. Feng Ming wasn't sure what the symbolism was, but he figured it was something along the lines of "shut up or I'll kill you." The chair of the meeting adjusted his spectacles before continuing. "Now that we've completed our free discussion on the topic, I'd like to invite each representative to state their positions. Let's start with True North Country, as they requested this meeting."

A middle-aged woman with hair wound up in a tight bun stood up. She was one of the weaker cultivators in the room, as True North Country didn't like mixing cultivation and politics. "Based on our intelligence, the fleet is heading north by looping around west. It'll take them two months to arrive, given that they left one month ago. If we don't respond appropriately, the Southern Alliance will set up a foothold on our Northern shores. It will be very difficult to chase them off if they do."

"With all due respect, I think you're overreacting," a man said, standing up. He wore a silk tang-style suit as opposed to cultivation robes. The man came from the Xia Empire, which happened to be as far inland as possible. They were also a respectable distance away from the battlefields between the two warring factions. "It's fair that you're concerned. I would be too if I were you. There are six suitable harbors where they can mount an offensive, and yours is the closest. To land anywhere else, they'd need to travel many more months.

"Unfortunately, mobilizing troops is expensive. Would it not be best if we were absolutely certain before committing our forces? For all we know, it's just a naval exercise. I, for one, do not wish to empty my country's coffers over such a possibility, as unlikely as it is."

"The possibility isn't unlikely," an older, bearded man said. "Our sources have uncovered plans that are years in the making. They'll be attacking Beihai City, mark my words. Huoshan stands with True North." His stance brought about a few claps. Far too few.

"But Beihai Port is only accessible via Haijing's territorial waters," another man said. He was short and balding. He was also an alchemist, the most prestigious occupation in the Evergreen Kingdom, which he represented. "It's the only port in their waters, and they've enforced a strict demilitarization policy for these oceans for over ten thousand years. Even True North Country, who owns the port, is only allowed a few dozen warships in case of emergency. Do you really think they'll let the South invade it? Meanwhile, we're bleeding actual blood in the Evergreen Battlefield. We can't afford to divert any experts on hearsay."

"Anything is possible after a change of government," a lady said.

The tall lady wore a black qipao with golden cloud patterns. She was the representative of the Quicksilver Empire, the Song Kingdom's strongest ally. "I think it's worth taking this seriously. We should at least send an expeditionary force that can slow them down and buy us time to mobilize additional troops. We stand with True North."

"We're fighting on too many fronts," a man with unkempt gray hair said. The man, who was from the Long Kingdom, shook his head. "We can't do it. If we reinforce Beihai, our battlefield will fall."

"Same here," another voice said. Many others piped in. Meanwhile, many countries farther away from the Southern border kept silent as always. They didn't know firsthand how steep a price their Southern neighbors paid to keep them safe. Sometimes, it seemed like they didn't care. They were content to send a little money every now and then, and send bodies as well.

"The Song Kingdom will reinforce Beihai," Feng Ming said, standing up.

The Quicksilver Empire's representative, Li Fei, frowned. "You're already fighting on the Southern Battlefield," she said. "And even though five years have passed, the Song Kingdom still hasn't recovered from its civil war. Let us do the fighting."

"This time's different," Feng Ming said. "I feel it in my bones. We can't spare much, but we need to send some help. I'll personally set out in two months to join the battle." He looked around the room at those who hadn't yet spoken. "I've heard some good arguments from many other kingdoms. The Evergreen Kingdom, the Long Kingdom, and the Phoenix Cry Empire are all busy with their battlefields. The Quicksilver Empire has agreed to support the North's defense despite having the Song Kingdom as a shield and buffer. But what about you?"

"What *about* us?" a tall man with blue cultivation robes and long black hair said. He carried a yellow fan and wore a golden sword at his waist. "We're not blessed with the resources to aid. While you all enjoy a certain enmity against the South, we're always in a constant state of upheaval. Shifting borders and rebellious vassal states are the norm. All to fight over scarce quarries, small spirit woods, and tiny bodies of water. We send you what resources we can every year."

"We don't need money; we need bodies," Feng Ming said, staring him down. He placed his hands on the table, an aggressive gesture in such a setting. "Mark my words, they'll attack Beihai City. We'll bleed in this war."

"Ha," the man said. "You're sending one man up, and you say you're unsatisfied with our response?"

"I'm worth more than half your army," Feng Ming said.

The room went quiet.

"You are just a single man from a backwater country," the man spat back. "You might be a marshal, but we have twenty cultivators that are just as strong if not stronger than you."

"I could take on half your army with my eyes closed and you know it," Feng Ming said. "Now tell me, are you a man or are you a coward?"

The man turned red with rage, and it seemed like a fight would break out at any moment. "Calm yourself, Marshal Feng," Li Fei said. "Now is not the time for posturing. We need to work together, not bring up petty grudges."

Feng Ming had never gotten along with Jiao Ming, likely because he could never accept sharing a given name with him. The man was cheap, petty, and vindictive. And prideful, of course. That was the man's most useful trait, a trait he strived hard to manipulate."

"You're right," Feng Ming said. "I forgot my place. I'm just from a small backwater kingdom with a shortage of cultivators and resources. One of me is all we can afford to send. I'm sure everyone else can afford to do more."

Everyone around the table grumbled. To avoid losing face, all of them would have to send at least one peak-core-formation cultivator. Alternatively, they could send an assortment of core-formation cultivators and foundation-establishment experts that matched one in power. The price would be far from negligible.

"The Desert Wind Kingdom will send ten men, headed by my brother," Jiao Ming said. "They might not be as strong individually, but as a team, they can more than take you on. In addition, we'll send a brigade of one thousand foundation-establishment cultivators. Qi-condensation cultivators are too expensive to ship around."

One by one, the others followed. The few dozen kingdoms quickly formed a patchwork army. Once the details had been settled, there was only one final matter: leadership. Feng Ming was selected unanimously.

The meeting was adjourned, and they all started chatting, laughing, and drinking. Feng Ming was willing to do many things, but pretending to socialize with these snakes was not one of them.

"You should really stop fighting with Jiao Ming," Li Fei said. "He's a strong fighter, and his kingdom is powerful. Think of what you could accomplish by working together." She'd grabbed a glass of red wine in one hand and handed him a small cup of baiju with her other. He took it and shot the burning liquid down in a single gulp.

"Why should I work with him when I can accomplish more by fighting him?" Feng Ming asked. "Just insult his honor and bam—instant army."

She rolled her eyes. "Now you'll just have to explain yourself to Princess Guo. No doubt she'll be wondering exactly what possessed her husband to volunteer for this expedition just after she gave birth to her third child."

Feng Ming grinned. "I'm just the best damn marshal out there, and everyone knows it. Even Jiao Ming concedes to that, as much as we disagree on many things."

"There's that," Li Fei said. "Now tell me, what does your gut tell you about this 'naval exercise'?"

"Honestly?" Feng Ming said, raising his hands helplessly. "If I could get three times as many men to go up with me, I would."

"That bad?" Li Fei asked.

"It's not just a routine exercise, and definitely not a normal battle," Feng Ming said. "They have something up their sleeves, I'm sure of it. But what can we do? We're tapped out. The South's been pressing us hard for the past few years, and many of us are at our breaking point. What I'm getting for this battle isn't enough, but it's all we can spare."

"Then why go?" Li Fei said. "Why put your kingdom in jeopardy to fight for Beihai City?"

"Because I have to," Feng Ming said. "If we lose Beihai, they won't need to limit themselves to the battlefields—they'll be able to send forces in from all their seafaring cities. Based on our most conservative estimates, their army is massive. At best, I'll be able to buy us time."

"I can respect that," Li Fei said. She sighed. "I'll be sure to press our emperor to send more reinforcements south while you're gone."

"Many thanks," Feng Ming said. "Now if you'll excuse me, it's high time I pick another fight with Jiao Ming."

Li Fei raised an eyebrow.

"He owes me a few bottles of wine," Feng Ming explained. "Battles and funding are good and all, but a man needs to pay off his gambling debts."

"What gambling debts?" Li Fei asked.

"The one's he'll be owing me soon," Feng Ming said. "Wish me luck."

Chapter 29: Progress

The solitary clock ticked in Hong Xin's office as she looked over paper after paper. She was exhausted, as were the other women in the room. Despite their fatigue, she, Bai Ling, and Ji Bingxue went over the documents together as they made sure they hadn't missed anything.

Her office, though small, was comfortable and well-furnished. A solid wood desk, complete with runic engravings, sat in front of the window. A small cinnamon-wood fireplace crackled heartily in a corner. A tall grandfather clock ticked away every second, letting out a larger set of tolls every hour or so. She preferred the smaller room to the spacious audience hall, where everyone and their dog could hear you if you so much as sneezed. It was quiet and comfortable. Relaxing even.

Hours passed, and after an exhausting triple-check, they finally relaxed. The last of the small evidence trails had been erased, and they would no longer have to step on eggshells when speaking to the Church of Justice or government officials. The last of the investigations following their foiling of the Spirit Temple's plans had finally died down. Now they only had to worry about assassins in the dark.

Most importantly, they'd finished preparing. The plan they'd worked on for the past few years was finally finished. The Spirit

Temple would move soon, and they would strike hard and fast. Their survival depended on it.

A large map filled with annotations was sprawled over her desk. They'd worked over the plan again and again, running over the different contingencies in case of unforeseen events. Secret passageways most people didn't know existed were shown as thin red lines on a floorplan of the Spirit Temple. Some of these paths had been discovered by questioning their recaptured sisters. Others were the result of a careful infiltration of the temple's staff.

"Are you *sure* they'll use that same storage room?" Ji Bingxue asked. "They've used other storage rooms before."

"Only because they didn't have a choice," Hong Xin said. "Over the past twenty years, they've collected seventeen batches of souls. They've used this room all but two times, and that was only because of regular maintenance. Maintenance isn't due on the rooms for another three years, so they'll use their main one. They prefer it because it's warded with ample protective formations. It's also deep within the temple, so their forces can respond at a moment's notice."

"I'm only saying that we should consider the possibility," Ji Bingxue said.

"We have backup plans to infiltrate the secondary storage room," Hong Xin said. "They've never used a third."

"I agree with the headmistress," Bai Ling said. "The best predictor of future behavior is past behavior."

Ji Bingxue rolled her eyes. "I just think they might change things up this time. What if our people let something slip?"

"Impossible," Hong Xin said. "They've been charmed by the best of us, and they're all low-level and mid-level servants. They aren't important enough to be bound by strict oaths. Besides, what can they say when they don't even know they work for us?"

"Fair. To be honest, I'm more worried about the last piece of the puzzle," Ji Bingxue said. "Will he cooperate?"

"He should," Hong Xin said. "Worst case, I'll... He should."

"There's just a lot riding on this," Ji Bingxue said. "If we have to pay a certain price to get his help, I'm willing to pay it."

Hong Xin rolled her eyes. "Still upset that he isn't fawning over you like everyone else is?"

"Not upset, just disappointed," Ji Bingxue said, pouting cutely like she did with some of their customers. Both Hong Xin and Bai Ling were immune to such charms.

Hong Xin looked up at the clock, whose hands showed just a half hour remained before his arrival. "We'll know if he'll help soon enough. If not, we'll just find another way. Now if you'll excuse me, I need to put my face on."

The two women left Hong Xin in her study. She ran her finger along the wall where a hidden vanity mirror was located. Runic paints and powders, essential tools for glamour arts, lay in front of it. Sighing, she picked up a brush and began applying a coat of plain makeup.

The first layer she put on was blank, as no one could wear two faces at the same time. Concealing her prior appearance was necessary as a foundation for the second. Once she looked as plain as plain could be, she picked up a thin brush and dipped it in a golden ink pot. It flowed across her face as she gave it structure. The many runes she inscribed caused the bones of her façade to distort and move around, thinning in some places and thickening in others.

Texture came second. She picked up a brush with brown ink and adjusted the softness of her skin, adding wrinkles where required and smoothing it out where not. She then used green ink to breathe life into her painting and blue runes that caused others' eyes to flow over her face, barely remembering her features after they saw them.

Finally, she painted red. Red was the color of passion, emotions, and desire. It was the detail in a masterpiece painting. A slight reddening of her cheeks and cherry lips. These small things accented all her other beautiful features. They also gave a familiar feeling to those who saw them.

It was a pity she couldn't show her real face. While it wasn't as pretty, it wasn't the lie she wore day in and day out. Unfortunately, that lie protected her friends and family. It also protected the careful game she played with Wang Jun. She'd gone this far without giving away her identity, and she wouldn't unless she had no choice in the matter.

Hong Xin fastened her hair with a red pin and donned her beautiful red-and-gold robes. She then picked out a red fan with mauve highlights. The door opened just as she finished. It was Bai Ling.

"He's here," Bai Ling said.

Hong Xin nodded.

"Give me five minutes and then let him in," Hong Xin said.

Bai Ling nodded and retreated, leaving Hong Xin to agonize over the most difficult task: choosing which tea to brew.

"Not bad," Wang Jun said as he sipped at his cup of tea. "Sea God's Wrath, aged twenty-six years. A good year."

It wasn't actually a good year, and the tea was terrible, but sometimes it was poor form to tell the truth. Something about the choice seemed desperate to impress him, something he found ridiculous since the person in question was the headmistress of the Red Dust Pavilion. Countless men would fight over her with a snap of her fingers.

"The date of the exchange has been finalized," Hong Xin said. "This year's order is particularly large. You may do what you wish with this information—anything *except* interrupt the exchange. It's vital for us that it goes through."

Wang Jun nodded slowly. He accepted the folio from across the tea table and reviewed the information. He frowned when he saw much additional information. Things related to noble families and merchant houses. Helpful things, but gratuitous. She'd been doing this for a while now.

"This is exactly what I was looking for," Wang Jun said. "As for the rest of this information, I confess myself confused. It's outside the scope of our agreement, and the Red Dust Pavilion isn't usually known for its generosity." He didn't like free things. Nothing was ever truly free.

"We exchanged information for a peak-core-grade concealment treasure," the headmistress said. "We still want it, of course, but we were wondering if you could obtain another seven such treasures for us."

He frowned.

"They don't need to hide people, only objects."

His brow relaxed.

"You know this information isn't worth that much," Wang Jun said. "Nor is the rest of the information you've slipped my way over the years."

"Then tell me what is," the headmistress said.

Now that's different, Wang Jun thought. *She's really desperate.* He thought for a moment before summoning a small box from his spatial treasure. "Let's first settle debts owed before talking about further exchanges." He opened the box, revealing a mauve hairclip inscribed with black runes. He looked for a reaction, but to his disappointment, didn't find one.

The headmistress's hand trembled slightly as she reached toward the box. She took the mauve hairclip and placed it on her head. The headmistress vanished, leaving him alone inside the room. He could see her, of course—shadows could never hide from him. But any other person in this city wouldn't be able to see her unless they physically bumped into each other.

"It might seem easy to make, but I had to infuse it with my own blood essence," Wang Jun said. "I can only make a few such treasures. Then again, objects are much easier to conceal. Why do you require such a thing?"

"I can't tell you that," the headmistress said, reappearing before him. "I need them to hide seven individual objects. They're roughly one foot tall with a half-foot-by-half-foot base. Each object is stationary. I need people to actively avoid them while not realizing it."

Wang Jun nodded. "Doable, but expensive." He tapped his finger on his lips. "But I suppose there's a piece of information you could give me that's worth the trouble."

"Oh?" the headmistress said. "What might that be?"

"I want to see your face," Wang Jun said. "Your true face. No one outside the pavilion has ever seen you without glamour, and even my astute senses can't pierce your veil."

It was a simple favor, worth far less than what he was offering. But the tells were adding up, and he wanted to confirm his suspicions were baseless. Anything to ease his uncertain heart.

The headmistress thought for a while before speaking. "Change your request. Many other things are negotiable."

"Are you sure you can't satisfy this one simple request?" Wang Jun pressed.

She hesitated, then spoke. "I can't show you my face, but I can show you something none of our patrons have seen."

"And what might that be?" Wang Jun asked.

"A personal performance," the headmistress replied. "By yours truly. This might not be my true appearance, but there's a saying: a face is only a mask, but a dance tells all."

"You're a dancer?" Wang Jun asked. He hadn't expected that. Instruments and singing were proper entertainment, while dancing was considered lewd and base. For the headmistress of the Red Dust Pavilion to admit to such a fact was surprising.

He hesitated. A dance wouldn't give him the answer he wanted, and it certainly wasn't worth the price of seven obscurity formations. But his heart couldn't help but beat a little faster when he thought of the Red Dust Mistress performing just for him. He checked his emotional state for tampering and found none.

As Wang Jun agonized over the decision, the headmistress stood up and walked out from behind the short tea table. Every step she took caused his mind to shake and his heart to pound. "Are you sure you won't reconsider?"

His mind was in chaos for reasons he couldn't fathom. He stood up hurriedly and presumptuously put a hand on her shoulder and held her at bay. The shoulder felt familiar yet foreign, and to his surprise, she didn't brush his hand off. Still, Wang Jun was a calm man. He never made decisions in the heat of the moment. He had to do what he was best at. He had to hide and escape.

"I might take you up on that offer," Wang Jun said, calming himself. "Or maybe another favor." He pulled his hand back. "The personal cost in making these obscurity formations is high, so it won't just be a matter of money. We've dealt with each other for long enough; I know you'll repay a favor. Will delivery in one week be fine?"

Silence, then a nod.

"Then I bid you good day, Headmistress."

Wang Jun's pounding heart finally calmed once he was out of the building. He detected no tampering with his emotions, so that could only mean they were genuine. Whether they were the result of infatuation or something else, however, was an entirely different matter.

As he walked back to the Jade Bamboo Headquarters pavilion under cover of darkness, he looked back at the Red Dust Pavilion, where patrons flocked despite the late hour. He somewhat understood their persistent yet irrational behavior. *Stupid,* he thought to himself. He couldn't allow himself to fall for someone else.

His heart couldn't take it.

Chapter 30: Elation

Silence reigned in the inheritance chamber as time flowed like a gushing river. As Huxian and his friends slept, Gong Shuren slowly but surely attuned to the Sea God Clock Tower. What had originally been a plain stone clock with golden highlights now glowed with blue runes starting from the base. The tower portion was completely covered in glowing blue runes, while gold-and-blue ones were slowly creeping onto the clock's circular face, complete with frame, numbers, and needles. The clock's backdrop remained plain as ever.

In the background, the ticking of the Sea God Clock was a constant buzz that most couldn't perceive. Cha Ming had only noticed it after two and a half long months of waiting, during which he'd done things like craft pills, craft talismans, and stock up on time essence. He now possessed a large pool of it, safely nestled inside the Clear Sky World.

The white noise muffled most sounds here. But today, an entirely different sound broke that silence: a pulse, then a soft trickle of liquid. Cha Ming's eyes slowly opened. He turned his gaze to the two objects just beneath the clock and noticed one had changed. The transparent blue orb that Huxian had found in the fissure was glowing. Where there once was nothing, a few drops had condensed at the center of the gem. The soft blue light they generated shone through the Water Essence Core's transparent material.

Then drops appeared one after another. Each one resembled tears of reality leaking out from an invisible gash in the firmament. Three... seven... fifteen... The dripping intensified. It continued for a few minutes until a small blob of Water Source Marrow floated in the center of the gem. The Water Source Core then let out a final pulse. The dripping stopped.

Cha Ming took a deep, shaking breath as he willed the orb over. It was a struggle at first, since the distorted space-time made it difficult to control his transcendent force. "After all this time, I finally have you," he whispered as he gripped the gem in his palm, feeling its cool surface with expectation.

"Looks like I underestimated how much time the Runic Nirvana Pill required," Sun Wukong said. "But this is ideal. You can strengthen your body to better withstand healing your core."

Cha Ming nodded. He took out his Clear Sky Brush and expertly extracted the glowing blue stream. Then he painted a flowing blue script in the air. He painted it one rune at a time in three dimensions. As his soul was now a transcendent one, the process was much faster than last time. Only a single day passed before the 1,080-rune script was completed. The moment the last character was painted, it burst into its component runes and rushed into Cha Ming's three-colored marrow.

A thousand and eighty hints of blue light began growing where red, green, and brown coexisted. The blue lights brought flow to the marrow, which had originally been still and lively. It complemented the energetic, vibrant, and solid marrow from before. His blood changed over several times as the marrow transformed. The bad blood was expunged by his body through his pores, and though it was messy at first, the ooze generated diminished with every cycle.

The process took three days, much longer than last time. The transformation stopped once his blood was completely replaced. Then the blue runes, which still contained most of their original energy, dove into the voids in his bones. Living water runes filled the depths of space; they split and recombined, forming their own cycle.

Meanwhile, a smaller portion intruded on the once-stable worlds of blistering sands and scarce vegetation. Lakes, rivers, and oceans appeared on the once-dry planets, destroying the subtle balance that had been achieved over many years. But water was flow, and flow always proceeded to equilibrium. Soon, a cycle finished forming. It was a water cycle that flowed around and between pieces of land. Plants thrived, while the blistering heat was tempered by the quenching liquid.

But the world was missing something. Cha Ming knew what it was, but he was in no position to supply it yet. He would introduce himself to this makeshift universe once he found the Gold Source Marrow. In the meantime, he reveled in his increased strength.

Cha Ming's flesh crackled as his body broke through to peak marrow-refining realm. His strength surged until it finally reached what he'd wielded in the Bridge of Stars. At initial bone forging, his strength had hovered around 4,320 jin, as his strength was one rank higher than other body cultivators'. It had increased gradually until he'd broken through to initial marrow refining, where he'd possessed a strength of 43,200 jin. One hour ago, his strength had sat at 87,200 jin. Now, his strength had grown to 108,000 jin, that of a half-step-blood-awakening cultivator's.

One hundred and eight thousand jin. He knew that was a lot, but he also knew that it was far from what a mortal plane could support. Though transcending would increase his strength by a factor of ten, his journey on the Bridge of Stars told a different story. By completing a precarving on a core, his strength as a qi cultivator could increase by as much as three times and a third. He wondered if a similar thing was possible between peak marrow refining and blood awakening.

Regardless, Cha Ming felt nigh invincible on the Ling Nan Plane. His bones were as hard as half-step-transcendent treasures, which meant that only transcendent treasures or attacks that approached the transcendent realm could mortally wound him in a single attack. The only other way to kill his body was through attrition. His enemy would need to deplete the many small worlds of vitality within his bones. Even if half his body was somehow destroyed, including his internal organs, he could regrow them in just a few seconds. But mere flesh wounds? He couldn't care less about them.

The surge in strength was very welcome, but with his newfound ability, Cha Ming discovered something else: a small speck of hope he'd gained with the boost in strength. If he found four portions of elemental marrow, he should be lucky enough to find a fifth, shouldn't he? And even if he didn't, did it even matter, since the Runic Nirvana Pill would be completed soon?

They waited. Some time later, a soft gray light appeared near the Sea God Clock Tower. The Runic Nirvana Pill had finally reached maturity. A maelstrom that sucked in all ambient energy didn't appear around the pill like before. Such a surge of energy wasn't required, as the pill had taken tens of thousands of years to absorb ambient energy from the plane. What did appear was a gray seal—a Grandmist seal. It slowly etched itself onto the pill over the span of a few seconds before the glow finally died down.

Cha Ming summoned the pill with his transcendent force and stared at it. He'd been fighting for this pill for many years. He'd braved the Bridge of Stars and Jade Moon Planet for it. He'd crafted its transcendent version but failed, only to have to settle for this pale imitation. A shadow of doubt still lingered in his heart, but he smothered it like an unwelcome ember in a doused fire.

"It'll work," Sun Wukong said, appearing again. "You have to trust in yourself, trust in your work. It won't be perfect like the original Nirvana Pill, but what's really perfect in this world? Even if it's only a third as strong as the transcendent pill, it'll be enough to mend your core and let you transcend."

Cha Ming nodded. Then, after taking a deep, relaxing breath, he sat cross-legged and popped the pill in his mouth. It dissolved into several streams, one stream for each of the five elements. They meandered through his qi pathways before finally settling inside his Dantian and floating around his core. Only a small amount of medicinal potency began attaching itself to his fractured core and mending it. He needed time. Lots of it.

Teacher Sun, how much time acceleration can a mortal body handle? Cha Ming asked.

I'm really not sure, Sun Wukong said. *Normally not too much, but you're a body cultivator. You should at least be able to handle what the princess is handling.*

Cha Ming nodded and walked into the time-contracted space around the Sea God Clock. He walked past where Gong Shuren was sitting while attuning to the Sea God Clock and closer to Mr. Mountain, who had grown to a respectable 330 feet. It was small for a mountain but rather large for a demon.

Cha Ming's body began to twitch as he walked, and he soon realized why: He was existing in many different time-accelerated zones simultaneously, and the strain on his body was massive. In fact, it would be impossible for him to stand there without a very strong body. Thanking his lucky stars, Cha Ming proceeded closer and closer to Mr. Mountain. His body broke and rebuilt itself repeatedly, and when the strain seemed to be at the limits of what his core could handle, he stopped.

The multicolored medicinal mist in his Dantian continued its slow work; being in the time-accelerated zone didn't change that. What *could* be changed was how time passed in the outside world. Cha Ming continued cultivating calmly and entered the longest period of cultivation he'd ever undergone in his life.

His first stretch of cultivation lasted a whole year before he couldn't take the solitude.

"What, you can't handle a little bit of closed-door seclusion?" Sun Wukong said, laughing. "That's nothing. In the future, you'll have to seclude yourself for thousands of years to make any progress. Think of this as a warmup. While you're at it, you can think about things that have been bothering you and sort them out."

Cha Ming reflected on this advice as he played a few games of *Angels and Devils* and socialized with Huxian and his friends. Then he returned to cultivating. This time, he cultivated for ten solid years. While he did so, he ruminated over his staff arts, his various techniques, and theorized several formations that might or might not work. Since he had a goal to work toward, time passed quickly. Still, only about half of the pill's medicinal potency had been absorbed by his core after ten years. Many of the exterior cracks had visibly mended, but many imperfections still remained. Therefore, he repeated the process many times. Another ten years passed, and a quarter of the original medicinal potency remained. Then twelve and a half percent, then six and a quarter.

Soon, a hundred years had passed for Cha Ming. The medicinal absorption had slowed to a trickle, and while much of the damage had been healed, he could still see many important cracks remaining in his core. If his cultivation increased, the cracks would widen.

Despite the lack of progress, Cha Ming continued. He'd gained a sort of patience and unshakable focus in the process. While cultivating, he spent time deciding what he'd do for his rune carving. He also decided on his next course of action, assuming he managed to thwart Zhou Li's plans for Haijing City.

Finally, on the 108th year since he started absorbing the Runic Nirvana Pill, Cha Ming noticed a change in his Dantian. A small gray flame appeared near a thin crack on his core. The flame moved along the crack, and as it did, the crack disappeared as though it had never existed. True to the name of the pill, his core was being reborn as fire destroyed its imperfections.

The process was much faster than the initial absorption of the medicine had been. In only three hours, most of the smaller cracks were eliminated. After three more, the larger ones also disappeared. Little by little, major holes that had appeared at the center of his core began to shrink until finally, only five small imperfections remained. They were infinitesimally small, but Cha Ming could clearly sense them. Still, he also sensed that they wouldn't threaten this stage of his cultivation. His core could grow unimpeded and would survive rune carving. That was more than enough.

Cha Ming wept as the greatest burden on his heart was lifted. With this, he could cultivate normally and transcend this plane. Once he transcended, he would slowly cultivate until he became an immortal. Once he did, he would find Yu Wen again.

Excited, Cha Ming urged his qi and moved to break through. His qi circulated in his body and rushed to impact against his healed core.

"Stop!" Sun Wukong yelled.

Startled, Cha Ming reluctantly halted the breakthrough process and looked at the belligerent Monkey King.

"You can't break through here. A time-accelerated area like this is great for absorbing medicinal efficiency and great for tempering your resistance to pain since your body can barely handle it, but if you try cultivating here, you'll tear your meridians apart."

Cha Ming looked at Sun Wukong doubtfully. "My meridians look fine. Why can't I take the opportunity to break through to the peak of core formation while we're here?"

Sun Wukong shook his head. "Always so greedy for a quick boost in strength. It doesn't work that way. In fact, there's a reason why your Clear Sky Brush can only support accelerating time by a multiple of five. That remained unchanged while you were in this field of contracted time."

Cha Ming glanced inside the Clear Sky World and noticed that this was indeed the case. While a hundred years had passed for him, only six weeks had passed on the outside. "Is five times the limit for normal mortals?" he asked.

"It is," Sun Wukong said, nodding. "But if you want to push the limits, ten times is also possible. If you sit at the very edge of the time-contraction field, you can still cultivate."

By now, most of the adrenaline at having healed his core had faded. Sighing, Cha Ming walked over to the comfortable edge of the time-contraction field and sat down once more. He circulated his qi and built up momentum before impacting his core. The breakthrough was effortless.

Unlike last time, which had been so painful he'd nearly passed out, it only took a single pop. His qi was as pure as possible due to the long stabilization period. His core expanded as he reached late core formation and a vacuum appeared around him, gathering ambient energy. Cha Ming popped one of the many pills he'd crafted and began feeding his deficient core.

Ten pills later, he was done. He was once again at the limits of a cultivation realm. Tiny specks of impurity filled the qi as usual, and only cultivation and exertion could fix that. Unfortunately, he was out of time.

Cha Ming exited the time-contraction field only to be pounced on by Huxian. For the first time in a long time, he laughed and cried tears of joy. He'd spent over a hundred years of blood, sweat, and tears to finally heal himself and get back on the right track. They laughed for over an hour before Cha Ming looked back to Gong Shuren and the Sea God Clock, whose shortest hand was now fully covered in runes, and whose long hand was halfway covered. He couldn't help but feel uneasy at their shrinking deadline.

"Maybe we should head back early," Cha Ming said. "Just in case. She should be fine here alone, shouldn't she?"

"It's never a bad idea to be cautious," Sun Wukong said. "Besides, there aren't many people who can harm you anymore, the Sea God Emperor included. As for her..." He chuckled. "I'd hate to be the poor fool who tries to cut off her connection with the clock tower."

"My thoughts exactly," Cha Ming said. "Huxian?"

The small fox yawned. Then he called out to Mr. Mountain, who grumbled and turned into a violet mist that shot into Huxian along with Lei Jiang, Silverwing, and Gua. Cha Ming pressed a finger on the pale-blue mark on his forehead, and Huxian pressed a claw on his. Both marks shattered and sent them outside the Sea God Clock Tower.

Chapter 31: Challenge

Cha Ming and Huxian appeared in Clock Tower Square, prompting gasps from those around them. They surveyed the city as cultivators watched. The city had changed, and not in a good way. He cast out his transcendent soul and mapped out the city. Of his four disciples, only three were in the city, and none were in Haijing Academy. He and Huxian rushed through crowded city streets until they arrived at an assortment of rundown buildings. He was greeted by familiar people—students he'd taught in Haijing Academy, some elders, and other members of the Alabaster Group.

"Master!" Yue Bing yelled as Cha Ming entered a small house where many of them were gathered. She was busy treating a young man whose body was covered in cuts and bruises. A bloody stump where his hand used to be was steadily growing into a new limb, courtesy of Yue Bing's blood vitality. The process continued, and a few minutes later, the young man's condition finally stabilized.

"It happened in an alley seven blocks from here," the man said to Elder Gan, who'd been waiting as Yue Bing treated him. "The City Guard wasn't patrolling the area, and some ruffians robbed me. I was outmatched, so I gave them everything I had. Unfortunately, it wasn't enough. They cut off my hand in their displeasure and told me to bring more next time."

"They dare to be so brazen so close to our headquarters?" Elder

Gan said angrily. "Do they think we won't hunt them down?"

"We have no proof," Zi Long said. The violet-robed man had been sitting cross-legged in a corner during the treatment. "The City Guard will intervene if we act against them. It's nothing we haven't already seen in the past two months."

Elder Gan clenched his fists and breathed deeply. Then he frowned and looked up at Cha Ming in surprise. "Your cultivation. It's increased."

Cha Ming grinned. "I experienced a fortuitous encounter in the Sea God Trials. I don't dare say I'm invincible, but there aren't many in this city who would dare tangle with me. Even then, I think it would take a transcendent to kill me."

"Good, good," Elder Gan said, laughing heartily. "We might not be able to retake our place in the academy, but with you here, we should be able to leave the city alive."

"Leave the city alive?" Cha Ming asked. First their members were getting attacked, and now they were talking about leaving the city? "What happened while I was gone? Why is no one in Haijing Academy?"

"What's the point?" Elder Gan said, shrugging. "The headmaster has changed. Elder Dai is nothing more than a senior member of a neutral faction, while the Alabaster Group can only maintain a token presence in the academy. We've been cleared out to make way for those who wish to dedicate themselves to science instead of ideals, and we have no funding or facilities to operate with. The only reason we haven't left yet is because we've been expecting an ambush just outside the city."

"That bad?" Cha Ming asked, aghast. "Who the hell gave them that courage?"

"Zhou Li and his cronies, not to mention the support of the Sea God Emperor," Elder Gan said. "He turns a blind eye to everything Zhou Li does, and the bearer of the Sea God Scales appointed Yao Lan as headmaster. He interprets Haijing Academy's core directives in ways that have completely dismantled our organization while favoring his own. There's nothing we as elders can do to stop him.

Once the neutral elders saw where the wind was blowing, they quickly sided with the headmaster."

Cha Ming massaged the middle of his brow. Just as he was about to ask another question, he heard screams outside the door, along with the clanking of armor. He summoned his Clear Sky Staff in case of trouble but noticed they were carrying a familiar person. The door burst open, and four armored men brought Ling Dong inside. Or what was left of him.

"Please save him, Blood Doctor!" one of the guardsmen said.

Before he'd even said these words, however, Yue Bing had charged in to heal him, and Cha Ming had already fed him a runic pill and stabbed formation flags around him to assist Yue Bing however she needed. Zi Long was also there, helping however he could, and Jin Huang had rushed into the building as well.

Cha Ming sighed in relief as Ling Dong's body began to heal. Many of his fingers had been amputated, and his feet were missing. This normally wouldn't have been a problem for a cultivator of Ling Dong's caliber, but special restrictive devices had been set in place to prevent these injuries from recovering. Further, many spikes had been jammed into him. Even his eyes weren't spared from the torture.

Fortunately, Yue Bing was a miracle doctor. She first removed the spikes going through his torso and aided his body in healing the most critical damage. Then she moved on to his hands and feet. As she did so, Cha Ming used his transcendent force to break the manacles that were restraining what was left of his arms. He used his thumb and middle finger to destroy his collar, giving vision to the blind man. The blindness was temporary, of course, as Yue Bing healed his eyes shortly after.

Ling Dong shuddered but grinned when he saw Cha Ming. "I knew you hadn't died. Those guardsmen and marshals were full of shit."

"Who did this to you?" Cha Ming asked, barely containing his anger.

"The three newly appointed marshals and their cronies," Ling Dong said. He stood up and stretched out, shadowboxing in the air to test out his newly grown limbs. "From what I gathered, they're the head of the new elite corps, a wing of the City Guard."

"Elite corps, my fins," one of the guardsmen spat. "They're only more powerful than us because they've done the unthinkable. They've 'tamed' fiendish sharks as mounts. Sharks! Those are bad enough, but fiendish ones? Is it even possible to tame them?"

It is, Huxian said. The guardsman wanted to object, but Huxian continued. *I can do it, and several of my friends can. Ling Dong can do it. But aside from that, no human could. Unless... unless they used a devil-binding contract on them.*

"What's required for such a contract?" Cha Ming asked, his headache mounting.

"A devilish cultivator adept with fate affinity," Huxian said. "If he pays a high enough price. We even know one who's had ample time in this city and ample resources to work with. He could have been making them for years without us knowing."

"This keeps getting better and better," Cha Ming said. He looked to one of the guards. "How big is this elite corps?"

"Only a few hundred members," the guardsman said. "But every one of them is a middle-formation body cultivator mounted on at least a middle-formation fiendish demon. They're almost unmatched in the sea."

"Great," Cha Ming said. "Just great. This is madness. I'm half tempted to go over to the palace and just kick in the Emperor's face."

Elder Gan paled and looked toward the guards. They looked surprisingly amenable to the idea but shook their heads helplessly. "The Sea God Emperor is out to witness a military demonstration on the surface. I heard they were heading to Beihai City, where an armada of the Southern Alliance will be arriving a day from now."

"You have *got* to be kidding me," Cha Ming hissed. "That's not a military demonstration, that's an invasion of the North. We need to stop this."

"With what army?" Elder Gan asked.

It was a good point. They didn't have an army, and apparently their enemies had two.

"Huxian, his friends, and I can hold our own against many senior cultivators, but you're right," Cha Ming said. "It's not enough. What about the Alabaster Group's forces in the city? Will they fight?"

"We'll all help, of course," Elder Gan said. "And some neutral cultivators might as well, if just to maintain Haijing's neutral status. Unfortunately, they're currently being suppressed by the headmaster."

"Then that's where we'll start," Cha Ming said. "We need as much help as we can get."

"If I might suggest," the leader of the guardsmen said, "most of us guardsmen don't like the direction we're heading in. This military demonstration—this invasion, as you called it—flies in the face of tens of thousands of years of neutrality. It's madness. If what you're saying is true, and they'll either be attacking a coastal city or getting drawn into the conflict unwillingly, it's best if the City Guard confronts the Emperor. He might be strong, but without us, what can he accomplish?"

"That's surprisingly helpful," Cha Ming said. "What do you need?"

"We need Ling Dong," the guardsman said.

Cha Ming raised an eyebrow, but he continued.

"Ling Dong is highly respected amongst all the guardsmen. He's armed many of our senior members and would be a good rallying point. Moreover, you might not know this, but Ling Dong is a huge benefactor of the City Guard. He's tamed over twenty percent of the mounts currently in service.

"Twenty percent? How?" Cha Ming asked.

The kid's got talent, Huxian said in a haughty tone. *It's why I picked him. Now, I'd like to add that I happen to know some friends who hate sharks, especially fiendish ones. If I leave now, I should be able to convince them to fight. I'll just say they're colluding with human whalers or something.*

"Can't you just be honest?" Cha Ming asked.

Demons love embellishment, Huxian said. *And dolphins are notoriously lazy. Anyway, I need to run. This is going to take a lot of time.* The demonic fox fully flexed his Godbeast muscles and zoomed out the door. He left the city before the City Guard could even register his absence.

"We'll go now as well," Ling Dong said. "Will you be fine going to the academy?"

"Of course," Cha Ming said. "I have a few aces up my sleeve."

"Then Yue Bing and I will go visit the nobles we know," Zi Long said. "I've been laying formations for many of them, so we've developed good relationships. Yue Bing's healed severe injuries many of them have sustained, so they owe her a blood debt. That's not something taken lightly in Haijing."

Cha Ming nodded and looked to Jin Huang.

"I'll come with you, Master," Jin Huang said. "I have a few friends at the academy that are willing to help."

"Then let's not waste time," Cha Ming said.

Elder Gan barked instructions as they left. Members of the Alabaster Group immediately began packing up and collecting others around the city while Elder Gan followed after Cha Ming. They arrived at the door of Haijing Academy where guards stood with weapons drawn.

"Please show your identification," the guards said.

Cha Ming glared at them and walked up to the door. He searched for a flaw in the formation, and after finding one, kicked the door open with a powerful kick. Splinters of wood flew inside as the door was smashed to bits.

"Stop! You're breaking the peace!" the guards said. They rushed in to attack him, but Cha Ming simply slapped out with both palms and sent them flying into the city streets. The wide-eyed Elder Gan followed him into Haijing Academy, where guards came pouring into the streets to meet him. He dispatched each one with palms that smashed armor and crashed into their chests. One of them was even a qi cultivator, so he went a little lighter—slightly more strength and the guard would have perished.

"What's going on?" a voice boomed.

Over a hundred figures flew out. They were all elders of the academy, many of whom Cha Ming recognized. At their head stood a tall, skinny man. Headmaster Yan. "Who gave you the courage to barge in here? As headmaster of Haijing Academy, I demand to know what's going on. Otherwise, prepare to receive my wrath."

"Some headmaster you are," Cha Ming said. "You're just a glorified elder, and you've dared to lay hands on members of the Alabaster Group."

"I've done no such thing," Yao Lan said. "They've all refused to disseminate knowledge, and thus, we've made room for others who are willing to share."

"Everyone has secrets," Cha Ming said. "What you've done is abuse your power to kick them out and grow your Obsidian Syndicate. What you've done is clear as day. Not only were our members forced to take refuge in the city, but the guard has conveniently been absent while our members have been attacked. They don't even dare leave the city for fear of being killed."

Many elders muttered behind Yao Lan, whose eyes narrowed. They'd clearly not been aware of the full situation. "You have no proof," Yao Lan said. "These are all baseless accusations."

"The truth is clear for everyone to see," Cha Ming said. "But I don't have business with a glorified elder. Using my right as a grand elder, I wish to challenge the Nine Illusions professional trial."

More muttering.

Yao Lan couldn't help but grin and then laugh heartily when he heard this. "You want to try and usurp me using the Nine Illusions professional trial? Do you think my position is a joke? You might be a grand elder, but no one has bested the transcendent trial in thousands of years. It's there only as a carrot, to show the desperate that anything is achievable if you set your mind to it."

"Nothing is impossible," Cha Ming said. "And unlike you, I've already successfully crafted a transcendent item."

"And failed," Yao Lan said. "You couldn't even defend it against a heavenly tribulation. Do you think you can avoid it by hiding inside the formation? I'm sorry to disappoint you, but it doesn't work that way. Every single one of those who've succeeded had to fight a simulated heavenly tribulation. You failed before, and you'll fail this time as well."

"We'll know if I try," Cha Ming said. "Now tell me, will you cooperate, or do I have to make you?"

Yao Lan opened then closed his mouth. He looked around and was met with stares from the many elders. They held high respect for Cha Ming as a professional, and the headmaster medallion didn't change that one bit.

"You can naturally challenge the formation," Yao Lan said. "I take it you have the requisite fee?"

Cha Ming tossed a hundred top-grade spirit stones to him.

"Then follow me."

While there were originally one hundred elders gathered, the crowd grew as they made their way to the formation. The grand elder didn't stand on ceremony and tossed the stones on the formation and gestured toward it. "Go ahead. Don't cry when you come out."

Cha Ming nodded and stepped toward the portal. He stepped through it onto a large stone platform. A few runes floated around him: herbology, alchemy, runic arts, talisman arts, and formation arts. "I wish to challenge a transcendent trial. Talisman arts."

"Are you sure?" a voice said from all directions at once.

"I am," Cha Ming said.

"You meet the required soul strength and have cleared the elder trial," the voice said. "The trial will begin momentarily." His surroundings distorted, and Cha Ming found himself in Elder Ling's cabin once again. He looked around the comfortable living room and saw the *Angels and Devils* board as well as Mr. Mao Mao's perch. Then, he walked over to a table and summoned the Clear Sky Brush.

Cha Ming thought for a moment. He'd already painted a Flow Talisman at transcendent grade, so logic dictated that he try that. Moreover, a hundred years had passed since his last attempt. However, he felt inspiration tugging at him like nothing else ever had. He was brimming with hope, brimming with energy. He *would* see Yu Wen in the future.

But that was just a background issue in his current emotional state. He wasn't feeling hope right now; he was angry. He was *furious* at Zhou Li and disappointed with the Sea God Emperor. He wanted nothing more than to tear Headmaster Yao to shreds along with the City Guard marshals who had dared touch his disciples. It was this seething rage that made him summon red ink instead of blue.

It splashed across the page despite his slow movements. He poured his heart and soul into every stroke of the three-dimensional poem. Every character resonated with him, as did the whole. It seared itself into his soul as he wrote.

> *Disappointment douses the hearts of the needy;*
> *Man is left wanting and ever-yearning.*
> *Kindling the flames of love and caring;*
> *Never questioning his devotion.*

Devotion was key. Strong emotions were everything. Whereas before it was love that drove him, now it was a burning desire to avenge his disciples, the Alabaster Group, and this city. Moreover, he wanted to avenge himself. Like before, the characters created their own paper as they solidified into a talisman. And the heavens raged above him as it formed.

Cha Ming looked up and grinned. Then he did something most would consider insane. He stored the talisman in the Clear Sky World. "If this were the real world, I'd be very afraid of you," he said. "But this isn't the real world. There is no plane backing you. You're just an illusion, and you can't exceed your maker. The plane is unlimited, but you are not."

The heavens roared, and a lightning dragon smashed down on Elder Ling's cabin. The cabin, which was littered with protective formations, lasted a surprising length of time against the torrent of lightning. Cha Ming didn't defend against it; he simply grinned. He was a peak-marrow-refining cultivator, and his skeleton was practically indestructible. Forget his fist strength, his vitality was overwhelming compared to most cultivators, on par with a half-step transcendent. One level higher, and he'd be able to regenerate his body from a single drop of blood. If he was facing the plane, he wouldn't dare do something so risky. But against a mere formation powered by top-grade spirit stones? Even all its stored energy couldn't fight against him.

But that wouldn't stop it from trying. The heavens raged and sent strike after strike against him. The world crumbled around him as the formation sent everything it had. He flicked from world to world, setting to setting, and in each one, he met fiercer and fiercer lightning. Still, there was one thing he didn't face: the mystical gray lightning at the end of the transcendent tribulation. The formation was incapable of it, so Cha Ming simply bore with the strikes, and eventually, they weakened.

Several hundred strikes later, Cha Ming was standing on a stone platform. His badly scorched body regenerated in an instant. "Do I pass?" Cha Ming asked.

"You do," the voices said. The golden characters representing talisman artists turned a light shade of violet. Then they turned to gray. "No further trials are available until energy stores have recuperated. You may go."

A portal appeared, and Cha Ming walked through it. He caught the gray emblem in front of the awestruck elders. It was the same gray as the headmaster emblem. As a transcendent elder, his station matched that of the headmaster and exceeded it in some ways.

"You only hold your position because of a corrupt prime minister," Cha Ming said. "You're just a glorified elder pushing your peers around for your selfish motives. Step down peacefully, and I won't make things difficult for you."

Yao Lan glared at him as though Cha Ming had killed his mother. "I'm still the headmaster, so your words mean nothing. Besides, everything I did, I did for *science.*"

"Science is meaningless on its own," Cha Ming bit back. "It's only useful when it helps people better their lives. You rejected our faction because we prioritized good over science, and you chased us out. You tried to have us killed so you could monopolize resources. Who's the true enemy of science then, you or me?

"For what you've done, I'm throwing everything right back at you. You've called into question Haijing Academy's neutrality and conspired against the Alabaster Group? Fine. As punishment, I swear now that if the Obsidian Syndicate doesn't vacate Haijing Academy immediately, I'll make them. Do any of the elders disagree?"

Headmaster Yao looked back, but they all looked the other way. A couple dozen elders flew down to support the headmaster, who was now coughing up blood and pale as a sheet. "You've gone too far," one of them said.

"Have I?" Cha Ming asked. "Complain to someone who cares."

They struggled to retort but couldn't. Cha Ming simply didn't want to waste time with their perverse reasoning. They tried helping up the collapsed elder, who, to Cha Ming's surprise, began chuckling. His laughter became increasingly high pitched, and his eyes suddenly filled with lightning. Cha Ming's eyes narrowed as he saw that Headmaster Yao had undergone a devilish transformation. He'd also activated a consumption ability.

"Good, good, very good," Headmaster Yao said. "I've never been bested at anything in my life. It's a real eye-opener." He took out the gray medallion that represented his authority over Haijing Academy. "Since you've bested me, there's no need to keep you around. When you disappear from this plane, I'll be the true winner." He poured qi and soul force into the medallion, and Haijing Academy's formation began to glow. All the energy in Haijing Academy gathered toward Headmaster Yao.

Cha Ming looked at him almost pityingly. With his strong soul and formation arts, he knew the formation inside and out. He poured a wisp of transcendent qi into his grand-elder medallion, and as swiftly as the power had come to Headmaster Yao, it left. Headmaster Yao stammered as he tried to think up a reasonable explanation as Cha Ming summoned a mass of power in his own hand. "Since you dared try to kill me after I showed mercy, there's no need to remain. You can die now."

He gripped his palm tight, and before anyone could react, wave after wave of energy hit Headmaster Yao's crackling body. Due to his identity as a pride devil, his body simply dissociated and tried to move away, but Cha Ming altered the formation and surrounded the devil with five-element energy that he supplemented with white creation energy. It clashed with the lightning, and Headmaster Yao's body trembled.

Simultaneously, many members of the Obsidian Syndicate acted. They charged toward Cha Ming, but an unexpected person intercepted them. It was Jin Huang.

"My friends!" Jin Huang said excitedly.

The attackers seemed confused, but Cha Ming soon saw what he meant. He wasn't speaking to these people, but the several living poisons that were now escaping their bodies. The men shrivelled up as the poisons left them, completely draining away their vitality and cultivation.

Meanwhile, he heard shrieks from everywhere in Haijing Academy. Many were shrieks of pain from minor members of the Obsidian Syndicate, but many others were screams of joy. Thousands of tiny blobs of poison were pouring out from every room, every building, and most people in the academy. They were all converging on their creator. Jin Huang laughed as they jumped into his body of their own accord, and his cultivation began to rise. It leaped up to late core formation and proceeded straight to peak core formation. It was an effortless double breakthrough!

After merging with the poisons, Jin Huang grinned devilishly at the remaining members of the Obsidian Syndicate. "No need to bother with these, Master. I'll take care of them."

Cha Ming nodded and harnessed the power of the formation once more. He clasped his hand into a fist, and a similar fist appeared above the headmaster. Power from all around Haijing Academy hammered down atop the poor man, who could only shriek in despair as he was destroyed, body and soul.

"You dare?" a voice yelled above them.

Cha Ming looked up and saw a figure descend from the clouds. Through his Eyes of Pure Jade, he could see the devilish apparition with ochre wings that floated behind him. Cha Ming snorted and slashed with his hand. This time, he struck at the Obsidian Syndicate's remaining members. Over half of them were decapitated. He only left those with mild sin glows.

Seeing that he was being ignored, the transcendent who had just appeared roared in indignation. The sky rumbled as he struck down at Cha Ming with a mighty blade of flame. Cha Ming raised his Clear Sky Staff to resist the strike and moved the formation to protect those around him. His bones creaked as the transcendent struck down, and much of the flesh was seared off his body. It grew back almost instantly, leaving the surprised transcendent wrestling with heavenly lightning from above.

"Do you think I'm afraid of you?" Cha Ming asked. "The plane loathes you and wants nothing more than your death." Cha Ming clenched his fist, and the formation mobilized against the transcendent. As he tried to fight back, the heavens rumbled again and struck him with lightning, forcing him to retreat far above the formation's limits.

A chuckling man with angel wings appeared beside him. "By all means," the man said, "continue to fight with him. Many transcendents will die attempting it. I might just swoop in and finish off any survivors."

The devil's eyes narrowed. "We should have smothered you in your cradle," he spat at Cha Ming, who shrugged.

"But you didn't," Cha Ming said. "Whose fault is that? Now, are you going to stick around for me to keep attacking you, or will you get lost?"

The transcendent glared at him murderously. "This isn't over. We'll see you dead." He disappeared in a burst of flame. After confirming the transcendent had gone, the angel also vanished, presumably to follow him. All was quiet once more.

"I suggest you quit now while you're ahead," Cha Ming said to the Obsidian Syndicate's remaining members. "Leave the city. You're not welcome at Haijing Academy anymore."

The sulking men and women immediately fled without picking up their belongings. Cha Ming turned to the other elders once they'd cleared out. "You might be interested to know that the Sea God Emperor is on his way to witness a military demonstration by the Southern Alliance near Beihai City."

"Have they gone mad?" Elder Dai exclaimed. "That's just asking to get sucked into a war. Haijing City is neutral. It always has been."

"Therefore, I was hoping to take a large contingent of elders to try and convince the Sea God Emperor otherwise," Cha Ming said. "Are you willing?"

Many hesitated. The Sea God Emperor was a very intimidating individual. Moreover, most of them only wanted to pursue scientific truths. They didn't want to get embroiled in a war if they didn't have to.

"I'll go," Elder Dai said almost immediately.

"As will I," another said. Soon, a few dozen elder-level figures separated themselves from the main group and stood before Cha Ming. Many full members followed them. "When are we leaving?"

"We have no time to waste," Cha Ming said. "The demonstration is in a day."

Elder Dai nodded. "As a transcendent elder, you are our representative until the Haijing royal family says otherwise. We'll come and support you, but be warned—we won't fight against the Emperor."

"That's fine," Cha Ming said. He hoped he could stop any fighting before it came to that. They flew outside Haijing Academy, and after collecting members of the Alabaster Group, they flew out of Haijing City. As they stepped out, they were joined by thousands of Haijing citizens in golden armor. They were City Guardsmen, and each one of them was accompanied by a powerful demonic beast. Beside them stood a group of Haijing nobles. They were following Yue Bing and Zi Long.

"Are they a match for the elite corps?" Cha Ming asked as he surveyed the City Guard's forces.

"Not quite, but they can put up a fight," one of the guardsmen who'd swam up beside him said. The man wore different epaulettes than the others, which Cha Ming figured indicated rank. "If fighting breaks out on the surface, we'll give them something to remember."

"This man used to be a marshal before the new grand marshal was appointed," Ling Dong said, swimming up beside him. "He's very dissatisfied with their current military management."

"Good," Cha Ming said. "Is everyone ready?" He looked behind him and received nods from the people he'd gathered. "Then let's swim."

Chapter 32: Reality

*T*ick. *Tick. Tick.*

The clock in Wang Jun's office counted the seconds as he reviewed his plan. He would never write it down, of course; it was all in his mind, and not even his most trusted aides knew of it. It was a simple plan, a good plan. But too much of it relied on one person.

His nervousness was evident, to the point that even Elder Bai noticed it as he poured tea for his young master. He and Wang Bing reported, but Wang Jun mostly nodded and gave simple directives. They were doing well, so their businesses could practically run themselves.

"I just don't understand it," Elder Bai said, capturing Wang Jun's attention. "Given our asset base and the profitability of our businesses, there should be no way your brother can keep up. But our informants say his customer base is stable and vibrant despite the obvious mismanagement of his businesses."

Wang Bing snorted. "He's obviously resorting to some illicit means. His inflated 'customer base' is just a result of money laundering. It's a pity we haven't been able to discover what they've been trading in."

"Would it even matter?" Wang Jun asked. The other two stared at him. He shrugged and continued. "The council of elders clearly doesn't care about deliberate wrongdoing no matter the magnitude.

They've stopped rewarding us for finding mistakes, and they've even begun using our recommendations to help Wang Ling improve his businesses. No matter what we do, unless it's a mistake so severe it can't be excused, it's all meaningless."

"Money laundering seems like a big deal," Elder Bai noted.

Wang Bing shook her head. "Only if the source of the illicit income is exposed and sufficiently damning."

"And that, Elder Bai, is why I've stopped investigating," Wang Jun said. "Unless I find ironclad evidence of wrongdoing that breaks the Golden Kingdom's major laws, I won't say anything to the council."

"Won't they accuse you of neglecting your duties?" Elder Bai asked.

Wang Jun shrugged. "They've already admitted on paper that what we've found isn't worth a reward. According to our family rules, worthwhile things have rewards while worthless things do not. I have good reason to believe they think investigations are a waste of my time. Therefore, it follows that my time is better spent generating income for the family."

Elder Bai frowned. He peered at Wang Jun carefully, looking at him from many different angles. When Wang Jun finally raised an eyebrow, he scowled. "You're up to something. I can feel it."

"I am, but I can't talk about it," Wang Jun said. "You should know better than to pry."

"Is it so important that you can't even tell little old me?" Elder Bai said, putting on a false wounded expression.

Wang Bing nudged him. Hard. "If he hasn't shared it with us, that means we'd be the opposite of helpful. He's trusted us with everything else. It's obviously not an issue of loyalty."

Wang Jun smiled. "You're right. Though if I die tonight, I highly recommend you recuse yourselves from family businesses and sell your assets at a discount."

That comment brought an uncomfortable silence to their table. Eventually, Elder Bai coughed and began picking up their teacups and putting everything away. Wang Bing also began putting documents in her briefcase.

"My apologies for the short and uncomfortable meeting," Wang Jun said. "You'll be able to tell how it went based on my mood tomorrow."

"Regardless of your mood, make sure you get back in one piece," Elder Bai said. "These old bones have lost far too many family members. My heart won't be able to take it if I lose you too." His eyes were misty and red.

Wang Jun placed his hand on Elder Bai's shoulder. "Don't you worry. There aren't many people on this plane who can catch me if I want to escape."

The older man nodded, and soon Wang Jun was alone in his office. His clock ticked away the seconds as he waited for nightfall.

Darkness was difficult to come by in the streets of Gold Leaf City. As the capital of the Golden Kingdom and the base of operations for the Church of Justice, every nook and cranny was well illuminated. It was as though not doing so was admitting defeat against the darkness. The lights were like tiny city guardians, fulfilling their nightly duty by keeping the enemy at bay.

Despite the lack of shade, two people rushed through the streets undetected. They were surrounded by an unnatural shadow that hid them from the light. The small pocket of darkness proceeded unnoticed through eastern streets until it finally arrived at a small chapel, a spirit chapel. Such chapels were unusual in this city since the kingdom barely tolerated the Spirit Temple's existence.

Why have you brought me here? one of the people said. It was the Wang clan's Patriarch, Wang Wuling. *If it's not important enough to warrant my attention, you will be punished.*

They rounded a corner and found a decent bit of shade, which they entered. They then jumped over to another shadow inside the chapel proper. No alarms went off, and no one was alerted. They hid in a deep darkness within the temple, despite being surrounded by protective formations that even a transcendent would hesitate to trip. *I keep forgetting how good you are at hiding and evasion.*

We're here to witness wrongdoing by a family member, Wang Jun said. *They'll be here within the hour. Now, if you'll excuse me, I have work to do.*

The Patriarch hmphed and crossed his arms, but Wang Jun focused on manipulating nearby shadows into formations. He casually observed the Patriarch's reaction—the man was evidently surprised by the news, even nervous. That could mean many things, but at least it meant he hadn't been expecting this little show.

Strings of shadow and fate worked their way around the chapel, undetected by the few priests that patrolled its halls. Here and there, Wang Jun saw spirit scouts. While very perceptive, their intelligence was too low to detect anything amiss.

A half hour later, two formations hummed to life. One was an obscurity formation, while the other used an expensive golden treasure as its base.

"An eavesdropping device?" the Patriarch asked.

"You can't expect them to say words out loud if they can say them mentally," Wang Jun said. "Unlike us, who are hidden so deeply a chaplain couldn't detect us, they still fear the Church of Justice. The chaplains might tolerate the temple's assassins out of fear of losing their heads, but to zealots, some things can't be ignored. It's one of those things we'll be witnessing tonight."

The Patriarch didn't say anything, and they both waited for another quarter hour. Finally, several figures filed in. Three of the men were high priests of the Spirit Temple, all peak-core-formation cultivators. Another four weren't initially visible, but Wang Jun's formations revealed four peak-core-formation Spectral Assassins. They and their gear were only half corporeal due to their ghostly heritage.

Another quarter hour passed before a second group finally walked in. They wore black concealment cloaks, and high-grade ones at that. Wang Jun's formations revealed three figures—two peak-core-formation Wang family protectors and a much younger figure: Wang Ling.

I see you managed to make it—on time and unfollowed, one of the high priests said.

Our business relationship is a very important one, Wang Ling said. *I wouldn't miss it for the world.*

Then you have the goods requested? another high priest said.

Wang Ling nodded. He waved his hand, and seven black-and-red urns appeared between them. The third high priest grabbed one of the urns and unstoppered it. A few wailing wisps floated out from inside it, scrambling to escape.

Hmph. The high priest waved his hand and caught the escapees and forced them back inside the container. He then repeated the process for the six others. *The goods are legitimate. Seventy thousand resentful souls with sufficiently dense negative karma. As promised.*

I take it our goods are satisfactory? Wang Ling said.

As always, but you can understand why we want to verify them in person, the high priest said. *The nature of our trades is extremely sensitive.*

I understand, Wang Ling said. *And the payment?*

I've already arranged for it, the high priest said. *The money will be laundered through your businesses over the course of a year. We'll meet in approximately one year once you've accumulated the next shipment.*

Pleasure doing business with you, Wang Ling said, bowing.

As always, the high priest said, bowing back. Wang Ling left the premises, and soon the Spectral Assassins and the high priests did as well. A crystal orb in Wang Jun's hand stopped recording soon after. "I assume you can see the problem. The soul trade is lucrative, but failure means the eradication of our entire family."

The Patriarch sighed. He waved his hand and urged the recording globe over. "Are you the only one who knows about it? Does Elder Bai, Wang Bing, or Protector Ren know?"

Wang Jun's eyes narrowed. "I wouldn't dare tell them about such sensitive information."

"Good," the Patriarch said. He clenched his fist, and the orb shattered.

Wang Jun shook slightly but restrained himself.

"You knew all along," Wang Jun said.

"I did," the Patriarch said. "And so does the grand elder. From now on, you are to stop investigating this matter and continue competing with Wang Ling using profits, not wasting your time on such petty things as justice and crime."

Wang Jun clenched his jaw. For a moment, he was overwhelmed with an urge to just kill the man. *But that wouldn't solve the problem, now would it?* He should have expected this. If the grand elder was complicit with even this, then it wasn't surprising the council of elders wasn't concerned about smaller issues of fraud. "I humbly request to be relieved of my position as auditor."

"Denied," the Patriarch said. "You chose to go against the will of our elders, the will of our family, and compete for the family leadership. You could have obediently followed your brother's lead and helped us reach greater heights. Instead, you chose to fracture the family. If you want the family leadership, you'll have to earn it."

"Understood," Wang Jun said with a quavering voice. He held out a hand and retrieved the strings of shadow and karma from the room. Then their surroundings shifted, and they were outside the chapel once more. The Patriarch flew off on his own.

Wang Jun summoned a familiar crystal sphere in his hand. The one he'd given the Patriarch was a fake, of course, leaving him with the original evidence. If he wanted to, he could incriminate his entire family. Every single one of them would be burned in the Church of Justice's inquisition, and not even their grand elder could stop it. Sweet revenge would be so easy to obtain. All he would need to do was abandon Elder Bai, Wang Bing, and many people he cared about.

Uncertain, Wang Jun stowed the sphere and turned his attention toward a shadow making its way toward the main Spirit Temple. The shadow had been there during the exchange and had avoided detection just like he had. It made its way through various sentries, and to his surprise, it vanished. A lady in plain acolyte robes appeared and walked across a deserted street and entered the Spirit Temple through a side door.

Interesting, Wang Jun thought. He became one with the shadows and followed. He needed something, anything, to distract him.

Chapter 33: Support

Hong Xin entered the Spirit Temple's hallowed halls in broad daylight. Or she would have, if it wasn't night. She, the new servant girl, was welcomed by the steward and shown to her room where she would rest before reporting in the morning. After a few quick assurances and a dousing spell to soothe his worries, she was left in a small stone room, where she took out a small kit of paint and powder.

A few careful strokes below her eyes made her look sleep deprived and sallow. Some pale powder gave her a sickly aura, while a few other well-placed runes changed the rest of her features to that of a man, whose hair was tied in a top knot with a bone clasp. She then touched her simple clothes, transforming them into acolyte robes. A cursory inspection in the mirror assured her that she'd done her job well.

She opened the door and walked out with the confidence of an acolyte. She held her head high but bowed it whenever she passed by any priests. No one recognized her, of course, but neither did they see her as a stranger. Her powerful glamour caused them to recall her as a familiar thrall, no one worthy of attention.

The Spirit Temple was built like a large stone labyrinth; some even said lesser acolytes could get lost if they wandered in too deep. Fortunately, her information had been supplemented by many insiders. She knew the layout by heart, and before long, she arrived at a long hallway where only important members were allowed.

High priests were too difficult to imitate, so Hong Xin activated the power of her brooch. Dark runes spread out from the mauve artifact that shrouded her in darkness that even the magical torches in the hallway couldn't illuminate.

One step at a time, she thought, making her way along a secret path not many men or women knew. Her feet avoided key stones and stepped on the ones that allowed safe passage. Her surroundings shifted as she passed one magical obstacle after another. She soon reached the halfway point.

Suddenly, she heard a shifting sound. A tall man in dark robes walked toward her while muttering something dark and incomprehensible. His feet fell on all the right spots by instinct as he read a book he held close to his nose. She froze when she realized what he was—a medium. Priests were one thing, but mediums were especially troublesome due to their sensing capabilities. If he got within a few feet of her, her cover might be blown.

She bit her lip as he continued walking, and soon it was clear that he wouldn't alter his path. Gritting her teeth, she reached out with her soul and qi. She felt at his heart, probing it for worries and doubts, anything she could work with. Her icy powers dulled his perception as she worked, and finally, she found something—he'd forgotten one of his books. She could work with that.

She urged the flames in her heart to kindle that feeling. His steps faltered, then paused. He hesitated, then turned back toward the room he'd just left. It was now or never. Hong Xin sprang from stone to stone, using the darkness around her to leap through the veritable maze of magical traps. She passed the man just as he entered the room, causing him to look back briefly in confusion.

You didn't notice a thing, she thought as she doused his suspicions. She was just a feeling, and nothing more.

Breathing in deeply, Hong Xin walked down the rest of the hallway until she reached a large door that led to the main altar. She ignored it and chose to enter the door on the left where offerings were prepared. It would still be a few hours before they began the ceremony that caused the resentful souls to feed on each other, resulting in an influx of evil spirits for the temple. Most people in the kingdom didn't know this dark secret, but she did. Her captives had told her everything eagerly as they pleaded for swift death.

Hong Xin summoned a golden key as she approached the locked door. She inserted the expensive artifact into the door's formation and deactivated it. The door creaked open, revealing a warmly lit area filled with perfume, religious artifacts, and what she was looking for: seven black-and-red urns waiting to be emptied.

She stepped forward to retrieve the urns, but as she did, her sixth sense warned her. She paused and looked around but saw nothing. Confused, she took out a patch of red dust and blew it into the room. It scattered throughout every cubic foot of air, confirming that no spirits had been stationed here on short notice.

Sighing in relief, Hong Xin stowed the urns. Something seemed to latch on to her, but as she batted at it, she found nothing.

Strange, she thought. *It must be my imagination.* She double-checked the room for traps and, finding none, she left it. She then walked over to a wall and pressed her finger on three separate spots, pouring qi and resplendent force into them. The stone sank into the wall, and the wall opened. She jumped through the secret entrance and closed it behind her before running through the stone tunnel at a brisk pace.

A gust of fresh air welcomed Hong Xin as she emerged from the catacombs. Her red robes were soaked in sweat, and her gaze was wary. Everything had gone smoothly, and she should be happy. Yet something seemed wrong.

Despite the shadows covering her, she felt followed. The feeling had only intensified in the catacombs. Now that she was out in the open, the sensation was more vivid. Just to be sure, she took out a pouch and retrieved a pinch of red dust. She scattered it around her as she probed with her resplendent force. A leaf fell from a nearby tree as she did. Curious, she picked it up to examine it. A hiss of wind sounded as a blade barely missed her head, severing two hairs in the process.

Hong Xin sprang into action. She summoned twin fans just in time to catch a dagger that appeared right behind her. As she moved, she noticed figures materializing in the red dust.

Spectral Assassins, she thought. A dozen ghostly figures, creatures of the night no one dared belittle, had somehow surrounded her. She'd followed the plan perfectly, and there had been no spirits in the room when she'd stored the urns. Yet somehow, they'd found her. Not only that—they could see her clearly despite the shadows obscuring her. Even a medium would have trouble spotting her in this situation.

Is it a transcendent? Hong Xin thought. She immediately dismissed the idea. Transcendents were lofty beings, but more to the point, they kept each other in check. It was difficult for one to move without alerting the others.

As she thought this, the assassins pounced on her once more. This time, they fought together. She dodged them with fiery steps while slowing others with a burst of cold. A dagger nicked her arm as she blasted one of them with a plume of flame. Then, sensing danger, she ducked and summoned a forest of icy spikes that stabbed into three nearby specters. Two of them phased out of the material world and avoided the stab, but one of them howled as an ice spike pierced his heart. He might seem like a ghost, but his flesh was as real as any.

Hong Xin's small victory brought her no comfort. She was surrounded, and a noncombatant like her didn't stand a chance against these strange assassins. They renewed their attacks once more, and this time, they summoned crimson awls affixed to long black chains. She knocked three out of the air as they hurled toward her, but six more snuck through her defenses. She closed her eyes and prepared for the inevitable. Then she blinked when the inevitable didn't happen.

Shadows writhed before her as another figure appeared. A familiar man with blond hair carrying a familiar black longsword in his hands.

"I hope I'm not too late," Wang Jun said.

Hong Xin panicked for a moment before remembering that she was still wearing a glamour, albeit a different one. Her heart fluttered, but she cooled her emotions and spoke different words than what had originally come to mind. "What are you doing here?" she asked.

"I thought you'd be happy to see a friendly face," Wang Jun said. "Why the cold shoulder?"

She continued glaring at him, and he coughed uncomfortably. The Spectral Assassins looked at them cautiously as they reevaluated the situation. "I happened to be in the area when I saw you getting attacked by a bunch of ugly ghosts. Then I remembered that you owe me a favor. A wise man never discards a worthwhile investment."

Hong Xin smiled lightly. "I see. I seem to recall owing you a dance, is that correct?"

"Yes, you promised a dance," Wang Jun said. "That's negotiable, of course. We never ironed out the details."

"A dance is convenient," Hong Xin said. She urged her qi and activated the glamour runes on her face and within her clothes. They transformed into regal red-and-gold robes that flowed while hugging her curves. The fans she carried also took on a red-and-golden hue. Flames appeared around them as she cracked the fans open. "Let's dance."

Shadows oozed around Wang Jun as he charged at the specters. They disappeared and appeared at random as they sought vulnerabilities in his armor. Unfortunately for them, he didn't wear any. What he had was a cloak—a cloak of shadows. And it was shadows they struck instead of flesh, and each time they struck, it slowed them down. One of them, a ghostly figure with a large blade, grinned as he finally found flesh.

Wang Jun grinned back. They were surrounded by shadows, so

he naturally surrounded them. He slashed in the air, and a black blade of shadow qi cut through space. It reappeared behind the attacking specter before his blade caused much damage, extinguishing the strange being's half-life in the process.

Though he was busy fighting, Wang Jun took careful note of the headmistress. Her every step contained a charm that wooed man and spirit alike. The specters faltered when they tried attacking her, and her lithe movements easily evaded their jaunting steps. The headmistress was obviously not a trained fighter, but that didn't mean she wasn't effective. As she danced, she swept out with her fans, covering the specters in tiny red lights that resembled dust.

The Red Dust Pavilion had earned its name from these red flames, a little-known fact since the headmistress before her had initiated a coup on the previous headmistress, Hong Yinyue. But the records remembered, and now the specters did as well. Every flap of her fans thickened the layer of red dust that ate away at their spectral cloaks. Meanwhile, Wang Jun bound them to the material world, where there was nowhere to hide.

The headmistress shot him a smile that could stop hearts and topple nations, but surprisingly, he only felt warmth and comfort. They danced together, and for a brief moment, everything seemed well in the world.

Suddenly, a chill ran down Wang Jun's spine. *Danger.* Wang Jun's fate qi resonated with his surroundings, and he shouted a warning to the headmistress, who retreated beside him. They turned their backs to each other as another flood of two dozen specters emerged.

"They must have tracked something you carry through karma," Wang Jun said. "Give me the urns."

The headmistress looked at him for a moment, then tossed him a small ring. He looked inside and found not only the urns but many other personal items. Mirrors, makeup, brushes, clothes. Hairclips, jewelry, shoes, and scarves.

"I need thirty seconds," he said, before sitting cross-legged.

His eyes darted to a mauve hairclip buried in a mountain of other accessories. It was of a familiar design, like the one his sister had worn on the day she died. The same one he'd given Hong Xin.

No, it's not similar, Wang Jun thought. He inspected it more closely. *It's identical.* He forced this thought away and called out the seven urns.

Wang Jun formed swift hand seals and coughed up a mouthful of black blood. Another lock of his golden hair faded to white as another bit of his lifespan poured into the blood, but he didn't care. The betrayal he'd felt with the Patriarch had cut him deeply, and the loss of lifespan barely meant anything in comparison. So he split the lifeblood into seven portions and splashed it onto the urns. Then he summoned the seven formations he'd given the headmistress earlier. Had he known they'd be dealing with karmic tracking, he'd have made them stronger or refused the favor. Still, there was no sense regretting.

The aura on the urns faded rapidly as he cycled his shadow and fate qi to reinforce the formations. Whether it was due to lack of caring or dire need, he withdrew his senses and completely focused on the darkness. His life was in the headmistress's hands. It was risky, but death would be a sweet mercy.

Hong Xin danced a furious dance. She was ice and flame incarnate. Twin phoenixes, both red and blue, danced around her as she twirled with her fans, blocking out the blades and daggers from the specters. Chains of red metal assaulted her impromptu barrier; ice and fire barely repelled them.

Though she was bitter that he hadn't consulted her, she sensed pain in Wang Jun's heart unlike anything she'd ever felt before. She sensed betrayal, hurt, and heartache. The man she loved was on the verge of breaking; he was a shattered vase barely held together by cheap mortal glue.

Unfortunately, she could do nothing about that while they were still under attack. So, she danced. Forests of ice shards emerged around her, and blazing fruits grew inside it. They burst on contact with the specters, slaying some while scorching others. Another awl flew toward the stationary Wang Jun, and she summoned a wall of ice, trapping the awl in the process. The specter tugged, and the wall was yanked free.

She dove toward Wang Jun and flapped her fans, sending a sea of flames to repel a half dozen foes. Many shrieked, but two stronger assassins managed to evade the flames. They dove in for the kill. If she dodged, Wang Jun would die. That was something she couldn't live with, so she readied her fans and faced them. She would defend him or die trying.

Almost there, Wang Jun thought as he finished the last few weaves of shadow and fate. The formations hummed to life, and the urns were hidden. He remembered the battle and stood up from his seated position. As his awareness expanded, he noticed two specters stabbing toward the headmistress. He formed rapid hand seals, and the shadows around him shot out to impale them. The two specters disappeared, and their weapons and cloaks clattered to the ground. He looked at the headmistress and noticed something pooling beneath her. Blood.

His eyes narrowed as he spotted the two weapons lodged in her abdomen. He swept out his cloak and wreathed the area in darkness. Now that the karmic links were broken, they completely disappeared from the specters' sights. Wang Jun took out an emergency potion and poured it around the headmistress's wounds before feeding her a pill. Then he pulled out both swords in her abdomen. She gasped and cried out in pain as they cut her on the way out.

Fortunately, the healing potion was a good one. The wound closed and halted any further bleeding. Still, she wasn't out of the woods yet. He picked up her small body and entered the shadow plane, linking their current location with the shadows outside the Red Dust Pavilion. He ran through the door of the perpetually open establishment, maintaining the cloak of shadows as he walked. He didn't move to avoid the customers but used his qi to force them away, leaving them confused and unsure of what was happening.

After entering the main reception hall, he spotted a familiar figure who was trying her best to remain composed.

"Mistress Bai Ling," Wang Jun said, his voice hidden.

She looked around, wondering what was happening.

"Head to the hallway behind you and wait for me. Your headmistress is dying."

She jumped at that and obediently made her way over. The moment she entered the hallway, Wang Jun dragged her into their concealing shadows. She yelped when she saw the headmistress's wounded body.

"Lead the way to her bedchambers and call over a spirit doctor. She requires immediate medical attention."

Bai Ling bit her lips and nodded. She led Wang Jun down familiar corridors, and just before reaching the chambers he usually visited, they stopped by another set of doors.

"Place her on the bed," Bai Ling said. "I'll need to heal her personally. She doesn't allow anyone but me or a few select mistresses to touch her body." She then looked to the door. He looked to it as well and realized he was being a bit rude.

"I'll wait outside," he said, coughing lightly. Though his robes were covered in her blood, seeing her naked body was a bit improper. Minutes crawled by as he sensed familiar surges of water qi and smelled faint medicinal ingredients. After some time, Bai Ling walked out of the room looking pale as a sheet.

"I'll send servants to fetch clothes and cleaning water. You're welcome to stay until the headmistress recovers, as she's in no position to see anyone."

"Of course," Wang Jun said, smiling. "I was about to return home in any case."

"Invite him in," a voice suddenly said. The voice seemed familiar, but Wang Jun couldn't put his finger on it.

Bai Ling looked back toward the room, then to Wang Jun. "Don't try anything funny, or I'll stab you in the heart." Judging from the look she gave him, she meant it.

Confused, Wang Jun walked back into the bedroom. He noticed the headmistress preferred simple chambers and decorations, something he himself appreciated.

"Please open a drawer to your right," the headmistress said. He nodded and opened the small drawer, revealing a tea set and what he recognized as high-quality tea.

"There's no need to entertain me," Wang Jun said. "You were mortally wounded by Spectral Assassins. Their ghostly wounds aren't something that's easy to recover from."

"Please, I insist," the headmistress said. "After all, I'm about to ask you for yet another favor. This time, however, I agree to your terms."

"Splendid," Wang Jun said. He picked up the tea set and turned toward the only light in the bedchamber.

Then he saw her. The woman he'd dreamed of for years. In his surprise, he dropped the tea set. Shadows caught it and brought it back to his shaking hands as he looked at the pretty girl in a red nightgown.

"I imagined many ways in which we'd meet again, but this wasn't one of them," Hong Xin said with a light smile. She motioned to the other chair. "Please. Sit."

Though her appearance was mostly unchanged since they'd last met, her demeanor had changed tremendously. She held herself with a poise he couldn't hope to imitate and grace that belied her years. He sat down weakly as she calmly poured him tea.

"How? Why? When?" Wang Jun mumbled.

"It's a bit of a long story, and for now, I can only tell you the shortened version," Hong Xin said. "When we parted ways last time, I was devastated. I felt useless and unwanted. It wasn't your fault, but that I simply didn't have the heart of a cultivator. I wallowed in self-pity, and it took a cruel man and his disgusting desires to give me the courage to fight back. I set fire to an inn and decided it was best that I disappear for a while."

"Stonefell," Wang Jun said.

"That's right," Hong Xin said. "Looking back, it makes sense that you'd try to find me. I'm glad you didn't."

"Not for lack of trying," Wang Jun muttered.

"So I've gathered through my associates," Hong Xin said. "In my travels, I met Hong Yinyue, a past headmistress of the Red Dust Pavilion. Through her heritage and her help, I infiltrated the organization and deposed the old headmistress. Then, after gaining control of what was left of that wretched place, I traveled to Gold Leaf City to stamp out what remained of the Red Dust mistresses. Which is how I got involved in this dirty business with the Spirit Temple."

Wang Jun looked around, and once again he noticed how truly poor the place seemed. Not just the decorations, but even what the mistresses wore. Everything was superficial, completely lacking value and power. "I take it the poverty isn't voluntary."

Hong Xin shook her head. "We were instigated by the noble factions who'd lost out in the previous headmistress's fall. They made us an offer we couldn't refuse, and as a result, we began fighting the Spirit Temple. They have dirt on us, Wang Jun, dirt that the Church of Justice would stop at nothing to cleanse."

"The soul trade," Wang Jun said.

Hong Xin nodded. "Before Wang Ling began dealing in souls, it was the Red Dust Pavilion who did it. We would lure helpless victims away and use unforgivable methods to corrupt their spirits. With our knowledge of the heart, we were very good at it. But we were careless. We left evidence."

"Thus the urns," Wang Jun said.

Hong Xin nodded and summoned them beside the table. She poured them both another cup of tea. "By planting these urns in unknown locations in the seven houses, we are evening the playing field. They can expose us all they want, but we'll implicate them in return. The Golden Kingdom won't allow them to escape unharmed if they've dealt in the soul trade."

She held her hand to her freshly bandaged wounds. "Ideally, I would have been planting the evidence right now. But I'm injured, and time is limited. I trust Bai Ling and Ji Bingxue with my life, of course. But you're good at this sort of thing, aren't you? If you hid them well and set up contingencies in case we were exposed or killed…"

"I can do that," Wang Jun said. "I'll do it right away." He swept up the urns and gave Hong Xin a reassuring smile. "I should go now, though, to minimize the risk of getting caught."

Hong Xin nodded. "Thank you. My sisters and I don't have anywhere else to go, Wang Jun. The Red Dust Pavilion changed us. That wretched place leaves dreadful scars that won't disappear no matter how hard you try."

"Don't worry," Wang Jun said. "You'll be safe. I'll make sure of it." He waved his hand, and a portal of shadows appeared. Just as he was about to step through, however, a hand suddenly grabbed him and pulled him back.

Hong Xin pulled him into her embrace. She kissed him deeply, and her lips were like fire that burned through his very soul. He felt warmth unlike anything he'd ever experienced, and for a moment, he forgot about the betrayal he'd experienced a few hours prior. When he opened his eyes, he noticed Hong Xin had her hand on his heart.

"I can see you're hurting so badly you can barely stand it," Hong Xin whispered. "But you shouldn't let it break you. It's just a setback, nothing more. Remember that if your heart hurts, I can fix it. Just trust that I can always fix it."

Wang Jun closed his eyes and basked in the warmth of her touch. He felt his emotions normalize and his rage subside. He began thinking a little more clearly and remembered that it wasn't all bad. He still had Elder Bai, Wang Bing, and a host of capable assistants. His brother might be trading in souls, but they were now evenly matched. A few more good plays, and they would *win*. Besides, he'd found her. He'd found her at long last.

"Thank you," Wang Jun said, walking back toward the portal.

"Wang Jun," Hong Xin called out. He looked back and saw her waving shyly at him. "Don't take so long to come see me next time, all right?"

Wang Jun smiled. "I'll come visit soon. I promise." He then walked through the portal of shadows toward his first destination. He wasn't sure how he was going to do it yet, but if he was going to blackmail someone, he'd do it properly.

The wheels in his mind began turning, and by the time he reached their front door, the plan was perfect. It was going to be a busy night.

Chapter 34: Crossing Swords

Four men floated above crashing waves just north of Beihai City. They looked on as hundreds of black ships slowly made their way toward the harbor. The massive black vessels barely skimmed the ocean as they cut through it. The sky was clear despite the turbulent sea.

The four men had a working relationship, one that benefited each side greatly. Zhou Li just wished it were more than that. Unfortunately, a half dozen years of buttering up hadn't worked quite as well as he'd hoped. Such was life.

"I must thank the Sea God Emperor for taking the time to see this demonstration," Zhou Li said. The Sea God Emperor, Gong Xuandi, grunted. He was disinterested with the whole affair and was only here because his prime minister and grand marshal had convinced him to come along.

"We're confident that this excursion will be well worth our time," the prime minister, Gong Luoyang, said. "Haijing City has historically limited financial cooperation with the mainland. The planned increase in trade more than makes up for the inconvenience."

"Not to mention your offer for hired naval support," the grand marshal, Gong Huan, said. "I must admit that I'm a little skeptical about the so-called naval power you've touted. I'm grateful for the Emperor's support in evaluating it. If things are as you've said, we'll be able to clear out large amounts of territory around Haijing at a much faster rate."

Fortunately, the Sea God Emperor's trusted advisors were more than friendly with Zhou Li. As such, they could be counted on for timely support if the Sea God Emperor felt the urge to return to Haijing City. That would be a disaster. There were other ways to instigate the Sea God Empire, of course, but those ways were much messier. Instigation worked best when both parties actively hated each other.

As the ships approached, Zhou Li stared at Beihai City. The coastal nation was practically defenseless, as they'd never built more than the maximum number of ships their treaties with Haijing allowed. Yet he felt unease as he looked at the harbor. The single image projecting far into the future suddenly distorted, splitting up into tens of images. Uncertainty.

Zhou Li hated uncertainty more than anything else. He quickly sifted through the tangle of images, following likely karmic threads to their logical destinations. He changed his script to better railroad the upcoming conversation, and to his relief, the plan was saved. Barely.

At that moment, a glimmer of light appeared at the docks, followed by a few dozen more. Thousands of other lights poured in behind them. These were all cultivators, and he already knew every one of them, their stories and their vices. One of them was particularly irritating, but another was very easy to manipulate. It was a worthwhile trade-off in his opinion.

"It seems the North has sent a delegation to greet us," Zhou Li said. "Shall we greet them back?"

The Sea God Emperor shrugged. "To do otherwise would be discourteous. Please signal for parley. Instruct our guardsmen to allow them to pass."

"A wise decision, Your Grace," Gong Luoyang said.

"Gong Jian," the Sea God grand marshal said. "Have your men control those sharks and form orderly lines. I don't want them biting anyone by accident."

"Understood!" Gong Jian said. The marshal, who served under Gong Huan, issued quick instructions. Before long, the few hundred men and mounts that had accompanied them floated at attention behind the Sea God royalty and Zhou Li. The ships slowed down, and the bright lights advanced.

"Marshal Feng Ming of the Song Kingdom, Marshal Jiao Meng of the Desert Wind Kingdom, and Ambassador Li Fei of the Quicksilver Empire all send greetings and request a parley!" a loud voice said from the approaching lights.

"Granted!" Gong Jian shouted back.

Zhou Li looked at the three men, then at the guards and their feral mounts. All the elements were in place: important people, something important to burn down, and ample gasoline. All he needed now were sparks to start the blaze. They would arrive shortly.

Feng Ming's foreboding headache proved accurate. Not only did several hundred black ships appear on the horizon as expected, four powerful individuals and a few hundred guardsmen with demonic mounts had come along with them. They hadn't expected anyone from Haijing.

"This is no longer a naval skirmish but an extremely delicate political situation," Li Fei said from behind their protective formation. "Please try to behave yourselves."

"It might be best if you do the talking," Feng Ming suggested.

"That would be a great sign of disrespect to the Sea God Emperor, his prime minister, and his grand marshal," Li Fei said. "They respect strength, not political maneuvering and cunning. I will send you mental advice as we speak, but could you please promise me you won't say anything stupid?"

The question was pointed both at Feng Ming and the man beside him, Jiao Meng. Jiao Meng was Jiao Ming's brother, and they were alike in more ways than one. He disliked Feng Ming very much and wanted nothing more to embarrass him at every turn. "I definitely won't step out of line," Feng Ming said.

"Spoken like a coward," Jiao Meng mumbled. He followed up with a quick apology as Li Fei glared at him coldly.

Meanwhile, Feng Ming evaluated their respective positions. Assuming the Sea God's people chose to distance themselves from the conflict, they could hold their own for some time. The South's fleet was impressive, and this was mostly due to their superior spiritual blacksmithing capabilities. Their basic troops' weapons were on a higher level than the North's, but this advantage didn't apply as much to higher-tier weapons since the Northern Alliance had Huoshan's blacksmiths. Overall, the South's elite troops were stronger due to better access to alchemical goods and unsavory practices that favored the few over the many.

But these weren't their elite corps—those were stationed at the battlefields. This was a naval army that emphasized massive artillery and numerical superiority. Moreover, Feng Ming's group was the cream of the crop and didn't have to worry about getting bogged down by weapon superiority. Their group was skilled in military formations, which the North excelled at; they were also armed with weapons they'd specially prepared to destroy ships.

"Marshal Feng Ming pays his respects to the Sea God Emperor," Feng Ming said, bowing lightly. His companions followed suit, as did the elite army behind them.

The Sea God Emperor nodded. "I see the South's naval demonstration has attracted the attention of the North. We are happy to inform Marshal Feng that this is not an attack. They are simply mobilizing in Haijing's waters as permitted by our treaty."

Feng Ming frowned. Though the Sea God Emperor seemed genial enough, the man beside him was not. "Many thanks for your reassurances," Feng Ming said. "It's just that the presence of the South's ships so close to a Northern Alliance territory is unnerving. Moreover, you might not know this, but Zhou Li and I hail from the same kingdom. He's not from the South, but rather from the

Song Kingdom in the North. He fled after betraying our king and unleashing a civil war in our lands."

The Sea God Emperor frowned. He looked to Zhou Li, then to his advisors, who nodded silently. He gave them a scolding look. "We were already aware of this," the Sea God Emperor said as he turned back to Feng Ming. The surprised expression on his face had vanished. "While it might make you uncomfortable, we'd like to remind you that the sea near Haijing is our territory. It is necessary for us to claim a port to maintain trade with the mainland."

Feng Ming floated closer to the Sea God Emperor as though to say something in private when suddenly a gold shape zipped through the air. He summoned his spear just in time to absorb a blow from a man in golden armor. Haijing's grand marshal, who'd been standing off to the side, had suddenly attacked him with no provocation.

A fire raged in his eyes. A sweltering sandstorm erupted around him as he activated the Magma God's Spear. Though it was on loan from his father-in-law, it was perfectly suited to his abilities. His marshal's cloak billowed behind him, lending his body great strength to complement his ample qi reserves. "Your attack was uncalled for and unprovoked. I was having a peaceful conversation with your emperor. Know your place." Feng Ming heard a mental groan from Li Fei as he realized his mistake.

The Sea God Emperor's eyes narrowed. "Gong Huan is my trusted brother and second only to me in the Sea God Empire. You would do well to remember that even as my lesser, he is your better."

Feng Ming sweated as he sought a way to deescalate. Fortunately, Li Fei stepped in. "My apologies to His Highness the Sea God Emperor," Li Fei said. She bowed very low as she stood beside Feng Ming, though she remained a few inches back, probably due to some strange custom. "Marshal Feng intended no disrespect; his words were sharp because he focuses on battle, proving himself day in and day out through spear rather than pen."

The Emperor's expression softened at her words. Unfortunately, Gong Huan would have none of it. "This disrespect cannot go unaddressed. I demand a ritual combat to resolve it."

Ritual combat? Feng Ming asked. *What's that?*

When a Haijing noble suffers dishonor, he will often seek to redeem himself through combat, Li Fei explained.

That doesn't sound like it could go wrong at all, Feng Ming said. *Besides, he attacked me unprovoked.*

It's a little uncalled for, but since he mentioned it, the Emperor can't let it go unaddressed, Li Fei explained. She issued some instructions on how to navigate the thorny situation.

"Though my rank isn't as esteemed as the grand marshal's, it still holds some weight in the eyes of the North," Feng Ming said. "It would be unfortunate if I were injured. I humbly request that our subordinates fight in our stead." He gestured to Jiao Meng. "Marshal Jiao is second only to me in this expedition, but his strength is mighty. He would be happy to fight against a subordinate of your choosing."

The Sea God Emperor nodded. "His words ring true. We can't have a conflict at our level over a small affair. Choose your representative."

Surprisingly, Gong Huan didn't press the issue. "Marshal Jian is my right-hand man. He will fight you, without his mount, of course."

A man to the side bowed and summoned a trident. He stood close to Jiao Meng, sizing him up.

"Please!" Jiao Meng said.

"Please!" Gong Jian echoed.

They began exchanging blows off to the side. Gong Jian was a strong body cultivator, but Jiao Meng was no slouch. He cultivated qi primarily, which he supplemented with body cultivation on the side. His spear exchanged multiple blows with Gong Jian's trident.

Things are going too smoothly, Feng Ming thought as he looked around. *Aside from the unprovoked attack.*

Zhou Li hadn't moved from his spot. He wore his usual light smile as he surveyed the cultivators. Feng Ming noticed the man's fingers were twitching continuously. It was unusual for cultivators to retain body twitches, but seeing no hand seals, he dismissed them.

"I heard that the Sea God Emperor finished his ascension in

record time," Feng Ming said. "Congratulations on your smooth victory."

"Hardly smooth," the Sea God Emperor said in an unusual display of humility. "My sister almost won. It's a pity she chose her champion poorly."

"Oh?" Feng Ming said. "I only heard of the news in passing. I'd love to hear more about the Sea God's ascension ritual firsthand."

"Certainly," the Sea God Emperor said. The two other men continued fighting. "The first trials were much easier than I'd ever imagined. With Advisor Zhou hiding our karma from the enemy, we passed in record time. I thought we'd have trouble in the second round, but that was where his capabilities really shone through. We managed to get through days before the crown princess. When they'd finally gotten through—"

The Sea God Emperor suddenly stopped and looked toward the dueling pair.

Feng Ming looked over as well. His hands were itching fiercely. He immediately detected the problem. Jiao Meng had wounded Gong Jian with his spear, but as a result, the man's mount had attacked him in a fit of rage. Gong Jian had taken the opportunity to counterattack, so it was now two against one.

"Restrain your mount!" the Sea God Emperor bellowed.

"Hold!" Feng Ming shouted. He dashed forward, but it was too late. The opponent's trident had already lodged itself into Jiao Meng's shoulder, and the vicious-looking shark that made his skin crawl took a deep bite and bit off one of his legs. Jiao Meng screamed.

"What the hell happened?" the Sea God Emperor demanded.

Before the man could reply, one of the South's ships exploded.

"Enemy attack!" a voice yelled. Drums began beating in the background as the South's ships reacted to the explosion. Several more explosions rang out, and suddenly several men appeared on the prow of some Southern ships. They were dressed like Feng Ming's troops, but he recognized none of them.

Trouble, Feng Ming sent to Li Fei.

"Genius move, Marshal. Let's strike while they're recovering!" a voice yelled from his own ranks.

"Stand down and sheathe your weapons!" Feng Ming roared. "And someone kill the man who just spoke." As he sent out the order, however, he detected a few dozen beams of sword light coming from among his men. He dove into action, deflecting most of the blows with a well-timed and extremely lucky sweep of his spear.

Just as it seemed like he would intercept them all, however, a string tugged at his arm. His spear halted, allowing the blade through to pierce the wounded Marshal Jian, who was still bleeding from his wound and being restrained by the Sea God Emperor. Feng Ming traced the string and discovered it emanated from Zhou Li. Then he realized in horror that the blade light was also tethered. It was tethered to Marshal Jian's head.

The man's head exploded. His strong body didn't have a chance to save him.

"You dare!" the Sea God Emperor shouted, his presence mounting. "You'd better give me a good explanation for this."

Feng Ming shuddered at the man's pressure but stood his ground.

"We're obviously being instigated," Feng Ming said. "I recommend you pull your men back. Unless you want to get dragged into a war, that is." He heard another mental groan.

"You think we fear war?" the Sea God Emperor asked. "You think we fear anyone on this mortal plane?"

"I urge the Sea God Emperor to retreat," an unexpected voice suddenly cut in. "This lowly advisor didn't expect such a situation. It would be best if you let us deal with these sneaky Northern saboteurs before we resume negotiations. We wouldn't want you to get dragged into a war."

"If it's a war they want, it's a war they'll get," the Sea God Emperor said with a heated voice. A large blue trident appeared in his right hand, and his crown began glowing with a soft blue light. "I might not care for your petty squabbles, but I've never been so insulted in my life."

At this point, Feng Ming felt another thread. This one was invisible, but it ran between him and the Sea God Emperor. The malevolent karma emanating from the thread made him want to retch.

Then he felt it. It wasn't just him that was covered in threads, but everyone else as well. Every last one of his men were entangled with both the Southern forces and the Sea God Emperor's men.

The strings were also connected to one other man: Zhou Li. Feng Ming suddenly realized that the man's fingers weren't forming hand seals—they were controlling karma. He'd been playing them like puppets the entire time.

As the Sea God Emperor's presence bore down on him, his prime minister attacked Feng Ming's men with his Sea God Scales. Meanwhile, the grand marshal rallied their elite troops. Their mounts, vicious demonic sharks from the deep, began emanating a baleful aura Feng Ming hadn't noticed before.

"Fiendish demons!" Feng Ming exclaimed.

But it was too late. The Sea God Emperor let out a beam of blue light from his trident that swept toward him. He wanted to avoid it, but if he did, Li Fei would take the hit. And she wasn't nearly as strong as he was.

Seven hells, he thought. He readied his Magma God's Spear and prepared to accept a blow from the strongest mortal on the plane. It covered half the distance in a split second, and for a moment, Feng Ming was sure he was going to die.

Then he felt a shift in the waves below him. A pillar of water burst out, revealing a staff-wielding man in cultivation robes. He recognized that man.

"Cha Ming!" he called out in warning. The blue light enveloped Cha Ming's body as thousands of robed men and guards in golden armor emptied out from the ocean. Every one of them bore Haijing's emblem.

This battlefield was lost. He knew it when he saw them. But more than that, he felt utter despair. For the second time in his life, he was watching his friend die before his very eyes.

And once again, despite the many fortuitous encounters he'd had and all the hard work he'd put in, there was nothing he could do about it.

Cha Ming felt pain unlike any he'd ever felt. His bones had sustained hairline fractures from blocking the Sea God Emperor's blow, and most of the flesh had been seared from his bones. Fortunately, he was a peak-marrow-refining cultivator, and a very durable one at that. His flesh recovered in seconds, and his bones healed over. By the time the blue mist faded, Cha Ming was standing before the Sea God Emperor, staff in hand, his clothes immaculate.

"Pardon my intrusion, Your Majesty," Cha Ming said, bowing lightly. "This entire situation seems orchestrated to pit the North and Haijing against each other, so I think we should take the time to sort out the situation. Would Your Majesty be willing to stay his hand?"

The Sea God Emperor frowned when he saw that his blow had been blocked with no residual damage. "Cha Ming, I truly didn't expect to see you here," the Sea God Emperor said. "How is my sister? Is she well?" Fortunately, the Emperor seemed to have none of the animosity Cha Ming had detected when they'd first met.

"Reporting to Your Majesty, she is well but cultivating in the Sea God Clock Tower," Cha Ming said. "She should be out at any moment. I'm sure she will be happy to hear of your concern for her. About the current conflict…"

"You aren't qualified to discuss the current conflict," the prime minister cut in, stepping up beside the Emperor. "You are a mere elder of Haijing Academy." He then looked over the currently assembled scholars from Haijing. "Where is Headmaster Yao?"

"My apologies, I forgot to clarify," Cha Ming said. "Headmaster Yao is no longer in this world, and as the only *transcendent* elder at Haijing Academy, I've replaced him temporarily." He pointed to his gray identity medallion. "As the only transcendent elder in the past few millennia who's earned his position, I believe I'm uniquely suited to represent Haijing Academy."

Then he summoned an Alabaster badge given to him by Lu Tianhao. "Moreover, as a junior partner of the Alabaster Group, I represent the North's angelic faction. Since I belong to both factions, I would hate to see us come to blows."

"It's too late for tha—" the prime minister said. He was cut off before he could continue, however.

"My sister may have made a mistake when selecting you as her champion, but she has always been an excellent judge of character," the Sea God Emperor said. "Speak. What is it you wish to discuss?"

Cha Ming nodded and held his hand out to the assembled group of scholars, and a group of white-robed scholars to the side. "As you know, Haijing Academy has always maintained neutrality. This has allowed it to flourish as this plane's premier research institution, greatly benefiting both the continent and the Sea God Empire, since the Sea God Empire prefers to focus on body cultivation."

"And that's not about to change," the Sea God Emperor said. "The relationship has always been beneficial to all sides involved. I care not for the conflict between the North and the South. Borders shift between angelic and devilish forces, but the Sea God Empire is eternal."

"An admirable position," Cha Ming said. "One I'd normally agree with. But did you know that over the past two months, members of the Alabaster Group were ostracized, denied research budgets, denied workshops, and finally, had ninety percent of their members evicted from the academy under pretense of making room for more productive members? This is all despite having generated a competitive amount of knowledge and grooming many proud citizens of Haijing."

"Is this true?" the Sea God Emperor asked the prime minister.

The prime minister shrugged. "I'm not fully aware of Headmaster Yao's actions after his appointment."

"I find that very hard to believe, given that you chose his appointment," Cha Ming said. "Furthermore, his faction worked closely with your longtime advisor, Zhou Li. To make matters worse, we were forced to flee to a remote part of the city for our safety. The City Guard avoided our areas, making us prime targets for thugs and criminal organizations. Many of our members died. We would have left the city temporarily, but we feared we'd be killed on the way to Beihai. Am I to believe that this is also not something the grand marshal is aware of?"

"I've heard of no such thing," the grand marshal said. "We've always supported the neutrality of Haijing Academy."

"Until now," Cha Ming said. "Elders, can you serve as witnesses and assert that everything I've said is true?"

"Yes!" they shouted in response, bowing to the Sea God Emperor, whose frown deepened.

"Regardless of these civil matters, this is a military engagement," the grand marshal said. He extended his hand to the group of cultivators who'd prepared for battle under Feng Ming's leadership. "They've infringed on our sovereignty. We cannot allow this insult to remain."

"What's infringed on our sovereignty is our new grand marshal's reckless actions," a man said, stepping up beside Cha Ming. He wore elaborate golden epaulettes not seen on most guardsmen. "Ever since the grand marshal took over the guard and replaced us old marshals, over twenty percent of our mounts have been replaced by fiendish mounts from the fissure. Fiendish mounts!"

"I don't see a problem with fiendish mounts," the Sea God Emperor said. "Explain yourself."

"Our ancestors didn't tame fiendish mounts, and for good reason," the old marshal said. "I've invited the foremost beast tamer in the city to testify." With that, Ling Dong appeared beside him. "Ling Dong is the city's best beast tamer and has armed many of our finest soldiers with his skills as the world's only demonic smith. Yet he was imprisoned and tortured for two months!"

"For refusing to arm our new elite corps," the grand marshal said. "This was obviously politically motivated, so we had to make an example of him."

"I refused to arm your elite corps because they are despicable creatures who aren't even under Haijing's control," Ling Dong said. He turned to the Sea God Emperor, and unlike the scholars, he stared him straight in the eyes. "Taming demons requires three things: power, respect, and a reciprocal relationship. Since part of a fiend's nature is demonic, I can tame them. However, this is due to my special abilities. Ask any other beast tamer, and they will say the same thing: it cannot be done."

"But it clearly *has* been done," the Sea God Emperor said, gesturing to the fiendish shark squad.

"It looks like taming on the surface," Ling Dong said. "But in fact, it is not. They are actually bound by a devilish contract, a common way to control lesser devils in the South. And the Southern Alliance is the only place that can produce and enforce such contracts. Or dissolve them, for that matter."

He pointed to Zhou Li. "By replacing your demonic mounts with fiendish creatures, Zhou Li has both increased the guard's might and made it dependent on the South. Given a few more years, they could completely replace your mounts. Then your entire guard's mobility would be at the South's mercy."

"Is this true?" the Sea God Emperor said, looking gravely at his grand marshal.

"The dependence on devil-binding contracts is a minor affair," the grand marshal said dismissively. "Once we have our own devil binders, it won't matter."

"And you didn't inform me first?" the Emperor growled.

The marshal paled and stepped back as the Sea God Crown's power flared.

This entire time, Cha Ming hadn't been paying full attention to the Emperor and the others. He'd kept his attention on one man: Zhou Li. The annoying, all-knowing man had been quiet. If past behavior was any indication, that didn't bode well for them.

Still, despite spreading out his transcendent force and keeping his Devil-Sealing, Demon-Subduing Eyes active, he saw nothing out of the ordinary. Unfortunately, there was little he could do about the man's karmic powers. He wished Wang Jun were here, or even Gong Lan. They would know what Zhou Li was up to.

Brother, we're here! Huxian's voice suddenly said.

Cha Ming thanked the heavens for their mercy when he suddenly thought of something. It wasn't a reassuring thought. *Huxian, how badly do those dolphins you spoke of hate fiendish demons again?*

No reply.

Huxian?

Silence.

Cha Ming looked to Zhou Li, who smirked. The waters bubbled, and suddenly hundreds of dolphins burst out of the water and pounced on the elite corps and their mounts, including the grand marshal.

Stop them! Cha Ming yelled.

I can't! Huxian said. *They won't cooperate!*

"Looks like you lose again," Zhou Li said, suddenly stepping up and back. He summoned a large scroll, which rapidly began unfurling behind him. It was filled with scenes of blood and slaughter, where devils wreaked carnage on lesser mortals. Then, to Cha Ming's amazement, the vivid images began peeling off from the scroll. They radiated a sinister aura, and a malevolent ochre halo emanated from every fiber of their being.

Hell's gates might as well have opened. A tide of devilish creatures poured out and attacked the Northern cultivators. Cha Ming looked over to the Sea God Emperor, who'd stopped berating his advisors and had begun fighting back against the demonic dolphins. Huxian and friends, seeing they could do no good there, leaped into the flood of devilish creatures and began tearing them apart alongside Feng Ming.

They started a fight, but it's far from unsalvageable, Cha Ming thought. *We haven't directly attacked the Sea God Empire.*

Warning bells rang in his mind, and as he moved to place himself between the Northern cultivators and Haijing's City Guard, he realized there was another group from Haijing. One that he'd brought over personally. A burst of sword light left the group of

Northern cultivators and smashed into them, killing a full fifth of their members.

Cha Ming wasted no time. He flashed into the group of surprised cultivators, who relaxed when they saw him. Dozens of black staves appeared in the air, and to their surprise, stabbed down on a few select cultivators. "These men attacked the Sea God Emperor's men. They are plants by the enemy and deserved to die." He disappeared as they began arguing in confusion.

As he rushed to calm down the Haijing City Guard, however, a voice bellowed from where the elite corps were fighting dolphins. "Who dares kill members of my guard? I'll have their heads!"

A blue blur rushed out toward the North's forces, and both Cha Ming and Feng Ming rushed to intercept it. Cha Ming's staff and Feng Ming's spear struck out at the same time, barely blocking the Sea God Emperor's trident. "Get. Out. Of. My. Way."

The Sea God Emperor's eyes were crimson and filled with madness. He'd lost all sense of reason and was already preparing for another strike.

"Just like Songjing," Feng Ming said bitterly.

"Just like Songjing," Cha Ming said, preparing to take another blow. They'd tried their best to dissuade everyone, but it was all for naught. The North, the South, Haijing, and rogue demons were fighting each other in a mad frenzy. Even if they won the battle, the results would be catastrophic.

Zhou Li had played them all for fools yet again.

Chapter 35: The Stillness of Time

Now that dialogue was no longer an option, Cha Ming allowed his transcendent force to fill the entire battlefield. Streams of small golden gliders zipped out from the hundreds of black ships not far away; the South's ships were evidently carriers for these smaller contraptions that were piloted by cultivators.

With rehearsed prevision, they swarmed the North's cultivators, who clashed with them in formation. Several gliders fell into the sea on impact, but it was just a drop in the bucket. They stung at the Northern cultivators like bees, crashing toward them on bladed treasures as they tried to pierce them with spears. Dozens fell with each wave.

Cha Ming and Feng Ming had no time or breathing space to help these Northern cultivators. Cha Ming might be strong, but his endurance and regenerative capabilities were his most powerful assets. He used these to tank blows from the Sea God Emperor to grant opportunities to Feng Ming, who often got lucky and scored substantial strikes against the powerful body cultivator.

Unfortunately, the Sea God Emperor was the most powerful mortal body cultivator on the plane. Each time Cha Ming blocked his dreadful trident, it felt like getting struck by a mountain. His flesh broke apart and his ligaments tore, only to heal over again just as quickly. The ocean below them was stained in blood. His blood. The power of the Sea God Crown was simply too potent; his disadvantage in body cultivation would only keep increasing.

As these titans fought, the guardsmen who had accompanied Cha Ming had joined forces with the dolphins in attacking the fiendish sharks. Thousands of guardsmen clashed with their elite counterparts while hundreds of dolphins ripped and tore at the few hundred sharks. All around them, fish of all kinds joined in to attack their dreaded foes.

Ling Dong was fighting alongside the guards, as was Jin Huang, Yue Bing, and Zi Long. Ling Dong clashed with shark after shark while projecting his Demon-Subduing Intent, both bolstering nearby friendly demons and reducing the fiendish sharks' combat effectiveness. Devil-Sealing Intent shone out from all over them, further weakening the sharks, but they were too powerful. The evil means that had given them birth allowed them to grow much faster than their tamer counterparts, so even weakened, they still managed to take down one dolphin after another.

But not without paying a bloody price. For each few dolphins they felled, one of the fiendish sharks was destroyed. While this might not seem like a win in most people's books, the dolphins cackled gleefully with every kill. As Huxian had suspected, they held a terrible secret—their bloodlust and their hatred for sharks. If you put the two species in the same place, the dolphins wouldn't rest until the sharks were dead. This applied doubly so to fiendish ones.

Yue Bing was an unexpected star of the battle. If not for her, they would have already fallen. The blood doctor flew around on her bloody wings, siphoning blood from enemies and healing allies as they fought over the bloody ocean. Appendages that had been bitten off, deep bites, and gashes—all could be healed by her miraculous powers. The guardsmen had noticed this, but every time they tried to close in on her, Zi Long's illusions interfered.

Meanwhile, Jin Huang roamed the battlefield practically unhindered. Even the fiendish demons feared him and his poisons, so he sowed them with impunity. He didn't kill scores of foes but weakened them. The rest would be up to his allies.

Cha Ming defended with Splitting Heaven and Earth as the Sea God Emperor crashed down with his trident. A residual blade of water struck Cha Ming's body and split it vertically. Cha Ming quickly reformed and summoned a combat formation. Sand blew around him as his freshly summoned Desiccation Formation attempted to suck all the moisture out of the air and the Sea God Emperor himself.

The Sea God Emperor would have none of it. He kicked Cha Ming away, nearly breaking his ribs in the process, before slashing at key points in the combat formation and breaking it apart. He finished just in time to notice Feng Ming's spear stabbing at his face, which he grabbed with his bare hand then flung Feng Ming away.

We can't win this battle, Cha Ming thought. *Not without help.* He looked at the heavens above, where three angels and three devils floated as though unaffected by the terrible battle. They would interfere if they had to, but the cost was steep; with the mounting conflict between the North and South, they didn't dare waste their transcendent lives. Likely, they would only interfere to save more important individuals before they died in battle. Cha Ming hoped it wouldn't come to that.

One last noteworthy battle was taking place. Huxian and his four friends were fighting the surprisingly powerful prime minister and the grand marshal. They weren't devils, he noticed, just practical individuals who had seen a chance and taken it. But did that make them any different?

Both were powerful body cultivators minoring in qi, and the Sea God Scales and the Sea God Shell were treasures that bordered on defying the plane's will. Whereas the Sea God Crown enhanced the body, the scales controlled space and the shell controlled force. The shell covered them in a golden glow that, with their peak-marrow-refining cultivation, made them almost impossible to harm. Meanwhile, under the protection of the grand marshal, the prime minister struck out at the assembled beasts with spatial fragments.

Blood flew all around them. Gua, with his fan, controlled flows of ocean water to obstruct and tangle the two's movements. Silverwing, on the other hand, felt practically useless. Despite his swift speed and powerful attacks, his moves were easy to predict. The fear of a spatial blade appearing before him midflight prompted the bird to fight in a more reserved fashion; he used a smaller form to fight and preferred to slash out with wings, talons, and blades of wind.

Unlike Silverwing, Lei Jiang was king in this battlefield. He zipped all around and used the nearby water to his advantage, constantly striking their two opponents with bolt after bolt of lightning. Huxian fought alongside him with tooth and paw, using his superiority as a Godbeast to match their physical strength. For every strike he received, he gave. Shadows and light danced around him, nibbling at the nearly infinite vitality of their opponents.

Mr. Mountain! Huxian shouted as he exchanged yet another round of blows. A violet mist, which had been absent all battle, suddenly materialized as a massive mountain. Several miles wide and tall, it was impossibly large for a demon. But why would Mr. Mountain care about what was possible or impossible? Mountains were big, and they were heavy, right? He came crashing down on the prime minister and the marshal, forcing them to cough up blood as it struck their combined field of space and force, shattering it in the process.

As they resisted the mountain's crushing weight, Huxian, Lei Jiang, and Silverwing quickened their assault while Gua supported. Thin gray lines appeared between them as their Greater Friendship Circle activated its Four Trigrams Suppression ability. The pseudo domain bogged the grand marshal and prime minister down and wore away at their treasures' effectiveness. All at once, the demons descended on them.

Seeing his companions threatened, the Sea God Emperor shoved Cha Ming and Feng Ming away with a sweep of his spear and darted toward the pseudo domain with frightening speed. His crown glowed brightly as he stabbed into it with his trident. The domain shattered, and the five beasts scattered. They retreated toward Cha Ming and grouped up with him and Feng Ming.

With the short respite, Cha Ming noticed that Zhou Li, who'd been missing this whole time, had been fighting with Jiao Meng.

The wounded marshal had somehow been separated from his allies and was fighting for dear life. His leg had already been healed with spirit medicines, but he was still in a weakened condition. Cha Ming moved to assist him, but it was too late. A clever trap by Zhou Li gave the sinister man the opportunity he needed. Black flame dragons pierced through Jiao Meng's back. The marshal's corpse tumbled into the ocean where demonic fish fought for it.

Cha Ming looked over the battlefield and realized that, on all fronts, they were losing. The scholars had been instigated to fight alongside the Alabaster Group and cooperate with the Northern forces, but they were slowly being whittled away by the innumerable gliders. Moreover, the black ships had taken to the field. They were more than transports, it seemed, and given the opportunity, they unleashed deadly blows from weapons mounted on their prows. The weapons looked like cannons, but sleeker, with inscribed runes. He'd heard of such things from Feng Ming before and knew how potent they could be.

Fight with Huxian and the others, Cha Ming said to Feng Ming. *Give me time.*

Cha Ming darted out toward the ships and used his Clear Sky Staff and Crushing Chaos to demolish a cannon. His strike tore a gouge in the ship, but it was nothing compared to its massive body. As the cultivators on board unleashed their techniques, Cha Ming retreated and struck another ship. Their main weapons fell one after another.

Zi Long, retreat with the guard and bolster the North's formations, Feng Ming shouted as Cha Ming worked. Since the suppressing fire had been alleviated, he took the opportunity to fix their weakness. Huxian and the others were buying them time with the Sea God royalty as they retreated from the battle with the fiendish sharks.

By now, most of the dolphins had perished, their blood dyeing the seas red. They died in satisfaction, however, as they'd killed over half of the fiendish sharks in the process. The guardsmen who'd survived the bloody confrontation retreated along with Cha Ming's disciples under cover of illusions, and by the time the elite corps knew what had happened, they'd joined with the North's cultivators.

The moment they stepped into the formation, Zi Long began manipulating their battle formation, while Yue Bing healed crippling injuries. Her face was pale and gaunt, and she was clearly overdrawing her own vitality. Fortunately, she never fully ran out. The battlefield lacked nothing if not blood. As Jin Huang aided Zi Long in altering the formations, Ling Dong joined the defensive line. With his presence, one glider after another fell.

We can't hold out anymore! Huxian shouted. He and his friends retreated, this time all darting into Huxian's tails. Time sped up around the fox, who barely escaped a killing blow from the Sea God Emperor as he dove into the North's formation. It hummed to life as Cha Ming destroyed the last cannon. He noticed Feng Ming managing to enter the formation unimpeded, but suddenly realized he'd lost track of Zhou Li once more.

A faint sensation of crisis alerted him to an incoming flame dragon. He dodged it, only to discover that another had taken its place. He absorbed the blow with his body, but as his flesh regenerated, yet *another* had appeared. As he looked around, he noticed that his surroundings looked much different than before. The ships were still there, and the cultivators were still fighting for their lives as the Sea God Emperor's men and the South's forces wore away at their defenses.

But around him, he noticed brush marks. The marks seemed to burn the very air around them, forming portals into a foreign world. Flaming dragons continuously crawled out from these portals. It was the most realistic painting he'd ever seen, and Zhou Li, who had gone missing, had painted it just for him.

Cha Ming moved to attack Zhou Li but was interrupted by another half dozen flame dragons. As soon as he managed to destroy them, more came, forcing him back to the center of the painting. He found himself surrounded by black flames in three dimensions. Feeling a tinge of dread, he focused on evasion, using an Origin Strike to pierce his way through. Unfortunately, the Origin Strike was too narrow, and while he struck many flame dragons, many more took their places and forced him back. He was trapped.

"It's truly too difficult to kill a body cultivator at your level," Zhou Li said from outside the painting. "Only the Sea God and his right and left hands are harder to kill. You have no idea how much time and effort I put into this painting, how much blood, sweat, and tears I put into refining it. You should be proud."

"Don't think you can stop me," Cha Ming said. He cast out his sigils and summoned a peak-grade combat formation. An icy field surrounded him, and though it didn't harm the black flame dragons, it slowed them. Cha Ming beat his way through the surrounding dragons, but just as he was about to reach the outside, he noticed a distortion. His body shifted, and he found himself back in the center of the painting.

Cha Ming's face darkened. "What have you done?"

Zhou Li shrugged. "It's so difficult to predict a karmic anomaly's actions, and almost impossible to kill you in a reasonable amount of time. The only way is to trap you. If you don't fight, you'll die, but if you fight, you'll stay trapped. I've accounted for everything you're capable of and more."

Cha Ming, not resigned to his fate, continued beating the dragons around him. His qi reserves were deep, so he pushed them to their limits. He alternated between all five elements, pushing to find a weakness in the painting. He considered using the Space-Time Camera for a brief moment but discarded that thought. Zhou Li could easily deal with it, as he'd shown in the precious fight.

"I think you can break through, eventually," Zhou Li said. "Fortunately, you don't have enough time."

Cha Ming knew this was true. During his battle, he'd kept an eye on the North's battle formation. Their opponents were slowly but surely slaughtering their way to the center. It was no longer possible for them to flee, and he could see angels flying above them, ready to interfere if they absolutely had to. The ships had also mounted secondary cannons and began firing at their forces. They were losing men, and fast.

As Cha Ming fought the dragons, he let out his rage. He raged at Zhou Li, who'd defeated him time and time again. He'd predicted his every move and stopped his progress, and for what? Was it for spite? Zhou Li wasn't much older than him, but his eyes were filled with vicissitudes Cha Ming couldn't comprehend. And based on his words, he remembered many past lives. His plans were the work of many generations, while Cha Ming was only a fly trapped in his carefully woven net. The net hadn't even been laid for him; he was incidental, a problem not worth mentioning. All hope seemed lost. As the sea turned increasingly red with blood, and the black ships approached, the North's forces dwindled.

And then they felt it.

It was a subtle shift in the tides, a slight alteration in the waves. The ocean, which had been churning fiercely during their battle, suddenly grew calm. Moreover, it became deathly still, as though the waves didn't dare upset its crystal-clear surface.

An object appeared between the black ships that fired on the formation of cultivators with impunity. It was small and thin, and it rose slowly. But as it did, everything seemed to freeze around it. The weapons, which had just been loaded and were in the process of firing, slowed down to a crawl. Their runes refused to shift, and their operators, who wanted to look around in confusion, could only stare dimly at their weapons.

The small object broke through the still ocean, creating not a single wave in the process. It rose higher and higher until finally, a much larger object poked out. It looked square, like a large block of smooth concrete one expected to find in a city center. It rose from the ocean, revealing a large semitransparent clock, whose every tick took an eternity to hear.

The moment it pierced the ocean's surface, the ships around it were forced out of the way by something akin to waves of water. But they weren't waves; waves were not permitted around the clock, only stillness. But these fresh gushes of water pushed the boats outward like they were nothing more than children's toys. Most flipped over to their sides, but many were completely overturned.

The clock's large body rose from the ocean, its entire structure covered in blue-and-gold runes. It rose higher and higher until finally, a figure emerged with it. Gong Shuren, who'd been attuning to the Sea God Clock Tower, finally rose from the deep. Her eyes were blue, and her white hair had also turned a light shade of gold. It complemented the blue-gold runes on her skin that pulsed with the inviolable might of a sea god.

"Stop right this instant," she said in a voice that carried throughout the battlefield. It was a soft voice, but everyone heard it. Northern, Southern, and Sea God forces alike suddenly stopped what they were doing. It wasn't that they wanted to—murder flashed in their eyes as they sought to slay their enemies—but that they *couldn't* do otherwise. Time had frozen for them, and the fact that their minds could even register her words was impressive enough.

"Who gave you the courage to violate our ancestors' directives?" she said, turning to the Sea God Emperor.

The Sea God Emperor gulped as he stared at the Sea God Clock Tower. Then, to everyone's surprise, he fought its suppression and bent down on one knee of his own accord.

"This lowly one greets the Sea God Emissary," he said, his voice filled with reverence.

"These lowly ones greet the Sea God Emissary," the prime minister and grand marshal said, kneeling then kowtowing. The time-freezing field left the remaining Sea God's forces, and they too kowtowed in her direction.

"It seems you all have some sense left," she said, looking at them dispassionately. "For all the mistakes you've made."

"We have erred," the Sea God Emperor said with his head still bowed. "Please instruct us on how to proceed."

Gong Shuren, the new Sea God Emissary, looked to the two figures beside him like a god amongst mortals. "Speak. You have something you wish to say."

The prime minister trembled, then spoke. "Everything I have done was for the benefit of the kingdom," he said. "The South—it's far more powerful than you could imagine. Only by allying ourselves with them could we survive. Now that you control the Sea God

Clock Tower, however, things are different. How could we possibly fear them?"

He stood up with a zealous look and overlooked those frozen mid-battle. Cha Ming was one of the few who had shaken free from her control and escaped his predicament.

"And you feel the same?" Gon Shuren asked the grand marshal.

Emboldened by the prime minister, he stood up and nodded. "There were downsides in allying with the South, but the benefits were substantial. Our ancestors were neutral, but was that not due to helplessness? No kingdom could help us achieve our full potential and claim the vast swaths of ocean all around us. Now that the opportunity has come, why not grasp it?"

"I see…" Gon Shuren said. The Emperor was still kneeling and awaiting her command. "How low we have fallen, where we need allies who would abandon us the moment trouble arises."

Both the prime minister and grand marshal looked around at these words. To their surprise, Zhou Li, who'd orchestrated the entire battle, had vanished.

"We have erred," the prime minister said. "But everything we did was for our empire."

Gong Shuren sighed and shook her head. "Don't waste your breath. With the Sea God Clock Tower comes power and knowledge that completely exposes you."

She waved her hand, and an image appeared. It was of the prime minister conversing with Zhou Li, who held a black crystal.

"I may not have been there, but the clock remembers. It remembers when your thirst for power, combined with your fear, overcame your benevolent heart. You succumbed to your deepest desires, and from that moment on, you cared little for your clansmen. You only cared about yourself and your descendants."

"And you," she said, looking at the grand marshal. "You grew up dreaming of conquest, and just the mention of battle would boil your blood. Your weakness was easy to exploit; you became the lynchpin that embroiled us in a war."

"I'm guilty," the grand marshal said. "Please punish me. But know that I did sincerely want our empire to return to its former glory."

Gong Shuren looked at him for a moment but shook her head. "Glory? Is glory necessary? You broke our ancestors' edicts and put us in danger. The road to ruin is paved in good intentions."

She then looked to the Emperor. "What of you, Sea God Emperor? Do you have anything to say for yourself?"

"Nothing," he said after a moment.

"Nothing in your defense?" Gong Shuren said. "Gong Xuandi, your life is in my hands."

"I am aware," the Sea God Emperor said. "I'm also aware that my actions have endangered our empire. They went against the edicts of our ancestors. I was blind, and I regret my actions. Only death can absolve our sins."

Gong Shuren walked over slowly. Her every step was synchronized with the ticking clock tower behind her. As she walked, swords leveled against cultivators, and leaping sharks inched toward their targets at a snail's pace. She stopped inches away from the bowing Sea God Emperor.

"You made a grave mistake. You all did." Her gaze turned to the prime minister, who was still standing. "Gong Luoyang, your mistakes were both self-centered and irredeemable. You manipulated the grand marshal with Zhou Li's help and caused this entire situation. The matter with the scholars was your doing, but it is nothing compared to the karma you have sown for the empire. I sentence you to death."

"I—" Gong Luoyang started.

The clock tower tolled, and the toll resonated with everyone containing the Sea God's bloodline. The sound was sinister, like a reaper's scythe, and dissonant like a macabre orchestra. It was the sound of death itself. Gong Luoyang collapsed to the ground, lifeless.

Gong Shuren then turned to the grand marshal, Gong Huan, who was still shivering. She sighed before speaking, and her sigh carried across the battlefield. "Your situation pains me the most," she said. "You were clearly manipulated, and you did all these hurtful things for our kingdom."

"Please have mercy," Gong Huan said, trembling with closed eyes.

"But you'd do it over again in a heartbeat, wouldn't you?" Gon Shuren said.

"Yes," the grand marshal replied. "For the glory of our empire."

"I'm sorry, then, for I must wrong you," Gon Shuren said. A tear fell from her left eye as the clock tolled a second time. The reaper struck once more, and the newly appointed grand marshal of the Sea God Empire was dead.

She sighed again. "Now's your last chance. Your life is in my hands." Time, which had already slowed to a crawl, seemed to freeze even further. Endless moments passed as those on the battlefield awaited his answer.

"I will yield to your judgment, Emissary," the Sea God Emperor said, not raising his head. "May our empire flourish under your reign."

Gong Shuren nodded. Then she reached out and placed her hand on his shoulder. "You... have erred. You have endangered our kingdom by sowing karma, and there's no telling what the consequences will be for the Sea God lineage if this karma isn't rectified. The purpose of our empire was never to thrive, but to breed proper and upright descendants for the Sea God. Every emperor, prime minister, and grand marshal is appointed through the Sea God Trials and tempered through their reign. When they transcend, they are judged according to their actions.

"Unfortunately, your death will do little to appease the karma sown. Furthermore, your brothers were unrelenting. You are different. You regret your actions, and that is why you are still alive."

Gong Shuren lifted her hand, and the Sea God Shell and the Sea God Scales floated up beside the clock tower. The power of force and space they emanated merged with the tower's aura and strengthened it. Then she picked the crown off the Emperor's head, looked at it for a moment, and placed it on her own.

The crown attuned the moment it touched her brow, and a wave of crushing pressure swept over the elite corps of the guard. The clock tolled a third time, and their lives were no more. A wave of her hand caused time to quicken around the fiendish sharks, even as the time in their surroundings was frozen. They aged at a rate visible to the naked eye, with millennia passing every second. Finally, they became nothing more than skeletons.

The remaining guards trembled in fear, but their mood lightened when the powerful Sea God Emissary smiled at them. "You did the right thing in rebelling against the Emperor. And you, scholars, also did the right thing. You were unfairly treated, but instead of running to the mainland, you confronted the Emperor. For that, you have my thanks."

She then turned her sights on the frozen gliders and black ships. She clenched her fist, and large spikes of ice erupted around them and pierced the still-frozen artifacts and those within them. Time resumed, and the battlefield erupted in a garden of ice and blood. The sea around them began to move once more, but everyone could only stare in awe at the frightening display of power. Only Huxian seemed undaunted.

"Sister Shuren, that was awesome!" he yelped and jumped over to her. "Can you teach me?"

She ignored him for now and looked gravely at the bowing man who used to be the Emperor. He'd been berated, defeated, and uncrowned. The moment she took away her suppression, he'd likely try to end his own life. "You have sown karma for our kingdom, Xuandi, and for that, you have lost your crown. You have always yearned for it, and I cannot fault you for that; it's how we were raised.

"But that doesn't change the fact that we owe karma. We meddled in the North's affairs, and they have lost many cultivators. The scholars in Haijing have also suffered, the scholars we rely on for our benefit. Much of the suffering can be alleviated with benefits, but the North was still severely weakened by our actions. Therefore, you and the two remaining marshals in Haijing, as well as the strongest from each family, are hereby exiled. You are not to return until one hundred years have passed, and you will support Marshal Feng in all his endeavours, laying down your lives if required."

The man formerly known as the Sea God Emperor trembled. "I, Gong Xuandi, will end my life instead," he said, breathing hoarsely. "Fighting is one thing, but living on land is a punishment worse than death."

"That wasn't a request," Gong Shuren said. "It was an order." The crown on her head glowed blue once more, and he kneeled immediately.

"As you wish, Emissary," Gong Xuandi said. He then stood up, bowed, and walked over to the astonished Feng Ming.

"Cha Ming, come with me," Gong Shuren said. She walked off toward the clock tower and beckoned for him to follow.

The remaining troops, under Feng Ming's direction, began clearing the battlefield and collecting their dead.

Epilogue: The Taotie Rises

Cha Ming and Huxian followed Gong Shuren into the clock tower, and as they did, they felt a change in the space around them. A sensation of crashing waves now permeated the entire structure, further lending to its mystical charm. "No one in our family knew what would happen if the clock tower was attuned," she said as they walked. "They tried it in vain for tens of thousands of years, but little did they know that it has happened far more often than they realized."

"Just how old is the Sea God Empire?" Cha Ming asked.

"Hundreds of millions of years old," Gong Shuren said, visibly shivering. "And I saw it all—the clashing fates on the plane, the destiny of our nation, the rise of heroes and the fall of villains. Not every generation successfully passes on the crown. Sometimes it is lost for tens of thousands of years before it is earned back."

"That's a long time," Cha Ming said. "Is that why you changed? It seemed like you wanted revenge when you began attuning the tower."

"I did," Gong Shuren admitted. "But I had time to think about it. Much more time than you could even imagine. And when I saw the past, I also saw the future. It was unclear, undetermined, but I saw a general trend. That's why everything I did today was measured and proportional. I couldn't bring back the lives of those who perished today, but I could bring balance to the karma our kingdom owes.

The situation is unfavorable for the South, but they have harmed us much over the past thousand years. Even the prime minister's turning was the product of dozens of years of effort that went far beyond Zhou Li."

"But why bother with balance?" Cha Ming asked. "You saw how the South is. They'd stop at nothing, even kidnapping and taking hostages and murdering countless innocents to achieve their goals."

"And they always will," Gong Shuren said. "They are despicable, and I don't like them. But over hundreds of millions of years, our empire has experienced much. Just like we shouldn't ally ourselves with devils, we shouldn't ally ourselves with angels either."

"Can't kingdoms use all the merit they can get?" Cha Ming asked. From what he'd gathered, it was the lack of providence, the lack of merit that caused kingdoms to crumble.

"You haven't lived long, so you don't know," Gong Shuren said. "In this age, the good are rewarded, but the evil are punished. Do you think it will stay this way forever? For all eternity?"

"Shouldn't it?" Cha Ming asked. "Isn't this a rule of the universe?"

"The universe was painted in black and white, Cha Ming," Gong Shuren said. "What goes up must come down, and what rises must fall. Good and evil are shifting tides in the sea of destiny. Every shift is a trial that must be weathered."

Cha Ming frowned. "Are you saying the rules will change? When? And for how long?"

"Does it matter?" Gong Shuren asked, looking him in the eyes. "Will you change the way you act if they do? Do you want others to change?"

Cha Ming, speechless, shook his head. No, he wouldn't change even if the situations were reversed. If he was punished for doing good, so be it.

"Soon," Gong Shuren said. "It could be as little as fifty years, and as much as a million. But it will happen, and when it does, everything you know will be called into question."

Gong Shuren raised her hand, and a blue mist floated out from the clock tower's walls. They pressed together until they solidified and formed what looked like a little pocket watch. "Huxian, this is for you. You've touched on the essence of time, but it isn't enough. Absorb this, and it will take you to the limits of what this realm has to offer."

Then she looked out at the empty air in the clock tower's halls, and for a moment, Cha Ming thought he saw something. A slight glimmer, tiny strings connecting it to countless lives on this plane. "Everything is balanced at last," she said. "You can keep your academy medallions, but I'm sure you know my stance by now. You eliminated scholars from the South for their actions, which was well within reason. But it must stop from now on. They must be permitted back into Haijing. That's nonnegotiable."

Cha Ming sighed. He picked the medallion off his robes, smiled, and stored it in his Clear Sky World. "There's no need. I'm sure you'll find someone adequate to be headmaster. I won't be coming back."

"All right," Gong Shuren said. "Be careful out there. You have a path to follow, and a good chance of succeeding. But things are changing. You might find yourself invincible right now, but I assure you that you are not. I like you. Don't get yourself killed."

Another wave, another shift. The next thing they knew, Cha Ming and Huxian were back outside, floating above the red ocean waves. The battlefield had been cleared, but the blood remained. For a moment, they wondered if that spot of blood would ever fade.

"Huxian?" Cha Ming asked the fox, who jumped on his shoulder. "Let's go visit Wang Jun. I owe him a favor, and I think it's high time I repay it."

Zither music sounded throughout the Red Dust Pavilion as it always did. Hong Xin sat on her balcony, looking over the mistresses and newly recruited trainees fawning over their clients. She trained them in kindling arts, of course. Though some would learn dousing arts as a minor, only those who could handle it learned both.

Everyone below was chatting while waiting for the main attraction: Ji Bingxue would be playing again, and her performances always gathered a sizeable crowd. Many of the watchers were just normal cultivators—men and women alike. Even core-formation cultivators scrambled to obtain a seat in the crowded venue. Never too crowded, of course. The breathing space was necessary for customer satisfaction, and the shortage was necessary for their bottom line.

As she looked at them socializing, she felt a presence behind her. "It's been too long, Master Mu," Hong Xin said as the man walked up beside her. She'd been expecting him.

"We hadn't heard from you in a while, and your courtesans stopped showing up for their regular appointments," Mu Feilong said. "I thought there might be a problem, so I thought I'd pop by."

"There is a problem, and I instructed them to stay here until you came by to resolve it," Hong Xin said.

A serving girl, who'd been waiting for this moment, brought them refreshments with lightning speed. There were two ruby-red wineglasses. She grabbed one and motioned to the other.

"And what might that problem be?" Mu Feilong said, swirling his own glass. He took a sip and nodded appreciatively.

"We need to renegotiate our rates," Hong Xin said. "We have no problem working with you, but I'm afraid we haven't been adequately compensated of late. The envelope on the tray is what I had in mind."

Mu Feilong frowned and set his glass back on the tray. He opened the envelope and withdrew a red piece of paper from it. He laughed when he saw the numbers. "Your appetite is impressive. The Red Dust Pavilion never dared ask so much when it was at its peak, much less now."

Hong Xin shrugged. "Consider it backpay for all the cheap work you've been getting over the years."

Mu Feilong looked at her incredulously. He tapped his fingers on his temple. "I really don't know what's going through that head of yours. You've seen our trump card, so I'm sure you're aware of your situation."

"That's true," Hong Xin said. "You could destroy us in a blink of an eye. But might I pass on some information of my own? For free, of course."

"Please," Mu Feilong said.

"Last night, there was a break-in at the Spirit Temple," Hong Xin said. "It's a very carefully kept secret, mostly due to the dreadful trade involved. I heard that seven very special urns went missing. They're very important to the Spirit Temple, and I'm sure they'll be scrambling to shore up their supply. It would be a pity if anyone were caught assisting them."

Mu Feilong frowned. "The Spirit Temple is impossible to break into."

"Not nearly as impossible as you think," Hong Xin said sweetly. "I happened to obtain the identities of seven houses scrambling to supply the Spirit Temple with their illicit goods. They're all in the process of gathering them, of course, but the goods in transit are kept very secret. It would be a *shame* if these storage locations became known to the Church of Justice. The consequences would be *devastating*."

"You're mad," Mu Feilong said. "No, I don't believe you. No one will."

"You don't have to," Hong Xin said. "But I'd carefully consider our offer for services if I were you. Women have many wonderful qualities, forbearance being one of them. But I'm afraid we're also vengeful creatures. Either you give us back what we're owed, or we'll burn both our houses to the ground. You decide."

Hong Xin didn't wait for him to reply. She walked back to her room under cover of darkness. As the sweaty Mu Feilong pondered her revelation, the lights dimmed, and the curtain opened. Ji Bingxue's zither filled the room with music, rousing everyone's spirits and inspiring everyone's dormant ambitions.

One man, however, heard a very different tune. It fanned the flames of his greatest worries and the consequences if Hong Xin's words proved true. It was hardly the nicest thing to do to a man you just threatened, but the Red Dust Pavilion was beyond playing fair. They'd flipped the board, and it was time to start a new game.

Wang Jun left the cold night and entered the Wang family estate. He didn't exit the shadows, however, but clung to them like a loving blanket. He took comfort in them, for it hid away the people he hated and shielded those he loved. And if not for finding Hong Xin, perhaps the shadows would be all he had left.

He didn't return to his study. Instead he directly entered the dark corridor. He followed it to the dark door that opened into the room where his dark master sat on a dark chair. The man, who'd just been playing what could have been the world's tiniest violin—for it didn't make a sound—looked at him in surprise. "And here I thought you'd be sulking for the next few days. Did something wonderful happen?"

Wang Jun smiled. "A fortunate turn of events, that's all. Don't pretend you don't know what it was and what I was up to last night."

The man sighed, and it was a silent sigh devoid of any sound. "I warned you it would happen."

"And I didn't listen," Wang Jun said. "The consequences were obvious."

Daoist Obscurus put down what he'd been holding. To Wang Jun's surprise, it was indeed a tiny violin, or something that looked a lot like it. He'd have liked to hear it, but the shadowy man only took pleasure in quiet things. "Did you learn your lesson?"

Wang Jun smiled wryly. "I learned that my family hates me more than I thought. I also learned that nothing is beyond them when it comes to making money. The rules are there to protect those in power, and nothing more. If I follow the rules, they'll likely find some other excuse to disqualify me from the family leadership."

Then he summoned the recording sphere detailing the exchange he'd seen with the Spirit Temple. He crushed the crystal, which shattered into small fragments that fell onto the cobblestone floor. "But I have my bottom line. Revenge by exposing Wang Ling would be easy, but the price is too high. I won't damn my family by taking the easy way out. I know I can do better than that."

Daoist Obscurus clapped his hands, making no sound in the process. He grinned with white teeth, and Wang Jun could have sworn he saw the smile stretch from eye to eye. "Spot on," the man said. "The rules are rigged, and the best way to win is to break them, or better yet, avoid them entirely. And you're right, you're practically a god among ants. What can't you achieve if you set your mind to it?"

He snapped his fingers inaudibly, and to Wang Jun's surprise, lights lit up all over the chamber. They barely gave off any light, but their presence seemed to intensify the shadows. They also lit up one other thing: a map of the continent with all its finest details. If one looked closely enough, one could see tiny people moving about on its exquisite surface. Each one was tethered to a fine string leading back to the one it represented.

"What I taught you before was the basics, simple parlor tricks," Daoist Obscurus said. "Things to avoid detection, ways to travel unseen. But shadow and fate can let us do so much more. They allow us to work around everything—nature, the elements, people, and even the heavens if you're strong enough.

"I taught you tricks to survive and learn the greater picture. I wanted you to experience joy and suffering, and the bitterness of life. You're now drenched in bitterness, with only a small candle to light your way. The bitterness is key, but the candle—well, a candle to reach for is the best motivator man could ask for.

"You learned the parlor tricks, but it's time to grow up. Now I'll teach you everything." He tapped his finger on Wang Jun's forehead and then the map. Everything blurred around him: the fates of countless people, the multitude of demons, the earth and all its riches, the sea and all its fullness. Every bit of information was a light that somehow deepened the shadow within him. It grew and grew until he could barely see anything.

And then he couldn't. Only darkness.

In the mountains near Easthaven Fortress, a presence stirred in a pit of blackness. It drank light, darkness, and time itself. Around it lay an egg, broken open, nothing more than an empty shell.

The beast had just hatched, and it hungered. It slipped out of the prison that had kept it trapped for ten thousand years and into the nearby valley.

A day later, an avian demon flew by the familiar valley. It swooped down to view its territory, but to its surprise, there was hardly anything left inside it. There was a valley, yes, but there were no trees. There were no demons, and there was no life.

Only a shifting tide of emptiness.

– End Book 7 –

A Note to Readers

If you've enjoyed this book, I would greatly appreciate it if you left a rating and/or review on the site where you purchased it. Ratings lead to credibility in this competitive marketplace, and by leaving one, you signal to the world that this book is worth reading.

Cha Ming's disciples grew a great deal between Book 6 and Book 7. That's because, during their master's absence, they had their own adventures. It's difficult to do them justice as part of the main series. If you're interested, you can find out more about them in *Violet Heart* (Book 1 of 2 in the Violet Fate Duology).

I send out updates to readers from time to time, such as writing progress, release announcements, and the like. If you're interested in receiving these updates, subscribe to the Painting the Mists newsletter at:

http://eepurl.com/dymvO1

You can also find a link to the newsletter at www.paintingthemists.com. As a bonus for subscribing, you'll receive exclusive biography sketches for each of the key characters, starting with Huxian!

Here are other ways to keep up to date on the latest news:

Facebook: https://www.facebook.com/RedMiragePtM/
Twitter: @RedMirage_PtM

The Cultivation Systems

This record is a summary of the cultivation systems on the Ling Nan Plane. Note that cultivation systems can change depending on the type of plane or the stability of the plane.

Qi Cultivation (Human)

Some humans are talented in harvesting the ambient energies of heaven and earth. They cultivate qi, enabling them to perform fierce magics by bending the elements themselves. Angelic cultivators gravitate toward this powerful but complex path.

Qi Condensation – Cultivators start their cultivation journey by condensing qi from their surroundings into their Dantian. They can circulate this qi in their qi pathways, executing qi techniques by expending it. A cultivator's qi pool expands and deepens as they cultivate. Many schools separate each step of the process into grades.

Foundation Establishment – After forming a sufficiently large qi pool, cultivators solidify it into solid pillars known as a foundation. Their foundation grows from the bottom of their Dantian and eventually grow tall enough to reach the top. Their qi thickens, and the amount of thickened qi they control depends on the height of their foundation. Foundation-establishment cultivators can fly a short distance from the ground using treasures like flying swords or special boots.

Core Formation – When their pillars reach their maximum height, cultivators melt them into a core, the most efficient way to store qi. Qi now takes the form of a fluid that travels in and out of their core. The core grows until it reaches its maximum size. At this point, cultivators are able to use their potent qi to fly unaided.

Rune Carving – By carving runes onto their core, moral humans can transcend. Not much is known about this realm, but legends say rune carving cultivators can generate a "domain."

Body Cultivation (Human)

Let's face it, some people aren't as they are strong. For those people, body cultivation is the preferred way to get ahead. Devilish cultivators and descendants of deities are drawn toward this brutal, straightforward path. Body cultivation makes one physically stronger, tougher, and nearly unkillable at higher cultivation levels.

Body Strengthening – Body cultivators start off by performing a basic strengthening of their body, purifying it in the process. Typically, the body is nourished with qi and then refined with an opposing qi, removing any impurities.

Bone Forging – After sufficiently strengthening their body, body cultivators must forge their bones to further support their growth. Bones are the basis of strength and durability. They traditionally subject their bones to intense quantities of qi, strengthening and tempering them in the process. They become akin to magic treasures, making it extremely difficult to shatter them using strength of an equivalent realm. Bone-forging cultivators gain the ability to manipulate their weight by using voids that are formed in their bones, making it easier to wield heavy weapons and use their immense strength to their advantage.

Marrow Refining – Once the bones are strong enough, it is necessary for cultivators to refine their marrow. Marrow is the basis of their blood, which feeds the remainder of their body in turn. Marrow-refining cultivators gain powerful regeneration abilities stemming from the deep pool of vitality hidden within their marrow and the voids in their bones.

Blood Awakening – To transcend, body cultivators must awaken the divinity within their blood. How this is done is uncertain, though descendants of a god have a much easier time in doing so.

Soul Cultivation (Human)

The foundation of a cultivator is their soul. Sufficient soul force is necessary to become a professional, such as an alchemist or spiritual blacksmith. In some cases, a sufficiently strong soul is required to advance in cultivation. Buddhists and evil spirits often lean toward soul cultivation.

Innate Soul – Cultivators are born with an innate soul, and it grows as the cultivator advances in qi condensation. Eventually, with sufficient cultivation, the soul will make a rapid breakthrough into incandescence.

Incandescent Soul – In the incandescent realm, the soul begins to shine with incandescent light. Advanced soul manipulation of objects and mental communication is then possible.

Resplendent Soul – Once the soul is sufficiently incandescent, it becomes resplendent. A wrapping appears around the soul, which is called a resplendent vestment. It embellishes the soul and prepares it to transcend. Long-range scanning is possible at this realm.
Transcendent Soul – A transcendent soul grows sufficiently large and gains the ability to move. Since it has broken free from its shackles, it can then leave the mortal body and operate independently from it.

Demonic Cultivation

Humans aren't the only ones who can cultivate. Demons, manifestations of natural forces in the material world, take a different path. They are incapable of cultivating their qi, body, and soul separately. For demons, these three components are part of a complete cultivation system. Demon bodies can grow to massive sizes.

Demonification – Spirit beasts are products of nature. By gaining demonic qi from their natural surroundings, they grow in power. If their bloodline is sufficiently potent, they can break through and become demon beasts.

Purification – Bloodline purity is essential for a demon's advancement. Demons in the purification realm continuously purify their bloodline with demonic energy they gain by either consuming other demons, humans, or natural treasures. They can also do this by living on a demonic mountain, but the process is much slower. Demons who possess sufficiently pure and potent bloodlines can awaken ancestral memories.

Core Formation – When a demon's bloodline is sufficiently pure, it can be crystalized into a demonic core. By feeding this core with demonic energy, a demon grows stronger. Core-formation demons can fly.

Initiation - ???

About the Author

Patrick Georges Laplante was born in a small town in the Canadian prairies in 1987. He began publishing Painting the Mists online under the pseudonym RedMirage in January 2018.

An engineer by trade, he graduated from the University of Alberta in 2009 and completed his master's degree in 2011. While writing and engineering have little in common, he actively utilizes his experiences and attention to detail in fleshing out a vivid world and answering the "whys," which are often left unanswered in xianxia fiction.

As an avid vegan, he aims to prompt internal reflection in his readers through various themes like non-violence, choice, and begging the question: Is personhood restricted to humanity? And what is proper conduct, morality, and love?

His work is inspired by a combination of Western fiction, *Dungeons and Dragons*, Chinese web novels, and various Japanese, Korean, and Chinese comics and illustrated novels.

www.ingramcontent.com/pod-product-compliance
Lightning Source LLC
Chambersburg PA
CBHW051514250626
47156CB00001B/85